LOVE

PUNKED

A novel by Nia Lucas

For Wendy, Helen, Fi and of course Lees. Legends, the bloody lot of you.

Cover Artwork by Fiona Bridges

Follow Nia Lucas @ Nia Lucas Books on Facebook, @BooksNia on Twitter and nialucasbooks on Instagram.

15th February 2003

It's been an uncomfortable ten minutes sat next to Maureen, I won't lie. It's not in the same league as that time I got trapped for an hour in a shopping centre lift with a woman that I'd written a pretty damning Parenting Assessment about two weeks previously. *That* incident saw my toes curl so badly, I feared they'd be permanently permed.

Maureen, against whose shoulder I am smooshed for the next eight hours until we land at LAX for our connecting flight, is however emitting a level of disdain that makes this particular interaction a close contender.

It's my own stupid fault. Most things are to be fair, it's been a twenty-two year unbroken run of well-earned culpability.

New-Zealand native Maureen and I had chatted pleasantly as around us our fellow passengers passively aggressively exchanged '*excuse me'*s as they stowed their luggage. Seated, belted and safely lifted-off, she'd innocuously enquired,

"So what's bringing you to our lovely New Zealand?"

There are many responses I could have offered, all of them inoffensive and bland. I could have gone for simple honesty,

"*Well Maureen, my father has developed an addiction to entering competitions and the other day he*

2

won a return flight for one person to New Zealand. It wasn't the most useful win frankly as he has a pathological fear of planes although it's still better than the bronze head-casting experience he won at Christmas. Thanks to that little victory, my father's bronzed, disembodied head now resides in my parents' downstairs loo, scaring the absolute shit out of anyone who goes for a wee. You see Maureen, in my twenty-two years on this earth the furthest I've travelled is to Ayia Napa with my brother-in-law because I'm a single mum and we only ever holiday in Wales. However, as my boyfriend cheated on me in his hallway while I was upstairs in his bed last weekend, Dad gave the flight to me and well, here I am".

However as my mother, my rapidly enlarging children and their father would animatedly attest to, inoffensive and bland are attributes I aspire to. I generally run with calamitous and astonishing. With that in mind, I'd blurted out,

"I'm going to see the boy who should have been the one to get me pregnant at sixteen, rather than the drug-dealing ex-con stranger who knocked me up in my Dad's garage and then turned my world inside out. I mean, after all Maureen, I've technically been married to Daniel McNamara since we were seven so instead of shagging morons and unfaithful dickheads AND being in love with unavailable and disinterested *No-Names* all these years, it should have been Daniel all along".

Her eyes had widened, she'd coughed and croaked out a simple, "Oh".

I'd smiled ruefully and in seeking to distract from the sudden awkwardness, I'd opened my pretzels in an inept manner that saw them launched over my travelling companions. Beside me, Maureen sniffs meaningfully and starts to finger knit.

I stare out of the window and pray that my stinkers are behaving for their grandparents and their newly-engaged father.

Chapter One

March 1995

I love Daniel McNamara, I have done since we were seven and we made our First Holy Communion together. I'd broken my arm the week previously whilst trying to impress Gio Romano and the lads on my street by roller-skating at speed over 'Bertha', the most feared manhole cover of any child within a two-street radius. Bertha won, my ulna and radius lost. When Gio drew pictures of bums and willies and then wrote *'Erin smells of shit'* all over my plaster cast just two days before my First Holy Communion, my mother's conniption was felt in the Vatican.

My unholy cast concealed in silky white bandages, I stood in my immaculate white dress next to Daniel and Gio as Father Eamon gazed at us sternly and asked us if we repented the sins I'm not entirely sure we'd actually committed. In his smart shirt and tie with his lovely blond hair gelled stylishly, Daniel looked like a Prince and me, with my stupidly thick curly auburn mop hair-sprayed into Ozone-destroying concrete, I felt like a Princess at his side. I stared at Daniel and imagined that he and I were getting married. My loud, 'I dos' in response to Father Eamon's questions, were captured by my father on his new Camcorder, amusing everybody as I delivered them staring cow-eyed at an oblivious Daniel. Gio Romano, his coal-coloured hair unruly and his shirt untucked, just picked his nose and looked bored before treading on my toes.

I truly believe that my declarations, in the presence of a Priest, render Daniel and I at least fifty-percent married.

My semi-husband and I have had limited interaction since our 'wedding' all those years ago. We're now fourteen which means as social norms dictate, we have studiously ignored each other for years

4

despite having spent significant portions of our childhood sharing the same classroom oxygen. I've watched him grow taller, spotty then not-so-spotty, voice honking and then calming until he finally, overnight as it happens, transformed into a hunk. I have not grown any taller, my hair remains auburn and mop-like, I have the grace of carthorse and the bust of a Page Three model. To any teenage lad, I must present a startling and alarming conflict of interests. No allure whatsoever but possessing boobs that call to them like a Siren's Song.

Daniel has been going out with perfectly-poised Carolyn Gregory since they snogged at the Youth Club Christmas Disco. In her Levi's, Kookai crop-top and her immaculately styled hair, the poor lad was powerless to her charms. I observed his adultery from the darkened corner near to the snack kiosk, weeping into a Sherbert Dib Dab and washing it down with Panda Pop as Lees copped off with Adam Jones against the wall-bars.

Giddy on Dib Dabs, I made the critical error of engaging Gio Romano in conversation over the pool table. He spent twenty minutes snarling insults at me which initially I sought to counter with sassy comebacks and returned barbs. Only he was better at it than me. And more cruel. *And more accurate.* I couldn't make my barbs wound like he did, I don't have the stomach for that degree of nastiness. His parody of my walk, miming grossly oversized bust, horrendous hair and pulling a face reminiscent of a gargoyle, it *stung*. He didn't take it too far, he simply took it as far as the readily-available material allowed him to and it *hurt*.

Humiliation is a strong word, implying a degree of self-blame that is unnecessary given the circumstances in which it is generally used. With all its syllables, it's a bit fecking smug too. I picture humiliation as a sturdy, horsey Head Girl from a private school, Miss. Humiliation Palmer-Smart, wagging her finger and looking disapproving. *Judgemental cow.* Humiliation is not a word that inspires affection but we're no passing acquaintances, Humiliation Palmer-Smart and I. We are travelling companions of sorts, pen-pals if you wish. We know each other intimately.

With Gio's insults and ego-shredding impressions ringing in my ears, I left Lees snogging Adam at the disco and sloped home, Humiliation Palmer-Smart trotting behind me on her imaginary steed. In fairness to Gio, at least he distracted me from Daniel's adultery but he also made me cry every night for weeks.

Three months on, the Under 18's Night at 'Pulse' tonight was Lees' idea. Our desperation to enter the Valhalla of the only nightclub in a twenty mile radius drove us to beg and plead for permission with persistence that propelled both our sets of parents into eventual weary agreement. We billed it as my fifteenth birthday celebration, the actual day occurring next week, my Dad depositing us at the club door with stern warnings and Lees' Dad on collection duty having pulled the short straw.

Everyone is here, the Local Radio Station's enthusiastic promotion of the night ensuring that we all fully expected this evening to be the Woodstock of our generation. As cheesy pop bombards us from the speakers and the middle-aged DJ makes inappropriate comments over the PA system, we all quickly realise that we have been somewhat misled. The watered down Coke at £2 for a thimble worth, does nothing to improve our consumer satisfaction. Daniel McNamara is here, with the cool-crowd regulars who form his friendship group. Carolyn and the Practically-Perfects (Lees' name for the group of five Queen Bees in our year) are laughing too loudly at the boys and tossing hair in a manner likely to elicit brain damage if they're not very careful.

Lees and I hit the dance floor straight away, our placement in the social shadowlands of our year group allowing us freedoms that the Practically-Perfects will never know. We are at liberty to prat around, to dance like muppets, to make absolute tits of ourselves because honestly, who cares? We have no reputations to maintain, no cool credentials to earn. Even Lees' leggy brunette gorgeousness has not provided her a pass into the upper Social Echelons. I strongly suspect that her association with me holds her back but as I watch the Perfects pout and look deeply bored, I know for certain that I would rather be attempting booty-shakes with my best mate than be one of them.

Apart that is from the bit about snogging Daniel McNamara. *I think I might quite like that bit.*

Eventually the promised Foam Party element of the evening is delivered with unsanitary looking cannons oozing out sticky, lung-burning foam which simultaneously melts inexpertly applied teenage makeup whilst blinding everybody to the resultant mess. It's *horrendous*. Lees clutches me to her like an anchor as the lads from our year belly-slide around the place like greased weasels, toppling girls in heels like skittles. It is a Health and Safety Officer's worst nightmare.

Cannons cease, mass exits are made to repair makeup and we all wonder who on earth thought this was a good idea.

"Rinny, this is total bollocks. Should I get Dad to come early?", Lees is sat next to the wash basin as I try to re-ponytail my bubble-sticky mop.

Before I can respond in agreement, a wall of indignant shrieking announces the arrival in the loos of the Perfects, all their attention focussed on a weeping Carolyn in their midst.

"I just don't get it, why did *he kiss me*? And, I mean, *New Zealand?* Who moves *there?*", Carolyn sobs as sycophantic reassurances fill the room.

I look at Lees who rolls her eyes and head bobs towards the door, seeking our exit but I am intrigued. Who's moving? The label in my hastily purchased Miss. Selfridge lycra sausage-dress is irritating me,

"Lees, just sort this label out can you?", I turn as Lees rolls her eyes and rummages in around my spine, tickling me on purpose and making me shriek.

"Er, *s'cuse* me, we're trying to have a *private* conversation here", Carolyn ceases her bawling enough to cock an eyebrow and find me lacking.

Lees jumps off the vanity counter and stands at my side, her hands on her hips. Lees is taller than me but I've got these stupid platform heels on so we're almost equal and arm in arm, we pettily snigger our way out of the door. Back on the dance floor, Lees and I attempt a Bobby Brown one-legged chicken move, spiced up with an inadvertent MC Hammer wiggle which is impressive frankly given the lack of traction on the sud-soaked vinyl. In our silliness, I spot Daniel McNamara looking miserable and I get a little tummy flutter. His lads have separated a bit from him and his shoulders are slumped.

"Lees", I nudge her and nod in his direction.

Her eye roll is massive, "Oh for God's sake. McNamara? Woman, you start spouting that marriage bollocks again and I will not hesitate to tell your mother that you played Doctors and Nurses with Gio Romano in the home corner when we were four. I'll bloody do it, I will", she nods her conviction.

I mock wail, "It's destiny Lee, DESTINY"

She takes me by the shoulders, "It's not destiny, it's obsession and it'll see you locked up. Look, McNamara's too fit for you Rinny, I love you but he is. He's a *ten* and you're working up to an *eight*. I know you'll be a bloody *twelve* by the time we do our A Levels but right now, aim for I dunno......", she's scanning round the room as her eyes widen and she nods, "Romano. Aim for Gio Romano, he's on your level and you've already seen his willy in the Home Corner all those years ago", she winks and laughs like she's hilarious.

I am not hurt by this brutality, I'm genuinely not. I love Lees more than anyone, even Daniel and honesty feeds our mutual devotion. I told her last week that her new jumper made her look like a female sex offender and that when she's on the blob, she smells like defrosting mince. She'd grinned and made me Mars Bar popcorn.

I shrug my acceptance, "Fair enough but not bloody Romano, Jesus, anybody but him. He's vile", I wrinkle my nose and grab her hand to go get a drink.

As we slip and slide our way across the suds, I am used as a sort of balance post by the unstable person behind me on the dance floor, risking my own nasty slip. As the body behind me appears to find its centre of gravity, I turn to berate them for their selfish use of my counterweight only to be met by bloody *Romano's* face.

"Shit, sorry Roberts", he looks genuinely remorseful.

I observe that this evening Gio Romano actually looks quite good. He's got an inoffensive shirt on, he's pretty tall, his freckles are nice and his coal-coloured curls are cut in a trendy manner. Lees' assessment of our comparative physical attractiveness suddenly seems less insulting. However, I'm still smarting from the pool table incident,

"Tsk, don't touch what you can't afford Romano", I sneer.

His eyes go wide and I see a smirk starting. He reaches into his pocket and pulls out a coin, "Fifty-pence here, I'll need change though yeah?", as he laughs at his own hilarity.

I splutter, searching for a witty response. I find none, "Screw you Romano".

"You offering?", he nods at my chest and my outrage is such that it requires backup but Lees has gone ahead to the bar and is out of range.

As I plan how best to de-bollock Gio Romano, I turn away only to be met by the unexpected but welcome sight of Daniel McNamara, who appears to be *watching us* from a few yards away.

Butterflies in my chest, I turn back to Gio to offer him my middle finger, when I find myself in the middle of an entirely alarming and frankly unwelcome kiss.

I am being kissed by Gio *bloody* Romano. That twat is kissing me. How *very* fucking dare he. Dry lips, hands mid-air like startled birds and eyes open, it is disconcertingly like being kissed by an angry distant relative. *Eeurrgghh.* Wide eyed, I shove him, the momentum making both of us slip slightly.

"What are you DOING Gio?!", my shriek sounds horribly like my mother's but it just gets weirder.

"What the hell Romano, you kissed her?", Daniel McNamara, like my Prince Charming, has suddenly appeared and I am gormlessly staring until my brain kicks in.

"Er, hiya Daniel", I gulp, frantically trying to signal Lees discreetly but bloody Adam Jones is chatting her up again and she's oblivious. Daniel is not looking at me though. He is looking at Gio, who has his fists clenched and his face angry.

Daniel's angry tone is accusing, "Why did you do it? You kissed her? You know how much I like her, you're supposed to be my mate but then you kiss her?"

I may swoon, it's a very real possibility. I am staring at Daniel, gob-smacked by my crush's declaration, overwhelmed at this sudden shift in my mundane circumstances.

I hear Gio snarl, "You can sod off Mac, you're leaving, you don't give a shit about your mates or her so what does it matter, eh?", and he goes to grab my hand, to pull me closer to him.

I yelp and '*oi'* Gio, wrenching my hand from his grasp, "NO, not you, I want to be with Daniel. You *like* me Daniel?", I look hopefully at Daniel but he's not looking at me, which is weird but perhaps he's embarrassed by his emotional exposure. Perhaps he is worried I don't return his feelings? I should reassure him,

"Daniel, I feel the same, I lo……", but he's not listening, he's shoving Gio.

"That's bullshit, don't do this, you're my best mate. It's not my fault, it's Dad's job", Daniel sounds really upset and I am touched by his clearly deep rooted affection although I don't know what his Dad's job has got to do with the price of fish but frankly, I don't give a toss. Daniel McNamara *likes* me. I've read that fourteen-year-olds can marry with their parent's consent in America. Maybe we can go there and then honeymoon at Disney? Lees could wear an Ariel Bridesmaid costume, she's a bit obsessed.

Just as I mentally plan our Little Mermaid themed Wedding Cake, Gio Romano takes a swing at Daniel McNamara in the middle of the Under 18's night and as a protective spouse does, I jump to Daniel's defence, my hands restrainedly on both of their chests as I stand between them,

"NO! Gio, NO! Back off, leave Daniel alone. I like him and he likes me and…..", I don't get to finish because Daniel *shoves* me aside and lands a punch on Gio's torso.

I have always struggled to take a hint. I reposition myself between them, the heroine of this drama, the object of their mutual jealousy,

"NO!! Daniel, Gio's not worth it, he doesn't matter. I don't like Gio, the kiss meant nothing. I'm………..", and then *it* happens.

The bouncers racing over to split them up, encounter the terminal lack of traction that the bubbles afford. The four of them, large and moving at high speed, are unable to slow down as they approach our little menage-a-trois and the seven of us explode in a shower of limbs, crashing to the floor in a slippery pile.

I'm not sure whose nose made sharp contact with my chin but it was an impressive spurt of blood that decorated my cleavage. I did hear the bone-crunch of a jaw slamming together and skulls bumping but I was distracted by my first horizontal embrace with Daniel McNamara whose head was currently smooshed into my tits, the shine *somewhat* rubbed off it as it took place beneath four bouncers, Gio Romano and four feet of chemical foam. My dress up around my waist, I suspect that the bloody awful boy-shorts I bought in Peacocks are now getting their moment in the limelight. Somewhere, in this retail-park-located, neon-lit disco-hell, Humiliation Palmer-Smart is prancing round on her pony, guffawing into her overbite.

"Erin? Rinny? Where are you?", the chemical bubbles currently dissolving my eardrum still allow me to hear the panicked tones of my best friend.

I belatedly realise that oxygen is an issue for me, the weight of six male bodies not something that my ribcage is trained to deal with. I swallow foam, blood and Daniel's hair as I scrabble in desperation for release. Just as my peripheral vision starts to go a bit fuzzy, I feel the release of pressure, bodies shifting above me. Oxygen re-accessed, I wrap my arms briefly round Daniel, only to have him cruelly ripped from my embrace as '*Mick*' is ordered to take '*that one*' out.

Pressure removed entirely from person, I am left here, hidden beneath these bubbles that are burning my lungs, dress up round my waist, knickers on display, somebody's blood dripping into my under-wiring. *Christ the glamour.* I can't stop smiling though. I am here, in the midst of Humiliation Palmer-Smart's latest bulldozer ride through my life but it doesn't matter, it doesn't bloody matter, because Daniel McNamara *likes me* and he just got into a bloody *fight* because of how he 'feels' about me. God, I feel like I'm in a John Hughes film. With what little dignity I can muster, I sit up, yanking my dress down as I clamber awkwardly to my knees.

"RINNY!! Jesus you're BLEEDING!! What the hell? Ohmygod we need to get you to first aid", Lees bends down and offers me her hand.

As I stand, Lees gasps and tugs my dress into position whilst wiping my hair back off my face and wincing at the melted makeup beneath.

"LEES, it's not my blood, it's…..well, I'm not sure whose it is BUT Daniel LIKES me Lees and he got in a fight with Gio Romano for kissing ME. They just got taken out by the bouncers", I gasp for oxygen and note that Lees is giving me the exact same look that she gave the old lady on the bus who got on with a pram full of ferrets last week. *Disbelief mixed with pity.*

"Rinny, did you hit your head mate….?", she's patting my arm and leading me towards a nearby bouncer, ignoring me as I spout my happiness and my desire to find Daniel.

On the sticky, lurid carpet near the doorway, I manage to pull her to a halt, "LEES, I am fine. I mean, everyone's seen my knickers but I'm fine. This isn't my blood and…….DANIEL!", I point, spotting him through the tinted doors of the club entrance sitting on the raised flower beds outside.

"God's sake Rinny, just leave it……", Lees pleads but I'm already heading out of the door.

It's absolutely freezing outside, I can see puffs of frosty breath coming out of Daniel's lips as he sits in the distance. Shivering in my tiny dress I go to move towards him but before I can get into his line of sight, he jumps up and jogs off towards something. Lees joins me, her arms crossed over her chest. *She's pissed off.*

I hear Daniel shout, "Gio…….G, wait there mate.", as he shoots off down the steps between the stores in the retail park.

Like some sort of demented penguin, I try and run in my stacked heels, a stupid plan really given that I can barely walk in them and I'm screeching, "Noooo, Daniel, DANIEL, don't hit him again, it's you I li………", but as he approaches Gio, who is stood in the car park, I hear Daniel shout,

"You KISSED Carolyn mate, I can't believe you did that. I'm moving to New Zealand and my best mate snogs my girlfriend because he's pissed off with me. This is the most shit night EVER", Daniel's head slumps as Lees catches up with me, her hand on my shoulder as I hear the distant sound of imaginary hooves clip-clopping towards me.

Daniel's words are clear in the chilly air, "I mean what are you doing G? You kiss Carolyn because you're angry with me but then you pull bloody ugly ginger Roberts too. Have you lost it?", as Daniel's shout echoes around the retail park, I feel the blood in my veins turning to ice, the sharp needles of frost piercing delicate flesh as my heart starts to crack.

"What are YOU doing, eh Mac? You're my best mate and you're moving to New Zealand? You tell us you're leaving in like *days* and it's like you don't give a shit", Gio's shout is pained but then I hear him sigh, "I'm sorry 'bout Carolyn mate and Christ knows what I was doing with Roberts, she's, y'know, *rank*", Gio shakes his head and toes at the tarmac as he looks down.

"Oh", my whispered voice cracks and I feel Lees slip her hand in mine as she rests her head on my shoulder.

Humiliation Palmer-Smart really is an 'invites herself in' sort of girl. She only gets to rear up her horsey head when somebody is too nice to tell her to sod off. Cruel or unkind people can't be humiliated, they sneer and snarl and repel her with the lack of chuffs that they give about hurting or blaming others. To truly be humiliated, you have to forgo a counter-attack, you have to decide not to deflect it elsewhere.

I could style it out with Lees, tell her about Romano being a shit snog, make fun, deride, deny that I genuinely like Daniel, make out like I'm not in pain but I don't. There's no point anyway, Lees knows me too well. I'll just shoulder the humiliation. Taking Lees' hand I take a final look at the object of my brutally rejected affections before turning and walking away.

Rank, ugly, ginger Roberts.

As we turn the corner, I feel Lees look at me kindly, "Rinny, just ignore….", but she doesn't get to finish.

"Roberts, hang on", I hear Gio's voice and it makes me jump and turn, a frown and a snarl on my lips.

I don't get to attack though because bloody Romano lunges forward and *hugs* me. He pulls me close and *hugs* me. I make the same noise the cat did, when the vet stuck that thermometer up its arse last week. A squawk of surprise, tempered with confusion.

"Sorry for getting you knocked over and for the shit snog Roberts", and he runs back off down the steps before I have a chance to draw astonished breath.

I turn to Lees, who looks like she's just been slapped with a frozen cod. I have to close my mouth because the cold is making my teeth tingle and I belatedly remember that I am entirely frozen. Shaking my head and rolling my eyes, I catch hold of her hand and drag her back towards the inviting warmth of the foam-filled nightclub, so that we can fetch our bloody coats and go home.

"Rinny", Lee beside me is struggling to contain her laughter, "Rinny, you might want to go find a mirror. Your mascara is all over your face chick and you've got loo paper stuck to your shoe"

Ah, of course I have. Humiliation Palmer-Smart canters off into the distance, braying with laughter

15th April 1996

"Erin ROBERTS!! You cannot lie down on your desk when the Bunsen Burner's are on, you stupid girl. Good heavens, with all that hair you are a fire risk as it is. Either wake up and do your work or leave this lab immediately and only return when you are able to function appropriately", Mr. Gibson is aubergine-hued with rage but I'm honestly too heartbroken and knackered to give many shits.

Lees hisses at me to '*wake up Rinny*' but I just can't and I'm going to grab, with both weary hands, the offer that my teacher has just inadvertently made me. Grabbing my books and the Morgan backpack that Lees bought me for my sixteenth birthday earlier this month, I mutter something incomprehensible that is shaped like an apology and zigzag out of the lab, my classmates jeers making me flip them the bird.

"OUT ROBERTS, NOW!!", Mr. Gibson saw the bird. *Bugger*.

When Miss. Stanley had her heart attack in assembly last month, nobody thought to lock her office door while she is on sick leave. I discovered this by accident the other day when I leant against the door handle, trying to look vaguely alluring in the presence of the Upper Sixth lads and instead disappeared from view like a crap magician's assistant. Lees found me, flat on my back amidst rolls of Miss. Stanley's motivational posters, trying to style it out.

Whilst prone on her carpet, I noticed that stowed under Miss. Stanley's desk was a very cosy looking duvet and a small camping mat. *Absolute result*. It is there that I now head, desperate for the sleep I missed last night.

Lees and bloody Adam Jones have been going out for nearly a year. He's nice, I like him. *I approve.* He's gently good looking, funny, nice to his mum, kind to animals and he treats my Lees like she's a present that he can't believe he got given. I therefore tolerate his addition to my life. His older brother however, back from his first year at Uni for Easter, is *not* such a nice boy.

Ryan Jones is the ultimate suburban bad boy, good looking in the slightly grubby, sharp way that the *wrong* boys often are and with an arrogance that sends shivers through my muscles. At Adam's house with Lees four weeks ago, Ryan had sloped down the stairs mid-way through some awful action film that Adam chose, marking his unexpected arrival in my life.

After staring at my tits for longer than a nice boy would, he slumped next to me on my lonely spot on the sofa and began his surly infringement of my sphere of reference, making stilted small talk and exuding cockiness. He smelt of Joop and shower gel and as his bare arm brushed mine, I swear I saw sparks come off our skin.

As teenagers, when your best mate is *attached* and you are single, you frequently enter into an interaction during social gatherings known as the 'filler snog'. It's a way of passing the time whilst avoiding painful small-talk that frankly, neither of you nor your lip-lock partner can be arsed with, as you wait for your attached friends to return their attention to you. It is a conversational cop-out.

I have filler-snogged a significant number of lads in my year. And the year above. *And the year above that*. It turned out that long-departed Daniel McNamara, happily ensconced this past year in his life in New Zealand, left a deeper scar than perhaps I realised. Don't start me on Romano either, all that pseudo-Italian twat does is take the piss. Their assessment of me as *'rank, ugly ginger Roberts'* echoed in my ears for months, it still does if I'm honest. Lees' enthusiastic rebuttal and dismissal of their opinions rang hollow. I knew they weren't far wrong.

So I made some changes. I saved up my wages from my Saturday waitressing job and got myself an appointment at the posh salon in town. Fringe eventually grown out and curls weighed down by increasing the length as advised, my ginger hair no longer reminds my peers of a 1980's housewife. I started to join Lees on her training runs, engaging in the first voluntary exercise of my life and I've gradually replaced my M&S stocked bra-drawer with Wonderbra lace fripperies, to my mother's abject horror.

My latest padded purchase dangling from her fingers, my Mum was astonished all those months ago,

"Good *God* girl, what in the name of merciful Jesus is this contraption? Erin Hannah Mary Roberts, you've got more than your due in the chest department, what on earth possessed you to buy this? You are NOT wearing it to school, I'll tell you that now my girl", my poor mother stared at my bra like she wanted to wash it in Holy Water and have it exorcised.

My Welsh-Valleys-bred mother, a fierce, sharp but ultimately kind lady who is trying to navigate my adolescence with as few conniptions as she can manage, is struggling recently. She's seen the make-up I increasingly wear, she caught me snogging Chris Ainsley in Lees' garden when she came to collect me from her party, she clocked the poorly-disguised love bite on my neck several months ago. I catch her fiddling with her Rosary beads more than she used to and she eyes me with suspicion when she thinks I'm not looking. At night, she kisses me on the forehead as I head to bed and tells me I'm '*a good girl*'. Increasingly, it sounds like she's convincing herself as opposed to offering praise.

So the filler-snogs started to mount up at the discos, parties and park visits. Nothing life-changing, no blossoming romances or devastating crushes. Just an absence of painful small talk and an increase in my lip-balm purchase. *Until Ryan Jones.*

6th April 1996

"You got a story sorted yeah? For your folks? We won't be back until the morning Erin, you know that?", sat in Ryan's decrepit Vauxhall Nova, I am trying to look nonchalant but honestly, I think it probably comes across as mild constipation.

I perform a jerky hair flick and smile weakly, "Yeah, I told you, they think I'm at Lees' tonight".

My heart is very possibly going to beat its way out of my latest padded boulder-holder because I *know* what tonight means. As I look at Ryan, all gelled blond spiky hair, Adidas top and cool jeans like a budget David Beckham, I know that tonight after this rave, we will be sleeping together in the back-seat of this crappy Nova. If I wasn't scared half to death by the threat of parental discovery, my lack of sexual allure or indeed my impending *performance*, I might be looking forward to spending time with this *cool* older lad but right now, I'm bricking it.

Kissing Ryan Jones is my favourite thing to do. We only do it in secret because Ryan does not want '*grief*' off his parents for dating a younger girl but we do manage to do it *a lot*. He made me promise not to tell Lees and for me, this was almost a deal breaker but then he told me that I was *fit* and I melted into agreement. *Absolute moron.*

Truth is, I *have* told Lees. I told her the night that I saw Ryan naked for the first time. I couldn't hold the information in, I needed to offload my astonishment. She was not impressed, furnishing me with Adam's anecdotes about his older brother's less than stellar personality traits. I nodded and made a fantastic impression of sincerity and contemplation, a performance that I wish I'd been able to video for my GCSE drama practical but the whole time, all I was picturing what Ryan's mouth looked like as I made him come with my hand and just how hard he'd kissed me in gratitude. *And the things he'd then done to me with his fingers.*

To be honest, sex is pretty much the last thing on my 'first time' list as Ryan has, over the last few weeks, efficiently worked me through the pre-sex milestones. It's been fun but it does mean that when my Mum looks at me, I feel waves of guilt as opposed to the righteous indignation that I once felt under her scrutiny. Ryan's enthusiasm for my erotic ministrations has been something of an ego stroker and my quest for further knowledge has driven me happily onwards.

This will be the second rave that I've been to with Ryan. The first one ended early with the loud and *utterly terrifying* arrival of what felt like every police officer in Wiltshire who burst into the smoke-filled disused agricultural warehouse and scattered its teenage contents like sugar sprinkles.

Ryan, momentarily forgetting that he's a bit of a shit, had protectively grabbed my hand and had raced us through the chaos, speeding us to eventual safety in the Nova. When I'd cried, he'd held me in a cuddle and I felt his heart racing in his chest. That little display of attentive-boyfriend behaviour saw things crossed off my pre-sex to-do list that made him swear fiercely and gasp his orgasmic gratitude.

Tonight, as Ryan points towards what looks like a disused cattle market, I feel little sparks of adrenaline. Before the police arrived, I'd found myself *loving* the music at the last rave, dancing with an enthusiasm and skill which surprised both me *and* Ryan. *It was amazing.*

As Ryan parks the Nova precariously on a muddy grass bank down a lane, this event looks more organised than the last one. As we walk towards the wall of noise and humanity in the distance, I can see that the main area seems to be under the protection of a low, wide expanse of corrugated iron roof, patches of clear corrugated plastic allowing the lasers to pierce the roof and project into the night sky. The football pitch sized concrete forecourt is where, led by the hand, Ryan takes me over to a group of slightly older guys, all smoking in a huddle. Greeting them with fist bumps, Ryan buys the E's that he, not I, will take.

My inability to take tablets causes my mother endless despair, bemoaning my inability to ingest paracetamol as it results in truly pathetic displays of hopelessness when I am unwell or injured. Right now, as Ryan knocks back his first E with a Red Bull, I would suggest to Mum that perhaps my ineptitude is an asset after all.

In my Levi's and the crochet crop top that Lees told me, "*Makes it look like you've wrapped your tits in doilies Rinny, you sure it's the look you're going for?"*, I feel pretty good. My crazy hair is trailing down to my hips in its more restrained format these days and Ryan's fiddling with it as he chats to his mates. I've got my new Airwalks on and this is possibly as put together as I've ever managed.

There's a lad in the group, the one that Ryan bought the E's off, who seems to be throwing me the occasional look. He's tall, mixed race and his dark hair is styled into a crown of soft spikes. He is good-looking in the sort of way that makes me nervous. Ryan is *cocky* good-looking, exuding the sort of irritating brashness that lets you forget his fitness long enough to engage with him. *This* lad? He is *intimidatingly* gorgeous and small, naive ginger people with improbable proportions and chipmunk cheeks, we are physically unable to engage with the likes of *him*. His frowning glances are drawing the attention of the other lads,

"Who's this then Ry?", one of the group nods at me, a derisive smirk on his lips.

I feel myself frown slightly and reach for Ryan's hand but he has stepped away from me, dropping the curl he'd been fiddling with.

"This is Erin, she's just a mate of my brother's, I gave her a lift here", Ryan looks uncomfortable and I feel a sting in the air.

Smirker snorts his derision, "Yeah, babysittin' are ya Ry? Hope it pays well"

Ryan laughs. He *laughs*. I've sucked his dick and let him see me naked and now he's dismissing me as nothing more than a juvenile encumbrance. I feel the bile burn in my throat and the fibre-glass itch of embarrassment tickle in my chest. *I hear Humiliation Palmer-Smart cantering towards me.*

Ryan sniggers, "It doesn't pay much but there's a few benefits if you get what I mean. Mind you, I reckon *she* should be paying *me*, eh?"

That's it.

As his mates and he chuckle, I feel the '*chopsy little madam'* that my Nana always complains about, rearing her head.

I am not aware of my foot pulling back in a kick but I do feel my foot connect *hard* with Ryan's shin. I see him as he spins in pained astonishment to face me only to be met by the feel of my knee connecting equally hard with the very dick that only two nights ago, he *begged* me to suck.

"You wanker, suck your own tiny dick from now on. Y'know, once you've fetched it out your kidneys", all five-foot-nothing of me towers over Ryan's prone, writhing form on the muddy concrete floor of this bovine-scented derelict space as he clasps his crotch and moans.

I turn and walk off, ignoring his groans of pain and his mates whoops of hilarity, motorising your carcass hard to do when you realise that your legs are numb from the regret that is sweeping your muscles.

How in God's name will I get home now that I've just neutered my lift?

I wobble-walk off towards the enclosed space under the corrugated roof, collapsing against the wet brick wall as I contemplate how on earth to get myself out of *this* latest cataclysm. Around me the music pumps and the bodies pulse and the lasers pull my attention like a magpie to precious metal.

I take stock of my situation. Ryan will not now be taking me home, of that I am certain. I am strangely unaffected by my assumed split from Mr. Jones. I have £20 in my bra, I know that we are a thirty minute drive from home and so as long as the taxi stops at a cash machine, I probably have enough wages in the bank to get myself home. What I *don't* have is the first clue where I actually am, where a phone box is or how I would explain my unexpected late-night arrival home to my parents. *Shit shit shit.*

The sensible part of me should really take stock, make plans, get home. The part of me that seeks out shitstorms like a pig looking for truffles merely shrugs and allows myself to get drawn into the writhing mass of bodies as the beat takes me. I dance. I forget that I am in *way* over my head as far as life is concerned and I throw myself into this sea of sweaty teenage humanity and it is bloody *delicious*.

I don't care that I am on my own, years messing about with Lees has taught me that giving a stuff about looking a tit only limits the fun that you have in any given situation. Mind you, it helps that every person in my immediate vicinity looks like they dropped a pill or seven so their awareness of my solo, friendless status is significantly dulled.

The beat takes me to a dreamy sort of place where for several hours, my body moves of its own volition and my heart soars with each crescendo and accompanying drop. *This is amazing.*

Eyes closed, hands raised in adulation and hips doing things that I was unaware they had been instructed to engage in, I am belatedly aware of a pair of hands gently placed on my waist.

"You got some fuckin' balls girl, y'know", the voice rumbling in my ear is deep, soothing even in this noise and I immediately get goosebumps over my scalp.
Sloe eyed from the dance sub-space I have entered, I turn, feeling alien lips brush against my temple with the movement.

Sweet. Baby. Jesus.

It's *him*. The lad that Ryan bought the drugs off, the incredible looking, brooding mate, he's *here and he's talking to me.*

I try to arrange my features into less of a stunned-mullet stare but again, I fear I just manage to look constipated. His dark brown eyes are holding my gaze, I can smell CK One and fabric conditioner and I watch as he slowly licks his lips before he bends towards my ear again,

"You're a feisty one, eh ginger? You beat up blokes often?", I feel his cheek move where it's touching the skin on my face, it feels like he's smiling.

I turn and look up at him, his full lips quirked up in a smirk and I feel my own lips twitch.

My voice wobbly with nerves, I shout over the music, "Only dickheads who deserve it".

He stands back, slowly folding his arms over his chest as he nods nonchalantly but I note that his gaze rakes up and down my body briefly. He's even taller up close and he's wearing a Stussy Sweatshirt under a black bomber jacket. He's got a single diamond stud in his left ear, a scar that bisects his right eyebrow and I'm belatedly aware that being near him makes my palms sweaty.

I feel that anxiety start to rise in my chest again and I blurt out, "D'you know where Ryan went?"

He smirks again and nods over towards the other side of the space, making me turn swiftly. I spot Ryan and his sniggering mates a short distance away. Ryan's looking at me with poorly-concealed rage while his mates all dance in a manner which suggests the E's have *properly* kicked in.

I mutter under my breath, "Oh shit, definitely no lift for me. Oh!", as I turn back to him, I'm astonished to find that he's stepped even closer to me, to the extent that we are now chest to chest.

Too flummoxed to know what to do, I look at him gormlessly as he bends his head and whispers,

"You wanna piss that cocky dickhead off even more?", his smirk is entirely feral.

With a cartoon gulp, I attempt a shaky shrug. Honestly, I think it just looks like some form of spasm but as he leans closer, as his breath starts to puff against my face, I panic.

"I DON'T KNOW YOUR NAME", my alarm gives my words a volume which scares even me. He jolts and looks briefly baffled before his lips twitch in a small smile.

"I'm Jamel, what's your name then eh, Ginger Feist?", he smiles as his head lowers again, warm puffs brushing my skin.

I whisper a wobbly, "Erin, my name's Erin"

I feel his lips touch my cheek, one hand in my thick curls, the other snaking around my waist as he chuckles against my skin,

"Nah, you're Ginger Feist, sweetness", and that's the last thing he says before his lips press against mine and the world explodes in shards of the brightest glitter.

Chapter Two

7th April 1996

I can't stop smiling, I think I probably look a bit mental. Sat next to me, in the driver's seat of this impossibly bad-boy VW Golf, is the *fittest lad I have ever seen*. Jamel. The lad I have just spent hours snogging at an illegal rave, royally pissing off the twat I *actually* arrived with and now I, *rank, ugly, ginger Roberts*, am being driven home by him at 2am on a Sunday morning. It's very possible that I might die from the giddiness of it all. It's like I am every kind of cool that teen magazines drone on about. *Me*.

Humiliation Palmer-Smart can bloody do one.

"So Ginger Feist, we gonna hook up again, eh? You going next week, that big one in Oxford?", in the darkness, I see him turn briefly to look at me and my heart races from his attention.

I have not got the first clue what he's on about, "Er, I don't know. I mean, Ryan used to be the one that took me to these and now he's er, not. So I guess…...not"

It's a certainty that Ryan Jones will be having nothing further to do with me. As Jamel snogged me into some sort of lip-chapped lock-jaw, I saw Ryan's fury in the distance. I heard his shouts and insults and then, two hours later, I saw him shagging a girl against the wall of the cattle market as Jamel led me by the hand to his car to take me home. With Jamel's large warm hand in mine, I floated past.

"I'll come fetch you, yeah? I'll take you on Saturday", and with Jamel's words, my fate is sealed.

I know that Jamel is nineteen, that he lives in Bristol but that he's '*not from there*'. His accent is a bit hard to place, Brummy perhaps but he is pretty cagey. He mentions brothers in passing, in response to me talking about my own fourteen-year-old fraternal burden Dylan but I don't have a clear picture about who he actually is. He mentions a Nigerian Nan but frankly, I'm too mesmerised by him to care about anything other than how long it will be until he snogs me again.

My plan, haphazardly formulated as Jamel's fingers toyed with my knickers in the back-seat of the Golf, is that Jamel will drop me home and I'll sleep in Dad's garage (always unlocked) until such time as I can reasonably walk in the door, pretending to arrive home from Lees'.

It doesn't turn out like that though. *It never does with me.*

In so many of the 80's films that have shaped my expectations of romance and love, the loss of virginity is generally undertaken in a variety of covert, parental-avoiding scenarios but with the key uniting ingredient of a bed and some degree of comfort. I'd always expected my *deflowering* to be in Johnny's cabin at Kellerman's or perhaps it would be in Tom Cruise's bed after the big football game. This dream has adapted in recent days, morphing into Ryan's back-seat with an Enya CD playing in the background.

Think again Roberts.

In Dad's garage, bumbling about in the dark so as not to attract any neighbours' attention, Jamel helps me reach down the bloody recliner patio chair from the ceiling rack, the chair on which I intend to sleep tonight. We're snogging again, I'm melting into a pile of hormonal goo as his large, muscular frame drapes around me and his hands are wandering into all sorts of forbidden territories. He keeps muttering against my lips that he needs to '*get going*' but the only place he *actually* goes is into my underwear and the part of him that I can feel '*getting going*'? Good LORD it's huge.

I, Erin Roberts, lose my virginity to Jamel Don't-know-his-surname on my mother's floral Argos patio recliner in a dark spider-filled garage at 3am in the morning. Jamel's kisses taste like Dr. Pepper and his mocha-toned skin tastes like fizzy sweets. He has hard ropey muscles that move under my fingers and when he likes something, his breath goes jagged and his kisses get wetter. In the dark, his hair feels like sponge and when he slowly slips inside me, he whisper swears. Whilst relatively painless, it is nonetheless the most astonishing and disconcerting event of my life thus far. Jamel, a well-endowed young man compared to Ryan, does an applaudable job of making it as pleasant as it could possibly be. If I'm honest, I could have been convinced to have another go afterwards given the brevity of the event itself but in the post-coital awkwardness, Jamel just busies himself in re-dressing and asking for directions back to the motorway.

As I adjust my own clothing, I feel awash with emotions that are too complex for words. I have never felt this *vulnerable* before. I want him to hug me, reassure me and kiss me but it doesn't seem to be on offer. As we gently open the up-and-over garage door enough to allow Jamel's exit, the words bubble unbidden from my mouth.

"What happens now?", I feel lost in this new adult landscape.

He turns, his hands shoved deep into his pockets and I can taste the uncertainty, it's like copper in my mouth.

"Er, I'll pick you up yeah? 'Bout 10 o'clock next Saturday night for that one in Oxford? Meet me at the end of this road?", he's gently kicking at the gravel on Dad's driveway.

"OK", I don't know what else to say.

He darts forward so fast that it makes me jump, as he presses a decidedly '*Distant relative at a wedding*' kiss on my cheek before muttering '*bye then*' and jogging off to his Golf.

The sound of his engine has faded to nothing before my tears start to fall. It's an hour later when I wake, swearing fiercely into the frosty dark of the garage, as I realise that not only did we not use any protection but that I also just had sex with somebody whose surname, occupation, familial history and indeed their basic information, I know nothing about. I cry until my head throbs.

8th April 1996

My garage deception pulled off with astonishing luck of which I am undeserving, Lees is wide eyed and pale as she rocks me gently in her arms on her bed as I sob snot over her truly awful chenille jumper.

"Rinny, chick, it'll be OK. You'll see him next Saturday and you can learn more about him. You just got the order of things a bit muddled up, that's all, sex came before the *knowing* but it'll be OK. Look, we'll get you to the GP on Monday for the Morning After pill, it'll be OK", I feel her nodding assertively against my hair but I know, *I just know*, that this particular calamity is not going to be quite so easily remedied.

We both forgot that Monday is a Bank Holiday. No GP for me. Tuesday comes around and I ring for an appointment but when the receptionist, a woman from my mother's church, tells me that it is 'emergencies only' for a same-day appointment, I am unable to formulate the words to explain that this *is* an emergency. *A sex related emergency.* I bottle it. I convince myself that you don't get pregnant your first time. On a sun lounger. In a garage. With a gorgeous stranger. At sixteen years and three days old. You just don't. There's no point risking the receptionist blabbing to my Mum for an outcome so unlikely.

I invest hours that following week devising elaborate cover stories, sleepover lies and machinations which allow me to be able to wait, undetected, at the end of my road at 10pm on Saturday for an all nighter with the only boy I've ever had sex with. I wait for three and half hours in the cold and the dark but Jamel never comes. I imagine emergencies, road works, navigational mishaps. I cry silent tears and then I excuse. He's ill, he doesn't have my phone number to let me know, I got the night wrong, the car broke down, he meant *Sunday* night not *Saturday*. As I creep into my poor, deceived father's garage and onto the fateful sun lounger for the second Saturday night in a row, I hear warning claxons in my head. I hear the gentle sound of horses hooves galloping towards me.

I don't sleep a wink.

Sunday night, I don't bother with a cover story. I simply sneak out at 10pm, undetected by my parents and I wait, desperation overwhelming what little logic I possess. I wait until 2am on a freezing cold street corner less than a hundred yards from my house as I feel my self-esteem leach from my bones with each passing minute. Jamel never comes.

Pulling every muscle in my body climbing in through my bedroom window, I lie on my bed and sob deep, aching silent tears. *Ugly, rank ginger Roberts.*

A flamey Bunsen-Burner death in Mr. Gibson's Physics lesson the next morning was therefore the least of my worries frankly. I curled up under Miss. Stanley's desk and slept until the bell rang, my heart hurting.

3rd May 1996

I can't lie, it's not been the most *chilled* build up to our GCSE's over the last few weeks. As if revision, coursework deadlines, hysteria, teacher nervous breakdowns and general teenage lunacy were not enough to deal with, I have had a little extra *fun and games* to navigate.

Ryan Jones is a proper twat.

My thwarted Romeo decided prior to his return to University post-Easter, to inform all of Adam's mates during a drunken 'boys night in' at their house just exactly what he and I had got up to prior to our 'split' and what, as far as he suspected, I had also got up to with 'Jamel the E Dealer'. My *goodness*, this was information that caused some interest, for a variety of different reasons.

There have been three broad themes.

Girls in my year: "*Fit Ryan Jones was only with her because she's a slag and she's easy. Let's make sure we're as bitchy as we can be, in both looks and comments every time we see her so that she knows we think very little of her*".

Boys in my year: "*Erin Roberts is well easy, she gives blow jobs and shags drug dealers. Let's make lewd and offensive comments every single second of the day when she's around*"

Everyone else: "*Have you heard about Erin Roberts? Let's whisper things that are entirely improbable about her as she walks past us*".

Oh yes, it's been a *hoot*. Miss. Humiliation Palmer-Smart has barely dismounted her steed for more than a few passing seconds for weeks now.

The are however some good things that have come out of this entire débâcle. My not-so-little brother Dylan has become my unexpected protector, my kindly defender. He's a pretty big lad Dyls, at fourteen he's already hitting six foot. We've always got on well, he's got a gentle and affable nature and as siblings, we rub along nicely. In recent weeks however, he's been hauled into the Head's office for a number of fights, prompting my mother into conniptions and my gentle father into mild scoldings.

Dyls has stayed schtum about the cause of all of these ruckus' but I know why he's been lamping all of these older lads. I know and I love him for it. I buy him chocolate bars at break time and I've been

31

doing his chores at home as an unspoken '*thank you*'. Last night, when he heard me having a pathetic little weep in my bedroom, he walked in and just hugged me. Not a word exchanged, he just hugged me and then walked back out muttering,

"They know fuck all 'bout you Rinny. Just ignore the bastards, eh?"

Lees also dumped poor Adam in an overly dramatic response to my distress at the gossip. The focus of her anger, Ryan, was not wounded in the slightest by this romantic severance, a point I made repeatedly as she wept on my shoulder. Lees wanted Adam to know that he should have stopped his brother from spreading his bitterness, that he should have been a more vociferous defender of me to earn her continued love. Adam, poor soul, wanted Lees to understand that,

"*I was so drunk that night Ryan told everyone that shit about you Erin, I was unconscious in the loo before all the lads arrived and that when I woke up, I'd pissed my pants and thrown up all over my hair*"

He was in a position to defend nobody that night, not even himself.

They got back together. I gave Adam an incontinence pad from the nursing home where Mum works to show there was no hard feelings. He laughed and whispered in my ear that his brother is an arsehole. I whispered back that Adam might be interested to know that his brother's erect dick was less than five inches long by my calculations. Adam grinned like he'd won the lottery. Since this happened, Adam has interceded on my behalf in a most animated fashion and to be fair, the lads are far less aggravation now than the bloody girls in my year.

"EARTH TO ROBERTS! Jesus woman, you gonna write on my bloody shirt or what?", I am jolted out of my slightly nauseous daydreaming by Gio Romano, brandishing a marker pen and pointing at his graffiti-scrawled shirt.

Today is the last day before study leave starts and my peers have all lost the proverbial plot. Teacher's cars have been egged and ketchup'd in the car-park, leading to two of my classmates being led away in handcuffs following their arrest for criminal damage after the ketchup stripped the paint off the cars. *Well played lads.*

There has been a water fight which saw an entire corridor of art-displays ruined and another five of my peers being frog-marched home under suspensions and the pièce de résistance was the arrival of the two ambulances which were required when another group decided to try stacking the picnic benches on the hockey field. They managed to make it to five benches high before the pile collapsed on them and the resultant crush injuries required paramedics.

The remainder of the Class of '96 are now sat under armed guard in our common room, Mr. Gibson threatening bloody deaths to anyone who so much as farts out of turn.

"You 'kay Roberts? You look well peaky?", Gio's face is scrunched up in concern which surprises me.

As a rule, I avoid Gio Romano. After being at school together for our entire childhoods and adolescence, the coffin nail in our fractious association was that night at the Under 18's Disco last year, when he and Daniel McNamara rode roughshod over my fragile teenage ego. He always makes a point of taking the piss or catcalling me on the bus, winking at me like he's *hilarious* when I retaliate.

Gio, the grandson of Italian immigrants, has become a little bit of a heart-throb this year though. He's by far the most physically matured lad in Year 11, he's over six feet tall and whispers abound about an alleged six-pack. He's also got the olive skin and dark curls that give him a bit of an edge on his more doughy, rural peers. To me, he will always be annoying Gio Romano who used to pick his bogies in Mass and whose willy I reluctantly observed in the home corner at playgroup when we were four. He'd cried when I'd dropped my own knickers and showed him my *fairy*. To be fair, I think he was expecting a woodland creature with wings. They were probably tears of disappointment.

He still considers Daniel McNamara to be his 'best mate' and on the school bus, my ears prick up when I hear him reading aloud Daniel's letters to the lads. Daniel is loving life in New Zealand, a surfer apparently and in possession of a tanned, blonde girlfriend whose photo elicited whoops from the lads.

Today though, our interaction is a continuance of what I can only describe as a 'thawing' in our association. I think that Adam has said something to Gio, I'm actually certain that he has, because it's often Adam AND Gio who wade in when the comments directed my way get too bawdy or the girls looks become too vicious.

Right now though, he's not wrong. I do feel peaky. In fact, I feel proper poorly.

"Gio, I don't feel very well", as I stand to run to the nearby loo, I am astonished to see that the common room carpet has also decided to come for a little jog with me. In fact, it's jogging very fast towards my face.

When I start to come round, my body is gently bouncing, as if I'm on a horse. I can't open my eyes right now because they are too heavy and it's too hard but I'm definitely riding something. I can feel something warm and firm against my cheek, strong supports against my back and under my knees and I can smell something nice, like herbs and lemons.

I think I've got on that bloody horse with Humiliation Palmer-Smart.

Then my horse speaks, "Don't you chunder on me Roberts, we're nearly at sick bay, don't you bloody

34

hurl on me now", it turns out that when horses speak, they do it with Gio Romano's voice.

I find the energy to prise open one eye and peer out like a tortoise.

"Gio?", I think that Gio Romano is *carrying* me.

"Roberts, you wanna be grateful I caught you back there. Your face was headed right for that floor and honestly, you can't afford to get any uglier"

I've thrown up all over him before I even realise what's happened. To be fair, he doesn't stop moving nor does he drop me but he's *not* happy,

"FUCK'S SAKE ROBERTS!! That is pure rank". I'm not listening though, the darkness has claimed me again.

"Erin, Erin! Come on poppet, open your eyes for me, come on sweetheart, if you don't open your eyes right now, I'm going to have to call an ambulance. Erin!", I jump as somebody shouts in my ear and I feel a sharp pinch to my other earlobe.

"Owww!", I jolt and sit bolt upright, blinking in the bright florescent light of what I quickly realise is Miss. Harvey's sick bay.

I turn and see a concerned looking Miss. Harvey, a pretty twenty-something who multi-tasks as the school Bursar, sick bay manager and Head Teacher's PA. I groan as another wave of nausea sweeps over me although it's arrested by the sight of a shirtless Gio Romano thrusting a cardboard bowler hat under my chin, "In there Roberts, not all over any other bastard this time".

"MR. ROMANO! Mind your language and will you PLEASE go and put a shirt on", Miss, Harvey scolds him but I spot the slight blush in her cheeks. *Those six-pack rumours were spot on then Romano.*

Miss. Harvey runs through the standard checklist as Gio rinses his vomit covered shirt in the sick bay sink. Have I been sick before today? What did I last eat? Have I got a temperature? Have I banged my head today? Anyone else ill in my family? Blah, blah. Nothing of any significance.

As he rinses his shirt, Gio shouts over his shoulder from across the room, "This isn't the first time a woman's puked on me, y'know. My cousin did at Christmas, turns out she was knocked up but she had no clue until she chundered in my lap", he turns back to the sink sniggering.

I don't laugh. I don't move. I feel every single drop of blood drain from my upper body and pool in my feet as my veins re-fill with ice. I hear the Rolodex of my mental calendar ticking in my head and I realise that the small stockpile of Tampax in my bedside drawer has built up for a reason.

I turn, in almost comedic slow motion, to stare at Miss. Harvey. My eyes must look like saucers and I can feel my lip wobbling as my eyes fill with tears. To be fair, Miss. Harvey's facial expression is even funnier, I'd laugh if I wasn't on the verge of collapse. Her face drains of colour in response to my wide eyed panic and her jaw drops as if it lost the pin in its hinge.

I can't stop the sob that falls out of my mouth and Miss Harvey, her youth never more evident, claps her hand to her mouth in astonishment with no pretence of professional neutrality.

"Oh my fucking GOD Roberts, are you serious?", I swivel like the girl from the Exorcist to face a gob smacked Romano, who also looks like he's seen a ghost.

Miss. Harvey is roused into belated action, "MR ROMANO, OUT! Take your shirt and please leave, I need to speak to Erin on her own. Get a spare shirt from the office if you need one", she leaps up and makes ushering motions but Gio is just staring at me and not moving, his surprisingly broad chest heaving as he takes deep, shocked breaths.

My eyes must be broadcasting more info than the Time Square Billboards. Shock, panic, horror, shame, fear, astonishment- they're all there, flicker-taping across my features as loud as any shout. I gasp as Gio comes towards me, his face surprisingly kind and conciliatory looking,

"Want me to fetch Morris?", his voice is a gentle murmur.

Lees. I need my Lees. I nod frantically, prompting the spillage of more tears down my face. He nods and gently pats my arm before he heads swiftly out of the door, bare chested and clutching his dripping shirt. That hand-pat transmitted as much of a message as any words. "*Your secret's safe with me Roberts*", was what Gio meant and in these brief seconds, I trust him.

The door slams behind him and I turn to see Miss. Harvey rummaging around in her handbag, her arms visibly shaking as she shifts things around.

From its depths, she retrieves a slim cardboard package in shiny cellophane wrap. She looks nervous as she turns to me, biting her lip and a sort of beseeching look on her face.

She looks at me earnestly, "Have you done a test Erin?". My lip wobbles as I shake my head.

Miss. Harvey darts glances round the room and whispers, "Look, we're not allowed to give girls these here in school but I happen to have one in my bag", she suddenly blushes and looks uncomfortable, wincing as she looks at me.

"I don't er, need it now but Erin, take it and go and use it. Just please don't tell anyone you got it from me", her very pretty face is racked with what I know must be anxiety about professional boundaries being crossed and in response, I break a few of my own by throwing my arms around her and hugging her in gratitude. The squeeze she gives me in return gives me immeasurable comfort right now.

"I'll be back in a minute Erin, just use the staff loo through that door", Miss. Harvey straightens her skirt and walks off towards the door that leads to the photocopying room as I sit and stare at the packet in my lap.

Holy. Shit.

Two minutes later, Lees bursts through the door like a tornado, "OH MY GOD Rinny!! Did you really chunder on Romano?! I swear, Gio just walked into the art room half-naked and Mr. Dobbs nearly came in his trousers! He said you needed to see.......me......", Lees' voice loses its volume and tempo as she spots the box I'm holding in my lap.

She looks at me, aghast, "Oh Rinny, oh no, oh *shit*", as Lees launches herself at me, I collapse in her arms, sobbing out all of my hurt, my panic, my fear and my *fucking* humiliation.

She leads me to the loo, reading the instructions and holding my hand tightly as my sobs make my stream of pee stop and start like a learner driver bunny-hopping down a road.

When the second blue line slowly develops in the window, I howl in anguish, prompting Lees' own hysterical tears.

"Oh Erin, oh sweetheart, oh you poor thing", Miss. Harvey appears in the doorway and pulls us both into a shaky hug.

Lees and I don't go back to the morning's timetabled final exam prep classes. Miss. Harvey's professional training was limited to tea making and leaflets about Family Planning clinics and abortion helplines. I took them with a weak smile and let Lees lead me out of the gate and to the park near our school, where we sat cuddled on a bench, not speaking, as we absorbed the morning's events.

It's the rumble from Lees' stomach that elicits the first noise from either of us, quiet chuckles and moans about being 'starving' follow. As we stand and stretch our stressed-out muscles, Lees spots two familiar shapes lumbering towards us from across the park.

Gio is wearing a Hockey Team hoodie, stretched tight over his stupidly big body. Adam looks like an underpass on a London sink estate, so covered in graffiti is his uniform.

"Lees, I've been looking for you EVERYWHERE. I thought we were going to the chippy for lunch babe?", Adam's affable shout is relaxed as he sweeps Lees up into a gentle, sweet hug and a little snog.

Gio looks at me, his eyebrows raised in a silent question. My sad nod and lip wobble says all it needs to as he closes his eyes and nods slowly. *Pregnant.*

"Erin, I've brought you some chips too coz honestly, I'd pay you a good £20 if you throw up over this dickhead again- have you seen him in this shitty hoodie?", Adam's laugh elicits weak smiles from Gio and I.

Frowning, Adam looks back and forth between the three of us, all very sombre and quiet.

"Right, what's going on, eh? I know you're not that pissed off at Roberts for the chunder but you've said like three words Romano since it happened and now these two, who *never* fucking shut up, look like they're going to a funeral. Lees, babe? What's happened? Why did Gio fetch you out of art, why did you and Erin leave school before lunch?"

Both Lees and Gio look down at the grass, sweetly refusing to breach my confidentiality. I take a deep shaky breath and I say the words for the first time,

"Adam, I just found out that I'm pregnant, that's why I was sick on Gio and why Lees took me out of school. I'm pregnant Ads", and with those words, the tears claim me again.

I'm in Lees' arms and then it changes, the body changes and I hear other sobs that aren't mine but I'm too lost in my tearful terror to work out what's happened.

"It'll be okay Roberts, it'll work out okay, don't freak out, yeah?", it's Gio that's hugging me and as I crack an eye open, I see that Adam is now holding a sobbing Lees.

I hear Gio snort, the sound rumbles through his chest against my cheek, "Anyways, it should be me crying not you. I get bloody chunks blown all over the shirt that Carolyn Gregory wrote on saying that she'd give me a proper dirty shag after the prom. That's like a written contract innit? I could take her to court if she doesn't deliver on that promise but not now, not when the writing's all washed off coz you chundered on it. Jesus Roberts, your up-chuck just cost my dick big time".

In all this life-changing horror, it's bloody Gio Romano that makes me smile. That wannabe-Italian moron makes me smile.

I stand back, wiping snot across the back of my hand as he looks suitably grossed out and I smirk, "Don't kid yourself Romano, I doubt *anything* about your dick is 'big time'"

He smirks back with a chuckle, "Well, if there's an expert on dicks round here, you're probably the one to ask, eh Pramface?", and as I thump him on the chest laughing, I feel a tiny bit lighter than I did.

Adam eventually gets over the shock, although he does throw his chips in the air as he jumps to his feet at one point, "Oh Holy Shit, is it my brother's?".

I reassure him that it is not, his relief appears to be more for me than for his avoided Uncle-hood. My best friend, her boyfriend and my as-yet-uncategorised non-enemy Romano kindly don't ask me who the father *actually* is although you can almost taste the curiosity. Lees knows though, the squeeze of my hand tells me that she knows.

"What you gonna do Roberts? You gonna keep it?", Gio, his mouth filled with chips, asks the headline question, the one that Miss. Harvey's pamphlets have been silently shouting from my pocket.

I knew, the moment that second line started to appear, I *knew*. I will be having this baby. My Mum and Dad's reactions will be off the conniption Richter scale, my Nana will proclaim it as proof of my true *chopsy* nature and my Aunties will exchange meaningful looks about the niece that is always to blame for tribal-cousin misdemeanours (I organised all fourteen of us onto the roof of the Social Club in Port Talbot at my Auntie Eileen's Fiftieth last year, singing 'Come on Eileen' obnoxiously as we let off fireworks). Dad's family will purse their lips and tut into their Earl Grey.

I have no idea how I will support me and my baby or what our life together will look like but what I do know is that I will be a mum in about eight months and I *will* figure this all out.

"I'm having the baby Gio. I'm going to keep my baby", I nod determinedly and eat my chips, ignoring the slack-jawed stares of my companions.

I hear a deep gulp, "Fair play Roberts, fair play", Gio's tanned hand pats my knee and we all stare out over the playing field, digesting.

11th May 1996

I gave myself a weeks grace, I felt I needed to get my head together before I opened the wormhole in my universe. My friends and *Romano* sworn to secrecy, I allowed myself a week to work through my options before my parents were told.

I've bailed on the prom, a decision that caused Lees anguish. Mum was really shocked when I said that I wasn't going to go,

"But *cariad*, you'd picked such a pretty dress. Honestly Erin, the way you do change your mind is ridiculous, what are we going to do with that dress by there?", she'd nodded towards the wardrobe where my lovely Morgan dress hangs.

I'd sighed, "I've got the receipt Mum, I'll take it back in my lunch break on Saturday"

The returned dress and the un-purchased ticket will save me £100 of waitressing wages which I think I'll need for more important things. *Nappies for starters.* Pretty much all of my year will be staying on to Sixth Form so the prom has limited meaning if I'm honest. It's mainly an excuse for people to snog and shag on an artificial deadline and that is the *last* thing I have any interest in right now.

I only allow myself to cry at night, between the hours of midnight and 1am. I'm very strict about this, I have to limit my self-pity. In that hour, I see Jamel's smirk as he leaned in for that first kiss, I feel his lips against the skin of my neck, his deep rumbling voice, the gasps as our bodies slipped and slid together in the most intimate of conversations. I see those bright glitter shards of excitement and feel the tingle-thrill of being *desired.* The humiliation swiftly creeps in from the wings and I writhe under my duvet, in agony from the knowledge that it was all a pretty lie, that it was all entirely in my head and that I had been used, undesirable for anything other than a brief thrill. *Rank, ugly, ginger Roberts.*

What tips me into proper snotty sobs, every night, is the knowledge that *if* following the search that is now required Jamel is never found, the only story I can give my child is that their mother allowed herself to be impregnated by a stranger on their grandmother's patio recliner in a garage. I have nothing to offer them in terms of information, I don't even know his surname. What a *truly* auspicious conception and back story.

I quickly realised that the key to the future for me and *my baby* is getting my GCSE's, my A Levels and the place at University that I really want. How I will achieve this with a small child, I have no frikking clue but I feel, deep in my bones, that this is the path the two of us need to take. *Together.*

Yesterday I looked at myself in the mirror, naked. I'm a couple of inches over five foot, slim but not skinny, stupidly big boobs which *do my head in* and curly ginger hair that reaches my hips. My eyes are a coppery brown, they sort of match my hair and I have a smattering of freckles that no foundation can silence.

As I rested my palm over my not-flat-much-longer tummy, I felt an odd peace because I think, I *hope*, that when this little bundle of rapidly generating cells arrives, they will love me. They will *love* me and all the crazy aggro I cause and hopefully the daft situations that humiliation lures me into won't phase them. They'll be mine and I'll be theirs and we will link arms and face life together.

I just need to tell my parents now.

Today I struggled through the first few hours working my Saturday shift in the cafe, the Romano-Chunder incident marking the start of daily morning nausea which stalks me until lunchtime most days. Serving greasy fry-ups and soggy omelettes does little to assist me in coping and in the end I volunteer for laundry duties, keen to be away from anything edible for a bit.

I earn £40 every Saturday working as a waitress but I know that this summer will require me to ramp up my earning efforts, stockpiling cash to pay for the babygrow-requiring consequences of my actions. As I steam the thick tablecloths in the large press, I steel myself for the conversation that I must have tonight. Once my parents are told, I have to then focus on two things. My bloody revision that keeps me up at night in cold sweats and the search I must undertake for Jamel. I talked to Lees about it last night,

"Chick, I'll have to speak to *sodding* Ryan, he's the only person I know who is vaguely linked to Jamel. I.......I'll ask him once Mum and Dad know. Jesus, Ryan'll love this, eh? The ultimate revenge", I slumped against Lees' headboard as she patted my knee and agreed to get Ryan's Bristol number from Adam.

Waitressing shift over, I get on the bus home, my heart racing. My plan is to target Mum first, her reaction will be the biggest but the easiest to manage. Mum directs everything outwards, she lays it all on display. She's loud, incredulous and swift to emote but she is also straightforward and once she has vented and exploded, she calms and she plans routes through to solutions. *I need her.* My mum is the middle child of five children, she grew up in a pretty tough part of the Welsh Valleys, her resilience and plain talking leading her to a career as a Nurse. Mum now works as the Matron of a Nursing Home within walking distance of our house and I sometimes help out in the kitchens for extra cash.

Dad will be much harder to deal with. He will be so, so desperately disappointed in me. It's actually Dad's reaction that I am most fearful of, even though he will barely raise his voice. Dad will just look quietly devastated and it will *slay* me. Dad met Mum when she nursed him after a nasty car accident. Dad was a cocky Student from Cambridgeshire, studying Maths at Cardiff Uni. When he crashed his beloved motor into a brick wall, he awoke to see red-haired, trainee-nurse Bronwen Lewis scolding him for his stupidity as she tenderly wiped his face in a hospital bed. *Love at first sight.* He became a Chartered Accountant, bringing his new no-nonsense Welsh wife across the border to the sleepy Wiltshire town where we now live. Dad is a gentle, quiet guy and at well over six foot tall with thick tawny blonde hair, he and Dyls look almost identical. Mum is little and curvy, I suspect that my youthful slenderness will be short lived.

Mum finishes her shift at five, I'll get back at six and Dad is at the footie with Dyls until about seven so my window of opportunity to get her alone is slim.

"Hello love, how was work?", Mum is stirring chilli at the hob as I walk in the door.

A bit of small talk, a scolding for my failure to eat lunch, a concerned enquiry as to whether I'm *sure* I don't want to go to the prom tonight and then I feel the opportunity open up.

"Mum, I need to talk to you about something before Dad gets home and well, it's big so can we go and sit down?", I nod towards the lounge but my Mum is immediately wary.

"Oh Holy Mary, it was you wasn't it, with the bloody ketchup on those teacher's cars?! I bloody knew it, I said to your Dad I did, when the school sent out that letter, '*That's got Erin written **all** over it'*. Well my good girl, you are going to pay every penny yourself. Honestly, if you had an OUNCE of your Lisa's sense, I'd be *thrilled*", she's crossed her arms over her chest and has her lips pursed like Les Dawson.

I roll my eyes, "God's sake mother, if I was going to do *anything* to their cars, I'd be cutting the brake lines not decorating them with *condiments.* Mum, please, I need you", my cocky tone disappears as my voice cracks and I realise the truth, *I need my Mum.*

"Erin, what is it sweetheart?", Mum's tone immediately shifts, concern written all over her face as she rubs my arms.

Man up, Roberts. Out with it.

"Mum, I'm pregnant", it's a whisper that leaves my lips but it might as well be a scream.

Mum's hand covers her heart, dropping the tea-towel as she does it. She steps backwards and grasps the worktop, her mouth working soundlessly. I fill the silence with my own words, trying to delay her inevitable explosion,

"I'm about six weeks gone, I've got to go to the GP next week I guess. I, er, I'm going to keep the baby and I've spent the whole week thinking about it and so I'm sure that I don't want to get an abortion, or an adoption or anything else. I want my baby and if you and Dad don't want me here, I saw that there's a flat for rent near the cafe and with benefits I can probably afford...."

I'm cut off as Mum asks, "Whose is it Erin, who's the father?", I feel an icy trickle of undiluted horror spike through my heart at both the question and the solitary tear that is running down my mum's cheek.

I close my eyes and whisper, "His name is Jamel. It....it was a one off thing Mum, he.....he dumped me after we....y'know....I haven't seen him again", I feel my own tears, cool rivulets down my cheeks.

Mum covers her eyes with her hand and we stand in silence, for what feels like the rest of my adolescence. Mum eventually shakes her head, huffing out a series of deep breaths before she drops her hand and slowly walks towards me, reaching for my shoulders. I look up at her, she's taller than me by a few inches,

"You and my grandchild will be going nowhere Erin, at least not until I am certain that you can manage to keep you and little *cwtch* fed and properly cared for because Madam, I do still remember the life that poor bloody pet rabbit of yours endured and I will not have my grandchild going through *that*", she rolls her eyes at me but there is a smile in the corner of her mouth.

She nods with determination, "You will sit every one of those GCSEs and it'll be to Sixth Form with you lady, we will sort it all out between us and this Jamel's family. Now, that boy might be a little shit who needs a proper hiding for the way he's treated you but he's going to be a Dad and he'll just have to step up. He's at school with you? I've never heard his name before Erin, he wasn't at your Junior School, eh?", Mum is starting to turn back towards the chilli as she speaks.

I'm fighting too many emotions. Relief at my mother's efficient salvation, her acceptance, the *affection* in her words but now there's pain, there's regret and there is the terror of her impending disappointment in me. I shake my head slowly as the tears start anew.

"Erin?", Mum's seen my distress.

I look down, "He's not at school with me mum. He's……..older"

"How old?"

"Nineteen"

"Where's he from"

"I don't really know, Bristol I think"

"What does he do?"

"I don't know"

"Does he live with his parents?"

"I don't know"

"Erin, what *do* you know about this boy?", my Mum's voice is pitched just below hysteria.

"He's called Jamel, he's nineteen, he drives a Golf, he's got brothers and a Nigerian nan", *and he deals drugs.*

"SWEET FUCKING JESUS Erin!!", my mother has sworn like this only once before when I'd bought a pretty convincing fake tattoo at the market and a fake nose stud and I returned from a night at Lees' aged fourteen, faux-pierced and fake-branded. Mum had briefly lost it.

The rest of the night is a bit of a blur if I'm honest. Mum rages at my poor choices with stranger-boys, she nurse-scolds me for my lack of contraceptive wisdom, she belatedly panics for the risks I have taken and the deceptions I engaged in, she shouts, she hugs and then she cries with me.

I'm in bed before my Dad and Dyls get back, too wrung out to stay awake. Mum takes the hit for me, she'll tell Dad.

I lie in my childhood bed, feeling about a thousand years old despite the floor to ceiling evidence around me that I have lived only sixteen. As Tim Burgess and Keith Flint smile down at me from my walls, I contemplate the Prom based rite of passage that my friends are engaged in right now. I wonder if Lees got those chicken fillets to stay put in her new bra, I wonder if Gio will get his promised shag from Carolyn, I wonder if the Practically Perfects will wow in their collection of Miss. Selfridge's finest couture. I wonder if anyone will notice my absence.

I wonder if Jamel Don't-Know-His-Surname has any fucking clue about the true devastation that can be wrought by five minutes on an Argos patio recliner.

Chapter Three

15th May 1996

"Why the fuck are you ringing me, eh? Who gave you this number? Was it my dickhead brother?"

I roll my eyes to the ceiling, "Ryan, I'm really sorry to bother you, I just wondered if you had a number or any way of me getting hold of er, Jamel, that guy you bought drugs off back at the rave?"

I hear a derisive snort, "I'd have thought he'd have given you his digits, eh? I thought you were *with* him Erin, you were pretty much fucking him at the rave?"

I grit my teeth, "Er no, we aren't together but I need to get hold of him about something urgent. Ryan, I know you don't like me but please, this is important, do you have his number or even an address or *something*?"

I hear a bored sigh at the other end, "Look, he doesn't answer his pager any more, he hasn't done for weeks. Nobody's scored off him for ages. He lives in Bristol but that's all I know"

I manage to extract the pager number from Ryan and I'm about to thank him and swiftly end this most uncomfortable call when he jeers,

"When a girl wants to get hold of a bloke they don't see any more, it only means two things *Erin*. He's either given her a dose of something nasty or he's knocked her up. Which is it, eh?", he's laughing now. *Bastard.*

I hang up.

Within an hour, I'd sent Jamel's pager two messages with my phone number. Initially I just paged him my number but then, realising that he might not see that as anything of note, I prefixed the second message with '911'. I have done this every night since that first message but he's not rung back.

7th June 1996

When you look forward to entering the silent exam room because it's the only time you get any relief from the gossiping whispers and the hissed insults, you realise that it's perhaps time to move your pregnant, ginger butt to Peru.

I am indeed pregnant. Preggers. Preggo. The GP reckons that my due date is the 12th December but he told me that the scan I'm having today will confirm it.

My Dad cried. I didn't see it but I heard it. Mum sent Dyls to his mates house straight after football the night I told her and I heard her using the gentle voice that she does with my Uncle Gethin, who has Down's Syndrome, as she broke the news to my Dad. I heard her gentle voice and then the silence and then the hoarse, rusty, *broken* sound that my Dad made and I had to shove my fingers in my ears and muffle my tears in my pillow.

Dad came into my room very late that night and he pressed a whisky scented kiss on my forehead as he whispered, "I love you Princess" against my skin, before he walked out. I heard the rusty, broken sound again through the wall dividing our rooms.

Mum bought me prenatal vitamins. Mum took me to the GUM clinic and made me have the most humiliating appointment *ever* for STD tests, "*Yes, I'm sixteen and pregnant. Yes, I had unprotected sex with a complete stranger and I have no idea about his health or sexual histories. No, I have no clue how to get hold of him. Of course you can stick that swab there*". All clear, thank God.

Ryan came home from Uni and Adam, bless him, had not been able to adequately fake denial when his dickhead brother had aggressively asked him if I was pregnant. Adam's stumbling, unconvincing rebuttals simply confirmed what Ryan suspected and within two hours of him frequenting the first pub in our small town, the gossip waves started. Impressive really. By the end of the night, everyone knew that Erin Roberts was pregnant aged sixteen by a drug dealer who'd dumped her, you could literally see the phone lines crackling in our town.

Adam was told by eight separate people that I was knocked up within the space of twenty minutes. Gio, breaking his lip-lock with Carolyn for a few short seconds, rang me to say that the cat was well and truly bag-sprung. Lees turned up in red-cheeked fury, hugging me tight and threatening painful curses upon the head of her brother-in-law.

It's been a marvel for my GCSE performance however, this pregnancy malarkey. The gossip has rendered me housebound and I genuinely spend twelve hours a day revising. I have no other distractions, my friends invite me to parties that I have no desire to endure and as such, I am the *Queen* of the practice paper. I go into exam rooms with a confidence that renders me cocky, I will absolutely *nail* these bastard exams because right now, they are all I have control over in my life.

"You OK love, how did the English paper go?", Mum collected me at lunchtime to drive me to my 2pm scan at the hospital.

I have no idea how they will find anything worth looking at on this scan, I've lost so much weight from this morning sickness shite that my belly is perhaps flatter than it has ever been. I expect to see nothing more than a tiny pinhead dot, waving at me.

As we wait in the Antenatal Clinic, I become aware that this is the first time I have been publicly identified as a *pregnant person*. The school gossip and local whispers are one thing but my discreet midwife 'booking in' session at the GP surgery was undertaken when there was nobody but deaf old people in the waiting room to observe me being called in. *This* is my first foray into an official setting where my pregnancy is openly and legitimately acknowledged. As I peruse the 1993 editions of 'Home and Garden Magazine' on offer, I feel eyes on me. I slowly look over the pages of Slow Cooker recipes and I see a collection of *couples,* clutching hands but shooting me and my mother furtive glances. A couple of the women smile kindly but I can taste the judgement. I'm wearing school uniform, I might as well have a neon sign saying '*Guess what I got up to when I shouldn't have?'* pointed at me.

"Erin Roberts, is Erin Roberts here?", the Ultrasound technician calls my name and my mother's hand propels me from my seat.

Jesus Christ, I'm properly pregnant.

I'm ushered onto a very comfy looking leather bed, in a room that looks like the bridge of some sort of space shuttle. Madhoo the ultrasound technician takes some details and confirms the ones that she has already. She does a stirling job of looking unruffled when my answers expose just how little I know about the father of my unborn child and how he is not involved. Mum squeezes my hand in support and chats in an overly-jovial manner to mask everyone's discomfort.

"Right then Erin, this gel is a bit cold I'm afraid my love but let's see what your little one is up to shall we?", as she smothers my belly in chilly slime, a screen beside me flickers into life and Madhoo runs a large potato masher over my belly.

She's concentrating *really* hard, in the gloom I see the furrows of her brow. If I was staring at the screen I would have missed it but as I'm staring at Madhoo, I catch the widening of her eyes, the upward flick of her eyebrows, the slight inhalation that she makes. I feel my heart start to race.

What now? What the fuck now?

"Er, I'm just going to ask my colleague to join us for a second. Please excuse me, I'll only be a second Erin", and Madhoo shoots off out the door.

"Muuuuuuuuum", my wail is pathetic and my Mum's frantic reassurance is too brittle to do anything other than panic me further.

"It's OK Erin, it's OK cariad, this is normal. She's just checking that little cwtch is tip top. I expect it's all that weight you've lost, maybe they're going to say you do need to have a few more fluids", Mum's rambling.

A serious looking lady with short grey hair comes in with Madhoo and with curt nods to me and Mum, she takes the potato masher and does her own sweep of my now shaking belly. She looks at Madhoo and nods, her expression sombre. She nods again at me and walks off, exiting my life in a cloud of mystery. Mum and I swivel our heads to Madhoo who looks like she wished she'd rung in sick.

"Well, Erin, the great news is it looks as if both your babies are developing really well. Two good strong heartbeats and lovely developing bones and organs. Let me show you on the screen", she sits down a bit too quickly.

My mother finds her voice first, "Pardon love?"

Madhoo exhales, "Twins Mrs. Roberts, I'm pleased to tell you that Erin is having twins. Fraternal twins by the looks of things, two separate amniotic sacs, can you see here?".

Too shocked to do anything other than stare, Madhoo outlines what look like two pale grey balloons inside which are each housed a wriggling kidney bean with bits sprouting off it. Two of them.

Twins. Of course it's twins, why would Erin 'Calamity' Roberts just have the one baby?

"Oh my fucking Christ", well, my mother's clarified her position on the matter.

"FUCKING HELL MUM!! I'm having fucking twins!", me too it seems.

"ERIN ROBERTS! Mind your language madam!", oh for God's sake.

I'm pointing accusingly at the screen, sitting up slightly, pale faced and wobbly. Madhoo has a rictus smile on her face and I just know she's praying that the next woman is much less aggravation. She patiently shows me *both* my babies on the screen as I sob and snot pathetically. My mother looks as if somebody hit her with a large, wet fish.

With shaking hands and muttered thanks, we feed a vending machine about a dozen pound coins and in return, we get endless prints of two tiny, slightly fuzzy, button noses in profile, long-legged gremlins. I sit in the chair and stare at these life-changers, these tiny little secret parts of me.

Mum watches me, gentle tears rolling down her cheeks as I run my hands over my uniform clad tummy and whisper,

"Are you OK in there? Are you both OK? I'll try and eat a bit more I promise, now I know you have to share the food"

Mum and I don't say a word on the way home, not a single syllable. She holds my hand in between gear changes as I stare at the photos of little people who will now change my life *twice* over.

12th July 1996

Today was my final exam, I am eighteen weeks pregnant and I now have the belly to suggest that it's not all a figment of my imagination.

It seems an odd thing to say in light of recent events but my life over the last few weeks has been mind-numbingly dull. Outside of antenatal grenades being thrown, all I have done, every single damn day, is revise or go to work. I only see Lees really, the girls that I get on with in my year have all been a little wary of me, the risk of 'gossip taint' too strong it seems. Oddly, I have actually seen a fair bit of bloody Romano, our amicable truce since 'Vomit-fest' has seemingly developed further into a semi-friendship. He's been seeing Carolyn Gregory since the Prom but he gives me a ring a couple of times a week, mainly for revision advice and he pops over a fair bit.

I did manufacture my only recent bit of drama a few weeks back. Dragged to McDonalds the day after the scan, Lees wanted to see pictures of the *baby.* This unveiling was to be done with a big blow-out meal and our favourite milkshakes. She brought Adam, he brought Gio and Gio brought a slightly disgruntled Carolyn, who's fear of the 'Pramface Taint' meant that I only got cat-piss smiles off her when she arrived.

"So, c'mon Rinny, show us the pictures of Auntie Lee's little angel", Adam had rolled his eyes at Lees' daft baby voice that she adopts whenever she discusses my *baby.*

Gio's arm was slung over Carolyn and with Lees in Adams arms, I felt a little stab of self-pity that I had nobody to cuddle me but then I remembered my secret, my multiple *loves* and the stab faded away.

I lay the fuzzy, slightly baffling photo on the table as they all leant in.

"OK Roberts, 'fess up, you're not pregnant at all are you? This looks like a toddler drew bubbles in grey and black paint", Gio had looked baffled as he stared at the tiny picture.

Kissing my teeth, I pointed a freshly bitten nail at one half of the picture, "Here's the baby, look, its head is here, its nose is there and that's its leg", there were slightly confused '*ahhhs*' all round.

With a sly grin, I took a breath as I looked at the cluster of bowed heads as I pointed to the other half of the photo, "....and here, here is the *other* baby, there's its nose, its arm and its tummy". *I waited.*

Four incredulous faces slowly rose up to look at me as I nodded with a faux '*can you believe it?*' expression on my face.

"FUCKING HELL!!!", Gio was the loudest responder, earning hissed admonishments from the parents of the children surrounding us.

He turned to his fiercest critic, "Oh shut up woman, Pramface here is having TWINS!", making us all snort with laughter.

Carolyn was definitely the one who spread *that* news, she was too quick to dash off to 'meet friends'. By teatime, everyone knew that Erin Roberts had copped for a 'double dose'. My mother says she's no longer going to the supermarket during the daytime after she got stopped by no less than thirty-seven people all nosily enquiring as to the *health* of her family. The frozen veg was soggy by the time she got to the till.

Back in May, before all this bollocks kicked off, I secured full-time summer work and I start tomorrow, stuffing envelopes and filing at the local Water Board offices. It will be, without exception, the most dull thing I have ever done but it pays a startlingly good wage and combined with my

Saturday job, I will be bringing in the best part of £1000 per month. I have not told them I'm pregnant and I don't plan to mention it. I'm hoping they all just assume I'm fat.

The wage is good news because it turns out that baby stuff is bloody expensive. I mean, there are *some* benefits to being the family disgrace. I am the first of my generation to produce offspring. My three Aunties all have children of their own, my cousins aged between eight and twenty-four. None of them have produced kids yet and as soon as my mum hesitantly announced my pregnancy and later upgraded it to twins, I have been receiving massive bundles of clothes, equipment, toys and sundries as my Uncles make full use of my transgressions to empty their cluttered lofts and garages.

My Uncle, Mum's baby brother Gethin who has Downs Syndrome, has been taught to knit by his carer and he is furnishing me with the BEST baby hats and jumpers I have ever seen. Entirely lopsided, ambiguous holes for limbs and startling shades of cheap wool, I genuinely cannot wait to dress my babies like a drunk unicorn vomited rainbows all over them.

Dyls, my placid, gentle, quietly hilarious brother, has been a bit of a legend. He stopped beating people up at school for slagging me off. He begrudgingly admitted that it was too large a task to manage and he lacked the energy.

Instead he has got his best mate, a fantastically gobby little girl called Matty, to channel her talents into spreading outrageous rumours about anyone who is particularly nasty about me. Together, they have convinced the entire school populace that Ryan Jones was born with his penis inside his body and that his petite prick is the result of multiple attempts to provide him with a working phallus.

Adam informed me last week that when drunk, Ryan has started stripping to prove to people that the rumours are false but the truth is, he *doesn't* have a very big dick, it really is quite *underwhelming* and he has cemented his new nickname of '*Pixie Prick*' (Matty came up with that). He is spending the summer back at his Uni house in Bristol as a result.

Some of the nasty girls in my year have had similar treatment, vaginal boils an affliction I was unaware of until Matty got everyone believing that every time one particularly vicious girl sits down, she leaks puss and has to wear a sanitary towel every day. She has no non-humiliating way of proving this to be false and the title of '*Pus Pussy*' was bestowed upon her. Matty is genuinely terrifying, I have warned Dyls to always stay on the right side of her.

Dyls is nervous about the babies, I know this. He's scared about how it will impact on our pretty straightforward family life. I can't reassure him, I'm too terrified myself.

Mum and Dad have told me that they are giving me their bedroom for the twins and I. It's got the en-suite that my mum had always wanted and I cry hormonal tears of gratitude for her sacrifice. Their larger room can accommodate two cots and a double bed, as well as the endless baby crap I'll need.

We don't ever talk about what happens when my babies are too big for cots and my family of three no longer fit into the house. We leave that undiscussed.

I still send messages every day to Jamel's pager, telling him I'm pregnant and asking him to call me. It's become my little routine at bedtime, it gives me a weird sense of comfort. I spend a huge amount of my time now panicking about how the *actual fuck* I will manage the life that is hurtling towards me, bringing with me the two babies that I feel I already know. They're two boys, I know this with every fibre of my being despite the fact that my local hospital doesn't reveal genders during scans and I can't explain my certainty without sounding mental.

Paging Jamel every day, it makes me feel like some sort of rescue might still come, that I might not be left on my own with this, that I might get some help from an equally guilty party. Whenever Mum points out the cost of nappies, the cost of buggies, the cost of *anything* I feel this sick sort of guilt, this sense of imposition. I need Jamel to be here to feel this too because as time goes on, it's making me feel pretty shit and it's what spurs me on to earn as much money as possible.

My bump is very obvious now. In the course of the last six weeks, it has 'popped out' astonishingly quickly, almost as if the scan prompted it to 'perform'. I am losing clothing options by the day, as my wardrobe struggles to accommodate my rapidly expanding girth. My midwife says that this sometimes happens with twins, this astonishing inflation.

I've already been told that my two little goblins will be coming out 'via the sunroof'. There will be no lady-garden traumas for me, my small frame and the fact that there are two babies to navigate out have already led my midwife and the consultant I went to see to conclude that it is the butchers knife for me. I will be having a planned C-Section at 38 weeks, a decision that I was happy to go along with given the secret fear I'd been harbouring about baby-heads and my under-experienced fanny. This means that my babies are now due mid-November.

As we travel home this afternoon, exams finished, there's a deep, friendly shout from the back of the bus,

"OI! Roberts, you coming out tonight then? Eh? Celebrate the end of this nightmare?", Gio and the lads, entirely delirious from our exam freedom, are currently letting the girls who swarm them like flies on shit apply make-up to their faces. They honestly look like a Widow Twanky convention and the girls giggle and simper, flicking hair and looking coy as they take any excuse to touch the boys.

I notice that Carolyn is not sitting with them, she appeared to be getting into the car of one of the fit Lower Sixth lads as the bus pulled off.

I turn, breaking my horrible daydream about C-Sections and I scrunch my nose up, "Nah Romano, I start my job tomorrow, I need an early night". *I also do not want to be the sideshow attraction at a party of drunk people.*

Gio prises himself out of his seat and wobbles down the bus towards me, his decorated face looking more Coco The Clown as opposed to Coco Chanel. He slumps into the empty seat beside me,

"C'mon Rin, it'll be a laugh, don't be a Pramface Killjoy", he winks as I look boggled.

"Rin?", I cock an eyebrow

"Yeah, I'm trying it out. What do you reckon?", he smirks at me

"I reckon keep trying, *Giovanni*", I laugh as his smirk turns into a frown.

He nudges me, "C'mon, you don't need to stay long, just show your face, eh? I'll walk you back if you get knackered. Morris is coming with Ad......c'mon woman, you've been like a fucking hermit for weeks. Christ only knows how you ever got pregnant, you never go out", he grins but it falters when he sees the hurt flash across my face.

He squeezes my hand, "I'll pick you up with Morris and Ad at eight. Come in your slippers and nightie if you need to but just come, eh?", with a small smile as I nod my reluctant agreement.

I hear Gio getting hassle from the lads for talking to me but I ignore it as I stare out of the bus window. Knowing that Lees will be at the party (*"Erin, I thank God you're friends with Lisa Morris, that girl's got her head screwed on"*), Mum is pleased that I'm going out. Her joke that she doesn't need to worry about me snogging boys at parties now, falls flat when I burst into hormonal tears and run up the stairs. I find a slice of cake outside my door as an apology.

I manage to find a market knock-off Fred Perry polo shirt dress that I bought last summer which has enough 'give' in it to accommodate my bump although it is a wee bit shorter than could be deemed 'maternity modest'. Bare legged in my Airwalks, I apply party make-up and try and look a bit less bedraggled than I normally do.

I have started to talk to the *boys* when I'm alone, I do worry that I might be going a bit mental. I chat to them about the party and how I will try not to eat all the Doritos but that they need to ready themselves for a flood of cheese flavouring. I tell them that I love them very much. I tell them that I know their Nana is *wrong*.

"Erin, those poor girls will be traumatized if you keep referring to them as 'lads'. You forget madam that I have had two pregnancies and I'm telling you now, at least one of them is a girl. You're carrying weight in your face". Oh thank you very bloody much mother.

At 8pm, Lees arrives with Ad, the pair of them smiling knowingly like a pair of loons.

"What? What's with those dopey grins", I chuckle as I grab my bag and shout bye to mum.

I smirk, relishing an opportunity to provoke the easily embarrassed Adam, "Dude, did Lees try that position from her magazine's 'Position of the Fortnight' on you? Gotta say fella, you're pretty flexible if she did", Lees honks with laughter as Adam flushes magenta.

Lees pats me on the shoulder, "No Rinny, he'll need alcohol for that. No, we're just smiling because, y'know, it's nice to see you coming out. I mean, we're not as excited as *some* people are about it but it's good to see you", she and Ad exchange meaningful smirks. I let it go, whatever *this* is all about will come to light soon enough.

"Where's Gio? I thought he was coming?", I ask Adam who grins knowingly again.

"Oh, er, well we're going to stop at his on the way", Ad winks and I roll my eyes.

This party is at Matt and Rob Bronson's, the only twins in in our year and lucky enough to have very wealthy parents who have a massive basement in their Old Vicarage home. This basement is the scene of many parties and tonight's end of exam lollapalooza has an alleged marquee addition. As we walk and chat, I'm actually glad I let Gio talk me into this.

We arrive at Gio's, a neat 1980's semi on the executive estate near the leisure centre. Lees and Adam are still smiling like idiots but I'm convinced it's to do with sex so I'd rather not know.

Gio answers the door looking, quite honestly, a bit gorgeous. He's got on the tightest T-Shirt I've ever seen him wear and it's clear that those six-pack rumours should also have included comments on his arms because *Jesus*. His coal-coloured curls are shaggy around his ears and his eyes really are a startling shade of blue. We get ushered into his Mum's immaculate living room, which I remember vividly from our 'Holy Communion Preparation Classes'.

"Romano, is your loo still through there?", I point and he nods as I trundle off for a wee.

Upon my return, Lees and Ad have completely disappeared, causing me confusion.

"We'll meet them there, yeah? I just need to grab a jacket", Romano looks jittery, he keeps looking at me as if he's judging my reaction. I am baffled frankly but I plod on,

"You got that stuff off your face then dude? I saw a couple of the lads in Tesco after school buying drink for tonight, they still looked like circus rejects", I smile but Gio looks a bit distracted.

I roll my eyes, "Right, are we getting Carolyn on the way? I've only been to her house once, she told her Mum that I spilled my orange squash on their cat when we were eight and I never got invited back", I snigger at the memory.

Gio looks at me, his blue eyes surprisingly intense, "Oh, er, no. Me and Carolyn, we broke up a yesterday. Did you not hear? Well, anyway, we're finished so…..", he looks anywhere but at me and it's all a bit awkward.

"Oh, right, er sorry about that dude", my tone is questioning as Gio does not look particularly heartbroken by the breakup. As he shrugs and the silence becomes awkward, I make a move to go,

"RIGHT. Let's go Romano, time is money, c'mon, grab your coat, you've pulled", I try and crack a daft joke but Gio jumps as if I've shocked him.

"Eh?", he splutters and I roll my eyes,

"Christ's sake, I'm joking. You told Daniel McNamara last year that I was rank, you told me again I was ugly a while back and then I threw up on you. Plus with this", I point at my belly, "I do understand that I have the appeal of a swamp monster. It's OK Romano, you're immune to my entire lack of sexual allure, I do know mate", I pat his arm and head off to get my shoes back on.

My progress is halted by a restraining hand on my arm, "Don't, don't fucking say that 'bout yourself Rin, don't. Shit, y'know I only said that to Mac because I was…...because I was pissed off. I didn't mean it, I didn't know you'd heard me", Gio is shaking his head and looking at the floor, his voice low and soft.

I stand like a stunned mullet, my trainers dangling from my fingers. Gio slowly raises his eyes from the floor and his voice is husky, "You're fucking gorgeous Roberts, you gotta know that, right?", he looks sincere.

I have only one option in this toe-curler of a conversation. I snort through my nose like a prize porker at the County Fair, smack his arm and snigger, "Yeah, right. Tease the hungry, pregnant woman Romano and your bollocks will regret it. I neutered Ryan Jones, I can do the same to you. Party, *now*"

As we walk to the twins' house, Gio is still a bit shifty. I'm jabbering away about my job tomorrow, the exams, the summer events, Gio's Newquay holiday with the lads that has Lees terrified that Adam will waltz off with a surfer-chick but Gio, he's not really chatty. As I run out of material, he slows and turns to me.

"Rin, you're.......you're not with the dad are you?", he mods meaningfully at my bump. "I mean, I asked Jones and he said that you haven't seen the guy since, is that true?", Gio is staring at me.

I sigh and I look at my friend, this newly-pleasant associate and I tell him the truth.

"Yep, Romano you're looking at *Rank Roberts* who slept with an E Dealer she met at a rave. A guy she doesn't even know and who hasn't returned any of her pages for the last three months and now I'm having his twins. *By myself* because nobody has ever really wanted to be with me and they never will now that I'm having two kids. *Well done me",* I start walking again, I have to because otherwise I'm going to have a proper snotty cry and it took me *ages* to get this liquid eye-liner right.

Gio follows me, hands in pockets, "Rin, what….what if there was somebody who wanted to be with you? What….what if there was? What would you think of that? Would you go for it, if somebody wanted that, with you and, er them?", he points awkwardly at my bump again and his enquiry sounds a bit cruel right at this moment, it sounds like he's making fun of me, taunting me with something that won't ever happen. I feel suddenly hurt, like he's knifed me in the back.

I turn and snap, "Sod off Romano, I know I'm an easy target but seriously, don't take the piss out of me, I'm too hormonal not to twat you. Truth? I'd think if any lad was interested in me right now they'd probably only be after one thing. Either that or they'd just be a fucking idiot for wanting to get

tangled up in this shitstorm. So no, I wouldn't *go for it*. I've had enough of *fucking* idiots. Literally",
I storm off, Romano trailing far behind me.

Having lost Romano *en route*, I slope into the twins' party, hoping not to attract any attention. I spot
Lees and Adam locked in a snog on the patio, music pumping from an honest-to-God marquee and
bodies mingling everywhere.

I sneak into the expansive kitchen and grab a soft drink and squirrel away an unattended packet of
crisps for my own consumption. Hoisting my expanding form onto the worktop of this incredibly
posh space, I take great interest in a nearby CD box as I wonder how long I leave it until I disrupt
Lees and Ad's snogging.

"There is no *way* I'm skinny dipping", an irritatingly coy and coquettish squeal followed by trilling
laughter announces the arrival of the Practically Perfects, hotly pursued by their band of male
counterparts, *Romano* included.

Spotting me perched and chomping snacks, the noise and shit-flirting fades into silence. I stuff
another crisp in my mouth and wave sarcastically.

"Who invited her?", there's a whispered female hiss.

My eyes flick to Gio, who is having a weird staring competition with the wall. I roll my eyes and re-
read the CD box for the hundredth time. *My goodness the Bee Gees have quite the back catalogue.* I
am jolted by the sudden and unexpected proximity of Liam Merchant, who prior to Gio's
transformation, held the title of 'Year Group Heartthrob'.

"Well hello there *Erin*. It's nice to see you", his tawny blonde hair is immaculately styled and his
Brit-Pop outfit sharp as he cages me in on the worktop with his arms. I pull a boggled face and smile

weakly.

He leans forward and I shift backwards, as he faux-whispers so that everyone can hear, "Tell me, do you only shag drug dealers or are you not too fussy Erin? Those babies will need a Daddy, you'd better get off that worktop and get to work at this party", his smile is shark-like as he nicks one of my crisps and turns to his mates for the comedic accolades that he wants.

I feel my eyes fill with tears, *bloody hormones* and I place my palm over my belly, protecting what is precious to me from what feels like a threat. I sit there, eyes cast down and I stroke my bump, silently reassuring *my boys* that we are OK.

I belatedly realise that there is silence. Nobody is laughing much but similarly, there is an absent voice. No defence from Gio, the person whose protection has been on a par with Adam's in situations like this, whose defence I think I've started to rely upon. *Who I thought was my friend.*

I shove Liam away, a bit pathetically if I'm honest but I just want to get out of here now. *This was such a fucking mistake.*

I push myself down from the worktop, still cradling my bump like some sort of Madonna figurine but I need to feel them under my palm. I walk over to Gio, hurt and anger radiating from me as he in turn radiates unadulterated sullenness and disinterest.

I look up at him, as he towers above me not meeting my gaze, "You got anything you want to add, eh Romano? Eh, *mate?*", my words are dipped in acid, they scorch.

Then he looks down, his blue eyes cold and his sneer the same one from the long-ago Youth Club Disco, "Nah Roberts, I'm not enough of a *fucking idiot* to get involved with you and your *shitstorms"*

I nod sadly, averting my eyes from his angry face and I walk out of the kitchen, out of the house and home. Lees and Ads are too wrapped up in each other to notice me leave.

My feet take me not into the back door but instead into the garage. I unfold the patio recliner (I swear Mum's given it a wash) and wrapping my arms around my two little monsters, I cry myself into hysteria in the place where this latest shitstorm started.

Humiliation Palmer-Smart canters gently off into the distance.

Chapter Four

22nd October 1996

I miss my feet. I miss touching them, seeing them, knowing that they're still attached. I couldn't tell you what my body looks like in the area from my navel to my knees. Not seen it for a while, it might have sprouted feathers and answer to the name 'Duncan' by now for all I know.

I miss having boobs that don't have their own gravitational pull and atmosphere. I miss being certain that I would not wet myself during the twenty-four hours of the day. I miss having a belly that does not continually undulate with the gymnastics of the two lodgers within it.

Most of all, I just miss being *me,* I miss that unappreciated quietness of a body that is only inhabited by *me.* Everything fucking hurts. *Everything.* I had to finish Saturday waitressing last month, I couldn't reach over tables to serve food and I couldn't be on my feet for seven hours without something truly astonishing happening to the diameter of my lower legs.

My midwife has this laugh, this little chuckle, that she emits when she measures my bump. I will lamp her next week if she does it again. I am nearly thirty-four weeks pregnant and I am ready to murder *anyone* who is not currently pregnant with twins or more.

People talk about their post-GCSE summer being an incredible thing, the heady mix of freedom and youth eliciting adventures and experiences on which people will reflect with sentimentality for decades to come. Me? I read baby books this summer, I learnt how to cook. I went to the pictures with my younger brother, I worked over fifty hours a week doing three different jobs and I tried to keep a lid on the terror that threatened to overtake me every *fucking* minute of the day. I went nowhere, I saw nobody except Lees, Adam, the people I worked with, my family and the bloody cat.

And every night, I sent the same pager message to Jamel.

The looming return to the daily company of my oh-so-friendly-and-supportive peers as we swept into September, filled me with a sick sort of dread. My Mum, who has morphed into this person that I *want* to spend time with, has been coaching me in the art of sass, building my armour and readying me for the next eighteen years of protecting two children from the shit that life will throw at us all.

In order to be permitted to attend Sixth Form in my pregnant state, despite my qualifying clutch of eleven A and B grade GCSE's, I had to meet with the Headteacher and Mr. Gibson who is the Head of Sixth Form. They actually came to the house to see me, a few days before term started and gently explained that there were *rules* and *restrictions* that they wanted me to agree to, in the period from September until I start my expected six weeks maternity leave in November. These rules include being on school premises only for my allocated classes or study sessions, all of which are being *thoughtfully* scheduled to take place solely in the Sixth Form building. I am *politely* requested to refrain from entering any other part of the school and any 'free periods' between classes are to be spent in the Sixth Form common room and not the library (where the younger, impressionable students may see my presence as the school sanctioning feckless promiscuity and recklessness). I am essentially as welcome as herpes, although my teachers are quick to impress upon me that this lack of welcome is really only extended to my unborn children. Once they have deigned to exit my uterus, my red card is cancelled and I will be free to roam the school hallways with impunity.

My mother jumped up at one point, the instructions to shove their restrictions up their arses transmitting like telepathy. I grabbed her hand, fighting my own tears of shame-rage and I shook my head. Truth is, I don't want to go to a different College or Sixth Form. I want to be somewhere where people do actually have memories of Erin Roberts *before* she got knocked up. If I go anywhere else, all people will ever know is the pregnant or child-rearing me and honestly, I'm not sure if I want that.

Agreements given and teachers departed, my mother prepared tea like it had personally offended her, banging pots and chopping chicken with a viciousness that made my father wince and leave for the pub.

Pointing a spoon at me threateningly, Mum ground out between clenched teeth, "Cariad, it doesn't matter what those vicious little bastards at school throw your way or what those up-their-arse teachers say. In fifteen years time, all those little buggers in your class will going through this but they'll be doing it with mortgages and beer guts and mid-life crisis' looming. Those teachers by there are all wankers too. You sweetheart, are young and full of energy and you do have your father and me right behind you to help. Those little beauts are going to be so loved, *so loved* and those rotten arseholes at school are not allowed to affect any part of your future and that means your exams madam, so head up, books open, no chuffs given, okay love?"

I hugged Mum tight from behind her as she stirred a saucepan. She patted my hands and told me to *'bugger off and hoover something'*.

It was easier than I imagined, being back at school. For starters, very few people look at my face. My terrifying belly demands the majority of people's attention and for those who need a bit *extra*, my formidable tits will happily keep 'em busy. It means that I can float through the day, avoiding interactions.

Sixth Form studies also mean that people dip in and out of the day. We are not forced to spend any lengthy periods of time together because once your chosen classes are done, people often head off. I'm doing English, Sociology and Geography, none of which sadly are with Lees. I have a few friends in my classes, including Adam who is doing the same subjects as me. Although *Romano* is in Geography and all the *bloody* Practically Perfects are in my English and Sociology classes, my bump seems to have grown large enough to dull their taunts, I guess for them it's a bit like shooting fish in a barrel, the thrill of the chase is gone.

I have not spent time with or spoken to Gio Romano since that party. *Fucking snake in the grass.*

Today is a modular exam for Geography. Yesterday was English and I'm not feeling brilliant really. My parents have gone with Dyls, Lees and her parents to a National Athletics meet in Cardiff. My huge brother is an astonishing sprinter and Lees has always been a long-distance runner. The pair of them have gone to the same athletics club for years and regularly compete in the same meets and this one is a particularly major event.

"Erin love, we'll be at your Aunties for the two nights but any problems at all, Pat's next door and we'll just be at the end of the phone. It's only two nights love, try not to burn the place down and remember to feed that bloody cat, eh?!", Dad hugged and kissed me yesterday morning, slipping a cheeky £20 in my hand and whispering *'get a Chinese tonight'* in my ear. They'll be back tomorrow morning.

I didn't get a Chinese in the end, I felt a bit poorly last night and I'm only in today for this bloody exam. I power on through, stroking my unusually quiet lodgers and focussing on my exam answers and *not* on stabbing Giovanni Romano in the back with my fountain pen, his broad shoulders only two feet in front of my desk thanks to alphabetical seating plans.

Pens downed, my classmates slowly shuffle out of the room. *Christ I feel rank and sore.* When my lessons end mid-day, I normally get the bus home from the parade of shops near school. It's only a short walk but today it feels like a bloody Arctic expedition to get there, I feel proper weak and wobbly and my belly is really tender. Everyone has gone by the time I shuffle out of the door and as I wrap myself in the coat that no longer does up over my bump, I get a wave of unexpected, inexplicable fear. *Something isn't right.*

Swallowing tears, I wobble slowly down the drive towards the school gates, deafened by the screech of tyres as my newly licensed peers zoom past me in their cars. I realise, about halfway down the drive, that the coldness I feel on my inner thighs is not simply the October chilly breeze hitting my tight-clad legs. I cannot *fucking* see what is going on under my massive bump but as I subtly sweep my hand up my leg, I feel the evidence of some significant moisture. Heart thumping, I look down at my hand.

Blood.

I make an animalistic sound, it's like a long drawn out moan as I drop my bag and crash to my poor bony knees. I can't see anyone around, lessons are all still going on, the school building now looks *fucking* miles away from my position on the concrete pavement.

I'm crying, I'm pleading with the boys to stay safe, to stay where they are, to hang on. *Mummy's going to get this sorted.*

In the midst of this panic, I see two figures moving in the distant car-park, approaching a car and the *astonishing* scream that involuntarily leaves my lips makes them immediately start with shock. I see heads swivel, I see quick movement, I hear feet thundering in a run. *Salvation.*

"Erin? Erin? Oh my GOD, ROMANO GO GET THE CAR, NOW!", that's Ad's voice, that's my friend. *My friend is here.*

I feel so weird, like I'm underwater and then Adam has got his arms round me and he's lifting me up off the floor. I can't keep my eyes open but I turn to him and say, "I'm bleeding, there's blood Ad. The babies, it's the babies" and I hear him swear and I feel his panic.

There's a car pulling up,

"We'll get her to the medical centre down the road, QUICK AD. There's nurses there, they can help her. Oh fuck, OH FUCK look at all that blood Jones, why's she bleeding so much?", that's *Romano's* voice.

I'm in a car and we're moving too fast, *too fast.* The boys are talking at me, telling me to do things, to stay awake, to hold on. *Bossy.* The whole time, I'm whispering to my babies, *"Mummy will sort this, Mummy will sort it".* They don't kick me though, like they normally do when I talk to them. *They're not kicking.*

We stop, hands gently lift me, I smell those lemons and herbs again and there's soft-hardness against my cheek once more. Panic, voices raised, urges to move aside, gasps, *'ambulance service please', 'Can Dr. Harris, Dr. Matson and Dr. Khan please come immediately to Examination Room 2 where we have a patient emergency'.*

There is a hand holding mine. It's warm and it's strong and amidst all the chaos that I can't open my eyes to see, it's this hand that I concentrate on as the thumb strokes mine rhythmically. More noises, squeaky wheels, calmer voices, sharp scratches on my arms, lifting, moving. I lose hold of the warm, safe hand and I cry out, reaching for it. It comes back and I'm whispering *'Please help my babies, please help my babies'*, like a prayer.

"Right, are you the father?", there's a question that confuses me.

Jamel?

"Muuuuuuum", my words and tears come from deep within me and I hear the shock in the room.

"Ad, you go back to school, get hold of Morris to get her folks, get hold of everyone. I'll go to the hospital with her yeah? So she's not alone. Get them here, yeah, quick", that's Gio's voice. *Snake turned saviour?*

I start to feel more awake, I feel like I'm breaking the surface of the water. I open my eyes and see that I'm moving, there's sky and then there's a lifting and I'm in an ambulance.

Gio's face appears above me, "You hold on Roberts, you hear me, you fucking hang tight and I'll come up the hospital in the car. Just…….just hang on, 'kay?".

I'm too stunned by this to respond. More so when Gio presses a kiss to my cheek before he disappears from view.

It all goes a bit blurry after this. I hear the words, 'Placental abruption' and there are more scratches in my arms. I manage to answer questions about my pregnancy although my eyes are really heavy and tired.

"Erin, sweetheart, I think you need to be prepared for the fact that the doctors might decide to deliver your babies early after a bleed like this. Just be ready for that poppet", the kindly paramedic lady pats my hand and smiles at me.

Oh shit.

The whole journey, I repeatedly ask the paramedics if my babies are OK, are they OK? They give me platitudes about heartbeats and *'all the best care at the hospital'* but I know when I am being mollified. I talk to the boys, I don't care if the ambulance crew think I'm nuts, I tell them that we're going to all be OK and that they just need to sit tight. I cry for my Mum, I beg the crew to help me get my Mum. *More hand pats*.

I'm unloaded from the ambulance and wheeled into the Maternity triage, which is *fucking* terrifying. Women all around me are moaning, groaning and screaming and I am so scared that I can't stop shaking and crying. I have never, in my whole life, been this scared. *Ever.* Midwives and nurses keep patting me as I lie on this trolley but nobody is telling me anything and I need to know if my boys are alright. I feel it bubbling in me, like a volcano and when two midwives walk past chatting casually, I lose it,

"Will somebody tell me if my babies are OK? Are my babies alive? Are they? Are they OK? Please can somebody talk to me?", my voice is so raw and so scared and oh-so-fucking desperate that everyone in the area stops and that's when I cry like I have never cried before. It's like my heart is trying to leave my body via my eyes.

And then that hand is here.

That big warm hand is back and it's holding tight and the lemons and the herbs are all around me and there's the voice, there's this voice that makes me feel safe even though I don't know why,

"Will somebody tell her what's going on? Why aren't you talking to her? She's scared!". *Gio.*

I turn and look at him, the only familiar thing I have in this terrifying place and as he looks down at me, the fluorescent hospital light making his freckles stand out on his olive skin. I don't see cruelty or coldness or confusing things in his worried blue eyes. I see the only person I have on my side right now and I whisper through my tears,

"Thank you"

He shakes his head gently, as if he's chiding himself for something and then he reaches out and brushes my crazy hair out of my face before he wipes my tears with his thumb.

"I'm right here, *Rin*", his deep voice is soft and reassuring.

There are suddenly consultants, midwives, machines, weird strap things, monitors, bags of blood replenished. A kind looking doctor with a ring of white hair around his tanned head talks to me,

"Erin, my name is Dr. Banerjee and I am going to be looking after you and your babies while you are here. Erin, what a fright you must have had and I am sorry that we have not been clear with you, forgive us please, we are simply a busy place. Now, Erin, we believe that one of your babies' placentas has partially come away and caused you to bleed so very much. We have looked at the scans and we think that it would be best if we deliver your babies today. The abruption was a nasty one and we want you all to be as safe as possible so what we are going to do is prepare you for a C-Section in a short while", his voice is calm and gentle but his words are filling me with absolute terror.

Today. A short while.

I whimper and grip Gio's hand tighter.

"Young man, I will need to also get you prepared for the theatre. You will wish to be there?", he turns to Gio who's flabbergasted expression would be funny in any other setting.

I smile weakly, "Dr. Banerjee, he's not the father. If Mum doesn't get here in time then…...then it'll just be me in there", saying the words aloud makes me feel sick with fear and I tangle myself up in wires as I frantically wrap my arms around my babies, my *loves*, my co-passengers in this as the tears start.

"Dr. Bannerjee, will my babies be OK? Are they OK?", my words come out as hiccuping sobs.

He pats my arm kindly, "Erin, they are going to be small and they will need very special care for a few weeks but at the moment, their heart rates are acceptable and we do not see any complications other than their prematurity. Let's just concentrate on getting you ready for the caesarean section, has somebody contacted your mother for you?".

Gio, silent until now, wades in with explanations about Adam ringing people from the school office and how Gio's mum was going to alert my neighbours and try and get messages to my parents. My fear for my babies means I can't concentrate really on what he's saying, I feel a conflicted urgency. I'm desperate for that c-section, to get them out into daylight where I can see that they are OK and not silently dying inside me but I am also absolutely vomit-risingly terrified of the whole procedure.

Lots of people are talking around me and I feel the bed being moved, heading to the labour ward apparently to await my summons to theatre.

I am too distracted to realise that the hand is back, holding mine safe. Its large, warm presence keeping pace with my swiftly moving bed. Corridors, doors opened, more faces, brakes on, *"We'll just be a few minutes Erin and we'll come and speak to you again"*. Door shuts, silence.

I'm in a small side room, I can see one other bed next to me but the curtains are semi-drawn so I can only see the be-slippered feet of its occupant. I look to my side and see the drips and the wires that are now piercing my skin. I turn to the other side and do a sort of comedy startle when I see Gio looking down at me from his significant height, his handsome face looking genuinely worried.

"Gio? Thanks…….thanks for taking me to the medical centre and for coming up here but…...but you don't need to stay, I'll be okay now, you can go, it's OK", I'm so confused by his continued presence in this scenario.

He looks at me, those blue eyes pretty fierce as he whispers, "No, I'm not letting you down again Rin. I'll be here, until your mum comes. I can't let you handle this on your own", he's shaking his head again and he looks a bit broken as he whispers, "Roberts, I'm so, so fucking sorry about what happened at that party. I've felt like such a prick for months, I was ......I was just a bit pissed off but I didn't mean it and I'm so sorry I let that prick talk to you like that and *now* you're going through this....", I feel my eyes widen as I see Gio's jaw clench and his lip wobble.

He blows out a breath and looks at the ceiling for a moment, composing himself it would seem before he looks back at me,

"Those babies are gonna be fine, you're gonna be fine and if your mum doesn't get here from wherever it is, I'll come in there with you Rin....y'know, if you want me to?", he thumbs at the door and looks at me cautiously.

I meet his gaze as I stroke my belly and whisper, "Gio, are you really my friend or is this just coz you feel guilty? Is this a game?", it sounds so pathetic but I'm too scared to give a shit.

He winces and comes closer, shaking his head and gently pushing my hair away from my face, "There's no game Rin, I was a proper dickhead before but I'm definitely your mate yeah, for real", he holds my hands and I nod as the tears start and I howl all of my fear and sadness and shock into his stupidly strong, herb-scented shoulder as he sits on my bed and holds me tightly to him, 'shhh'-ing me and telling me how it will all be OK.

A weird calm settles. Monitors beep gently, people come in and out and tell me things, I am taken by a midwife to the loo and a humiliating moment in the bathroom takes place where she helps me to wash the dried blood from my legs and lady bits (neither of which I can see) and then she also helps me (*oh the humiliation*) to shave the necessary parts of my muff in readiness for the c-section. Gio snorts with poorly concealed laughter when I emerge from the bathroom in a hospital gown and pressure leggings.

"Looking glamorous Roberts, looking good!", he sniggers and I smack his chest in outrage.

There is a lot of activity at one point, causing Gio to be called out of the room by the midwife. It turns out that Pat-from-Next-door had arrived at the hospital with a bag of my stuff, the babies bag that has been packed for weeks, my maternity folder and the news that as yet, neither the athletics venue nor my Auntie have been able to locate my parents and brother, all of whom appear to have taken themselves off for lunch or some sort of activity in Cardiff. Lees *has* been located and she and her parents are also engaged in the hunt for them. Everyone in our town seems to now be trying to ring anyone they know in South Wales to help locate my family. Despite my tears at this news, I get a little warm glow from the idea that maybe, *just maybe*, people are helping because they do actually care about me and my two little goblins.

Pat leaves, Gio explaining, "I er, I told her that I'd be in there with you if your mum isn't.......is that what I should have said Roberts? I mean, shall I get her back? Do you want her with you instead?", he looks adorably uncertain.

I realise right then, that having Gio Romano at the birth of my babies is not actually that weird. It feels like it's *right* somehow. I can't explain it but I whisper,

"I want you there Gio", and I smile weakly at him as he nods and looks at his feet, a slight blush colouring his cheeks.

Shortly afterwards, Gio's mum arrives. A very glamorous lady, Sofia Romano scared me to death as a child as her scolds and instructions are loudly barked out with Italian flourishes. She is as round as she is tall and she bursts through the door of my room in a cloud of expensive perfume and a lot of bangle-jangling.

"Oh Erin *cara*, you poor little thing my love. What is happening to you and your *bambini*, eh?", Sofia has a thick West-Country accent which is peppered with Italian words and phrases. She genuinely sounds like she has accent schizophrenia.

Gio makes it clear that he wants to support me through the c-section, Sofia looks entirely baffled and then resolutely opposed, telling Gio that he cannot be in there with me, it is not his place, he gets queasy watching Casualty, he is seventeen years old and does not know what he is doing.

Gio pulls himself up to his full height, at several inches over six foot, he towers over his mum, "Ma, there's no way you'd let Rora go through this on her own and there's no way I'm letting Erin do it either", he nods affirmatively but his mum kisses her teeth,

"Tsk, Giovanni I *love* your sister, of course there's no way that you let somebody you *love* go through…....*oh…*oh caro, oh I see Gio, I see. Oh son…", Sofia and Gio are exchanging meaningful looks that I don't understand but suddenly there's a sharp *thump*, like somebody's just hit me in the stomach and I feel dread sweep my entire body.

"GIO!", I screech as I feel a rush of moisture between my legs.

Gio jumps in shock as Sofia gasps and runs for the door, shouting *'Nurse!'* at the top of her lungs.

My bed seems to be flooded with what I can only describe as muddy water and I gabble out, "I haven't pissed myself honest, I haven't pissed myself, what's this? It's not blood, what's this?", like a lunatic with the accompanying backing track of sudden alarms from the monitors.

Four midwives rush in an I see the alarm on their faces straight away. I hear words, *'Meconium', 'waters have gone', 'page theatre'*

A midwife comes and holds my hands and looks at me earnestly, "Erin, your waters have just broken and unfortunately, that brown colour means that the babies are in some distress, the monitors show that that their little heart rates are changing. We're going to get you down to theatre right now and get them safely delivered, OK sweetheart?"

I'm nodding but inside my head I'm screaming, "GET THEM OUT, GET THEM OUT AND MAKE THEM OK"

Gio, being hugged by his Mum in the corner looks terrified but as our eyes meet, he breaks from her hold and flies to my side, holding my hands and gabbling reassurances.

It's all a horrible, horrible blur, like I'm watching it through a thick glass window. Gio is taken away by the midwives, his Mum pressing kisses to his head and weeping softly as he leaves. She comes and hugs me, kisses me and whispers things in Italian as she covers my forehead with expensive lipstick.

I'm taken away, people tell me things that I don't digest, I'm given a weird hat thing and I'm led to a high bed in a room filled with lights and tables and steel and monitors. There are hundreds of people here, stood in what looks like two groups. They're each stood around a clear, plastic cot and….

"FUCKING HELL I'M HAVING TWO BABIES", my astonished scream makes the entire population of the room jolt, followed by wry smiles and meaningful looks.

"Erin, you *did* know it's twins, didn't you?", a very young, earnest looking midwife holds my hand and looks at me.

I nod like a moron but whisper, "Yeah but it's actually true, isn't it? I'm really having two babies, like, *right* now?", slack jawed, I catch people's eyes, they all smile kindly and nod.

There is this horrendous bit next where they make me lean over and hold a midwife's hands. The 'sharp scratch' they warn me is coming is *not* how I would describe your man in green trying to force a garden fork up my spinal cord. *Nope.* They'd be better off just saying, *"Brace yourself, this will hurt like a fucking bastard love"*. It'd be more honest.

My legs and body numbing rapidly, they lie me down and that, *that* is when I realise that I have not ever known panic before this moment. I did not realise that panic can make your heart turn to an acid that melts all of your ribs, it makes your bones turn to dust, it makes your vocal cords emit noises that you didn't know it could.

"I'm scared, I'm so scared, I want my mum, I want my mum. Are my babies OK? I'm scared", snotty, pathetic sobbing.

"Roberts, will you look at the fucking state of me?", a deep but nervous voice comes from across the room as a midwife leads Gio in and I briefly cease my emotional collapse, distracted by the sight of Romano in scrubs and a paper hat looking like an ER extra. He's actually smiling although he looks completely terrified. As he's ushered onto a stool near my head and I see a big green curtain go up over my chest, we clasp hands and stare at each other, both completely thunderstruck by the manner in which our afternoon has panned out.

Warnings are given, instructions shared between colleagues, noise, equipment hustle. *Terror.*

Gio leans down, his coal coloured curls tickling my forehead and he whispers,

"You just look at me, just look at me and hold my hand and it'll all be fucking OK Roberts, y'hear me? Just keep looking at me coz I'm not gonna be looking nowhere else in case I see shit that gives me nightmares for the rest of my days. Just hold my hand Rin".

And so I do.

I feel the pulling, the weirdness of a numb body being brutally manhandled, I hear instructions, fake-calm platitudes but all I see is blue eyes, freckles and *kindness*. I see the scar on his forehead that I know he got when he fell in the playground, I see a chicken-pox mark from when it swept our class when we were six and we all got spotty and irritable together. I see the lipstick marks from his mother, I see the lips that are surprisingly full and soft looking. I see Giovanni Romano.

"Erin, we are just going to deliver twin one now", it feels like there should be a drum roll as the capable looking surgeon does his magic, "Here we are, Erin".

As I pull my eyes away from Gio and I look up, the green sheet provides the curtain upon which the opening act on the stage of my life begins. Emerging from behind it, like the lead actor, is a tiny, very angry little person, covered in white stuff and slime and I realise, as they are swept quickly away, that they are not *mine*. I am *theirs*.

"It's a boy Erin, you have a little boy and goodness, he's not a bad size at all", I turn to a slack-jawed Gio and grin like a Cheshire cat.

"Right Erin, time for twin number two to join their brother. Here we go", there is more rummaging and then I hear a noise, it's the noise that the cat makes when it has a *really* good stretch..

"Goodness me, you're a feisty one young man, Erin, you have another boy and he's having a little shout which is a *very* good sign for a little man arriving early", I hear the chuckle in the surgeons voice and it warms me through with a reassurance that no words could. *People don't laugh when they lie.*

An upbeat female voice talks to me from far away as I grin broadly at the brightly lit ceiling, "Erin, we're just giving your little ones a quick check over but they both seem to be breathing nicely and they're good sizes for thirty-four weeks, I think you've got yourself a couple of little bruisers here".

I turn to Gio, who is grinning in a duality of relief and astonishment. In a rush of gratitude, I grab his hand again and I press my lips to it, "Gio, thank you, thank you so much for being here".

Gio's eyes glance from his hand to my lips and up to my eyes again as he croaks out, "You're amazing Rin, you're proper full-on incredible. I can't believe what you just did, I can't fucking believe how amazing you are", and with those startling words, he leans down and presses the *softest* of kisses to my lips for the *briefest* of seconds before pulling back to share my astonishment at the action.

The astonishment doesn't get time to ferment because in my life, good things don't last.

"CLAMPS! Nurse, we have a major bleed, can I get the........", but I don't hear the rest.

I hear Gio shout in alarm as my world suddenly goes very dark.

Chapter Five

22nd October 1996

'Jesus, you'd have thought they'd not have allowed trucks into operating theatres", is genuinely the first coherent thought I have.

I can't open my eyes but clearly, the truck that has hit me must have been moving at speed. My entire body is roaring in agony, the epicentre being my stomach.

My head is thumping, I feel like nothing in me is wired right and I have an odd, achy empty-weightless feeling that I do *not* like. Then my second thought hits me,

"WHERE ARE MY BABIES?", my eyes-still-closed yell causes a volley of responding yelps of alarm in whichever space I find myself. One shout in particular sounds familiar,

"Good God in heaven Erin Roberts, how is it you are always the loudest person in a room, even when you are unconscious?". *Hiya Mum.*

I slowly open my eyes and see a lot of darks shapes looming over me but none of them look like thirty-four-week-old babies.

"Where are my babies?", my sob is pathetic, eliciting lots of patting and stroking hands and reassurances that somebody called bloody *Sue* has them.

"Who's Sue? I want my babies back, MUUUUUUUM, get my babies off Sue, I want them here", I'm wailing like a paid mourner now.

"For heaven's sake, SCBU you daft apeth, *Special Care Baby Unit* not bloody *Sue*", my mum's laugh quickly turns into a proper sob and I am suddenly wrapped in a blanket of M&S jumper and Elizabeth Arden perfume as my mum weeps on me.

"We thought we'd lost you sweetheart, we thought we'd lost you. My baby, my poor baby. I'm so sorry we weren't there", mum is sobbing and as I focus my eyes a bit better, I see my Dad holding a similarly weepy Dyls as he strokes my hair and looks at me with love.

"What happened? Are the babies OK? When can I see them? Where's Gio?", I try to sit up but the pain is so immense that I make an involuntary noise of anguish and my mum immediately goes in to nurse mode.

"Erin, you need to lie still sweetheart, we'll raise the bed for you in a bit. The boys are fine, my goodness Erin, they are just perfect sweetheart, they are so beautiful", Mum sobs again but rapidly composes herself, "They are up by there in the SCBU but they're doing so tidy, they might not be there long. We'll go there just as soon as it's safe to get you in that chair by there", mum nods towards a wheelchair in the corner, patting my hand as she sits on the bed.

"Sweetheart, after the boys were born, you had a proper nasty bleed beaut, you lost a whole load of blood because of a problem with the placenta. We, we thought we'd lost you Erin, we really did", Mum sobs again and I see Dad wipe his eyes.

"It was all very upsetting from what I gather and poor Giovanni was there and was very shaken, poor love. He's with his Mam and Dad at home now, they thought it was best to take him home. I'll ring them in a bit, tell them you're awake", Mum smiles softly and pats my hand.

Oh shit, poor Gio.

With Mum, Dad and Dyls here, the scary hospital world becomes a lot less threatening. I have my *terrifying* Mother as my advocate and within a short space of time, she has got me painfully upright and into a wheelchair *("I'll bet you'll be swallowing those paracetamol tablets willingly enough now madam")* and as a family, we go to see the two new owners of the heart that was once just mine.

Jacob-Jamel Dylan Roberts and Alfred-James Gethin Roberts. Jake and AJ.

I knew them before I saw them. I have always been able to picture them, I have always known them. As Mum wheels me into the room, I know without being told that they are the two noisiest babies in the room, cuddled up snugly in their incubators.

Both of them have a shock of soft, dark hair and their eyes are the most serene brown. They might not be identical but honestly, I'm going to need name badges because they look pretty similar.

When I tell my family the names I've chosen for our newest tribal members, my Dad sniffs at the use of his name, Dyls grins like a loon and my mother's frown is epic.

"Why on earth would you use his name Erin? Eh? That boy has done nothing, NOTHING other than abandon you and his children. He never replied to those messages you sent him. You don't even know him Erin, why use his name?", Mum is gesticulating wildly.

As I look at my eldest son, who weighs in at an impressive 5lbs 5oz, I smile softly.

"Because he gave me them Mum, he gave me them", and I kiss little hands and feet.

Mum rolls her eyes and mutters, "Well, he'll just be Jake as far as I'm concerned"

I'm stroking any part of them that I can touch and their little squawks of fury start to noticeably lessen as I start to croon at them, telling them that we all made it, *'Mummy told you we would all be OK'* as I ignore my mother's blubbering and her whispers of, *'They know her Fred, look at them, they know her voice'*.

Holding them both, as they are gently placed in my arms, our respective wires all de-tangled, is the most incredible moment of my life.

They both have nasal tubes delivering oxygen but the very friendly nurse tells me that she has rarely seen thirty-four week old babies who are such a good size and such confident breathers. Their little chests look like they're running a marathon but the nurse says this is normal.

I kiss them, I keep crooning at them and I feel every part of my body memorising their faces and shapes. They both seem to turn to the sound of my voice and I press kisses to their little faces as I ask mum to grab Gethin's crazy hats to put on them as Dyls snaps photo after photo in his capacity as official documenter of his nephews' births.

I was 'out' for three hours, time in which my family were breaking innumerable traffic laws down the M4 and in which I was being patched up, sewn up and re-filled with blood. Gio was also in that time having his first brush with a nervous breakdown, his mum reassuring mine that he is now fine but is having to be restrained from returning to the hospital as he is in no fit state to do so.

My boys are hungry. I have no way of explaining how I know this but I *do* know this. I tell my mum, who informs me that newborns aren't often hungry for a while after birth, they are just sleepy. I tell the midwife this, she gives me the same answer. I look at the boys and whisper *'You tell them'* at which point they emit a volley of cat-screeches and I look smugly at my mother.

The tiny bottles they give me, make me feel a bit weird and I find myself asking Mum in a whisper,

"Can I use my boobs Mum? Will they work yet? Do I need to like, *do* something to them to turn the milk on?", I feel daft but I'd dismissed breastfeeding as an option so I'd ignored all the book chapters on it. Now, I want to give it a go.

"Oh sweetheart, I think they might find that hard, their sucking won't be strong enough", Mum looks at me proudly but sadly.

"Before thirty-four weeks, babies often can't manage it Erin but we can give it a try if you'd like?", the midwife starts to manhandle me as Dad and Dyls beat a rapid retreat out of the door.

No human other than Ryan *sodding* Jones has ever put their mouth on my boobs but when my sons, propped up on a whole construction site of pillows, latch on with my Mum and Midwife Claire's help, it feels perfect. Don't get me wrong, it's the biggest nightmare I've ever experienced regarding my tits, and that includes that 'multi-way' bra that I got stuck in once in the Top Shop changing rooms. It takes *forever* to get positions and mouths and nipples and heads and hands right. I am at the point of throwing the towel in when little 5lb 3oz AJ latches on like a hoover and sucks like he's been lost in the desert for days.

I try and look serene but with every fucking suck, some bastard is stabbing me in the belly. I tell Claire this and she assures me it's my uterus contracting. I point out that my uterus wants to give itself a day off, it's been enough of a drama queen today already.

Jake gets the hang of it shortly afterwards and my mother briefly beatific at her daughter's endeavours, is soon frowning and muttering, *"Stubborn, chopsy little know-it-all"*, as I poke my tongue out at her and wink.

My elation and excitement have masked some pretty serious pain and *knackered-ness* and in the silence of the boys feeding, I start to feel rapidly unwell.

"Mum, I feel weird", I whisper and Mum jerks her head up from where she's been stroking her grandsons.

"Oh love, you've gone very pale. Right, boys, you're pretty much done here I think. Your poor Mummy needs her bed", as Claire and Mum start to untangle us from pillows and catheter and oxygen tubes and all that nonsense, I realise that I cannot and will not be separated from my babies.

An argument follows. I tell Mum that I'm not leaving them, she tells me I have to go to my bed and that I cannot sleep here in SCBU in my wheelchair, she tries to negotiate with me, I refuse to budge. Claire intercedes and offers options, I refuse. My mother calls me a stubborn little madam, I tell her I will teach the boys to call her *'Nana Stink'*. We get nowhere fast.

Claire scuttles off and returns with the sort of stern looking gentleman who I just know is here to give me a bollocking. Mum does too, she turns with her arms folded to give a satisfied, *"I told you so Madam"* look.

"Hello Erin, my name's Dr. Anderson. I understand that you'd like your babies to join you, is that right?", I nod, looking as angelic and compliant as I can muster.

He flicks through the charts that Claire has given him.

"Well, premature twins are usually here in SCBU for a couple of days at least but I understand that these young men are breathing unaided and have breastfed, is that right?", Claire nods.

Dr. Anderson turns to the boys and pokes and prods them into indignant fury.

"You are good-sized lads for early arrivers. This gentleman also appears to have produced something in his nappy", he points at Jake and smiles.

"I'm happy for them to be moved into the SCBU annexe room, APGAR scores are good, Mum can be with them then. Close obs please on both mum and babies, can we make sure that this is religiously done but yes, after the pretty hairy day you lot have had, I see no reason why we need to be pedantic about this. Congratulations Erin on your twins, I hear from my colleagues that you overcame some nasty obstacles today", he pats my shoulder as I gabble my thanks.

Mum's eyes are raised to the ceiling as she walks over to my wheelchair and mutters, "You are the boldest little madam I know Erin Roberts", as she pushes me to the bed where I will sleep. *Next to my boys.*

November 1996

I love three things above all else in my life. I love my two tiny sons, despite their efforts to destroy my sanity and I love my bed, I love my bed *very* much, I just get to spend disappointingly little time in it.

The first few days of their lives floated by in a fog of love, terror, incompetence (mine) and almost non-stop tit-pluggage. Those little gobblers *do not stop eating*. Mum took time off work and pretty much moved into the hospital with me. I alternated between screaming at her for continually telling me what to do with *my* sons and clinging to her sobbing my gratitude that she was there to to help me manage my newborn stinkers.

There was those terrible, truly awful two days when both boys got infections, like a hidden, creeping menace in their tiny bodies. We ended up rushed to NICU and I spent the most terrified forty eight hours of my life grasping perspex incubators and desperately trying to transmit some of my own healthiness through the plastic. They rallied quickly but I realised, in those horrendous hours, that I am now entirely owned by those boys. Body, soul, heart and calamitous nature, it's all theirs. I give my whole self to them.

Nobody tells you, they just don't *fucking* tell you. Your body, after you've had babies, looks like you're wearing a badly-tailored skin suit. My agonisingly sliced belly looks like a melted cake, my tits are enormous and the huge veins and nipples make them look like erupting volcanoes. Don't start me on the *other* things. Those little buggers may not have tunnelled out my lady-garden but it has still got the *right* hump and I am waddling round the place with a sodding lilo of a sanitary mattress between my legs.

Gio came to see us the first morning after the birth, he was there the second that visiting hours started bringing with him a box of chocolates, two Teddy Bears and a look of abject terror.

I'd had three hours sleep, I was unshowered and undressed and AJ had just peed through his inexpertly applied nappy, all down my PJ's. Gio rushed over, hugging me too tightly and making me cry out in pain but I was overwhelmingly pleased to see him.

"Romano, I am so sorry I scared you, I.......", but he cuts me off with a much more gentle hug

"Roberts, I have never, ever been so fucking scared, you like *bled to death* right in front of me", he looks a bit wobbly, "You're OK yeah, you're all fixed now, yeah?", he held my hand, that big, warm hand of his wrapped round mine.

Jake started to squawk, setting off his brother and as I tried not to scream from the pain in my belly, I moved to inexpertly gather him up, this tiny little bundle of boy. I showed Gio how to hold a tiny baby as he stared in wonder. I picked up AJ and when Mum walked in, I caught the oddly soft look she projected at the sight of Gio and I each holding a tiny baby and chuckling, sat side by side.

Lees arrived within minutes and it all got a bit too emotional and hysterical. Mum spotted my weariness and played the 'Bad Cop', swiftly ejecting the pair of them before helping me wash and start the first day of the rest of my life as a *Mum*.

It's been three weeks. We came home three days ago, that infection setting them back a little bit. Our days in hospital were spent in an odd sort of isolation because all we had to shape our days were mealtimes, optimum showering times (before any other cow got in there) and visits from every member of our family.

My boys are two little brown-eyed bundles of trouble. Jake has held onto his dark fuzz of fluff and as their little bodies grow, I notice that Jake's skin has a slightly darker tone than AJ's. AJ lost his dark fuzz, it just seemed to evaporate, I never found traces of it in his bedding or on my clothes. In its place is a caramel coating of felt on his tiny little head, his skin tone a sort of shaded peach. I sit and hold them for hours, the three of us just staring at each other. I tell them stories, I whisper my love and I tell them that I am so, so, so sorry that I didn't do a better job on giving them a Daddy.

It's made me cry more than I thought it would, this absence. Don't get me wrong, I am not alone in my 'single parent' status, there were at least four other girls in hospital with me who had dumped their dead weight. My distinguishing feature, as we chatted over the Breakfast trolley, was that I had no back story to offer in denigrating Jamel. No relationship ending, no cheating, no nastiness or personality flaws. I just have nothing. He simply never came back for me. *I wasn't worth the effort.*

I'm also not alone in being a Young Mum. I met a girl who was even younger than me, her wide-eyed petrified boyfriend at her side by the maternity bed.

Now that we are home, the world is a bigger place than our hospital isolation. It's also a *kinder* place. My boys are the most gorgeous babies I've ever seen, *not that I'm biased or anything*. The entire hormonal female population of our town stops the pram to coo at them as we run errands.

Those people who had been prone to the *looks*, and the *whispers* and the sideways glances when I was a pregnant teenage trollop, they are now all gushes and cooing and *'Oh Erin, it's lovely to see you, how are you?".* It's nice and I'm polite but I won't ever forget the looks and the whispers.

I've had comments about Jake's gorgeous skin tone too. I've seen the looks. I've had the, "So where was their father from...?", enquiries. I've started to play dirty and I *fucking* love it.

"So Erin, where was their Dad from?", "I don't know, I never saw his face".
" He doesn't look like his mummy does he?" "That's coz I nicked them, my real ones were ugly"
"So I bet your mum is finding it a challenge helping such a young mum with two babies", "Yup, mind you she needs to get used to it because I went out on the raz the night they were born and there'll be another two along in nine months. Oh well, can't seem to keep 'em closed".

Gio laughed himself into astonishing hiccoughs when we went for a walk in the park the first Saturday after the boys were discharged. He was pushing the double pram that my Auntie had found in a Car Boot a few months back, chatting crap as we headed to meet Lees and Adam. When the Practically Perfects and male associates appeared, Gio chatted and joked as the girls made a fuss over my *gorgeous* sons who were offered immunity from their collective dislike of me due to Gio's command of the pram. Liam was there, smirking at me as I looked into the middle distance, willing Gio to *hurry the fuck along*.

"So Erin, how are you?", Liam sneered at me and in a comforting move, Gio grabbed my hand and growled, *'Back off Merchant''* at him. I noticed the entire group clock Gio's hand in mine, shocked looks all round. I've never had a boy hold my hand before in public, not like *this*. It gave me a warm glow.

I smirked, feeling the invisible 'Mummy Armour' that I've grown coating my skin, "Oh Liam, you know. How've you been? Eh? Still a big cunt with a small dick and a face like a fucking car crash? Ah well, life's a bitch and then you die. So nice to to see you all, ta-ta", and I commandeered my sons and strolled off up the road, Gio snorting himself into diaphragm-spasms beside me.

I grinned and whispered to the boys, *"You two ever use language like that and Mummy will tell Nana on you".*

Gio has been at my house a lot recently. Lees always mentions it, with that stupid knowing look that she had the night of the dreadful party and my demented mother always greets Gio like a long lost son when he calls round. I'm not stupid, I do know that there is *something* swirling around Gio and I but I genuinely, no kidding, do not have the energy to invest in thinking about that kind of nonsense. I will acknowledge that when Gio hugs me, I get butterfly flutters and that when he holds my hand or looks at me for any length of time, my skin tingles. There's also the fact that at night, he's featuring in more of my dreams than I'm comfortable with but I can't dwell on it all because I am a mother of two premature babies, with no let up in my A Level commitments or my constant desire to prove my maternal credentials to everyone, *especially* my mother.

Whatever it is that drives Giovanni Romano to seek out my baby-spew covered company, I will only be interpreting it as friendship for the foreseeable future.

Today, on this slightly wintry November morning as I wheel my sons to the baby clinic for their weigh-in, I am blindsided by a sudden realisation.

Jamel is really, properly gone.

He might as well never have existed. His DNA is sat here looking at me, both of them sporting a hilarious set of Uncle Gethin hats but Jamel is as real to me now as a ghost and like all ghosts, I need to help him cross over. The boys get weighed, get cooed over by everyone and we go home, whereupon I dial in the last pager message that I will ever send.

"Jamel, I had your babies. Thought you might want to know. Bye then. Erin"

I brush away a tear and head off to allow my boobs to be chewed on by the gifts that a ghost bestowed on me.

13th December 1996

My plans all went to pot, I was stupid to have considered that they would not. My class timetable, despite some genuinely helpful re-jigging by my teachers, still requires me to to be in school for the majority of the day, three days per week. My mum has changed her hours at work, another piece of guilt I shoulder, so that she can have them for two of the days. However, I am a day short on childcare. There is a saying that it takes a village to raise a child well, my children are being raised (for one day a week) by an entire common room of teenagers.

My Headteacher and Mr. Gibson, somewhat shamed by the story of my near-death, have agreed that on a Thursday, Godparents Lees and Gio can care for the twins in the Common room during their free periods in the morning while I am in English and then for the period when we are all in lessons in the afternoon, Miss. Harvey has them in the Headteacher's Office, the hope being that they snooze through this section of the day. Lees and Gio were my first choices as Godparents, Lees because she loves them more than anything and Gio because he is *so* good with them and he was there at their birth, earning him some credentials.

Their Christening was a Holy Horror which I have blotted from my memory although I do get flashbacks to the moment when AJ covered the Priest's immaculate white cassock in shit due to a nappy malfunction and then Jake topped it off with a quick spew in the font. My Auntie's elaborately decorated Christening cake had also gone mouldy, discovered only after every guest had been served a piece and the scoffing had commenced. *Aces.*

Today is the day of the Sixth Form Christmas Party. AJ has been poorly this week and I am reluctant to leave him, his little cries actually tear my heart in two and Jake gets really agitated when his brother is not right, you can literally see him frowning and crying with worry. Mum however, loudly reminds me that she is a trained nurse, these are her grandsons whose welfare she values more than mine and that raising of me qualifies her for Sainthood. She insisted that I go to the party tonight. She was oddly fierce about it all, informing me (as if I didn't know) that I have not been *out* since that horrendous party after GCSEs. She even went shopping, voluntarily venturing into Miss. Selfridge and bought me a *lush* dress to wear. I cried and tried to pretend it was a sneeze. She called me a *'pillock'* and then hugged me.

I gave up with the breastfeeding. The boys weren't putting on enough weight, I was looking like a pipe-cleaner from the loss of so many calories and I spent my life with my boobs hanging out. I only express milk now so that a couple of their bottles a day are my milk but the rest is formula and I am secretly relieved by the straightforwardness of it.

"Rin, I'll come and get you at eight tonight yeah?", Gio is bellowing across the car park at me as he leaves at lunchtime. His current romantic pursuer, one of the older Upper Sixth girls, is trailing him like a puppy to his car.

I nod and wave, desperate to get this essay written during school hours because honestly, I have got less than no chance of getting it done once I'm home.

Lees and Adam are having a little bit of an odd period. Lees has confessed to me that she has started to fancy one of the lads in her athletics club. I have seen him, he is fit and he clearly fancies the very arse off Lees. Adam and Lees have been together since the night of the disastrous foam party, a twenty-one month relationship. They have done everything together. They were each other's first kisses, first gropings, first loves, first shags. They are closer than any friendship and are viewed as a defining relationship within our peer group but now something is shifting and you can see the fear in Adam's eyes. Lees has chosen to go training tonight instead of coming to the party and I fear that this is an indication that her decision is made. I asked her if she wanted to talk about it last night, when she was helping me bath the boys. She said she didn't but she thinks she will need to talk to me about it tomorrow. *After.*

As a result, I am getting ready solo, no Lees to advise me. I have propped my sons up against these little sitting pillows on my bed. They look like cute, drunk, judgemental gnomes. I ask for their opinion as I do my hair and dance around in my dress. AJ, still a bit poorly and sorrowful looking, just stares and grizzles but Jake is dribbling and beaming at me.

My dress is so nice, it's deep green velvet lycra with a neckline that allows me to wear the ugly old bra that holds my breast pads in place. It's pretty short but right now, I've never been slimmer so I want to show off my legs before normality resumes. My hair is an absolute catastrophe. It is down to my arse now, bloody baby hormones sending into explosive growth mode but fortunately the weight of it means that the curls are stretched into ringlets rather than frizz.

I strip my goblins and put them into their PJ's, Dyls happily helping get them fed before I go. Dyls considers his nephews the best source of free entertainment he could possibly have. He will spend hours with them sat on his lap as he watches TV, like two little bookends. He tells them stories and most recently, has taken to trying to attract girls by taking them for walks in the pram.

The cat gives them a wide berth. Wise plan, I can see Jake eyeing up that tail every time it comes close.

I grab coat and keys and money as I hear my mother let Gio in the front door. I smile as I hear Gio greeting his 'God Goblins', he is always so funny with them and so gentle for such a big lad. AJ looks at him adoringly, it's proper cute. When I walk in the lounge door, I snigger as Romano's jaw drops.

"I *know* dude! Not a patch of baby sick or shit anywhere on my clothes, I've brushed my hair, I have both bra AND knickers on and I have even shaved my legs. Romano, this is as glamorous as Erin Roberts gets", I do a sarcastic twirl and cock a hip.

Gio's not laughing though, he's just staring with his blue eyes wide and his mouth gaping slightly. I turn in confusion to my mother but she is looking at Gio with an oddly affectionate expression. *Baffling.* I roll my eyes and tell good-looking Romano to 'move it', kissing my babies, my mum *and* the cat goodbye, so that it doesn't feel left out.

In the hallway, I wrestle my shoes on as Gio stands behind me.

"Do I get one then?", his whisper makes me turn in confusion.

"Eh? Get what dude?", I'm frowning.

Gio's blue eyes look a bit fierce and determined, "A kiss Rin. I mean even the bloody cat got one so do I get one too?"

I tut and roll my eyes, joke pouting and going up on tiptoes to kiss his cheek. *But he moves.*

Like lightning, Gio's hand is cupping my cheek and the cheek that I was aiming for twists away and it's replaced by soft, warm lips. Lips that move against mine as his other hand rests on my hip, lips that stroke and caress and make parts of me tingle that I should *not* allow to tingle in my mother's hallway. *Gio is kissing me.*

My heart is racing and his lips, *Christ those lips*, are so gentle and then there is the most hesitant flick of his tongue, like a feather, as mine part with a gasp.

The doorbell rings and I jump away from him in shock, both of us wide eyed and entirely stunned by what has just happened. As I reach for the door handle, I don't break his blue-eyed gaze, opening the door without looking, staring at Gio in confusion.

As the cold December air rushes in, I turn to see who it is.

"Ginger Feist, I got your message"

Jamel. Jamel is at my door.

Chapter Six

13th December 1996

He doesn't look like I remember and yet he's *exactly* the same. He's taller, he seems to be *bigger* than I remember and his hair is much shorter, he's got a fade cut and the twists have gone. His cheekbones look more pronounced than I recall but he's got those incredible full lips and his eyes are as brooding as my memories. He's still got that scar in his eyebrow and *Holy Shit*, he is *fit as*.

I am overwhelmed with words and so none come out.

"Rin?", I spin in panic and see Gio's face crumpled in a frown of confusion, his eyes darting to and from Jamel.

"Have you two not gone yet, you're letting all of the heat out of this house Erin, can you shut that..........YOU!!!", my Mum, walking out of the lounge stops mid scold to point a shaking finger at Jamel in the doorway, "Oh my God, you're HIM, Jake is the spitting image of you", the blood seems to be draining from my Mum's face.

"You useless, irresponsible bastard", my Mum suddenly launches herself towards the door, bumping into Gio who jolts against the wall as I instinctively jump over the threshold (impressive in heels) and pull my babies' father out of my mother's reach.

"BRON! What the hell is going on out here.....is that, is that HIM??!!", oh *Sweet Baby Jesus,* my father emerges from the kitchen, crisps in hand and points his own finger at Jamel.

I feel the arm of this *stranger*, whose coat sleeve I'm holding, tense and I see his fist clench. I look up at his face, a *stranger's* face and I see fury and confusion as he glares at me.

"You piece of shit, do you know what she's been through?", and now bloody massive Romano has belatedly cottoned on and presents a much more genuine threat than my parents, he rushes for the doorway and I feel Jamel take a shocked step backwards.

Jamel. Jamel is here. He's not a ghost, he's wearing Adidas trainers and jeans, ghosts don't wear those.

"STOP!! All of you just back off", the words leave my lips involuntarily as I step between them all.

Ignoring the three irate figures in my hallway, I turn to Jamel, blocking out the background noise of shouting and threats and I look into his angry glare,

"We need to talk, c'mon", and in my heels and my pretty party dress, I drag this angry *stranger man* to the one place we might get some peace. *The sodding garage.*

We are not followed, I guess even through their communal rage they understand that Jamel and I perhaps need to converse.

"What the fuck was that, eh? Who are them people? Why they got beef wiv' me, eh and what the fuck was that message?", Jamel's words are like staccato gunfire, he forces them out with venom as he paces angrily in the flickering light as the fluorescent garage strip-lights kick start into life.

I feel tears rising as I try to start at the beginning of my explanation, "You didn't come", my words are a whisper.

"Eh?", his jaw is clenched and it makes him look really scary to be honest, his silver earring glints in the light like a warning flash.

The wobble in my voice is more fear than distress, "That night, you were going to collect me but you never came. I waited for you", I have never felt so pathetic.

He steps forward and points a finger at me, I take a step back and have to swallow the urge to run, "Tha's bullshit. I *did* come for you, I was on my way when.......", he's shaking his head and looking at the floor.

"When what?", I feel this odd sort of anticipation, this warm fuzzy tingle at the potential offer of a new narrative.

He looks up through his lashes as he mutters, "I got pulled yeah, by the Feds, stopped and searched on the way to get you. The car, it was.....it was nicked and then they found the shit I were takin' wiv me, the gear for the rave an' tha'. Big quantities. I got held then remanded, I've done ten months yeah, got out yesterday", his words are soft, almost ashamed and as he looks at me, I don't have a clue what emotion I feel. *He was coming for me. He's been in fucking prison.*

I look up, through the tears that have started to fall unbidden and I whisper, "You got me pregnant Jamel. That night, *in here*, you got me pregnant and in October, I had your twins. You got me pregnant and I had your babies and they are my *world* and now you're here and I don't *know* you and I can't work out....I feel like.......I can't believe that...", and the tears take me under.

I stand my hands over my face and I weep, surprised at how much *relief* I feel, how comforted I am by what he has said, pathetic though that sounds. *I wasn't forgotten.*

I belatedly realise that he is pacing round, swearing, his hands over his own face but he's shocked as opposed to distressed. I hear him still his pacing,

"This is fucked up man. They're definitely mine you reckon?", his voice is a bit sharp with hope, as if he's praying that I might turn round and say, *"Actually, d'you know what, Jamel, I might have got it wrong all these months, silly me. They're actually the postman's, how remiss of me not to realise that before".*

I'm on him before I realise I've moved, "You FUCKING BASTARD, of course they're yours", he barely seems to register the slap across his face as his eyes widen comically.

I hiss like a scalded cat as I prod him in his solid chest, "Those babies are the most gorgeous things in the world. I should never have told you about them, you don't deserve to be their Dad, you piece of shit. FUCK OFF! Go on, just fuck off back to wherever you live. I've done this all myself until now, I don't need you, *they* don't need you", I mean it. I *bloody* mean it, I am suddenly furious.

I have been their Mum for nearly eight weeks and we are amazing together, we have worked shit out and we are getting a life built. *He* is not needed, I can't believe I ever thought he might be.

My tears are blinding me but I storm out of the garage and round to the back door, where I let myself in. I hear voices from the living room, indignant and loud, my mother and Gio seemingly encouraging their mutual dislike of the newly arrived complication in my life.

I hear a little squawk from upstairs and the sound of my brother swearing, which can only mean that a nappy catastrophe is occurring. I'd rather face a shitty bum than my family and as-yet-uncategorised kissing partner so I walk towards the stairs.

As I reach the bottom of the stairs, I see Jamel through the dappled glass of the front door, his arm reaching up to the doorbell. Not wishing to reignite the flames of my mother's ire, I open the door before he can ring it.

He's got his hands thrust deep in his pocket and he's biting his lip and looking nervous, toeing at the gravel on mum's path. I roll my eyes and step out, pulling it softly on the latch, so as not to be detected. I wrap my arms around my waist, stroking the velvet of my new dress in an attempt to calm my nerves.

"You still beating up lads that are bigger than you, eh Ginger Feist?", he looks up through his lashes, a lopsided smirk on his lips that is entirely too cute.

I get a flash of deja vu as I mutter, "Only the dickheads who deserve it", I roll my eyes.

He looks directly at me and for a second, I feel a flash of familiarity as he asks, "Are they...are they OK, the babies an' that?", he looks anxious.

I frown in confusion, "They're fine, I mean they were born four weeks premature and they were really poorly a few days after they were born plus AJ's got a cold at the minute but they're good, they're really amazing and Jake, well Mum's right, he does look just like you. I hadn't really realised that before", I feel my lip wobble as Jamel's eyes widen.

"Boys? Twin boys?", I see a smile at the corner of his mouth

I nod with a smile of my own, "They're not identical. Alfred-James and Jacob-Jamel", I hesitate on the last name, waiting for a reaction that I can't predict.

He physically jolts, I see him take a deep breath, "You used my name?", his eyes are really wide.

I smile and look down as I say, "You gave me the two most amazing things in my life, I felt like it was the right thing to do. Plus, you're their Dad so....y'know", I shrug and look up at the frosty sky.

He startles me by coming up close to me, his warmth reaching me across the small gap between our bodies. He's tall, about the same height as Gio but he feels bigger somehow, he is broad but he's a *man,* there is nothing boyish about him. He smells *amazing* and that incredibly cheeky smile is making me want to squirm.

"Erin", he pauses as if I might not give my permission for him to use my name, I smile encouragingly, "Can I meet them? Can I see my sons?", his Brummy accent is strong as he comes even closer and I feel like my heart might beat out of my chest.

I nod dumbly, I desperately want my boys to have everything they deserve and now that Jamel is here, that includes a *Dad*. I jerk my head indicating for him to follow me which he does compliantly as I lead him into the house, quietly shutting the door so as not to attract attention.

Pressing my finger to my lips as I lead him up the stairs, I can hear my mum talking,

"Giovanni love, I think maybe you should head to that party, I don't imagine for one second that Erin will get this sorted in time to be able to go with you and she wouldn't want you to miss out".

Gio's deep voice rumbles, *"Nah, I was only fussed about going if she was. I'll hang on if that's OK, check she's alright Mrs. Roberts?"*

I hear mum pat his knee, *"Of course sweetheart, she's lucky to have you Gio, chopsy little madam that she is"*

I can hear the snorts and snuffles of my little piglets as we reach the landing, Dyls seemingly having won the battle of the nappy and resettled whoever it was that had disgraced themselves. I hear music coming from Dyls room as I pull Jamel across the dark landing. I can feel his pulse beating against my fingers.

As I push open our bedroom door, I hold my breath. I am strangely nervous about this whole thing. What if the babies freak out? What if Jamel doesn't see how incredible they are? What if the babies love him and then he disappears again? What if they love him more than me?

The glow of the night-light is the only illumination that we have. Jamel overtakes me into the room, as I turn to slowly shut the door, softly enough not to wake the goblins. When I turn back, he is stood, hands braced on the side of the cot as he stares down at the mini-occupants who are snuffling and snorting in tandem. They started to co-sleep in hospital, I'd noticed that they fell asleep far quicker when they were in the same cot and if I'm honest, they looked proper gorgeous bundled up together.

When we got home, they didn't both fit in the Moses basket safely unless they were top'n'tailed and they did *not* like this. AJ is a wriggler and Jake got a foot in the nose once too often. I got a bigger cot and it sits right up against my bed, the side lowered by the bed so that I can reach them when I'm lying in mine.

"They're so fuckin' small", I look up at Jamel's whisper and see his wide-eyed astonishment.

Smiling, I walk over to join him and whisper back, "They were so, so tiny when they were born, they're both over seven and a half pounds now, they were five pounds when they were born and they lost weight when they were poorly", I shudder suddenly at the memory.

Jamel's looking at me, intensely scanning my face, it's a bit overwhelming. I smile awkwardly and point, "That's AJ, he's got lighter hair and even though he's the youngest he's the noisiest one of the two, he likes to be noticed. That's Jake, he's bigger but he's more chilled and he....he looks like you. He loves his food and his favourite thing in the world is having his arms and legs rubbed with baby oil after his bath. He goes all soppy and smiles", I grin as I talk, relishing any conversation that lets me gush about my babies.

On cue, AJ has a squawk, making Jamel jump slightly. Patting Jamel's broad shoulder, I reach in and lift out my little snotty goblin, kissing his little head and reaching for a cloth to clear his runny nose. Jamel watches me, agog, as *our son* yawns and stretches.

I have a massive lump in my throat as I whisper, "Do you want to hold him?". Jamel looks terrified but he nods nervously.

I pat the bed and Jamel sits and I shape his arms ready to receive his tiny son. I can't hold back the sob as AJ settles in his *Dad's* arms for the first time, Jamel looking at me with concern before staring in wonder at what he's holding.

"I've got….I've got two kids. I can't…...I can't believe this is fuckin' happenin'. I can't believe that you and me…….we did this? This is for real?", he's comically astonished and I smile,

"Jamel, I promise they're real, I've got the massive scar on my belly and the near death experience to prove it", I chuckle but Jamel frowns, I wave my hand in dismissal and Jamel looks back at AJ,

Jamel whispers, "He's like you, y'know? He's well cute, like his Mum", at that last word, Jamel's eyes meet mine and my blush is nuclear.

I'm saved by Jake's snort, the absence of his brother's warmth unsettling him. Gently lifting him out, I move Jamel's arms again, trying not to gulp at the granite muscles I feel beneath his hoodie. As I place Jake in his other arm, Jamel's face sort of collapses. He's not crying, Jamel's not really coming across as the *crying type* but he's certainly overwhelmed.

He looks up at me, his eyes glistening in the darkness, "He's like me, he looks like me, don't he?",

Jamel's smile is wide and in that moment, I get a glimpse of what my eldest son is going to look like when he's older and it makes me melt.

I wink, "Yup, he's a bit too gorgeous, *like his Dad*". It turns out that boys blush too, even when their skin is an incredibly gorgeous shade of mocha.

We sit in silence for ages, I hear all sorts of conversation and movement downstairs but I'm too absorbed in *my family* to pay attention. Jamel just stares at the boys, smiling and looking at me when they do something cute. When they both randomly crack an eye open each, looking like pissed-off tortoises, they fix their stare on Jamel and I see his mouth drop in wonder,

Stroking their impossibly soft little heads I whisper, "Goblins, this is a really important person, this is your Daddy. Your Daddy, he found us", I feel a lip wobble and Jamel's stare is too intense to hold.

A thought strikes me and I ask, "How *did* you find us? And why didn't you call before you came over?", frowning, I move and lift the boys out of Jamel's arms and back into their cot as I wait for his answer.

He shakes his head ruefully, "Shit man, you ever tried to find a place you only been once before, like ten months ago? I've been driving round this fuckin' place for hours, recognised that house with the shitty fountain in the end", he shakes his head and I laugh softly, *Pat's Roman fountain is proper shitty.*

He looks at me, "Anyways, you never gave me your number that night. I only got my shit back yesterday, when I got released. The pager was dead but your message was the one that come up when I got it going, it must have been the last one that got sent. It's been sat in a book-in locker in the nick for all them months. I just got this message from you, 'bout having my babies. I couldn't work out if you was serious so I come straight here, borrowed my mates car", I close my eyes and nod, contemplating the hundreds of now-lost pages that I sent to a lonely locker, deep within a prison.

Jamel cocks his head, "Downstairs, that big lad, who's he?", he raises an eyebrow as I fumble for my answer,

"Er that's my mate Gio, from school. He's actually the boys' Godfather, he was there with me when they were born but we're not together, we're not it's just.......complicated", I blush unexpectedly as my brain fires flashbacks to our very recent kiss.

That bloody lopsided grin again, "This *complicated* with this Godfather, it make you dress up like this a lot?", he gestures at my dress and sits back, arms crossed over his chest, cheeky smirk broad.

"OI! It's my Christmas Party tonight which I'm actually missing to be here, with you", I smack him gently on the chest and he chuckles.

"Well, just so you know Ginger Feist, you look fuckin' hot. Maybe I need to get a Godmother, eh?", my soft snort makes my sons snuffle and Jamel turns to look at them again, awe on his face.

I see the time and mutter, "Look, I think I'd better go and speak to them all and so, er, I guess maybe...", I look meaningfully towards the door.

Jamel nods slowly, "Yeah I'd best get back"

I am suddenly curious, "So do you still live in Bristol?"

He winces and fiddles with his nails, looking down, "Yeah I'm there but.....but I ain't *home.* I gotta stay at this probation hostel place coz while I was inside, my Iya, tha's my nan, she passed and her flat went back to the Council so....", I feel his pain travel across the bed. I recall the Nigerian nan comments from March and now I see there is a story that ends with his fairly recent loss.

"Oh Jamel, I'm so sorry", and without thinking, I pull him into a hug, like I would have done with any of my *friends*.

This hug, it's pretty weird. He doesn't move his arms initially and I am about to pull back, a bit embarrassed when he suddenly moves and I am clutched to him, his hands in my hair and his other arm so tight that it pulls on my ribs. Jamel is shaking, I feel it through his whole body and as I absorb the scent of his aftershave, the feel of his body and spiky feel of his chin against my cheek, I realise that perhaps the comfort I wanted to provide is needed more than either of us realise. I eventually pull away, looking at the carpet.

His voice is a soft croak, "I can come back though, yeah? See them, maybe spend time wiv' them?", his eyes are so hopeful that my heart cracks and I nod without hesitation.

He sighs, "I'd better go, you gotta be in by 11 at the hostel", he shakes his head and I feel a horrible lurch at the idea of him leaving our cosy room to go somewhere so alien. I feel sad at the idea of part of my boys *leaving* to go somewhere horrible.

He stands and goes over to the cot, ghosting his fingers over their little downy heads.

"See you soon boys, be good for your mum hey" and I watch him press a kiss to his fingers and touch each of them.

I sneak him downstairs and back out the front door, pulling it closed as I stand on the step.

He darts looks all around, jigging a bit on the spot before turning and staring at me, "Erin, you gotta know that I had no fuckin' idea yeah, I had no idea what had gone down wiv' you, what you was handlin'. If I did, I'd have fuckin' got word to you, tried to help. You know that girl, yeah?", his tone is pleading.

I smile and nod gently. *I believe him.*

I reach inside and grab the phone message pad and pen, scribbling my number on it and handing it to him.

"Ring me, tomorrow yeah and we'll sort out you coming to see them, OK?", I smile and impulsively lean forward and kiss him on the cheek, making him beam.

He starts to walk backwards, grinning at me with that gorgeous face, "I'm a Dad Erin, you made me a fuckin' Dad. I got two boys, twin boys", his smile is electric as my lips wobble in my nod.

"You're fuckin' amazin' Ginger Feist, I'll ring you tomorrow yeah", and with that, he jogs towards his parked car.

I go back inside to face the music.

My mum jumps up, "So? Where is he? Disappeared again has he?", hands on hips, she's vibrating with fury.

Three faces stare at me expectantly as I sit, my head in my hands and tell them what I know, what Jamel has told me, what we have discussed.

"PRISON?! Well that says a lot doesn't it, eh? For heaven's sake Erin, what possessed you to agree to him seeing the boys?", my Dad is on his feet, gesticulating wildly at the ceiling.

Mum wades in, "Now look here good girl, we're all a sucker for a sob story from a pretty face and that boy, well, I can see why my grandsons are quite so handsome as they are BUT he has been involved with things that landed him in prison and I don't think we know enough about him to let him near my grandsons just yet".

"My sons", my voice is a low growl as I look up. I see mum's jaw clench and dad close his eyes in exasperation. Gio's looking between us all like he's watching a tennis match.

I carry on, my nails digging into my palms, "AJ and Jake are *my sons* and within twenty-four hours of finding out that they were *his* sons too, Jamel got himself here, even though he's only driven here once and that was ten months ago. Doesn't that tell you something about him?"

Gio's voice rumbles beside me, "Yeah Rin, it says that he was too locked up to help you when you were pregnant, too locked up to watch you bleed to death having them and too locked up to be any use when they were ill in hospital", I feel a rush of fury when Mum nods animatedly and points at Gio, indicating her support of his statement.

I turn to Gio and I bite, "Why are you still here? Shouldn't you be at the party?"

Gio looks a bit stunned and mumbles, "I was just waiting to check you were OK and I thought maybe, er, maybe we should have a chat, y'know, about what has *happened* tonight", he nods meaningfully at me. *The kiss.* I close my eyes briefly, trying to muster up some calm.

"Erin, I do not want Jamel in this house until I know him better, do you understand? You do seem to lose what little common sense you have around him and I'm only thinking of the boys' well-being".

That's it. I'm on my feet, "YOU don't need to worry about their well-being *Mother* because that is what MY job is, all day every day. I don't *lose my common sense* around Jamel, don't give me that.

114

We had sex *once*, we didn't rob a bloody bank. Gio, we'll talk another time mate. You head off to the party, it's only nine o'clock. I'll see you tomorrow. I'm going to bed, I want to keep an eye on AJ with that cold, y'know with what *little common sense* I've got left after Jamel has drained it all out of me", I stomp off, trying to ignore the way that Gio's shoulders slump or the sad look on his face.

As I softly close my bedroom door, I peel myself out of the lush dress that I was stupid to imagine I would actually get to wear in public and I lie down, as close to my snuffling gnomes as I can. I reach out and hold their tiny hands, watching them breath until sleep claims me. In my dreams, I see sad blue eyes, soft lips and freckled olive skin, shards of glitter, smirks that melt and a deep voice that calls me 'Ginger Feist'.

Christmas Day 1996

It's not going well, I won't lie. It's been a twelve day PR mission that has ended with toe-curling discomfort over the sprouts.

Jamel looks like he's contemplating suicide with the carving knife, my mother can barely chew her dinner her lips are so tightly pursed and my father has taken to the Festive Beer Selection Pack like wino let loose in Oddbins. Dyls seems to think that solution lies in the bottom of the serving dishes and is hoovering up food like a tornado and my sons, cradled one-a-piece by Jamel and I, are slumped like little Festive Elves in the ridiculous outfits that their Godmother bought as we both eat one-handed.

Christ on a bike.

Jamel rang the very next day after that first visit. He then drove back over the following afternoon after school to meet me at a local cafe with the boys. Jamel has started the job his probation officer got him at a Pallet Building firm mainly doing night shifts, meaning that he can normally come over in the afternoons.

It's such an odd business, getting to know the father of your children from scratch. So much seems clunky and awkward. *"Yes we had sex but what is your surname?", "I gave birth to both of your children but where do you come from?"* Jamel's surname is Watson. In between my endless gushing about *our* sons, I learn that Jamel's mum lives with his step-Dad in Birmingham, a gentleman whose delightful racist views led to Jamel leaving her care when he was eight, moving to live with his Nigerian Dad in Bristol. However, his Dad's very strict views and inability to understand his angry and wayward son, meant that Jamel was thrown out at fourteen. He went to live with his Iya and there he remained until his first stay at her Majesty's Pleasure when he was sixteen, after he stole a car. Upon his release, things were apparently calm until the fateful night when he headed off to see me, recklessly driving a stolen car full of drugs to do so.

His nan's death is not a small issue. Jamel actually can't talk about his Iya much, I asked him a couple of questions and he clammed up, his jaw painfully clenched. There is deep, raw hurt there and I don't know him anywhere near well enough to poke that wound. He has four brothers, one of whom is a full sibling and three are half siblings. Jamel is smack bang in the middle of the five, just like my Mum in her family. When I pointed out this uniting similarity, my mothers derisive tut indicated that commonality with Jamel was unwelcome.

Jamel is nervous with the babies, I feel an ache for him when I see his wide eyed expression when they cry or they grizzle for something and I'm really anxious that my encouragement or tips come across as patronising. He changed a nappy the other day and got so frustrated with his own lack of skill that he walked off, radiating embarrassment.

I've never had to interact with somebody whose penis has a working knowledge of my vagina. It is not something I am equipped to manage with any sort of skill. There is this unspoken awkwardness that sits on us, the blushes, the stares that make the other self-conscious, the shocked jolts whenever our skin accidentally touches.

Gio has been a pain in the arse since the night of the party. He's been very vocal about his mistrust of Jamel's intentions, the volume of which has unfortunately meant that the return of my *Baby Daddy* and the reason for his previous absence are now common knowledge. Gio makes a massive show of posturing and flouting his skills with the babies and he keeps pestering me for *'a chat'* which I have ducked pretty skilfully. I look at Gio, as we sit in cars, hang out at my house or chat in the common room and I feel this pull towards him. I think the truth is that I actually fancy him pretty hard, I *care* about him, I *like* him an awful lot but it's like there's this wall that gets in the way. I just can't see past my babies right now, everything else feels a bit *petty*. Jamel is part of that baby wall, I am so invested in getting this whole relationship between the four of us more relaxed and easy. It's taking all my energy, leaving nothing for Gio right now.

My friends and Gio have not met Jamel, I can't cope with having to stage-manage a larger group yet. Sat with Lees on my bed the other night, hugging her and letting her weep into the only baby-sick free top I currently own, we dissected her tearful dumping of Adam and the subsequent enthusiastic snogging of her new sprinter boyfriend *Kiron*. After several hours chatting, I'd asked her what people are saying about me,

She'd winced, "Yeah Rinny, they pretty much think you're shacked up with your ex-con lover. I won't lie Rin, you are deemed a total bad-ass but it's not doing much to silence the gossips", she patted my arm soothingly.

She'd frowned, "But Romano and you, what gives?"

I told her about the kiss and about the brick wall of babies and she winced more, "Rinny, I know you probably don't want to hear this right now but surely you must know, Romano proper arse-over-massive-pec fancies you. You do know that, don't you? Ads always reckoned Gio's been into you since before you got pregnant, you're why he broke up with Carolyn?", she looks at me earnestly as I close my eyes and flap my hands like a jazz dancer.

"He is no such thing, that's bollocks and Lees even in the unlikely event that he does have feelings for me, this is so NOT the time", she'd nodded ruefully and then sobbed more about sad, broken-hearted Adam and the guilt she feels about choosing Kiron.

Jamel has now spent twenty-seven hours in the company of his sons and I, *not* that I'm counting. We meet in freezing cold parks where all their father sees of his sons is two little rosy snouts poking out of a pile of blankets, overheated cafés, the leisure centre and I even dragged the boys, pram and all, to the Out of Town McDonalds. These little escapades were observed by my tight-lipped mother who at the end of last week, announced that she wanted Jamel to come to Christmas lunch.

Arms crossed, tea-towel brandished like a weapon, she'd collared me in the kitchen, "Well, as that eejit shows no sign of disappearing just yet, I'm not having the boys dragged out in the cold to sit in cafés and be gawked at pointlessly for hours. Right madam, bring him here. When's he coming next? I want him at this table for the Boys' first Christmas dinner. If I am to be forced to not kill the feckless bastard, I might as well feed him", she's nodded in a manner that I knew meant there would be no discussion.

Jamel upon hearing that his future contact with his sons and indeed the integrity of his bollocks was dependent on appeasing my mother, swallowed thickly and agreed. When he muttered that he *'didn't have nowhere to go this year anyway'* and then looked impossibly sad, my heart broke for him and instead of it being a dreaded chore, I realised that I actually *wanted* Jamel to come.

The boys' first Christmas Eve was cute. Lees bought them these two little Elf babygrows and at midnight mass, the Priest actually had to bellow in a most un-Christian manner for *'Everyone to please take your seats and give as much deference to our Lord's birth as to the Roberts' twins arrival'.* Tens of hormonal Catholic women rushed to place arses on pews, shooting continued adoring looks my sons' way throughout Mass. Gio was there with his parents and sister Aurora, the urge to kiss him again strong when he sneaked to the back of the church to help me soothe the squawking pair of elves, both baffled by the absence of their warm cot at the late hour.

"Which one do I get then, eh, if you snuff it Rin? Which one is mine and which one does Morris get?", he'd whispered in my ear as he rhythmically patted AJ's nappy clad arse as he rocked him back and forth.

I'd smiled and looked up at his ridiculously handsome face, "You get whichever one doesn't coordinate with Lees' shoes at the funeral, you know how fussy she is", Gio snorted and nodded as Jake snuffled into my neck.

I nearly head butted Gio by accident when I jolted as I felt his warm breath against my ear, his big strong body suddenly flush against mine, "What about if I wanted both of them……..and you Rin? What if *you* are what I really want for Christmas?", his last words were drowned out by the sound of everyone scrabbling to their feet for a prayer.

I'd just stared at Gio, so confused because in my head all I could hear was his voice saying very different things, *"......you can't afford to get any uglier", "Christ knows what I was doing with Roberts, she's rank", "Roberts, I'm not enough of a fucking idiot to get involved with you".* I didn't feel like I could trust in what he was saying, I wondered if perhaps his genuine affection for my sons means that he's kidding himself about me. *I can't put faith in this.*

I winced as I attempted a smile and whispered, "I think you'd be better off asking Santa for a Playstation Romano, they're less aggravation".

I watched as some sort of shutter went down over his eyes, his jaw clenched and I saw his shoulders slump. He lay a sleeping AJ down gently in his pram and, without looking my way, muttered, "Merry Christmas yeah", and without a backwards glance, he walked out of the church.

My lips wobbling, I placed Jake down next to his brother and tucked them in. It's only when I finally looked up that I saw both Sofia Romano and my mother staring at me. Both of them had the same sad look on their faces. I concentrated on rocking the pram.

This morning, Dyls padded into my room like he always does, his stocking dangling from his hand. I felt a bit daft this year putting my stocking out but when I'd gone to protest, as we returned from Mass last night, my mother who had been at the Christmas sherry said in a wobbly voice,

"You're still my little girl despite all your shenanigans Erin and you will still have a bloody stocking madam", before she'd turned away to brutally assault the turkey, sniffing and wiping her eyes.

This year, I'd hung two tiny little stockings at the end of the cot. I've bought little cuddly toys and in an afternoon of daftness with Lees, I'd dragged my childhood craft sets out of the loft and have created little name plaques for the boys. Dyls had said that they look like a toddler made them. I ignored him.

A baby in each lap, Dyls and I opened our stockings, laughing hysterically at my mother's decision to partially fill mine with what Dyls called *'Boy-Repelling Pants'.*

"No more babies for you Rinny in those bad boys", Dyls snorted as he pointed at the truly gigantic floral monstrosities.

The boys, not the *slightest* clue what was occurring around them but smiling and dribbling adorably, were furnished with huge piles of presents. Mum and Dad bought them a photo session at a local studio, Dyls bought them some sort of ball popping machine that made them stare like zombies, Gio bought them some teddies with their names sewn into the jumpers and I'd bought them this twinkly light thing that they lie underneath and get dazzled (hopefully into sleep) by.

Once we've all opened presents and Mum's liberated the stash of Quality Street, a weird sort of anticipation settles on us, awaiting Jamel's first proper introduction to my family. His work has been too busy this week to coordinate with my mother's shifts so she has not met him. The rough treatment that the potatoes are currently receiving in the kitchen suggests that a warm festive welcome might be thin on the ground.

Jamel's bricking it. He rang yesterday before Mass, his lovely deep voice giving me giddy tingles despite the fact that he was asking about whether Jake's shitty nappies had calmed down, a poorly tummy having laid Jake a bit low for a few days. I felt a bit wobbly from the concern he was demonstrating, from his *investment.* He kept asking, *"You sure your mum's cool wiv me coming?"*. I'd lied repeatedly.

Jamel has known that he's a Dad for exactly fourteen days, he's also been my undefined *person* for this duration. Not a friend yet, not a mate, certainly not a boyfriend, he flinches slightly hurtfully whenever our skin touches. I don't know how to define him other than as *'the father of my sons'*.

When he smiles at me, with that incredible face, with the cheekbones and the impish grin, with the beautifully straight, sparkly teeth and the roguish scar in his eyebrow, with that body that looks so strong and the eyes that sometimes look so sad, when *all of that* looks my way, I feel my bones tingle.

However, because in my role of *'Parental Training Guide and Twin Induction Tutor'*, I feel like I am a continued irritation to him, a bit of a bore really. I feel a bit crushed with every furrow of his eyebrow, every distracted eye-wander when he tires of my chat. There is after all nothing sexy at all about a bossy, baby-stretched, ugly little ginger annoyance that you barely know. He calls me 'Ginger Feist' but in the way you might refer to a little sister or a younger cousin. I am increasingly certain that if I had *not* fallen pregnant with the twins and he *had* turned up that Saturday night a week after our 'garage bang' (Lees' delightful phrase) he would quickly have realised that he was not interested and our association would have ended. It makes me feel sick and wobbly when this thought sits with me.

I've made an effort today, he's only really ever seen me bundled up in a Parka or in jumpers covered in baby sick, my party dress and the long ago rave outfit are distant memories. Today, I have on my denim mini-skirt over thick tights and a tight-fit t-shirt that shows off the boobs that are still a bit ridiculous thanks to daily milk-expressing.

The door knocks and I hear all four of us gulp, even the twins gurgle.

I open the door and try to smile through a massive spasm in my knickers. Jamel has got on a tight grey t-shirt, some really nice dark jeans and a new Adidas jacket. He's been to the barbers and his short top with fade has got a couple of cool lines shaved in. It sort of matches his eyebrow scar. His earring is glinting and his terrified face makes me smile encouragingly.

I wink, "You ready for this?" but he just looks alarmed and shakes his head as I usher him in.

Mum is in that hallway like a missile, "You made it then?", arms are crossed.

Jamel's body in front of me goes completely rigid, he doesn't reply straight away and in my panic, I grab his hand. This is our first intentional contact since the hug, that first night he met the twins.

In that second, Jamel's grip tightens around my fingers and I feel an actual, genuine current of electricity travel down my arm. He does not let go as we follow mum into the lounge, Dad and Dyls smiling like they have truly awful wind. He nods his hellos and holds onto my hand like a clamp.

I walk him over to the twins, lying on their little play mat and in an effort to make him feel less exposed, I get down on the floor and pat the carpet.

With the sort of cool, effortless grace that I will never, *ever* possess, he folds his tall frame into a cross-legged sit, reaching over and picking up AJ in such a newly capable way that I feel my heart constrict.

He's bought the boys their Christmas Presents which are teeny-tiny little Nike tracksuits, quite possibly the cutest thing I've ever seen. I scowl at my mother's quiet tut of derision, as she walks off. Dyls got some new Playstation game for Christmas and he fires it up, Jamel darting glances too often to hide his interest. I smile,

"Dyls, you want some competition over there?", I look at Jamel who is fiddling with Jake's fingers.

Dyls snorts, "Rinny, you are complete shit at games. You wouldn't be competition, you'd be charity. Man, you wanna show her how it's done?", Dyls tilts his head at Jamel who shrugs and saunters over the grab the proffered controller.

I watch, grinning stupidly, as my brother and *my sons' father,* joke, chat and get slowly more relaxed in each other's company. It's *amazing* and it lasts for forty-five minutes until my mother calls us to the table.

"So Jamel, how long do you have to live at the probation hostel?", we've all literally *just* sat our bums on the chairs as she launches her attack.

Jamel, his first words under the scrutiny of all my entire family, holds Jake over his shoulder and mumbles, "I move out next month, they only let you stay there 'til your license finishes".

I turn to him as Mum spears meat and lobs it onto plates, whispering, "Where will you move to?"

He raises his deep brown eyes to mine and looks sad as he murmurs, "I dunno", and I shift AJ in my arms to reach under the table, taking Jamel's warm hand in mine.

His eyes jolt back up to mine, filled with questions but it's broken by my mother semi-shouting, "Do you want pigs in blankets?", making him jump.

The poor lad barely gets a mouthful of food in before Mum hits him with the headline question, "So young man, are you a professional drug dealer and car thief or was this a little bit of work experience by there that got you locked up?", Mum's eyebrow is raised as she waits for his response.

Jamel chews slowly as we all hold our breaths before he rumbles out quietly,

"The wheels stuff I'd been a part of before, I got sent down before for that. I was a thick dickhead kid and I should never have got involved nicking motors, I was a prick. The dealin', I was doin' that coz…...coz I got in wiv some people I should have stayed clear of and got into shit, er, got into *stuff* coz I weren't thinkin' straight. My head was a bit messed up 'round last Christmas and it played out bad", Jamel stares at the table for a moment as we all hold our breath.

He looks up at me, "But you gotta know, that ain't me, that ain't who I am. I got plans, I'm gonna build a life for me and for my boys now. I ain't that person no more", he darts a look at my Mum who looks at him sceptically. We all resume eating in silence.

Mum works through an entire *'Mastermind Special of Aggressive Questions'*, as Jamel tries to eat his lunch whilst holding his son. He's handling it OK, his jaw is tight and his responses are pretty monosyllabic but he's doing OK that is until Mum sees me taking a big mouthful that will prevent me interjecting and she goes for it,

"You're not saying anything today Jamel that makes me think you're a good enough man to be in my Grandsons' lives, let alone be their father. What are you going to say to convince me, eh?", she folds her arms across her chest as I furiously chew trying to swallow enough to be able to scream at her.

Jamel, just looks at the two babies snoozing on us and then he raises his head and locks those intense brown eyes on my mother as his deep, low voice rumbles,

"Mrs. Roberts, my Iya told me you gotta be respectful, you gotta respect people so she'd strap me I 'spect for this but honest? I don't give a fuck what you think 'bout me", I hear my brother drop his cutlery and my father make a sort of strangled gulp.

He carries on, "I only give a shit 'bout what she thinks of me", he thumbs at me, "an' what my boys think of me, when they get old enough. You? You worry 'bout your kids coz that's your job. Me, I'm gonna worry 'bout *my* kids and 'bout whether their Mum, who's fuckin' amazin', thinks I'm doin' OK. I'm gonna just be here givin' a fuck what *they* think 'bout me, not *you*", and with that, he takes a mouthful of lunch and adjusts Jake's position on his shoulder.

There's a silence the like of which the Robert's clan have never experienced. My Dad looks like he's waiting for the A Bomb to drop, Dyls looks like he wants to snog Jamel, Mum's eyes are narrowed into such thin slits, I'm not sure she can see out of them and I'm holding my son and praying that neither he nor his brother will remember the moment that their Nana slaughtered their Father over the Christmas dinner table.

My mum's voice is so quiet, I think I'm imagining it, "She sounds like she was a good lady, your Nana"

I turn to look at Jamel, who's stopped chewing and who nods stiffly. My mum purses her lips and looks up and down the table, "You'd better eat a bit faster Jamel, there's plenty more and you're a big lad who needs filling", and she picks up her knife and fork and resumes her lunch as if nothing has happened. Jamel nods and speeds up as requested.

I'm staring at Dyls across the table, he looks as entirely baffled as me. Shaking my head, I pick up my own fork and wonder if perhaps we've entered a parallel universe. It quickly becomes clear that we haven't when Mum resumes normal service,

"Mind you, with you two chopsy, gobby pair of disrespectful eejits as parents, those two do have not a hope", she points her fork meaningfully at the pair of us and then at the twins and shakes her head as she chews.

I smile into my sprouts, nearly choking when Jamel's hand reaches for mine under the table.

Jamel thanks Mum for the *'well nice food'*. She tells him it was her *'pleasure'*. I wash up voluntarily with Dyls' help, as Jamel attempts his first solo bum-change and twin settling upstairs.

"I thought she'd kill him Rinny, dead man walking I reckoned", Dyls is still slack jawed as he whispers, "He's quiet and that, you can tell he's not good around people but he's a nice guy".

Dyls stops drying and looks at me as he adds, "I always thought I'd hate him, that he'd be a proper dick but he's not. He's just a bit freaked out, isn't he? Guess I would be too", and with that, Dyls heads off to the loo.

There is silence coming from my room as I get to the landing. I gently open the door and an astonishing wave of 'shitty nappy' smell hits me as I see Jamel tidying up around two clean, dopey looking babies.

He looks up at me and smirks, "You dodged a fuckin' bullet there Ginger Feist. Proper fuckin' rancid"

Nappy bag tied up, he heads to the en suite to wash his hands as I lie down on the bed next to my two goblins. I'm chatting to them, telling them that I thought their Nana would kill their Daddy, that they are the cutest Christmas Babies ever and then I stroke their little noses as I sing 'We wish you a Merry Christmas' softly at them.

I had forgotten that Jamel was in my room until I hear the floorboard creak. I turn and he's staring at me, a smile quirking up those *gorgeous lips.* Embarrassed, I pick the boys up and deposit them gently in their cot. Not meeting Jamel's gaze, I walk over to my wardrobe and fetch out the gift bag that I'd been saving until we were on our own. I pat the bed and as he slowly walks over, I notice that his socks don't match.

I hand it to him, "This is for you, Merry Christmas", and I smile nervously. Jamel's eyebrows are in such a deep frown, that I genuinely panic that I have offended him but as he reaches in and pulls out the photo album within it, the frown morphs into astonishment.

I gabble, "Um, I thought you should have some photos of the boys so I copied a whole tonne of my favourite ones and there were so many that I thought I'd make you an album. I printed out the nicest one in a big size and that's in the frame there", I point at the smaller box.

Jamel is flicking gently through the huge album, I found one in Boots that had 'Precious Twin Boys' written on the front. As I look over his shoulder, I point out the pictures and tell him where they were taken, who by and the story behind them. It takes me a while to realise that he's staring at me and not the pictures, my voice trailing off in confusion. Jamel is shaking his head slightly, like he's having an argument in his head.

It's a few seconds before he speaks, "That night, at that rave, I was watchin' you, y'know? You fuckin' floored that dickhead you was wiv, he was like twice your size but you just nuked him and then you walked off and just danced. You was by yourself but you just had it, you were just havin' fun. I never saw a girl that was ballsy like that, it was like you never gave one little shit, you was just doin' your thing. That's you though, innit? Me, I got into shit, I'm *in* shit coz I do what I reckon people expect me to be or tell me to do, wiv'out Case I……..", he shakes his head again, cutting off his explanation or expanding who or what *'Case'* is, his face in a deep frown..

He gathers his thoughts and points at the cot, "These two, I want them to look at me like they're gonna look at you, I want them to learn to be strong men, do good things, be kind like this", he points at the album.

"Maybe they'll be feisty, like their mum", he smiles at me and my little teenage heart does a flip flop as I blush and busy myself straightening my room.

I stand still as I look at Jamel in the mirror, "You're a good man, y'know Watson. You came back for us. You could have ignored that message but you didn't. You came back and you keep coming. A weak man wouldn't do that, especially not when you have to face aggro like today", I roll my eyes.

Jamel snorts, "I like your Mum y'know, she says what she means"

I sneer, "You like her, you can take her, she's a bloody nightmare, I can't believe you got her to back down"

He shrugs non-committally as he looks at the babies. A sort of awkward silence falls over us as the boys' snorts and sniffles fade into soft tiny snores. I look at Jamel, his back turned to me. His shoulders are broad, he's got a lush bum and his tall frame is sleekly muscular. I feel horribly self-conscious in his presence and start folding babygrows to distract myself.

I jolt as he rumbles, "I'll get you something, y'know, from them, when I get paid and that. I only got a weeks pay so I couldn't get nothin' once I'd bought their stuff but.....I will y'know", I meet his eyes and I see his discomfort. I smile and take a step forward,

"Nah, you don't need to do that, it's kind but you don't need to. My Mum bought me a present from the boys, A Level revision books", I roll my eyes and wink cheekily. Jamel snorts,

"Fuck that shit, me and my boys, we buy decent stuff, no shitty school books", he looks so disgusted that I chuckle.

Awkwardness settles once more and I sense that Jamel is not looking to linger, "Do you......are you seeing your brothers today?", I ask quietly.

Jamel nods slowly and sighs, "Yeah, look I gotta be somewhere, Erin. I need to sort some stuff out. That'll be cool yeah, wiv' your Mum? I don't wanna piss her off", he winces and I chuckle again, in awe at Bronwen Roberts' ability to terrify.

He nods at the cot, "They're havin' a good Christmas eh? Saw them presents in the corner, those teddies with the names on 'em", he smiles.

I throw a weak smile in response, "Yeah, they were from Gio those bears, no clue where on earth I'm gonna store them in this room", I roll my eyes but I see the flicker of a frown cross Jamel's face.

He nods, "Their Godfather, yeah? That all he is Feist?"

I look up at Jamel's *startlingly* good looking face and I wince again, "Umm, it's complicated, I don't know really".

He kisses his teeth softly, nodding as he looks at the floor, "Yeah, I'm gettin' that. Look, I gotta go".

He strokes his sons heads and bends his tall frame over to kiss them both, eliciting little snorts that make us both smile fondly. Holding his photo album gift bag, Jamel gets a somewhat reserved goodbye from my parents and a sweetly disappointed *'See you soon for a rematch yeah?"* from Dyls before he walks to the front door with me.

"I'll ring you tomorrow Feist, maybe we can take the boys out when I'm off work?", he's looking for agreement which I give with a smile and a nod before a thought hits me.

"Jamel, do your brothers know about the twins?", in all the slightly stilted hours we've spent together, we have yet to really examine Jamel's somewhat fractured family life.

He looks up at me, those deep brown eyes a bit fierce looking, "Tonight. I'm seein' a bunch of mates and tha' tonight an'........I'll be tellin' everyone then. I wanted.....I needed to get my head straight 'bout it first. Now, after today, it's fuckin' time innit? I'm gonna.....I gotta tell people, show 'em these, show 'em my boys", he raises the bag in his hand with a small smirk before making me jump by shooting forward and pressing warm lips against my cheek again, for no longer than a heartbeat.

With furtive nods exchanged, he strides off towards yet *another* car I don't remember seeing before and heads off.

"Erin, I don't want you and Jamel in your room with the door shut in the future", I've barely shut the front door before my mother is on me.

"Eh?", I'm baffled as I slip my trainers off.

She tuts and the arms go across the chest, "I'm not stupid Erin, I saw you two holding hands at the table and I see the looks you do give each other. If you and Jamel are in a relationship, I do not want you in that bedroom with the door shut, you understand?", her lips are pursed and I feel like she's on the verge of an explosion.

With a cat-piss smile, I use my restrained tone, "Mum, Jamel and I are NOT in a relationship and even if we were, what is the worst that we can get up to behind closed doors that hasn't *already* happened? Eh? Plus, if we don't shut the door, the babies get woken up or they fill the house with shitty smells so…", my response is cut short by the shout I knew was coming,

"YOU ARE TOO YOUNG! You're bloody sixteen and that much older boy is trouble Erin and because he's their father, you'll never be free of him now…..he's already ruined your life, he's ruined your future. I won't let him do more damage to you. Jesus Erin, you should be mooning over pop stars and messing about with your friends *not* caring for babies", my mother's voice cracks and my Dad shoots out of the lounge, a Walnut Whip in his hand and looking panic stricken.

All I choose to hear right now is that my mother considers my beautiful, gorgeous, *stinky* sons to be a source of 'ruin'. My lip curls and I hear my father mutter *'oh Jesus'* as I launch,

"RUINED? My babies have ruined NOTHING! Is that what you think they are Mum? A mistake, my *ruination*?", I see her face fall because I know, with every part of me, that she would kill for those babies but she's let her deepest frustrations out, courtesy of a festive Baileys or two.

"No….I love those little cwtch…..no, that's not what I meant Erin. You just need to stay away from Jamel, I see it I do, I see it in your eyes Erin, you and he together are dangerous. He's too like you, gobby and reckless and stubborn and……", She's gesticulating wildly now, the two festive Baileys she's consumed adding to her animation.

I'm shaking my head, kissing my teeth, my own arms crossed over my engorged, express-due boobs.

Mum's still going though, ".......and poor Giovanni, what did you say to the poor boy last night at Mass, eh? He looked heartbroken he did. You need to wake up Erin and realise that Jamel has taken away options from you........", I am well and truly checking out of this conversation now.

I over-cut her, shouting upstairs, "DYLAN! I'll be back in a bit, if the boys wake up, can you just stick them in the bouncy chairs, I won't be long. Cheers mate", and ignoring my mothers shrieks of my name, I stick my shoes back on and I am out of that door, resisting the door slam that I *really* want to do lest it wakes my sons.

I thunder off down the road, fury making my skin spark and my hair crackle. *Shit I wish I'd brought a coat.* It's 4pm on Christmas Day and I can genuinely feel the sloth and the over-indulgence transmitting from every cosily-lit house on our estate. I love the frosty darkness of December, it's one of my favourite times of year. I love the anticipation of Christmas and the familiarity of my home town and my festive routines. I'm struggling tonight though. I feel like a trapdoor has been opened and that some of this excitement and magic has just been leached away and it's replaced by anger and adult weights and worries. *My bloody mother.*

I stomp towards the leisure centre, a scene of many a childhood memory. Last year, they built a 'Teen Shelter' on a bit of disused land behind the tennis courts, generous of the Council to provide a spot where we could all smoke and snog undetected. I figure that Christmas Teatime is likely to render me the lone visitor. *I am wrong.* I can hear crying as I approach and it sounds so sad, so hopeless that I am propelled forwards to try and offer whoever the distressed party is, comfort.

Adam. His head buried in his knees, he's sat on the bench with his arms wrapped around his legs and his increasingly broad frame is heaving with the effort of his sobs. I feel my eyes fill with tears for this friend of mine, this kind, *life saving,* friend. This recently dumped ex-boyfriend of my best friend.

He jumps and swears in deep embarrassment when my hand touches his shoulder but when he sees it's me, he loses the attempted battle with his face and he breaks down as I throw my arms round him and let him sob into my chilly shoulder, doing little to appease the pressure in my now milk-filled tits.

His words come out as uncontrolled hiccups of sound, his juddering breaths rendering almost incomprehensible, "Why….love her…..miss her…..he's a twat…...fitter…...bigger…..flash car….always loved…….nobody else…...want her back…..only ever been her…..why Erin?", it is truly, honestly heartbreaking and I start to cry too, his pain is just horrible.

I whisper useless platitudes about how he'll find somebody else lovely, how amazing he is, how I don't understand why Lees likes bloody *Kiron* but that she still cares about Adam and wants him to be happy. When his tears start again, I panic and blurt out,

"Mate, she smells of defrosting mince when she's on the blob, you won't miss that will you?", at which point Adam snorts with unexpected laughter and the snot explosion that this causes makes us both chuckle.

We sit in silence, listening to Ad's breathing calm, as he swears softly in embarrassment and puts his face to rights. I tuck into his shoulder and squeeze his hand in silent support.

I hear his tut, "Jesus, my shirt is soaked, what a twat", I wince and touch my own t-shirt with trepidation.

I grimace and whisper, "Sorry dude, I think that's my boob juice. You crying made me leak", and with that, we collapse laughing, the mood shifting.

I look at him in the dark, "Why did you come here for a breakdown, what's wrong with the comfort of your own room?".

He tuts softly, "Ryan's home"

I roll my eyes in the dark, "Uurrgghhh, say no more. Tell you what, how about you take me to yours and I'll demonstrate to you how I kicked the absolute shit out of your brother and then neutered his Pixie Prick", Ad's genuine laugh makes me feel warm.

He turns to me, "And you Rinny? Why are you here on Christmas night? Where's the babies?".

I tell him about Jamel, our weeks spent reacquainting, today's events, the babies, my Mother. I omit all and any references to Gio. Ads pats my knee in sympathy,

"D'you reckon you're gonna get together with this Jamel then?", he's asking me the obvious question.

I look at him and find honesty is, as always, my best policy, "I don't think so Ad. He's really fit, he's the only lad I've ever had sex with but I think he sees me as an annoying kid sister or something. My mother hates him, he's my sons' father and he is honestly turning out to be a good guy. I do really fancy him but I don't know him, I can't read him, I don't know what he thinks about me and it's all so complicated", I shrug hopelessly.

Adam gulps comically, "Oh…..oh right…...Christ, that *is* complicated", I can see his wide eyes glinting in the gloom as he mutters under his breath, almost too quiet for me to hear, *"Poor fucking Romano".*

I feel a steady 'seepage' and realise that if my boobs do not connect with a breast pump asap, I will rapidly become human fondue.

I pat his knee, "C'mon Jones, I need to go home and pump my tits", Adam falls over his own feet in a comedic manner as we exit the shelter.

We chat as we plod. Adam *does* understand that Lees did not want to hurt him, he appreciates that people change and that feelings change but the truth is, he just can't accept it and its making him miserable. He misses her every minute of every day,

"It's like I'm dying, honestly Rinny, it hurts so much it feels like dying", his shoulders slump as we plod to a halt and I hear the wobble in his voice.

I turn to him, hands on his shoulders and look into his kind, boy-next-door face, "Nah Ads, dying is easier. Believe me, I've given it a go", he gives me a wide eyed nod of comprehension.

"One foot in front of the other Ads, that's all you can do. Just keep your mates close, use them to moan at and know that it'll ease up eventually", I rub his arms.

He smiles, "Mates yeah, you and me? Still mates, even if me and Lee…... aren't together?", he sounds so vulnerable.

I pull him into a tight hug, nodding and reassuring. It's a few quiet seconds before Ad whispers, "Erin, your er…..my t-shirt…….there's…..*milk*?".

"Oh bollocks, soz dude. Gotta run", and with a kiss on his cheek, I peg it home, clutching my squirting boobs as I jog.

Chapter Seven

1st January 1997

Jamel did not ring me on Boxing Day. He did not ring me for four days, four days in which innumerable Welsh relatives filled our house, monopolising the babies and throwing us all off kilter. I tried to play it cool, tried not to panic, I lied to my mother when she asked when he was coming over, I paged messages to him but did not get any replies.

Then, on the evening of the 29th, he called. He rang me from a crackling payphone and in a monosyllabic exchange that left me tearful and feeling like I was a massive annoyance to him, he told me that he'd been *busy.* He snarled and sneered when I questioned why he'd not rung to let me know and when I asked him when he was coming to see me, a genuine slip of the tongue due to a sleepless night with *his* sons, he snapped back,

"I don't come to see *you* girl, I come to see my boys, yeah? I've got enough shit goin' on, enough hassle comin' my way coz of me an' you so I don't need you makin' out like we're more than we are. You got that Erin?"

Yup, message received.

I couldn't speak, my entire throat was clogged with outraged tears. He told me that he had to do a tonne of overtime so he'd be visiting on New Years Day at the earliest. Then he hung up on me.

Anger was an emotion that I was able to access pretty quickly. That night, as I cooed over my boys in their bath, contemplating just how few hours sleep I might get thanks to Jake's newly acquired cold, I realised that I was fucking *furious* with Jamel Watson. I *hated* him in that moment and I hated the

136

claim he had laid on *my* beautiful little grizzlers currently screeching in disgruntlement at the indignity of being washed.

My Mum often says that it's probably good that I don't know any different. In her softer, more vulnerable moments, she kisses my head and tells me that I am *'amazing'* when she watches me feed/bathe/change/soothe/forgo *all and any fucking sleep*. She tells me that if, like me, you have twins first you don't really comprehend how much harder it is than just having one baby. She told me, in a conversation before Christmas that made me teary, that she could not have managed twins at *any* age, let alone sixteen and that she was in awe of me. Her supportive words ringing in my ears, I ran upstairs, woke the boys and held them to my chest as they snorted and squawked their astonishment at the fervent kisses being bestowed upon them by their mother.

In that moment, with Jamel's snarled words echoing in my head, my inner voice was screaming that Jamel Watson couldn't handle any of this, he couldn't manage twins alone, he can't even manage to be civil. He's a useless piece of shit and I *fucking* hated him in that moment.

I also realised my power. The power of *'No'* as in *'No Jamel, you cannot visit' 'No Jamel, you cannot see the boys'.* I realised that I am their mother and what I say, it *goes*. So I ignored his calls. I asked my Mum to hang up on him if he rang, a request that made her beam like a Cheshire Cat.

After three days of me ignoring Jamel, an under-the-weather Jake was lethargic and just not himself and as a result, I bailed on the New Years Day Wales trip sending Mum, Dad and Dyls with my apologies.

The doorbell rang about three minutes after my parents' departure and I knew it was Jamel, I could sense it. I did not answer the door. I heard him calling my name through the letterbox, I heard him go round the back door and knock on that, I heard the confusion in his voice. I did not move off the bed, stroking a sleeping AJ and a grizzly, feverish Jake. The phone went a few minutes later, undoubtedly him. I ignored it. *I'm cutting you out Watson.*

However, it was at 4pm that afternoon that I realised that fear is a bottomless commodity. Until those awful two days in the NICU when the boys were poorly, I thought that the *most* frightened I'd ever been was those minutes before the c-section. I was wrong then and I was wrong to think that the NICU was as scary as it got because Jake's eyes rolling into the back of his head and him fitting in my arms on New Year's Day took me to the next level of hell.

He wasn't breathing. My mother who *lives in this house* is a trained nurse and yet then, *right fucking then*, she was not here and my son was dying in front of me. My '999' call was probably the one that they will use from now until the end of time as a training call. Guided by the telephone operator, a few mini-puffs in his mouth and some firm pushes with my fingertips on his chest and my eldest son screeched back into breathing but by then, his brother was screaming his own terror as his mother's hysteria turned into hysterics.

By the time the crew burst through my front door, I was praying like I have never prayed before. We were rushed into A&E, Jake's perfect little body was pierced with needles and wires as I howled and hugged AJ tighter than I imagine he ever wishes to be again.

In that moment, I realised that there was only one person I wanted next to me, the only other person who could be anywhere near as worried as me.

I found a phone and sent Jamel a page that said that Jake was in hospital and he needed to come immediately. He must have been close by because it was less than twenty minutes later when he flew through the hospital door, his face a mask of worry and his panic matching mine and in that instant, we both forgave the other for being a dickhead. As Jamel rushed to Jake's cot-side, simultaneously stroking AJ's little head, I realised that Jamel Watson and I, near strangers that we are, will always now be connected in ways that neither of us can deny. *Family.*

138

Jake was deemed to be stable, febrile convulsions due to his fever and a nasty virus the diagnosis. The doctor delivering this news was lovely, young and kind and reassuring and his manner was so pleasant that even Jamel's deep frown softened slightly. However, the nurse, a snarky looking woman who followed afterwards to take us up to the ward where Jake would stay for observations and to finish his drips, she was *not* so nice.

Her opening gambit was, "You teenage parents, if you actually attended some of these baby health classes that are laid on for you, our lives would be a lot easier". No *'hello'*, no *'oh, what a scare you've all had'*. No *'How's the little poorly baby doing?'* Nope.

I hand AJ to his father, performing the maternal equivalent of *'Hold my pint'*.

"I beg your pardon?", I tap her on the shoulder as I ask the question.

She turns around with an eyebrow raised, I notice the brief sneer and the flickering glance at Jamel.

"You know that we came here in an ambulance, because my son stopped breathing?", I can feel myself getting louder.

She rolls her eyes, "Febrile Convulsions are extremely common, perhaps if you'd monitored his temperature a bit more closely we could have avoided all this fuss", with another eyebrow raise, she turns to her chart writing.

Jamel, who does not know me very well, had already started to stand up, protectively shielding AJ from what his face suggests he knows is about to follow .

"Put my sons chart down, you ignorant bitch and take your shit advice the FUCK away from us and our babies", my voice is all shades of menacing, even Jamel visibly gulps.

Nurse Twatface goes very pale and clutches the clipboard to her chest as she backs away, her piggy eyes on Jamel the whole time. I look between the two of them and I sense that her response to my words is likely to be directed at him. I decide then and there that I am *not* having that.

I step closer to her, "It's not *him* you want to be scared of, this is between you and me. You can fuck off, I want to speak to your supervisor. NOW!", and off she scuttles.

A harassed looking older nurse arrived and she took the impact of my tidal wave of indignation. She did actually apologise and in a sort of recompense for the aggro I'd caused her, I apologised for swearing at her staff. I'm not sure who was more relieved, her or Jamel, when the porter arrived to take us up to the ward. Once there, Jamel and I sat in silence, watching both boys breathe.

Mum came flying in about three hours later, so overwrought with renewed guilt at another hospital crisis missed that she fails to spot Jamel for a few minutes, too busy checking on Jake's progress, interpreting his charts, doing her own once-overs on her grandson. When she spotted Jamel, her eyes narrowed,

"You're here?", she could not have sounded less welcoming.

Jamel just nodded and kissed AJ's sleeping head, his questioning gaze meeting mine. AJ stirred, his little skinny legs stretching and a squawk of discomfort loud.

Mum nodded at him, "Little man should be in his cot, he's still getting over that cold of his. How about I take him home?", Mum reaches out towards AJ but I feel a sudden wave of discomfort. I realise that I don't want either of my boys to be separated from a parent right now and I honestly can't explain it but right now, the only person I trust is the *moody dickhead arsehole* I wasn't speaking to

140

four hours ago.

I look at Jamel, his face tense and his arms protectively wrapped round AJ and I realise that he's struggling with something too.

I mutter, "Jamel, do you….do you want to take AJ back to mine and stay with him tonight? I….I can't leave Jake, I just can't but I don't want AJ on his own", I keep shooting furtive looks his way and I get a warm ripple of relief as Jamel starts nodding before I even finish my sentence.

"There's no need Erin, your Dad and I will have AJ in with us, he'll be fine. I don't think Jamel needs to stay with him", Mum is tight lipped in her rebuttal.

Jamel's voice is just a croak, "Mrs. Roberts, can I stay wiv him. I…..I'd appreciate it", Jamel looks pleadingly at my Mum and I see the moment that her soft, well-hidden-at times heart responds to his vulnerability, to his genuine concern.

She purses her lips and tuts like Les Dawson, "Fine. Erin's Dad will drive AJ though, I can't imagine for a moment that whichever Death Trap you have driven here in *today* is insured", and with kisses to my head and a stroke of Jake's, my mother steals AJ from Jamel, secures him into his baby carrier and flounces out with a threatened promise to return in the morning.

Jamel and I stand awkwardly, the beeping monitors our only soundtrack. I can see his jaw ticking, I can almost taste his discomfort and my chopsy self can't hold back now that the small source of my terror is sleeping peacefully with his monitors all behaving,

"You're a fucking dickhead", a hand goes to my hip and Jamel's frown is off the chart as I cock an eyebrow and gently kick his shin.

His eyes narrow and his earring glints in a flash of warning, "What you on about you mental woman, you're the one told me to stay wiv' AJ?"

I roll my eyes, "Not that, I'm glad you're staying with him although don't you dare touch anything in my room, y'hear? No, you're a dickhead for speaking to me like shit the other day, for hanging up on me, for thinking that YOU get to treat me like that", my tone is more vicious than I had intended, my hurt a bit too raw.

I'm on one now, hissing a whisper, "I don't know you Jamel Watson, you don't know me but we've got to work together because our uglies bumped on a patio chair and we made these gorgeous babies and now I'm fucking stuck with *you* in my life instead of marrying Daniel McNamara. You EVER treat me like a hassle again and I will fucking neuter you, you understand?", I am belatedly aware that the ward is silent and whilst I am being fairly quiet (*for me*), Jamel and I are providing the nights entertainment for the other worried parents on this ward and we have at least five pairs of eyes on us.

I am belatedly aware that Jamel's lips are twitching in a repressed smile as his rumbles out, "Whoever the fuck Daniel McNamara is, he's welcome to you Ginger Feist coz you are all shades of crazy woman", he can't hold in a chuckle as I gasp in outrage and smack him on the chest in reproach.

Our play walloping results in Jamel pulling me into a most unexpected cuddle, his lips pressing into my hair and making me suddenly warm.

He mutters softly, "I'm proper sorry girl, I had some shit come my way when I told people back home 'bout the boys. It messed me up a bit, needed to get my head straight but me an' you, we're cool yeah?", we pull back and smile bashfully at each other as I nod and roll my eyes. Jamel smirks at me,

"So Feist, any other fucker gonna get a coatin' off you tonight? I might sell tickets, make me some dough, call it *'Ginger Feist on Tour'*", he laughs at his own *hilarity,* as I huff and turn my attention to my small, sleeping son. With an evil grin, I turn back to him,

"Laugh it up chuckles, you're spending the night at mine with my parents and *I won't be there to protect you.* Enjoy your cosy breakfast with my mother", I snigger.

Jamel's face, his far-too-handsome cafe au lait skin visibly paling even in the fluorescent light, looks panic stricken.

I waggle my fingers at him, "Go look after our son, ta-ta sucker", as he scowls.

Jamel kisses Jake goodbye and turning back to my smirking face he whispers, "My boys, they're safe with you Feist, you keep them safe. You're crazy woman but there ain't nobody could look after them better. You're a good Mum", and with a kiss to my stunned lips, he's gone.

I sat and stared at Jake all night.

Jake was released the next morning, Jamel the one who came to get us with AJ, having allegedly produced DVLA paperwork and insurance documents over the breakfast table that proved that this battered Fiesta was indeed legitimately owned and insured, silencing my parents over the toast rack.

As he drove us home, I wallowed in the *niceness* of my sons' father transporting us, of the novelty of this *family journey.* When the boys started having a little shout in the back seat, my automatic reaction to coo and sing at them made Jamel grin broadly, my rendition of 'La Isla Bonita' as tuneful as always.

Jamel, upon hearing about my Thursday childcare issues, stepped up in a manner which even my mother had to acknowledge as *'helpful'.* He now stays at my house every Wednesday night after work, sleeping on a blow up mattress on the dining room floor and he looks after the boys on a

Thursday until I get home from school, shifting his working week so that he works on Sundays now instead. He also comes down early on a Saturday morning and spends the day with the boys, while I go to work in the local supermarket.

"I am so, so grateful to you guys for looking after the boys, I honestly am but this is such a good solution", three days after Jake's hospital stay, I am sat in the local cafe breaking the news to Lees and Gio about their newly liberated Thursdays. We met up to have a stab at this Diploma of Achievement group project before school starts on Monday but in all honesty, we all know that Lees will do it with Romano's help and I will be the gobby presenter as research was never my strongest suit.

Gio was cuddling the babies but he'd been deathly quiet since arriving, in fact he and I haven't directly spoken since Christmas Eve. I gave him his Christmas Present from the boys upon our arrival (a *'Godfather'* T-Shirt) and he'd barely looked at me.

He stood up, kissing the boys in a gesture that made me melt and then he lay them back down, grabbing his coat and his present, as he muttered, "Whatever Erin, yeah. You and Jamel sound pretty cosy so that's good for them", he nodded at my raspberry blowing progeny before he looked me dead in the eye, those blue eyes almost angry looking, "See you around Roberts", before he walked off.

I tried to fake astonishment at his behaviour but my B in GCSE Drama was mainly due to the teacher's fear that I would go into labour if he marked my dry-ham performances accurately. There is *stuff* between Gio and I, that kiss has never been addressed and Lees' comments about Gio having feelings for me makes me feel jittery. I just don't know what this is between Gio and I, where is came from, what it is based on or if I can have any faith in it and as a result, I can go *nowhere fucking near it* when I am still sorting out the dynamics of my new family. His exit and his tone of hurt makes me ache, the memory of that brief kiss makes me tingle and his Christmas Eve comments confuse me, those three things I *do* know.

January moved forward with both babies gaining weight like pros and Jamel's Thursday and Saturday childcare going pretty smoothly. My mother, Christ only knows how, discovered that Jamel's favourite dish is Roast Lamb, a dish that his Iya would make every Sunday. We've all noticed just how often Roast Lamb is cooked on a Wednesday night and we've all clocked that Jamel's pudding is twice the size of anyone else's, in stark contrast with the continued barbed hostility that he receives from Mum.

Jamel moved out of the Bail Hostel in mid-January and into a privately rented bedsit on the same estate as his older brother, Dion. Jamel is starting to slowly divulge bits and pieces about his family, for example I know that Dion, who is Jamel's full sibling, has a five year old daughter of his own with a girl that he has known since his school days. Jamel looked almost panic-stricken when I suggested that the boys should meet their cousin, a reaction that wounded me slightly.

Jamel and I are comfortable in our mutual discomfort. We can gently joke, we hug in greeting, cheeks are kissed in goodbye and when he helps me with the night feeds on a Wednesday night, we can sit side by side in our PJs without too much discomfort but it's still *delicate.*

29th January 1997

"Rinny, this is my birthday night out and I don't care if you look like battered death, you are *coming*", Lees is submerged in my wardrobe, hurling potential clothing choices at me like a leaf blower. Tonight is the weekly 'blind eye' night at 'Pulse', the ill-fated Foam Party club. Lees turned seventeen yesterday and tonight is her official birthday night out, our under-age status overlooked by the bouncers in this weekly free-for-all.

She turns and smiles at me, "You know that Kiron's mates will be there Rinny, that Nick proper fancies you and y'know, Romano will be there too", Lees looks at me waggling her eyebrows.

I don't like Kiron. *There, said it.* He's far too up himself and arrogant, he thinks he's funnier than he is and he makes digs about me that he isn't entitled to because he doesn't know me well enough. Lees is like a subdued puppy around him and *that* annoys me. With Adam, she was herself. With Kiron, she's *not.*

I tut, "Jesus, Nick looks about fourteen, he's met me twice and both times, I was pushing the pram. It's *pity* not lust he feels Lee", I start picking up the clothes she's tossing around.

She stills her destruction, "And Romano?"

I look Lees in the eye, "He *doesn't* look fourteen but he's seen me give birth so I think lust is low down on his list".

I took the boys to yet another playgroup today. I've been trying to find one where I don't feel like some sort of 'good-will' project. I am always, without exception, the only mother there aged under twenty-one. I am always the only one with tiny twins. I have now been to at least half a dozen of these bloody things and each time, it's the same pattern.

After the inevitable induction by a well-meaning, kindly, elderly member of the congregation of whichever place of worship this playgroup is hosted by, I am inevitably towed to meet clutches of mums. They fall into two broad groups: Middle Class Mums in their late- twenties to mid-Thirties who see playgroup as a weekly opportunity to convince themselves that they are not alone in feeling lost and scared shitless, whilst secretly condemning the child rearing practices of every other parent in the place. They are always sat on the chairs.

The second group is younger but equally terrified, so fearful of judgement on their parenting that they take the opportunity to play enthusiastically with their child using the exact toys they have at home to send everyone the message that they are 'doing the right things'. Their anxiety means they never sit on the chairs, they are always on the mats or hovering at the edges.

Me? I'm usually being lectured in the corner. It's a *fucking ball-ache.* These women, even the young, anxious ones, will all engage me by offering me advice, tips, pointers, ideas, activities as if I had *begged* them to furnish me with these gifts. But I hadn't, I don't, I won't. I don't want to be their trainee. I want to be their *equal.* I want to moan at them about the fact that my sons feel that 4am is the start of the day's activities, I want to ask them if *their* c-section scars make it look like their belly is smiling sarcastically. I want to ask them how you raise sons with somebody who you fancy but who sees you as a weird mate. I want to ask them if it's normal to love your babies so much that you sometimes just cry looking at them. I want to ask these women what you do when you're sixteen and you're beginning to think that the only boys who will ever love you are the ones who share your DNA. I want to ask them what you do when you think you might only ever get to have had sex once in your life and that it was on a patio chair.

I get told how I should be doing things, the things I should be buying, the books I need to have read. I get condescending encouragement for my A Levels, my parents are praised for their support but nobody ever *laughs* with me, nobody ever *confides* in me. I don't get included in requests for advice and in turn, I don't offer it. Friendship is not what I am being offered. I think most of these women speak to me only so that they can start a conversation with their mates at the *next* playgroup, telling them how they spent time giving the 'teenage single mum' some good advice, receiving praise and admiration for their efforts.

I sometimes want to stand in the middle of these rooms that smell of coffee, cheap Malted Milk biscuits and baby shit and scream, *"I cope with twins every FUCKING day, two of them, by myself pretty much for 5 days a week and I do it without panicking the shit out of myself about every tiny thing. You bitches want to ask ME for advice frankly".*

The weird thing is that when I sit there, feeling like the kid that isn't being picked in PE as my boys

147

lie like guppies on germ-coated play mats, the person that I wish was sat next to me isn't my mum, or Lees or Jamel.

It's Giovanni Romano.

The thought of Gio being at the club tonight, it does make me a bit giddy. He's been weird for a few weeks, a bit distant but the odd thing is that I find myself staring at him, watching him more than usual. I feel drawn to him since he said *I was all he wanted for Christmas*. I think I watch him because I'm trying to work out of he meant it because my doubts remain strong although memories of that kiss that *he instigated* make me tingle.

Jamel is going to be late getting to ours tonight, he'd already warned me of that so I'll be gone before he arrives. When Kiron's car beeps outside my house at 9pm, I'm wearing the green velvet lycra dress that has yet to have a public airing as I jump in.

"Well Erin, you look less like a car crash than usual tonight", Kiron grins like a smug knob at me.

I kiss my teeth and stare out of the window, "Well Kiron, *you* look *more* of a dick than usual so congrats"

Lees turns in the front seat and shoots me a death stare. I've gone for Adidas trainers tonight, a bold choice with a mini dress but I *love* them. Jamel turned up with them after pay day, muttering in embarrassed tones about them being *a 'Christmas present from the twins'.*

Lees and Kiron head off to speak to his jock mates as soon as we get in the club and I avoid them by heading to speak to some of the girls from geography. My hair is annoying me tonight, the crazy waist-length curls tangling in my bracelets and sticking to my lip gloss. A few hours pass, chatting with the girls, dancing with Lees but there is no sign of Romano or Adam for that matter.

I'm in the middle of a dull-as-arse conversation with a girl I don't know very well when I hear a ripple of gossip traverse the room. It's low key, nothing scandalous but there's definitely a stir occurring. I end the dull chat, looking to head over to talk to Lees when I see the cause of the ripples, the source of the gossip. Gio standing by the bar. *Kissing Carolyn Gregory*. Hot and heavy, hands roaming. People are interested, Carolyn's status as Queen of the Perfects and Gio's status as Year Group Hottie makes this re-ignited romance noteworthy.

For me, it seems to be an event which my body has a surprisingly violent reaction to. I feel inexplicably sick, I feel like my body's entire blood allowance is pooling in my shoes and I feel the needles of hurt pricking my skin and yet I can offer no explanation as to why my body feels entitlement to behave in this manner. Gio is not *mine*, he never purported to be *mine* and we are being weird with each other at the moment and yet as I close my eyes, I hear soft words encouraging me to,

"You just look at me, just look at me and hold my hand and it'll all be fucking OK ".

Tears, unbidden and without entitlement, prickle in my eyes and I hear another, perhaps more accurate and honest set of words, *"Roberts, she's rank".* Puffing out breaths to steady myself, I plaster on a fake smile and head over to Lees and bloody Kiron.

I end up pulling Kiron's baby-faced mate Nick, frankly it was inevitable. The need for a filler-snog became overwhelming, a placebo needed to mask my uninvited pain at Gio and Carolyn's animated reunification. I snog him and then a bit later, in a moment of pure, unadulterated stupidity, I permit the flattering attentions of a much older lad at the bar and proceed to snog him too.

Nick gets the hump and drunkenly approaches, calling me a variety of unpleasant but perhaps warranted names. This causes my second suitor of the evening to come to my defence, that is until Nick yells out,

"She's got two kids, did she tell you that? That slag has got two kids already", his finger pointing like an extra in *The Scarlet Letter*, Nick's shout is loud and my shell-shocked snogging partner's defence of me turns to incredulity,

"Two kids, what the fuck? You're only like what, eighteen? Jesus Christ", and he walks away, his hand held up in a surrender gesture. *I'm sixteen actually you wanker.*

Nick walks off too, muttering further slurs as I stand, alone and the centre of attention once more.

I can hear the sound of galloping hooves and a horsey bray.

Nodding at my own feet, I feel that my work here is probably done for the night. Fighting tears of regret and self-flagellation, I collect my coat from the cloakroom and I head outside, to wait for Lees' eventual departure from the scene of my latest self-inflicted humiliation.

Sat on the raised flowerbed outside the club, my rapidly freezing arse makes me walk around for warmth. I end up trotting down those same steps that I followed Gio and Daniel McNamara, two years ago. I'm jolted from my humiliation-reminiscence by the sound of voices emerging from the club.

"Gio, what was that all about? Who were those lads and why did you start a fight with *both* of them?", I'd recognise Carolyn's simpering tones anywhere.

I hear Gio's deep voice but from my hiding spot down the alleyway, I can't make out the words. Carolyn's response is clear as a bell though,

"FOR GOD'S SAKE GIO! Erin? Who cares what anyone says about *her*? If they were slagging her off, you can bet she probably deserved it. Look, I didn't want to bring it up, not when we are only just back together but you know there was always the rumour that you were into her and when we broke up, some people said it was because you wanted to be with her. I mean, you were with her at the hospital when she had those *babies*. So, is there more to this Gio? Hey? Is there?", you can almost hear her foot tapping and I'm holding my breath.

Gio's response sounds weak even from a distance, "No, no course not. Why the fuck would I want to be with Roberts, hey? You saw the shit she caused tonight, why the hell would I want to be any part of that? She's a mate and I love her kids coz they're cute and I'm their Godfather but no, I don't want *her,* she's too much *aggravatio*n", he spits this last bit out, almost bitterly.

He's saying other things but I don't really hear it though. I just hear the blood in my ears and the pain of a brutal reality check. *My suspicions were true after all.* Gio doesn't want me, he never did, his declarations were false flags induced by my sons' cuteness.

Like a zombie, I go to the cash point, I take out money and abandoning my best mate in the club with her annoying boyfriend, I get in a cab and go home. It's dark in the house, I can hear the soft sound of Jamel's breathing coming from the open dining room door as I slope in. I go up to my room, skilfully avoiding the creaking floorboards and I enter the room where my two most precious responsibilities lie snoring. I stare at them, the tears running down my face and I vow then and there, to just *try harder* to get a fucking clue.

I strip off the dress and my trainers and in my bra and pants, I lie atop my duvet and let sobs claim me, muted so as not to disturb the boys. I don't hear the bedroom door open but I hear the deep gasp that follows it.

I flip over, boobs *'boinging'* in my bra to be met by the sight of a shirtless Jamel staring gobsmacked in the doorway. He turns away, visibly wrestling with his decision before taking a deep breath and coming in the room, gently shutting the door behind him.

He whispers, "You 'kay Feist? I heard…..I heard noise on the monitor".

Oh Jesus Christ, the pigging baby monitor is on.

I'm too strung out to care that I'm in my bra and knickers, I'm too resigned to humiliation to give much of a damn and the tears claim me once more. I hear Jamel swear under his breath and come over to sit next to me on the bed. A warm, strong arm tentatively wraps round me as he rumbles nervously,

"You….you been hurt or anythin'? You need me to get someone?", his concern makes me sob a bit harder, the boys snuffling on undisturbed.

I shake my head and look up at his face, this oh-so-fit face and this body that could honestly make angels weep and I whimper,

"I always fuck it up Jamel. Nobody will ever want me because I do stupid shit and I've got two babies and I will always, always just be rank, ugly ginger Roberts. Gio was right, nobody will want to deal with the shitstorms I cause. *He* certainly doesn't", and with an almost comedic boo-hoo, I sob into my hands.

I'm too deep in my wallow to properly realise that Jamel has turned slightly and that both his arms are wrapped around me. His skin is warm and it smells of Lynx and deodorant and Mum's washing powder. I feel the tears from my cheeks smear into his hard chest and my own arms gently snake round him so that I am clutched to him tight.

I'm suddenly hit by an overwhelming wave of tiredness and before I can really cross-examine how it happens, I find myself lying on my pillow, clutched to Jamel's chest as my hiccups turn astonishingly fast into snores. As my eyes shutter closed, I hear Jamel's voice whispering into my hair,

"You're fucking cool Feist, don't take nobody's shit"

When I wake for the 4am feeds, he's back downstairs and when he joins me to feed his sons, we hold hands over the duvet in silence.

30th January 1997

Jamel's anxious eye contact over the breakfast toast suggested that he is aware of my reluctance to face my peers after my performance last night. As I kiss my sons goodbye and offer Jamel the list of instructions and ideas for activities, he pulls me into a hug that warms me far more than it should.

"Me and the boys, we'll come get you, yeah? From your school? Don't bovver wiv that bus shit, we'll come find you", his words are cemented with a firm nod and my smile is wide.

School sucks the exact quota I imagined it would. Greeted by the painful sight of Gio chewing on Carolyn's simpering face, I am then met with lots of raised eyebrows and a furious best friend who had expended an hour searching for me when the club closed, making her late home and causing her parents to ground her. Lees calls me selfish and a drama magnet. I have no evidence to provide in my defence. She does not sit next to me at lunch time. Nobody does.

At the end of the day, our tutor group is in our tutor room, finishing off a display for the Open Evening, when there is a knock on the window. We all turn but it's me who smiles. Jamel, holding a son in each arm, appears to have dressed the boys in his image today as he scowls through the glass. They both have identical little jeans on, their Nike booties and teeny-tiny hoodies which Jamel must have bought. They also have little baseball caps on and I wonder if it is possible to die from an overload of cuteness. I grin and wave, blowing kisses as Jamel rolls his eyes.

Jamel's head jerk indicates that I am needed and I gather my bags, belatedly realising that all eyes, including my tutor's, are on me.

I smile appeasingly, "Mr. Dobbs, do you mind if I head off. My er, my babies' Dad needs a hand I think", I grimace but Mr. Dobbs dismisses me with a wave.

As I grab my coat and head for the door, I see Gio sit back in his chair, arms folded, shooting me a glare. Still hurt from last night, my responding smile is weak. As I pass his chair, Carolyn next to him mutters to nobody in particular, *"He's with Erin? Prison must have made him desperate"*, as chuckles ripple through the room.

I allow my bag to snag her hair as I pass and I grin as she squeals.

"Ginger Feist, you got any nappies in that bag, I got a double dose right here", Jamel's appalled look as I walk outside makes me laugh and together, we head to the disabled loo to deal with the dual horror.

AJ farts loudly in the middle of his nappy change, allowing me to hear for the first time Jamel's unguarded laugh. It's deep and husky and does terrible damage to my knickers. AJ beams with pride and then chuckles as his Daddy blows raspberries on his belly. Jake, not to be outdone blows a raspberry of his own, going almost purple with the effort of it and Jamel and I laugh ourselves daft at the pair of them.

When our eyes meet, there is this *fizz* that makes my skin tingle. Jamel's eyes dart all over my face as I stare at his lips that are smiling broadly. I remember those lips on my neck, those lips on mine, I remember the *feel* of him.

"We should go yeah?", Jamel breaks the spell as he jumps athletically to his feet, scooping up twins as I wash my hands. With a baby over each of our shoulders, we head towards the car park, my peers all now exiting en mass. Dyls runs over, fist-bumping Jamel and puffing up with pride at the fact that this cool older lad is *family*, his friends looking on in awe before he joins them on the bus.

There's a crowd of the Practically Perfects and assorted male counterparts stood nearby, derisive looks thrown my way and I sigh in resignation. Jamel spots all of this, eyes like a hawk and before I can catch my breath, he's taken my hand in his large warm one as he tows me towards the car.

Twins strapped in, Jamel and I load the boot.

"You 'kay Feist?", he's frowning at me, darting glances at my detractors, Gio visibly uncomfortable in amidst the smirkers. "What's wiv' the Godfather? Eh? You guys are mates yeah? What's his beef?", Jamel looks adorably disgruntled on my behalf.

I can't hide the lip wobble as I shrug, my hurts from last night still a bit raw.

"Fuck this", Jamel is striding over to Gio.

"Oi, bruv", Jamel's aggressive shout makes most of the car park jump but his burning stare makes it clear who his intended target is. Gio doesn't look scared, he looks *tired.*

Jamel carries on, "You serious 'bout not havin' her back? Coz you ain't no mate if you don't have her back, if you ain't on her side. Godfather? Not to my boys you ain't, not if you're lettin' other people give her shit. You wanna watch *your* back bruv coz me and you, we ain't cool right now. You don't come near my boys 'til you get a fuckin' clue", Jamel is close enough to Gio to show he means business but far enough away that a potential assault charge is not an immediate danger.

With a nod, Jamel walks away and I watch as Gio slumps against the wall, his head in his hands. I stare in awe at Jamel, my emotions all over the place and with a kiss to my forehead, he gets in the driver's seat.

As I glance back, Gio is staring at me, his face pained. I drive off with my sons and their Dad.

When Jamel headed off after dropping us home, our goodbye hug went on a few seconds longer than normal, he pressed his lips to my hair, his fingertips stroked rather than patted and I found my own hands clutching at his top willing it to last longer.

Fizzing.

He leaves, as he always does, to return to a life that I cannot picture, to an existence that does not include his sons, to a familiar circle of people who I have never met. Me? I cannot imagine being without the twins, it would kill me to be removed from their orbit, to lie in a bed in a place where they are not near me. I don't know how Jamel can wave us off with a smirk because I'd be howling if I was him.

Chapter Eight

February 11th 1997

Lees forgave me for what we are calling *'The Birthday Bail'* and I sometimes catch Gio looking at me at school, his face sad. However aside from a few polite smiles and a couple of strained chats, we don't talk like we used to. I heard that he'd walloped both Nick and my older suitor after I walked out of the club, a fight that has allegedly seen him barred from 'Pulse' indefinitely. I'm not sure how to feel about that. I do know that I miss him. I miss being his friend. I miss the person who held my hand while I birthed my sons and I miss the gentle thrum of *possibility* that sat between us. It's gone now, replaced with a Carolyn-shaped full-stop.

Jamel's visits see me primp and preen in a manner that causes my mother to roll her eyes. When he smiles at me, I feel like I've won something. When he sits next to me and chats about the babies that we *share*, I feel giddy from the bond that I have with this incredible looking lad.

Valentine's Day looming, Lees has been fretting over Kiron, what to get him, how to impress him. I'd muttered under my breath about how lovely, kind Adam had only ever needed a night on the sofa with a film and a Mars Bar to feel chuffed to bits. She'd frowned and looked a bit hurt, prompting me to apologise.

"So the Health Visitor reckons we give it a couple of weeks and start them on that baby rice", I'm chatting to Jamel during what has become almost nightly phone calls.

Jamel has bought a mobile phone, a purchase that caused my mother a conniption as she issued strict instructions to never, EVER call him on it, lest the cost of the call tip my family into financial ruin. We've developed a system where if I need him, I give him three rings and he calls back. He's so quick to respond that I am careful not to exploit it by 'pestering' him unnecessarily.

"Feist, er, I was wondering, maybe 'bout comin' up Friday night, after work, y'know. Maybe we go do somethin'?", Jamel sounds oddly jittery and I'm boggled.

"Oh, OK but we shouldn't keep the boys up too late, they'll be grumpy all day Saturday for you if we go somewhere too late. What did you want to do with them?", I honestly can't think of anywhere baby-friendly to take them on a Friday evening.

I hear Jamel take a deep breath in, "Nah, I mean you an' me, maybe we go somewhere, the pictures or somethin'? Your mum would watch 'em, wouldn't she?".

I babbled a shocked acceptance and with a bit of awkward small talk, we ended the call with plans made to *go out together* on Friday night.

I think I'm going on a date with Jamel

14th February 1997

Lees has proven herself to be as much use as a fart in a lift with this date-preparation bollocks. She helped me pick my outfit of a strappy vest top, denim mini-skirt, tights and newly purchased knee-high boots but she's done my hair in this mega-sleek ponytail and I feel a bit self-conscious. She also told me that she didn't reckon it was possible to date the father of your children,

"I mean Rinny, how much more serious can two people get than having twins, eh? Dating is a daft word for you two. If you two *get together* tonight, what's that going to look like? You've already had sex, you might as well just go flat-hunting on your second date", at my pale face she chuckled, "And as for the whole *'does he like me, will he ring me?'* thing, well, he sleeps at your house two nights a week anyway so that answers that one".

When I recovered enough to respond, I thumped her but I had a question I needed to ask,

"Do you like him Lee?", I'm nervous suddenly.

Lees looks at me, her face softening and her hands on my shoulders, "Rinny, I don't get a choice, he's the father of the cutest Godchildren in the world, I have to at least tolerate him. I think the big question is, after ten weeks of hanging around him, do *you* like him?"

She frowns when my response stalls, "I fancy him Lee, I really fancy him and I like it when we're friendly and he's kind. I like looking after the boys with him and I like looking at him", she laughs at that bit but looks thoughtful as she asks,

"Do you trust him?"

I have no answer so I shrug at which point Lees sighs and looks me in the eye,

"I like Romano more, Rinny. I like the idea of you with him more than the idea of you with Jamel", she looks at me warily as my face hardens.

"Well, he's with Carolyn now and anyway, I don't think I ever really trusted Gio, I don't think that he means anything he says to me, apart from the bits about caring about the twins. I believe *that.* All the other stuff? I think the last few weeks proves that to be bullshit. He never wanted to be with me, he just likes having fun with the babies *",* Lees had sighed sadly and busied herself with my makeup.

I know Jamel is as nervous as me because he has not stood still since he arrived. Pant-meltingly gorgeous in jeans and a military style shirt with a thick gold chain round his neck, he literally looks like he has an electric current running through him and he jumps like he's been shot whenever anyone speaks to him,

"Good lord boy, what's got you so jumpy?", my mother is, as always, as subtle as a brick, "If you can't stand your arse still by there, do something useful and go get your sons' washing from Erin's room", Jamel bounds up the stairs, a little glow in my chest from how familiar my house has become to him in such a short space of time.

"RIGHT!", I'm startled by my mother turning full force towards me, "Now I don't know what is going on here, boyo by there looks like he's done something that will see him back in prison and you, well, you do look just as shifty my girl. Where are you two chopsy pair up to, eh? Which one of you do I need to wallop?", arms folded, she's ready for action.

I shrug in wide eyed innocence, "We're just going to the pictures, honest Mum. It's……..it's just y'know, mates going out together", I am aiming for nonchalance and flippant devil-may-care apathy but my Mum, she knows me too well.

Her whole face softens into a sort of sadness, "Oh sweetheart, I don't think that you and Jamel should….", but Jitter McShifty has returned with his sons' washing and she smiles tightly and ends it there.

We make an over-baked fuss of saying goodbye to the boys, my Mum frowning gently as she observes our unease. In Jamel's car, I turn the stereo up loud to avoid the uncomfortable silence. He keeps looking at me and smiling in a sort of pained way and I can feel the questions bubbling in my throat. I guide him to the large multiplex cinema on the same retail park as the bloody nightclub. I gets out of the car in silence, playing with his phone and not a glance my way as he taps at the keys. I look around and see scores of couples, hand in hand, laughing as they wend their way to some sort of romantic assignation at the various chain restaurants on this park. They all look happy, they look smitten by their partners and they look comfortable. Me and him? We look like awkward cousins,

Jamel the older one who got ordered to take the younger one out for the evening.

"WHAT the fuck are we *doing* Jamel?", well, my self-censoring is going *swimmingly* it appears, as the screech leaves my mouth.

Jamel looks up from his phone like he's just been caught shoplifting, "Eh? Wha' you on abou' now Feist", he's wary and in this strapless bra that is digging into me something murderous, I do not have the patience to play it coy.

"US! Here! Jamel, are we on a date? Coz I'm not sure what this is and I've only been on two dates in my whole life and the second one of those ended up with me assaulting my date and then letting a stranger knock me up", I see his wince and the jittery looks he throws around but he stays silent.

I have nothing much to lose, "Look, this was maybe a mistake, I think maybe we should head home, avoid Valentine's Day stuff and watch TV as mates", I'm looking down and shaking my head, feeling foolish.

When I dare to look up, he's right in front of me, shaking his head slowly, biting his lip and with a weird look in his eyes as his words quietly rumble,

"I don't want you to be no *mate* of mine Feist", his words make me hear that sodding horse again, I hear Humiliation Palmer-Smart galloping towards me, laughing.

I don't want you. I feel pathetic tears fill my lashes, I feel my heart hurt *again* and my feet are prompted into moving *anywhere* away from him but as I turn, a hand grabs my arm and I am pulled flush against his big, hard body as his hand cups my head and brings me closer to his face,

"Feist, the things I wanna do wiv you, they ain't things I wanna do wiv any of my mates", his minty breath is warm puffs across my skin as I whisper back,

"What things?", I look into his dark brown eyes and take a breath in from the heat I see in them

He licks his lips, "This for fuckin' starters", and with that, he lowers his face to mine and his warm, soft lips pull me into a kiss that makes my body melt.

This is not a languid filler snog or a frantic-fumble Ryan snog, this is not even a sex-on-the-patio-chair incredulous sloppy snog. This is a *hot* snog, burning every nerve and synapse in my body in the brightest showers of sparks.

His hands are everywhere and I find myself entirely insensible, unable to do anything more than try not to melt into a puddle on the floor of this car park. He lifts me up and presses me against the door of the car as my inexperienced legs wrap themselves around his waist and my hands grasp at his strong shoulders and broad back.

I feel him press against me *there* with a bulging insistence that renders me giddy and which in turn makes him groan in a deep rumble.

"I fuckin' want you Feist, been wantin' you even though we got shit to deal wiv and call me Jay will ya? Every other fucker does", his gabbled words against my skin make me tearful from the idea that somebody that I like, actually likes me in return.

His tongue is calm against mine, in contrast to his frantic lips and his wandering hands. The taste of him is familiar somehow, despite the brevity of our kissing history and as my hand snakes down to cup his bum, he pulls back slightly,

"Feist, this…..this wha' you want too? Is it? Coz you gotta tell me now if it ain't", he nods at me to reinforce his words.

Inside my head is a sort of shutter showreel of images. I see my babies with their parents *together,* I see Gio's face and I acknowledge the ache in my chest, I see Jay's strong body that night after the club when I cried on my bed, I see Lees' frown, I see my mother's disapproval and then I see Jay, squaring up to Gio, *on my side.* Gio told me in the hospital that he was on my side but then it turned out he…...wasn't.

Is this what I want? I think the most honest answer is, *"Why not?".* Looking him square in the eye, I nod and with a smirk that should be illegal frankly, Jamel *'call me Jay'* Watson snogs me into blissful dopiness against the door of his car.

Hand-in-self-conscious-hand, he eventually leads me into the cinema, nuzzling sweetly at my neck as he wraps his arms round me from behind while we queue for tickets. I'm giddy with the sheer novelty of being publicly *wanted.*

In the darkness of the cinema, I pay no attention to the crappy action film I let Jay choose and I pay a *lot* of attention to the feel of Jay under my hands, his lips on mine, his groans against my skin as I tease him in the gloom.

The film ends and with swollen lips and slightly glazed expressions, Jay leading me out of the cinema into the *'what on earth do we do now?'* portion of the evening. I don't need to worry too much because it appears that our first stop is to have another snog. Jay sits on a low wall by the cinema doors and pulls me into the cradle of his thighs, his seated position making our heads level. His hand is on my arse, the other one is up the front of my t-shirt, hidden from view by my jacket and I'm whispering, "I like kissing you Jay", as he smiles against my lips.

"Oh my GOD is that Erin?", I reluctantly extract myself from Jay's *very* addictive lips to the sight of a large cluster of the Practically Perfects and their male accomplices exiting the cinema but in all honesty, I only really see Gio, his hand in Carolyn's as he stands glaring at the back of the group.

That warm hand that held me safe as my sons were born.

I look at Jay, his frown oddly comforting and I look back at the raised eyebrows and the sneers and I realise in that moment that my side is chosen.

I feel my lips quirk in a smirk as I raise an eyebrow at them, "D'you mind? How about you all just fuck off, yeah? Nosey twats", as I turn back to Jay, his wide, astonished smile makes me bolder,

"C'mon Jay, let's go home", and as I take Jay by the hand, he wraps his arms round me from behind so that we are walking awkwardly as we laugh, Jay flipping them the bird as we go.

I can't look at Gio. I just can't.

As I look at Jay in the darkness as he drives us home to our babies, he turns and flashes me a wide smile, that *gorgeous* face making me melt.

"Feist, the shit you come out wiv, I never met no girl mouthy like you. You don't give the tiniest fuck do ya?", as he laughs and I smile tightly.

Oh Jay, if only you knew how many fucks I actually give.

We chat in a weirdly more relaxed manner than we have well, *ever*. Jay is funny and I feel able to take the piss a bit more, the odd near-stranger-eggshells that I have walked on until now, starting to dissolve. I make him laugh and the sound honestly warms my heart. We park up out of view of the house and things go, er, *up a notch.*

The blow job that I furnish an astonished, groaning Jay with is undoubtedly the best one of my incredibly brief sexual career. His penis is warm and smooth, he tastes of shower gel and clean skin and although its arresting size makes for a slightly sore jaw, I like him so much more than Ryan that I give it 100% effort and his moans and gasps are a proper turn on. He is swearing his disbelief and his hands are in my hair as he pets me, begging me to continue. When he gets close, he warns me,

"Oh fuck Feist, I'm gonna, I'm close….", his hands are trying to tug me away but I keep going, making him groaning his astonished release into my mouth.

I've never swallowed before but I find that the bland, slightly bitter gloop is unpleasant but not repulsive. The incredulous look on Jay's face, as I pull back and subtly wipe my lips, is entirely worth it.

"Holy Shit Feist, you….you're…..fuckin' hell", he's shaking his head, wide eyed.

I wink, "I'm putting this on my CV you know? Patio-chair-shagger, Baby-popper-outer and tornado-dick-gobbler", and as Jay laughs and pulls me into a kiss, I feel pretty chuffed with my lot. We sit holding hands for a bit, listening to the stereo until I ask,

"So do you want to go up and see the boys before you head off?", I look at Jay as he nods pleasantly.

As we walk through the back-door, I drop Jay's hand, an action that makes him frown.

"You're back then?", like a bloody homing pigeon, my mother is in the kitchen, her massive purple dressing gown making her look like a menacing blackcurrant.

I smile, a picture of innocence, "Can Jay come up and say night to the boys?"

Mum's eyebrow goes through the ceiling, "*Jay* is it now? Well, I've just done their bottles so take those up with you", and with a 'hurrumph' Mum nods and wanders back to her sofa-nest.

As we walk up the stairs, Jay's hands wander up my tight-clad thighs until he's got both my arse cheeks in his hands as I grin down at him. The boys are both chattering at each other as we creep into my room, cooing in a way that I *know* they both understand. It's been a couple of weeks since they started to sleep through the night but this midnight bottle is an insurance policy that I'm loath to abandon.

Jay, smiling shyly at me, grabs Jake and plugs him onto his bottle while I deal with AJ's stinky bum and then watch him torpedo his milk like a pro. Jay shifts on the bed so that we are closer than we have ever been before when co-feeding our sons. His nose nudges at my temple and he whispers,

"Wha's wiv the hair? It don't look like normal", he looks at me

I roll my eyes, "Lees got hold of me, she was trying to make me pretty but she had her work cut out", I smile.

Jay tuts and looks down at Jake, "Bruv, your Mum, she don't have the first clue how fuckin' fit she is", as he plays with Jake's bottle-clutching fingers, I try to hide my nuclear blush.

The boys chug their bottle with their usual greed and once burped and re-settled, Jay smirks at me in the cosy darkness before sauntering across the carpet and pulling me to him.

"How long you reckon we've got 'til the purple ninja comes to chuck me out?", his smirk makes me tingle.

I stutter, "M-m-m-m-maybe five minutes?"

"I can work wiv that", and suddenly he's kissing me again. I'm here, in the room where my sons sleep, being kissed by their father and I *bloody love it.*

He leans me back onto my bed, his amazing body crawling up until he's on top of me, kissing me into mindlessness on the duvet. Tongues stroking and hands roaming, we both simultaneously sense a *presence.* In comedic synchronisation we both turn our heads towards the cot where two sets of beady eyes are staring at us through the bars, both sucking their fingers and looking with interest at the scene before them.

"Oh my GOD!", I snort my amusement into my hand as Jay shifts off me, jumping up and heading to the en-suite. My confusion turns to laughter as he grabs a massive towel and pulls the cot side up, draping the towel over it to block their view.

"Sorry boys but for the next four fuckin' minutes, she's mine", he whispers at the boys and turns that smirk to me.

I'm not sure how Jay got my bra off if I'm honest, I was a bit busy undoing his shirt and acquainting myself with the lumps and bumps of his astonishing chest. However, he did get it off and judging by the increase in swearing, Jay is pleased with what he has discovered.

Then we hear the sound of a purple menace ascending the stairs and Jay flies off me like he's been shot, buttoning himself quickly and pretending to do something over the far side of my bedroom. I fling my bra under the bed and throw my vest top back on, Jay's eyes bugging out at the sight of my unfettered knockers.

The door is thrown open and my mother's look of thwarted fury is almost funny.

"Oh, I thought Jamel had gone already?", a shockingly weak lie from Bronwen Roberts makes me smirk.

Mum rolls her eyes, "Look boyo, it's nearly 1am so there's no point you going all the way back to Bristol now, is there? Eh? You'd be coming back later this morning anyway while Chopsy Knickers here goes to work so I've blown up the mattress downstairs and your duvet's on there already. I've left you one of Dylan's t-shirts to sleep in", she raises her eyebrows, inviting Jay to challenge her.

Hands in his pockets, he shoots me a quick smirk and nods, "Yeah, that'd be good, yeah, thanks".

Mum stands back, holding the door open and indicating that Jay needs to vacate the room.

As his tall form disappears down the stairs, my mum turns slowly to me, an expression of sad neutrality on her face, "Erin, I need you to…..I want you to…..", Mum looks up at the ceiling and gathers her thoughts, "Love, don't rush into something complicated. You and him, well, it's not just about you two is it?", she nods meaningfully at the cot.

She nods at me, "Night night love", as she reaches the landing she turns and whispers, "You'd best find that bra from wherever it ended up madam, you don't want to fall over that in dark", and she disappears into her room as I stand in wide eyed horror.

15th February 1997

Over breakfast, Jay and I exchanged covert smiles and in the kitchen he pressed me against the worktop and kissed me silly, walking off nonchalantly when my father approached from the lounge. I grinned like a sap and made more toast.

As I scan shopping and stack shelves in the weekly ten hour monotony that keeps my sons in nappies, I daydream about warm lips, strong bodies and the promise of *more.* Mum and Dad are out tonight at the Nursing Home's staff quiz night and Dyls has got Matty's fifteenth-birthday party. I was looking forward to a night of undisturbed film watching but *now* I tie myself up in knots wondering how I might invite Jay to hang around for a few hours before he heads home for work tomorrow.

I'm swearing under my breath at my inability to stop the value-packs of beans slumping at a drunken angle on the shelves when there's a gentle cough and a, *"Hey Rin",* mumbled behind me.

Gio.

I turn and see him looking tall and astonishingly uncomfortable behind me and he's fiddling with my bloody tins,

My heart double beats as I scowl, "Oi you, gerrof those tins, the little metal bastards hate me today and if you knock them over I'll scalp you Romano", and with that his discomfort seems to diminish as he smirks and rolls his eyes at me. It's my turn to feel uncomfortable now as I fiddle with the cardboard tray I'm holding.

He mumbles again, "So, how you been Roberts?"

I look up at him, those blue eyes looking guarded, set in that stupidly good-looking face and I feel my chest tighten. In my desperation to distract myself, I start babbling,

"Yeah, good. The boys sleep through now, so I look less like a zombie. Did you….did you have a good time at the pictures with Carolyn last night?", I'm toeing the floor with my shoes and staring around.

He shrugs, reaching out to interfere with the sodding tins again but then he takes a deep breath and looks at me forcing my gaze to meet his,

"Roberts, I feel like I'm always having to say sorry to you, d'you know that? I feel like even when it's you that does crazy shit, *all the fucking time*, it's still me that comes out of it looking like a dickhead. D'you know how shit that makes me feel?", his tone is a confusing blend of contrition and accusation and my face is unable to pick between astonishment or aggravation.

"Eh?", I opt for bafflement, it's served me well for sixteen years.

Gio steps forward making my breath hitch, "In that hospital, I said I was on your side, that I was your mate and I *fucking* meant it. When *he* said…...what he said that time about not having your back enough, it made me think. But it's not true Erin, it's not fucking true", his hands are now on his forehead, his fingers snaking into his thick dark hair in a good imitation of frustration until he looks up at me, his face a bit fierce as he carries on,

"See, I'm always on your side but you…...you don't want me there, you don't want *me* so what am I supposed to do? Eh? I get myself in aggro for you but why the fuck should I bother? You're with him right? Last night, you and him, you're together aren't you? Be honest with me Erin, are you?", he steps forward, his arms outstretched like he's imploring me.

I'm brandishing my cardboard tray like a shield as I look at him a bit rabbit-in the headlights. *Am I with Jay?*

Gio gets closer, his face softer, "I meant what I said at Mass Rin, I've always meant it. You gotta know, I'm only with Carolyn because…..", he looks down and shakes his head before looking back up, "Are you seriously with *him* Rin?", my heart is thumping wildly from Gio's proximity, from the scent of him. I open my mouth uselessly, my skin tingling when a hear a shout,

"Ginger Feist, where d'you find nappies in this place, eh?", I spin in comic astonishment to see Jay pushing the pram towards me, his first visit to my place of work. I see his expression darken as he spots Gio but I do get a giddy flush from how incredibly fit Jay looks pushing that pram.

"There's my answer I guess, eh Rin?", I turn back to Gio who's shaking his head, his strong, tall frame slumped. The look gives me is so sad, my breath hitches involuntarily and my hand, unbidden, reaches out to him but with his hands in his pockets and his head bowed, he walks off.

My heart actually aching, I plaster on a wobbly smile and walk towards *my boys* and the kiss that Jay gives me makes my knees tremble. Neither of us mention Gio. Nappies located and a few sneaky snogs against the dog food shelf, Jay goes to head off with the boys. He's given Dyls a lift into town and plans to meet him at McDonalds before they come back to collect me at teatime.

Still feeling very unsettled by Gio's visit, I blurt out, "Er, my lot are all out tonight. Do you want to er, hang out for a bit later, before you go home?", I'm fussing with the boys in their pram, disguising my discomfort.

I *feel* Jay's smirk before I look up, "You *want* me to hang out wiv you Feist?", he looks far too smug.

I roll my eyes and try to look bored, "Yeah but only coz you can cop for bath duty".

He pulls me into a kiss before whispering against my lips, "That ain't the duty I wanna cop for Feist but I'll be there", and with an eyebrow wiggle, he walks off.

"Erin Roberts, I need you on tills, NOW", with my spotty supervisor's nasal shout, I am propelled into action, my head filled with confusion.

After work, lying on the floor in the living room with my sons who find 'peek-a-boo' the most hilarious thing, I hear my Mum talking to Jay in the kitchen.

"I'd have thought you'd have more exciting places to be than to be sat by here on a Saturday night?", my Mum's tone is weird. I don't hear Jay's mumbled reply but I hear resignation in Mum's voice as she says, "Well, me and Fred'll be home about eleven so I expect you'll be gone by then, eh? You've got work tomorrow, those babies won't pay for themselves", there's warning in her tone and I hear Jay grunt his assent.

I kiss my babies and make them giggle, in an attempt to distract myself. Jay pays me £60 per week for the twins, which I pay to Mum for food and board and she buys the baby milk with the weekly shop. I earn £65 per week and my Child Benefit covers the rest of the babies expenses.

Jamel works at a tyre fitting place, a job he got after he left the bail hostel last month. It pays pretty well but his car insurance, petrol and his rent eat most of his wages. We never talk about the dealing, not since the Christmas assurances of change. I know that Dion and Jay's other older half-brother Obi helped pay for his car initially but other than that, Jamel's money, his *life* remains cloaked in mystery. Nobody from his world has met the boys, or me for that matter.

I don't have money for anything. It's a truth I'm OK with. Mum and Dad treat me to odds and ends but I'm fierce about not accepting too much of their generosity. I may have to use all my disposable income on my babies but that is my choice. If I don't have money for buying clothes, or treats or the latest trainers, I can live with that.

With lots of noise, my family exit the house, Dylan excited about the party and a night at his mates' house and my mother a ball of Welsh fury having confiscated the whisky that Dyls had secreted in his bag with lots of shouting and a clip round the ear. Dyls' shouts of, *"I'm calling bloody Childline"*, echoing through the hallway as they leave.

Jay is washing bottles, his big, strong body filling the space in Mum's rapidly dating melamine kitchen as he loads the steriliser. Mum taught him how to do it last month, her Nurses obsession with cleanliness driving her to instruct a wide-eyed Jay about the risks of poor hygiene for babies.

"You're such an old scrubber Watson", my words are garbled as both my sons stick their sticky paws in my mouth as I carry both of them in to see their Daddy.

Jay smirks, "See, them boys are on my team, they shut you right up Feist", drying his hands, he takes AJ off me, kissing his little head and letting him grab at his gold chain.

Jay leans in, "Maybe I'll find something else to stick in there and shut you up more, eh?", he laughs as I splutter in red-cheeked indignation, pressing a kiss to my lips before heading for the bathroom with AJ, the boys' bath time calling.

Honestly, this is the best bath time *ever*, a house to ourselves meaning that Jay relaxes a bit more. He's really funny, the boys propped up in their little seats like soapy gnomes are chuckling away at Jamel's duck impressions and when we smear bubbles over each other's faces, the boys do these baby belly-laughs that make me want to cry at the cuteness.

The *fizzing* between us is doing absolutely criminal things to my knickers, Jay's heated looks and the kisses he peppers onto my lips in between messing around, they're delicious and my grin is so wide that I fear some sort of injury.

For the first time ever, I imagine fleeting images of future where the four of us have our own place, where Jay and I mess around in our *own* bathroom, the boys sitting in a bath that is *ours*. I've never seen that future, it frightens me a bit with how comforting it looks.

Soaked from our silliness, we get the boys dry and wrestle the ever-vocal AJ into his babygrow, his love of being naked means that he gets the right hump whenever he is returned to a clothed state. When the squealing little toad is picked up by his Daddy, he nestles into Jay's neck and immediately quietens. Jay's response is to lean his head into his tiny sons and close his eyes as he rocks him gently. I have to distract myself with Jake to prevent myself bursting into hormonal tears.

Clothed, fed, burped and read to, the boys lie in their cot in the darkened room, cooing at each other like they always do when they're settling. I gesture at Jamel to leave the room with me and in the darkness, we head downstairs.

"You want a tea or a…..", but my over the shoulder question as I walk into the kitchen is cut short as Jamel pulls me against the wall and kisses me like I just cured cancer.

We are alone in a house, undisturbed for the first time, well, *ever* and we both seem to feel a need to exploit this. We walk-snog to the sofa whereupon I am unceremoniously hoofed onto my back as Jay presses his full body weight over me and kisses me through the cushions.

"They ain't coming back, yeah? No chance?", he gasps out in between tongue thrusts.

I don't need to respond as I tug at his sweatshirt and pull the grey marl away from the body that I want to see a *lot* more of. My top is gone, my bra is gone, Jay's sweatshirt is gone and I have got his incredible back under my hands. I fumble with his jeans, making him groan into my mouth until he pulls back. Here, in the TV and lamp-lit space of my childhood home, I shuffle my way out of my jeans and Jamel Watson's beautiful brown eyes try to bore laser beams through the fabric of my knickers as he wrestles with his own denims.

His black jockey shorts have the most ridiculous tent and in our mutual state of undress, I suddenly feel a bit scared and insecure. Jay's body is sculpted like Gio's, a thought that makes me feel briefly

174

uncomfortable but I'm distracted by the fact that it's too pretty to be real. As I run my palm over the ridges and planes of his abs, I want to laugh at the silliness that I, *rank, ugly, ginger Roberts* am here being mauled by this lad. I don't need to worry too much because at the moment that I hit the peak of my insecurity, one of my sons yells down the baby monitor, making Jay jump off the sofa in alarm. In possibly the least dignified move I have ever pulled off, I clutch a sofa cushion to my bare knockers and back out of the lounge, Jay looking torn between amusement and relief that we were interrupted by a baby and not my mother.

The source of Jake's distress appears to be his brother, who has somehow rolled aboard Jake, his sleepsack and his lack of mobility no hindrance to his mountaineering and AJ is now zonko, crushing his protesting twin.

I rearrange my sons, smiling at their sleepy faces and jolt slightly as a pair of warm, wandering hands reach from behind me to palm my bare boobs and groan obscenities into my neck.

"Feist, get that towel on the cot yeah", Jay groans and pushes his jockey-clad erection into my bum indicating his desire for haste.

I find myself under my duvet snogging a naked Jamel Watson in an astonishingly short space of time. Jay naked is much, *much* more exciting that Ryan naked. His body is beautiful, that cafe au lait skin so lickable and as our hands roam freely, he explores me with a freedom that we have never had before. My hands cover my c-section scar, it's something that I feel horribly self-conscious about but Jay pulls my hands away and kisses my belly reverently.

Jamel's exploration of my body leads to fingers in places that make me tingle, "Fuck Feist, you're so wet and fuckin' tight. You like that? You like me touchin' you?", his words are groaned out as I gasp against his warm neck.

My hand is wrapped around his incredibly large dick, now wet tipped and rock hard and whilst I know that it has fitted in me before, I am suddenly nervous. As Jay shifts on top of me, a number of alarm bells ring and the words are compelled from my lips,

"Jay, slow yeah? Please? It's only……..it's only ever been you. I'm…….I'm scared", Jay's head flips up to meet my gaze, his eyes wide.

"Feist, are you fuckin' serious?", he looks appalled and I feel suddenly very self conscious until he says,

"That time we….what, that was your first fuckin' time?", I'm reading lots of emotions in his face but thankfully none of them seem to be rejection.

When I nod, I find myself pulled tight against him as he whispers into my neck, "I'm so sorry, Erin, I'm so fuckin' sorry", and he kisses me so sweetly and tenderly, I lose my nerves all together.

The kisses gets hotter and more urgent and I feel his dick nudging at me and my legs spread wider in acceptance until the point at which my brain turns on.

"CONDOM! Oh fucking hell Jay, condom!", and we both snort in our mutual amusement at my horror.

Wrapped in each other's nakedness, being able to laugh feels like the loveliest treat. Jay leans out of the bed and pulls from his jeans a pack of condoms, leading to more giggles from me as he teaches me how to put it on,

"Feist you better get this fucker on right coz I can't afford no more cots and buggies", making me snort and mock wallop his chest.

In the darkness, his smirk and twinkling eyes become like beacons to me, they relax me. Jay kisses me as he gently slips his length all the way inside me and the long gasp I let loose is one of wonder rather than discomfort.

Hands clasped together, Jay is thrusting in and out of me in fluid ripples that make my skin tingle and the whole time, he's kissing me and whispering, *"So fuckin' good Feist"*, against my skin.

He moves my legs gently, groaning at the change in sensation that this causes and after a few minutes, I feel his back muscles tense and his kisses go sloppy and less focussed,

"I'm gonna come Feist, fuck, I'm gonna come", and with a roar that he muffles into my shoulder, Jay pushes deeply into me as his muscles tremble and he collapses on me.

I whimper with regret when he pulls out but his hands swiftly start to fiddle with me in ways that make me groan as he whispers into my shoulder,

"You never came that first time and I ain't showin' myself up two times Feist", as his fingers slip into me and around my clit, I feel the sparkle-rush of an orgasm ripple through me.

He pulls me into a cuddle, kissing my hair and whispering expletives that make me laugh. We joke over what to do with the condom, my mother's detective ninja skills a concern.

I feel more words bubble uncompelled from my lips, "Do you...do you have to go straight away?", I am suddenly beset with clinginess, not wanting to have a motorway and a whole other life between me and Jay Watson right now.

Jay silently gets up, depositing the condom in the nappy bin and pulling his jockeys on. I see him open the curtains and peer outside, opening the window to look for something.

He turns to me and grins, that smile bright in the gloom,. "Y'know, I could get down that drainpipe. If I shift the car so she don't see it, I could stay over till I gotta leave for work at like 6? D'ya reckon she'll come in here when she gets back?", he looks hopefully at me and my grin is feral as I shake my head,

"No, she always gets hammered at those quiz nights, her hangover is a stinker afterwards", I roll my eyes as Jay nods.

He throws on his jeans and heads off to move the car as I find my PJ's under the pillow. I'm tidying the boys washing when there is a sharp buzz from the carpet by my bed. Jay's phone lights up, having clearly fallen from his pocket.

I don't have any experience with mobile phones, I've never used one but there is a 'new message' alert on the screen. In my clueless attempt to try and turn it off to prevent it waking the boys, I press a button and I see the word, "Case" at the top of the message followed by the text message itself, *"I can't believe you're not here J. It's my birthday and you're not here. We said we'd be mates, I miss you. Call me xx".*

My first thought is simply, *"Oh".* In my post-coital glow, I'm not sure whether to be secretly chuffed that Jay gave up some sort of party to be here with me or whether I should feel aggravated by the fact that Jay has somebody close enough to him to send him kisses and make demands on his time. I realise in that moment that whilst Jay and I are a million times better acquainted than we were at our sons' conception, I still have massive knowledge gaps and his life in Bristol is a total mystery.

I don't feel secure enough to push though. Things are.....new with Jay. I have to swallow down my chopsy self and just bide my time for answers.

When Jay bounds up the stairs, I beam at him, genuinely chuffed to bits that he's here with me. I really fancy Jay, just that smile is enough to make me tingle and now that I've had a sex re-boot with him, I realise that I really like shagging him too *especially* when pregnancy is not a likely outcome. I am just conscious that things are new and not as *comfortable* between us as perhaps I would like for a person I am sleeping with.

In his warm arms, we chat gently about stuff we haven't talked about. I tell him that I still hope to go to Uni, I just haven't really got my head around the funding for students with kids or how far from my parents' support I will be able to be. Jay tells me that he doesn't ever plan to leave Bristol, he feels settled there and has no plans to return to Birmingham. He has not seen his two half brothers by his Mum and Step-Dad since he left their care. His younger brothers were only two and four when he left. Dion and Obi, who is his Dad's son from another relationship, are both several years older than Jay.

A few surreptitious eye glances and he mutters, "There's a Uni in Bristol, y'know?"

I manage a non-committal, "Uhuh", unsure about where this conversation might head.

I ask him about his job and he smiles wryly when he explains that his boss, aware of his criminal record, doesn't allow Jay to go near either the till or the keys to the cars. His faint blush and tooth-kiss belies what I suspect is genuine shame at being marked as 'dodgy'. He tells me that he's put a photo of the twins on his locker at work, resulting in a lot of hormonal clucking from the girls in the office.

As we talk about my job and the overtime I want to do in the holidays to earn extra cash to maybe take the boys away, I feel the question bubble across my lips,

"Why did you start dealing Jay? Was it the money?", I lie back against his chest under the warm duvet.

I feel his muscles tense and his voice sounds tight, "Yeah, I mean, fuck, the dough was sweet but nah, it started coz I got pissed off one night and went out with some boys from my Dad's manor instead of my usual boys. Them manor boys, they're fuckin' big names round my way and when you're seen wiv them, well, it takes you places. They needed an in wiv' them Uni students, wanted to start dealing to them. Wiv' this mug", Jay circles his face with his finger, winking at me as I roll my eyes, "They reckoned this pretty boy mug would get me in wiv' them posh student girls".

I look up at that *pretty boy mug* and ask, "Did it?"

Jay sighs and looks at the boys' cot, "Yeah, yeah it fuckin' did and once that dough and them deals started flowin', there weren't no way I was gettin' out of it".

Something clicks in my head, "So that's how Pixie Prick Ryan knew you?", Jay's smile is guarded as he queries the nickname and I explain.

I've also seen enough crap Police shows to ask another question, "Jay, if you got arrested carrying a tonne of gear, well, doesn't that mean that those lads are going to be pissed off with you for losing them money?"

His whole body tenses up and his face crumples in an angry frown as he nods, biting out, "Yeah, yeah they was pretty fucked off, they went after…...they went for people that I was tight wiv", Jay's fists clench and he pauses, his breath a bit ragged before he continues, "While I was inside, Dion, he...he got it dealt wiv, called in some old favours. It was proper risky for him, D, he's got a rep and was pretty y'know, *big name* time ago and he's got a kid. His missus, she…...she and some others are still proper pissed wiv' me right now, he took too many risks for me. I owe him too big", Jay's head is bowed and I feel his distress through his body.

I have no real comfort to offer him apart from the obvious so I go for that, leaning up and pulling him gently into a kiss as I whisper against his lips, "I had your two kids, I reckon you owe me bigger", and as I smile, I feel his lips quirk against mine and we fall back against the mattress, our bodies tangled.

I come with Jay inside me this time, an event which makes him smirk far too smugly and which makes me weirdly self-conscious. I also panic that even in whispered gasps, we may have scarred our sons emotionally by shagging in the same room as them. I tell Jay this and he snorts,

"Feist, your Mum in that dressin' gown is more fuckin' scary than me and you in this bed. Them boys, they ain't never gonna be able to drink blackcurrant wiv'out feelin' nervous", and as I laugh with my sons' father, cuddled under a duvet next to our babies, I feel like this is my own little brand of perfect.

Sleeping next to somebody else is weird. Jay sprawls whereas I always sleep curled in a ball. I forget he's under the duvet at one point and gasp when a hand covers my thigh. We both jolt awake when we hear my parents come in but true to form, Bronwen Roberts is three sheets to the wind and I hear her drunken chuckle as my father has to help her up the stairs. Jay had decided to hide on the floor as soon as we heard them and his relief and my piss taking lead to a mock-tussle that ends, dangerously, with his dick in my mouth and his fingers in me, as we muffle our groans of pleasure.

He's getting his t-shirt on in the gloomy dawn as I wake. The boys are starting to stir and Jay needs to get out before my hungover mother gets any sense of what is occurring in her daughter's room. Morning breath limits the snogging but Jay pulls me into a tight hug and whispers, "Last night was the bomb Feist, I…..I'm proper glad you asked me to stay", and as he kisses my hair and waves his sons goodbye, he launches himself out of the window and down the drainpipe in a pretty startling manner.

He kicks the window by accident and I hear a bedraggled, "What the bloody hell was that Erin?", from my father through the wall.

My sons decide that 5.30am and their father's departure marks the start of the day and the cacophony of noise they emit renders a response pointless. Despite the early hour, my day begins with a smug grin that I can't seem to wipe off my face.

Chapter Nine

17th March 1997

"I BLOODY KNEW IT!! Those flowers by there were squashed flat the other day and that drainpipe have been wonky for weeks. Your father even said, *'Bron, it looks like somebody's been swinging off that pipe'* and lo and behold, they bloody have. You've got some explaining to do Madam", my return from school today has been unusually *dramatic* and I wasn't properly prepared for this on a Monday afternoon.

Mum had the boys for me today as usual and in doing so, had gone to Pat's for coffee with the twins. Pat mentioned that she had seen *'the babies' father'* leaving our garden at 6am yesterday when she had been walking the dog and *'thought she should mention it'*.

Cow

With my coat and messenger bag still on, I take my youngest son from his Nana's arms, he's currently looking between me and his Nana like he's deciding which horse to back.

She's not done though, "Now I know that you two have been going on dates and we're not stupid, I can hear the two of you smooching in the kitchen when you do think nobody hears you but staying over?! Erin, you are sixteen years old, you are under my roof and I will not have you sneaking lads in your room overnight. Look at what can happen, eh?", she holds my eldest son aloft as some sort of evidence, who, giddy from his newly acquired altitude, squeals and giggles in a desperately cute way.

I can't argue with any of what she's saying. I *want* to but honestly, I can't. I have to play a more clever game. I nod acceptingly and the look of astonishment on her face makes me have to disguise a snort of humour as a cough.

She gawps at me, "That's it? No argument? No chopsy comeback? Jesus, you must be coming down with something Madam, I was sure you'd be a bit gobby", her eyes narrow as she smells the well-matured rat.

I shrug in faux nonchalance, "I'm too grateful to you and Dad for all that you do for me and the boys to go against you on this. I'm sorry that me and Jay snuck around behind your back but it's hard because like it or not, we're a family me, him and the boys and when the four of us are together and he stays over it feels, I dunno, *nice*. It feels like the sort of family that the boys deserve", although this started as a bit of a game-plan, my words are more genuine that I intended and I feel my eyes swimming as I continue,

"I don't have the right to ask you to go against your rules but this isn't just some daft teenage crush mum. Jay will always be in my life, we share two children and although this is all very new and yes, we're only teenagers, this is a much more complicated situation than just having a boyfriend staying over. Whatever happens between me and him, however this pans out, it feels like we need to *try*, as hard as we can, to give being a family a shot", I nod through a lip tremble.

Mum looks at me appraisingly, "And sleeping with him is part of this *trying* is it? Oh Erin, I know that hormones at your age do run wild but sweetheart, you are playing a grown up game by here now. You're right, this is not a teenage crush, this is more complicated and I worry that you're not mature enough to think it through carefully enough beaut. You're a bright girl but you're so young sweetheart", Mum looks so sad and she reaches out and wipes away the stray tear that has fallen down my face.

She adjusts Jake on her hip and when he reaches for me, I wriggle off my coat and my bag and take

Jake in my spare arm, both of my boys nestled into my neck, warm and sleepy. I kiss their little heads and whisper into their fluffy hair how much I love them. My Mum looks a bit broken as she clutches her face in her hands and watches us. Looking up at the ceiling, she takes a deep breath,

"Right, this is what we'll do. Jamel can stay here, no more bloody drainpipes, on Wednesday and Saturday nights in your room. He can only do this mind you, on a few conditions", she looks at me as I try to dampen down the grin I feel building in my lips.

"Those conditions are that you go to the GP this week and we get you on some proper contraception, the implant for you I reckon. Then I want you both to have STD tests, that boy more than you but if you've been sleeping with him already, you need to have them too. Then the third condition is that at no point, EVER during the hours of 10pm to 6am are your father or I to be *reminded* through that wall that Jamel is in your room. Do you understand what I'm saying Erin? Your father will find this hard enough, he doesn't need *sound effects*", Mum mother's no-nonsense nurse persona is incapable of embarrassment, it's a pity that this does not extend to her daughter as I am blushing at a *nuclear* level.

Red hot with shame, I nod into my sons scalps as they babble and grab my hair.

With that fresh level of mortification as our baptism, Jay and I are officially acknowledged by my family as being 'together'. On Wednesday night, when Jay arrives, he gives me a shy kiss in front of my eye-rolling mother and once the boys are bathed and in bed, we take a DVD into my room and we don't come out. It turns out that the best soundproofing is in the en-suite. and that shower sex, whilst tricky and requiring a degree of cooperation that Jay and I had to work at, does not make anything rattle or squeak. As I sleep, Jay's arms wrapped around me, I wonder how and when I will know if I am falling in love with him. It keeps me awake.

On the bus to school the next morning, Lees is unusually quiet, she's swamped in a massive sweatshirt and she looks pale and a bit poorly. She and Adam are on slightly awkward chatting terms now and as the three of us and my brother sit together, kind-faced Ad shoots me worried glances across the seats. Romano stopped getting the bus as soon as he got his car but Ad has to share his mum's car so his access is a bit hit and miss.

"You okay chick, you look a bit peaky?", I nudge Lees gently and her cat-piss smile and jerky nod do nothing to reassure me, her slender frame huddled in a protective slouch against the side of the bus. She looks out of the window as Adam mouths to me, *"Something's up"*.

At lunchtime, Lee is still silent and when I catch her gazing into the distance, her lip wobbling, my concern escalates. Adam is constantly watching her, bless him that's not unusual but he knows her so well and his worry makes me anxious.

Romano, sat with Carolyn at a nearby table, catches Ad's worried looks and frowns questioningly at me. I shrug in response.

I have to ignore the increase in my heart rate and the slightly sweaty feeling I get when Gio looks at me. I don't know where this silliness came from but his supermarket visit last month has confused me more, *"I'm only with Carolyn because…."*. He looks particularly gorgeous today, the bastard. He's got on what I consider to be my favourite of his t-shirts, it's a snug fitting grey granddad top and it makes his blue eyes even more blue. Carolyn's all over him but he doesn't break my gaze.

A Year 10 girl trips up behind us and grabs Lees' arms for balance at which point Lees' yelp of pain is so sharp and so loud that it makes me spill my drink in shock. For a minor grab, I can't help but be surprised by usually placid Lees' overreaction but when I look at her ashen face and the pain that is transmitting, I realise that her reaction was genuine. *Lees is hurt.*

"Christ Lee, you OK?", as the question leaves my mouth, Lees jumps up from the table, wincing and holding herself protectively as she rushes from the room.

Ad and I follow suit, as I call Lees' name and implore my marathon champ best mate to wait for us less athletic bods. She runs into the girls' loo, allowing only me to follow her.

"Chick, are you poorly? You really don't look well mate, maybe we should ask Romano to drive you home?", I'm talking to the only locked toilet door in the loos.

When I hear the first dry sobs, I plead for her to open the door.

"Rinny, I don't know what to do. I don't know what to do", her sobs become louder and more distressed. I feel the cold trickle of dread seep down my body. *Lees is pregnant.*

I try to stay calm, "Babe, it's OK, it's all going to be OK. I'm here, we'll get this all sorted. Does Kiron know?", I try to think rationally.

Her sobs hitch and she sounds frantic, "What? Why do you say that? What?"

I take a breath and talk to the door again, "Mate, if he's the father then it will really help if he's around to support you, whatever you decide to do", the words barely leave my mouth before Lees' jumps in,

"I'm not fucking pregnant Rinny!", silence follows.

I scrabble for a clue, "Oh….oh, phew, OK well that's good I guess but…….Lee, wassup babe? What's going on then?", I admit defeat, I've got no idea what's upset her so much.

The lock bolt slowly slides across and I hear a jagged intake of breath as Lees opens the door, her head bowed and her face a picture of misery. My first reaction is to pull her into a hug, which I do but she hisses and jumps back from me, clearly in a lot of pain.

As I frown in confusion, Lees closes her eyes and bites her lip as she slowly lifts up her t-shirt and what I see makes me gasp.

Lees has got bruises from her hips up around her ribs and I can see the discolouration spreading up under where she has currently got her t-shirt pulled to. I feel my mouth tightening and my eyes filling with tears as I reach slowly out and lift her shirt higher. I see bruises up under her bra strap and as I turn her gently, her back has a whole series of scattered bruises.

My voice is a whisper, "How….?", but Lees is crying now, shaking her head and she is trembling. Her whole body is trembling and as I step close to her and gently wrap my arms round her, I feel my own tears spill.

My cracked voice is soft against her hair, "Who?"

 I know though. I know what she's going to say. I see how nervous he makes her but I thought it was because she wanted to always impress him, because she is not *herself* when she's with him. She doesn't talk about him like she used to talk to me about Adam. There's no humour in her voice when she talks about him. I just assumed it was because she seemed so anxious about impressing him or because she knows I don't like him.

Kiron.

Lees' whole body sags against me and I find myself trying to hold her up without pressing on her bruises.

"Tell me", my words are sobs.

And she does. After training last night, she went to Kiron's for tea. His Mum and Dad were asking her about her plans for Uni and where she might like to go. She mentioned her new interest in going to Sheffield, a potential athletics link with Don Valley Stadium making her contemplate her options. This was news to Kiron. They have only been going out for three months but he has already been very vocal in his desire for Lees to follow him to Birmingham Uni, where he starts in September.

"He…...he just gets so angry, so fast. It comes from nowhere Rinny. We were in his car going home and he just pulled over, he did it so fast it actually made me think we were crashing. He grabbed me and told me that I don't make any plans without checking with him, that…...that I have to always check with him", Lees' whole body is shaking as she recalls the conversation.

"I started to say that it was only an option, that I was just looking at options and he just lost it. I tried to get out of the car, I turned away from him and that's when he got my back and my ribs", tears pour down her face.

She assures me that this was the first incident of violence. She tells me that whilst he has scared her with his anger recently, this was the first time that he has hurt her.

She whispers, "Rinny, I think…...there's this rumour at the club about the senior boys using steroids. Has Dyls said anything?"

I shake my head but wince at the realisation that I have not perhaps spent time alone with Dyls recently to allow such a disclosure.

Lees looks down, "I think Kiron's involved, he's got really built really fast and I don't think that's normal".

I shake off my shock and my anger and I tip Lees' chin with my finger so she looks at me, "We need to tell the police Lee, what he's done, it's assault. You need to speak to the police, please", I hold her hands, imploring her.

I know all of Lees' expressions and I know this one. *Mulish refusal.* She stands up a bit straighter, her pretty face tight with decisiveness,

"No, I don't want that fuss. He's coming here to school to collect me, he cried after it happened and he said that he wants to make it up to me but I'm going to finish with him today, when he gets here. Can I get a lift home with you and Jay?", I nod without hesitation, my relief that she's finishing with him pretty acute.

We stand, holding each other as I whisper into her hair, "I always fucking hated that twat", and her gentle snort gives me comfort.

As we pull back, I have one final attempt, "Lees, honestly, I still reckon you need to tell somebody, even if it's not the police. His parents maybe? The coaches at athletics?", her shaking head tells me I'm not going to win this.

"Rinny, I just want to be rid of him and forget that I was stupid enough to fall for his shitty charm. When I think about what I did, dumping Ad and throwing away what I had with him……", her lip goes again and I see the tears start.

The bell for afternoon lessons sounds loud and we need to move. She hurriedly dries her eyes as she pleads for me to keep this between us. Knowing that I'll be there with Jay when Lees has that chat with Kiron, is the only thing that makes me agree.

Adam is waiting for us outside the loos, slumped against the wall. As we emerge, he jumps to his feet his worried gaze darting questioningly between Lees and I. I smile tightly at him and pat his arm. He approaches Lees and so I walk a little way ahead, not wishing to intrude on this moment. When I turn around, I see Adam tentatively reach for Lees' hand as they walk to class together, looking anywhere but at each other.

When the bell sounds for tutor group at the end of the day, Lees is so jittery, she drops all of her books, Adam sweeping in to pick them all up as she blushes. As we're in separate tutor groups, I agree to meet Lee in the car park in fifteen minutes as Romano and I head to our mutual tutor room.

"What's going on there, eh Roberts?", Gio's deep voice rumbles next to me as we walk.

I look at him, his big strong body so familiar and those lovely blue eyes making me a bit sweaty as I say, "Lees has got a lot on her plate but I think we're going to get it sorted today, I hope so anyway", I bite my lip anxiously.

Gio stops and his hand on my arm makes me tingle, "Rin, you know how Jones still feels about her?", Gio looks a bit sad.

I smile gently and look at him, "Romano, I think things might just work out OK with them", I wink but he just stares at me.

There's a whiny voice behind us, "Gio, I'm going to get a lift back with……..oh, Erin, I didn't see you there", Carolyn walks up to Gio and plants a possessive snog on him as I look away awkwardly.

She steers him off and I troupe behind them, rolling my eyes. Fifteen minutes later and Lees and I are stood in the car park. Jay isn't here yet and neither is *fucking* Kiron but the buses have all started leaving and the car-park is emptying out. I'm fiddling with my geography folder when Lees gasps and grabs my arm. I look up to see Kiron's expensive BMW approaching, his eighteenth birthday present

191

from his wealthy parents.

My lips curl in a snarl but Lees has gone pale and she's shaking so I have to concentrate on supporting her. The car screeches to a halt and Kiron leaps out, his face looking worried. Lees is right, Kiron is looking *bigger* and there is no way that he's managed that through hard work alone since I last saw him only a few weeks ago. He is still good-looking but right now, I don't think I've ever seen anything more ugly.

"Lee, babe, y'ok?", his gaze is darting between my face, which is currently transmitting raw hatred and Lees' wide-eyed fearful tension.

Lees swallows with a gulp, "Kir, can we talk?"

He looks at me, his eyes narrowing, "Sure, not with *her* here though".

I open my mouth to start verbally gutting him but Lee grabs my arm, "Rinny, can you just wait for me over there?", I silently communicate my concern and reluctance but she nods urgently and so shooting Kiron my most effective *'Fuck off and die'* look, I back over to my allotted position a few feet away.

Kiron goes in first and wafting over the March wind I hear *"Sorry" "Love you" "Never again" "stressed".* Lee's voice is quiet, her head shaking as she looks down at her feet. She's got her arms wrapped around herself and she's transmitting fear but she's also projecting refusal. *Atta girl.*

He takes a step towards her and she jumps away, startled. I feel my feet tense in readiness to move but I pause as Kiron looks frozen in what seems like shame until something *shifts.*

Lees clearly says her final piece, I hear the words *'finished'* and *'goodbye'* and as she turns to walk away, I see Kiron's body *change*. His whole posture alters and it just screams aggression. I feel my muscles ready themselves for action and when Kiron's hand grabs Lees' arm, yanking her back to his side with a brutal force and making her yelp in pain, I lose it.

I'm yelling for him to *'fucking leave her alone'* as I run and I see Kiron release a whimpering Lees as I literally launch myself at him.

My older cousin Owain and I would fight as children. He's almost exactly a year older than me but as kids, we would physically fight over anything and everything. It earned me the nickname 'Hellcat' from my Uncle, who was torn between admiration and embarrassment that his small niece could reduce his hulking son to a whimpering puddle of scratches and bruises. I'm sure it's my fights with Owain that made me think I could separate Daniel and Gio that time, that gave me the confidence to go for Ryan and prompted the slap I gave Jay.

Now, I don't recall ever hating *anyone* as much as I hate Kiron and I go for him with a viciousness that clearly startles him. I feel my claws connect with flesh, my feet flailing as I push and grab but he's a big lad and he starts to fight back. I feel a punch connect with my arm but I've got a good shot at his bollocks so I ignore the pain and I go for it. He's on the floor and I hear Lees shouting, pleading with us to stop. I hear Kiron hissing and screaming insults and slurs. Distracted momentarily by a particularly loud plea of Lees', I make the mistake of turning away from Kiron.

The punch to my head dazed me but the hands around my throat were the thing that shocked me the most. I'm pulled to the ground and I look up to see Kiron's scratched, bleeding face absolutely puce with fury, his neck veins standing out and spittle frothing from his lips as he screams insults into my face.

Then he's gone.

Choking in much-missed air as the gravel bites into the back of my head, I hear voices. I hear a frantic

Adam shouting Gio's name and I hear the *'ooof'* sound of punches connecting.

"You never fucking touch her again, you hear me, you don't fucking touch her. I'll kill you you cunt, I'll fucking kill you", that's Gio's voice and I sit bolt upright, nearly head butting a weeping Lees by my side as I do.

Woozy from the head punch, I look over to see Gio Romano beating the ever-living shit out of Kiron, who now has blood pouring from his mouth and a nasty gash on his forehead.

"Gio, no, stop", my shout is a bit pathetic but it pauses him.

Kiron doesn't move as Gio jumps up and runs over to me, kneeling down and gently patting my head.

"Rin, you're bleeding, that bastard made you bleed", his hand comes away from my hair with a thin coating of blood.

Teachers are now running from all directions, their concern initially for the prostrate bleeding stranger in their school car-park until an entire choir of dissenting voices quickly appraise them of the fact that the wounded party had been trying to murder *me* before Gio intervened.

It all goes a bit mad and it takes me a few seconds to realise that I am in Gio's lap on the floor, that warm, strong hand in mine as his other hand pushes my blood-matted hair from my face. Lees is being held by Adam, who is cuddling her close and stroking her back as she sobs.

Kiron seems to have roused himself and with no affiliation to the school and his anonymity acting as a shield, he ignores all of the teachers pleas to await medical attention as he swears at us all, spits at Lees and walks over to his car. Adam is restrained by a shocked looking Mr. Dobbs, who has to prevent mild-mannered Ad from seeing through his threats to kill as Kiron's car squeals off out of the car-park.

I'm staring up at Gio from my position in his lap, his worried face is only inches from mine, "Rin, what the fuck was all that? What the fuck just happened?", Gio's deep voice makes me sleepy.

I whisper, "Thanks for saving me Gio, I reckon I could have taken him though", as I smirk. All around us is commotion and questioning voices but I only see Gio.

Gio snorts, stroking my face in a way that makes me tingle, even through my concussion, "Roberts, you went for him like a mental little ginger-ninja chipmunk. I've never seen anything like it. You are completely out of your tree, d'you know that? That twat was twice your size, you've got no sense of self fucking preservation have you? You were the same when we were kids, do you remember roller skating over that manhole cover?", he smiles as he looks at me like I'm mental, his hand tenderly stroking my hair.

I smile weakly, feeling a bit sick.

"ERIN ROBERTS! How did I guess that you were involved in this, eh?", Mr. Gibson strides across the car-park, "Good Lord, are you bleeding? Mr. Dobbs, I think we need to get Miss. Roberts some medical attention before she further befouls the car park. Mr. Romano, as you seem to have the new school boxing champion in containment, can I ask you to take her to the medical room. Miss. Morris and Mr. Jones, I'd like you to come with me and fill me in on this afternoon's little excitement please and let's make it snappy, I am missing out on a perfectly good cup of coffee"

Gio sweeps me up, lemons and herbs filling my nostrils as I whisper, "Dude you don't need to carry me", even though I'm loving the feel of his arms around me.

Gio's face is tense as he strides off with me, grinding out, "D'you know Roberts, every fight I've ever had has been because of you, did you know that? I hit my best mate in a nightclub because of you, I hit two wankers in that club after Christmas coz of you and now, *now* I'm lamping some dickhead in a car park because of you. You are a fucking menace Rin".

I wince up at him, "Eh?"

"Feist! What the fuck? You hurt?", I hear the sound of feet running and I feel Gio take a deep breath under my where my head is resting.

"Bruv, what's happened?", Jay, his good looking face genuinely worried, appears in my line of vision as his hand strokes my face.

In a clipped tone, Gio explains, "Something kicked off with Morris and that dickhead she's been seeing. Then *killer* here", Gio nods down at me, "decides to unleash ginger fury and rugby tackles the bastard in the car-park, kicking the shit out of him until he punches her, body slams her and strangles her. Now she's bleeding and here we are, *bruv*. I'm watching out for her *again* coz you weren't around", Gio isn't looking at Jay as he says this, he's staring in the middle distance.

Jay's jaw clenches and his scarred eyebrow raised, "He fuckin' hit her? You serious?"

I wriggle out of Gio's surprisingly firm grip and stand up, a bit dizzy, "OI! I'm right here you know. Jay, where are the boys?", I can't see my babies anywhere.

Jay looks at me, his hands examining my blood matted hair, "Your mum came back from work early, half day or somethin' so we went out wiv the boys. We got stuck in traffic and she's got the boys at home, that's why I was late. FUCK girl, you seen your neck?", Jay gently pushes my hair away and I hear Gio gasp and swear fiercely.

Jay looks absolutely furious, "I want his name, NOW bruv, you get me?", Jay looks at Gio and I see a shared nod of understanding.

Their reaction worries me and as I touch my neck, I realise for the first time that it hurts to swallow and that actually, my neck feels *bruised*.

Jay pulls me into a hug, kissing my forehead and then gently kissing my lips as he whispers, "Fuckin' hell Feist, you gotta stop this crazy shit, I ain't havin' you hurt", and as I look up into his worried brown eyes, I feel a momentary panic that has absolutely nothing to do with injuries or fights.

I want Gio to be the one kissing me, not you.

But Gio is backing away, muttering, "I'll see you later Roberts, get that head looked at yeah?".

I spin too quickly, making my head dizzy and my neck hurt as I blurt out, "Gio, don't go. I want to…..I need to say thank you, for helping me. For….for getting him off me", Gio just nods sadly.

Miss. Harvey panics when I arrive in the medical room after hours, bruised and bloodied with a strange male in tow. My head is merely a nasty scratch, the result of an abrupt arrival on the gravel. No stitches needed and a quick rinse and spritz with the iodine sees me sorted. My bruises on my arms, my neck and legs she can do little about but she asks me to go and see a doctor about my neck. I notice the covert looks she throws Jay and the slight blush on her cheeks. *For God's sake.*

Mr. Gibson with Lees, Gio and Ad flanking him, arrives in the sick bay shortly afterwards. Lees hugs me and holds my hand as the boys shuffle awkwardly.

"And who the hell are you?", Mr. Gibson looks Jay up and down.

Jay cocks an eyebrow and rumbles out, "I'm Erin's boyfriend", his eyes dart to me, this is the first time he's called himself that and it makes me feel a bit weird.

Mr. Gibson tuts, "Well, after today's little episode, you can consider yourself banned from site. There will be no unauthorised *boyfriends* on school premises for either Miss. Morris or Miss. Roberts from now on. Are you an associate of this as mystery, injured, disappearing male whose name neither Miss. Morris nor Mr. Jones strangely appear able to recollect? This male who I believe your *girlfriend* assaulted before becoming a victim herself?", Mr. Gibson raises his eyebrows at Jay.

Jay smirks, "Nah man, I got nothing to do wiv that fucker but me and him will have a little meet up soon I reckon", Jay looks at Gio and Ad, both of whom nod curtly at him.

Mr. Gibson scowls, "Charming. Right, in the absence of any grievances lodged, injured parties seeking redress or the cares that I frankly do not give, you are all dismissed. Miss. Roberts, if you wish to speak with the police regarding the injuries that you have sustained, please appraise me of this immediately", he raises an eyebrow in question and I shake my head, conscious that I would have to admit to the police that I started the fight and that isn't ideal.

Mr. Gibson nods firmly, "Right, do not ever repeat this sort of behaviour you lot and young man", he turns to Jay, "I do not wish to ever encounter you on my school premises again. Mr. Romano, as you managed to restrain the effervescent Miss. Roberts so skilfully earlier, you may consider a favourable UCAS reference dependent on your ability to ensure that she aggravates me no further whilst on this school's roll. Now bugger off, all of you".

As we leave the room, I hear Jay mumble something to Gio to which both Ad and Gio respond with nods and more mumbles. Jay takes my hand, wrapping his arm around me as we leave and with Gio offering to drop Ad and Lees home, we part ways, Gio's sad gaze meeting mine as we walk away.

In the car, begging his discretion, I tell Jay what Kiron did to Lees. Jay's jaw clamps and he looks furious.

"He hurt my Lees, Jay and then he tried to hurt her again. I couldn't let him get away with that", Jay just nods and holds my hand in between gear changes.

Word has already reached my brother by the time we get home, the grapevine a truly astonishing thing. He and Jay immediately fall into secretive chats which go silent whenever I come back in the room. My neck bruises concealed in a scarf and elaborate hair-styling, I manage to escape my mother becoming cognizant of my little foray into cage-fighting.

22nd March 1997

Dyls comes home from training, grinning like a lunatic. Over dinner, he blurts out,

"Rinny, you know that sprinter Kiron that Lees used to go out with? Well, he's had a bit of *bad luck*. Turns out, somebody tried to steal his car or something last night after training and he's proper banged up. They took baseball bats to him, he's got broken arms and a busted leg, his jaw and his nose are broken and Coach said that they proper smashed up his car, a write off apparently. Three big blokes he said, all in hoods and ski- masks. Nasty. He'll miss training for *months* and because he can't write, they don't know if he'll be able to sit his exams", Dyls shakes his head, stuffing food in his face with a *'what can you do?'* expression.

Mum starts talking about how awful it is, that poor boy, how the world is a dangerous place, blah blah. I however have turned to look at my *boyfriend*, who is animatedly fussing over our two high-chair occupying sons and I see the furtive smirks exchanged between my brother and he. My family distracted, I hiss under my breath,

"Where were you last night?", my eyebrow is raised.

Jay turns and shrugs but his smirk is a give-away, "I was just hanging out wiv' Obi and D, Feist. Y'know, brother stuff, we even played a bit of baseball", and with a wink, he turns back to fuss over our sons.

I literally don't know whether to laugh or cry.

That night, under my duvet, Jay strokes my skin as he kisses me gently, demonstrating a tenderness that we haven't really engaged in before. It makes me feel slightly uncomfortable, I'm not sure how I feel about it and he whispers against my skin,

"Feist, maybe you should come up town wiv' me, for my birthday?", his eyes meet mine in the darkness.

This is *big*. Jay's twentieth birthday which falls exactly a week before my seventeenth, is being celebrated with his brothers and his friends in Bristol. People I have never met, people who will mark my entrance into Jay's world. Dion, a pretty influential and popular character judging from Jay's comments, has organised some sort of trip to a club and Jay has been the closest thing to giddy that I've seen him when he talks about the night, it seems that the plans suggest that the friends and family members who were pissed off with him for the issues with the dealers may finally be offering Jay forgiveness.

I genuinely did not expect him to ask me, maybe that's odd? We sleep together several times a week, we share twin sons, he seems to be comfortable with my family and my home, we ring each other every day when we are apart and he does introduce himself as my 'boyfriend' but I never presume any sort of claim over him. A lady at work, who I don't know very well, asked me, *"Are you going out with your boyfriend tonight love?'.* I genuinely started saying, *"Oh, I don't have a boyfriend"* when I realised that this is not true. I laughed and corrected my mistake, blurting out that I'd forgotten that I *do* have a boyfriend and we actually have six-month-old twins together. She looked at me like I was mental and pretended to have a job to attend to. As I stared at the deli counter, I realised that when she'd said the word 'boyfriend', it had been Gio's face that I had linked to the word and *I don't have Gio.*

To be fair though, the idea of a cool night out in Bristol does appeal to me and it probably is time that I met his brothers. I smile happily and nod, leading to a responding grin and then some sweaty, naked silliness that ends up with us on the carpet as I ride Jay with our hands clapped over each other's mouths to prevent noise.

Jay's phone pings in the early hours of the morning, waking me. Whatever the message said, it makes his whole body tense and as he angrily throws on his t-shirt and boxers and goes to the loo, I reach over and press the button that illuminates his screen.

"It was a year ago J, sometimes I can't believe it went down the way it did. I wish every day that things were different, I miss you so much. Is it OK to be there Saturday? D and Megs said I should come. Text me xxx"

I turn it off and roll back over. I know who the text is from. *Case.*

I fall asleep but it's blue eyes, safe hands and dark curls that fill my head.

Chapter Ten

29th March 1997

I've never been this far away from the twins, *ever*. There is a motorway and towns and cities between me and my babies and I don't think I can handle it to be honest. I have rung Mum twice already on Jay's phone to check on them and Jay had to pull over at the last motorway junction because I didn't think I could see this through, I thought I needed to go back.

Mum was a bit weird when I asked if I could spend the night out with Jay in Bristol and if she could babysit. I had a fair bit of sympathy to be honest. I'm sixteen, Jay is now twenty, I don't know any of the people I'm going out with aside from my boyfriend and he has a fairly recent history of drug-dealing in the city in which we are to frequent. If I fast-forwarded sixteen years, I think that if Jake or AJ asked me the same question, I'd probably be saying 'no'.

However, Mum and Jay have a sort of peaceable truce thing going on. Mum went out with him, the day of 'Kiron-gate', to a baby activity session and it marked a turning point for their relationship. He's still scared shitless of her mind you, he accidentally groaned loudly on Wednesday night when I made him come *really* hard and he genuinely slept with one eye open the whole night, terrified that my mother would come in and de-bollock him.

Jay has been patient with my rambling as we head to Bristol but he's clearly pissed off, we're supposed to be meeting his brothers and friends at Dion's flat in less than an hour and I've been flapping about turning around and potentially adding at least another ninety minutes to his journey. He listened silently and then growled out,

"Look, are you fuckin' comin' or what Feist? Eh? I got no time for this shit tonight, I got people waitin' on us", his teeth kiss and frown make me feel a bit foolish.

I nod rapidly, contemplating what the night might hold. A few minutes later, he reaches over and takes my hand.

"They'll be OK y'know, those little bastards know better than to play up for your Mum", his smile, in this dark car, is so unbelievably gorgeous, set in that face that I genuinely can't believe sleeps next to mine voluntarily and I take a moment to appreciate what I have.

I smile at him and turn the radio up.

We enter the built up landscape of the city, busy streets and slick neon lights. I had a massive, epic panic about what to wear tonight. In a moment of unfettered madness I found myself talking to Carolyn Gregory at school last week as I perched beside Gio and Ad at lunchtime. I asked her advice and was pleasantly surprised when she gave me a small smile and some reluctant but genuinely useful help, even flicking through magazines to show me what to buy. As a result, I am now wearing possibly the coolest outfit I've ever managed.

My body changed after the boys were born. I lost a lot of weight from breast-feeding and then I've been a bit too frazzled to put the weight back, the boys routine means that meal times are often on the hoof, eating one handed not conducive to an overloaded plate. Jay, in our protected little duvet world, whispers things that make me believe that my body might be desirable but I struggle to match this with *rank, ugly ginger Roberts*. I have my scar and a couple of weird little ripples at the bottom of my belly, like it sort of melted a bit and I have a set of purple stretch marks under my belly button. My boobs are a different shape, a bit more bottom heavy than they were. Jay tells me he appreciates them with enough enthusiasm that I'm not too worried but tonight, in my basque top, black lycra hip-hugging trousers and the Fila trainers I bought with advance birthday money, I feel insecure.

We pull down roads lined with Victorian terraces, some small and cottage-like, some tall and thin. All of them are universally dilapidated and a bit menacing looking to a country girl from a semi.

"Tha's my place there", Jay points at one of the taller Victorian houses and I swivel in my seat, keen to see where my boyfriend spends the majority of his life.

Jay turns the car and the shift in the style buildings is acute. Several storeys high, the block of flats that he parks in front of has coloured panels in an attempt to gussy-up the drab pebble-dash façade. The windows are small and square with a tangle of railings going off in all different directions.

Jay turns to me, his whole body language transmitting the same nervousness that I feel. With rueful smiles, we close in for a kiss and there is something wonderfully comforting in this snog. Jay deepens it first, his tongue stroking mine soothingly as his hand tugs my loose curls. As his other bold paw has a little grope of my Lycra-clad tits, I feel his smile twitch against my lips,

"We're gonna have a good night tonight Feist", he pulls back and smirks at me, that scarred eyebrow looking unbelievably cheeky.

I smile and wink at him, "Happy Birthday bruv", as he laughs and with a final kiss, we leave the car.

My heart is in my mouth as Jay leads me through bleach-smelling stairwells and fluorescent-orange lit corridors. As we reach a battered white PVC doorway, Jay wraps his arm over my shoulder and as the door opens and a wave of voices and music hits me, I hold my breath.

"Bruv, you will be fuckin' late for your own funeral, swear down", a tall guy with his hair in cornrows stands at the door.

Judging by his resemblance to Jay, I have to assume that this is Dion, confirmed when an impossibly pretty girl approaches from behind him asking,

"D, you seen my bag man, can't find it nowhere and…...Jay, you fuckin' made it then and…….oh, this her?", the fierce looking blonde, her hair in a high ponytail, looks me up and down before looking at Jay for her answer. I feel my eye twitch at the brutal slight.

Jay's arm around my shoulder pulls me closer and his voice is tight, "This is Erin, D we comin' in or wha'?", Jay moves, taking my hand as his brother stands back with a sarcastic flourish to allow us to pass.

I look up at D with a nervous smile and squeak out, *"Hi"*, as I get a nod in response. I smile weakly at the blonde girl but she just quirks an eyebrow, still looking me up and down.

The hallway walls of this slightly steamy flat are filled with photos, mainly of a beautiful little girl as well as lots of photos of D and the blonde girl together and lots of group shots. I see a lot with Jay in them, in several his arm is slung possessively over a stunning brunette with a shy smile.

As we enter the lounge, I am overwhelmed with things to absorb. The room is pretty *statement,* with a black and chrome theme that runs through the furniture, décor and soft furnishings. It looks like a magazine shoot. In the room are a lot of people for a pretty average sized lounge. There are several lads, a few girls and oddly a middle-aged lady in a dressing gown.

"Look who decided to finally show up eh Ma", the blonde girl shouts from behind us and the middle aged lady, whose ill-advised jet-black hair dye and suspicious glare makes her look like a pissed off crow, looks up at Jay,

"Well, Jamel, it's been a while?", her tone suggests that she's not that chuffed to see Jay. Through his hand, I feel his body tense.

He grinds out, "Hi Sash".

The lady sits back on the sofa and folds her arms, "So this is her, hey? What's your name love?", she looks at me with interest.

Before I can speak, blondie pushes past us, her incredible bum vacuum packed into a tiny miniskirt, distractedly looking for something as she talks, "It's *Erin*. D, where the fuck is my bag, eh? Obi, you seen my bag?", at that name, I look over to see who it applies to and am relieved to see a more friendly expression greeting me.

A tall but stocky lad with very dark toned skin and short braids jumps to his feet and comes over, "Megs, why the fuck would I have your bag girl? Hey Erin, I'm Obi", I sag with relief at his kind smile and beam back at him.

He smiles again, "Gotta say girl, I heard you ain't to be messed wiv. Wheels here", he nods at Jay, "He told us 'bout you takin' on lads and fuckin' smokin' them, you're a proper Bruce Lee I heard. I'm gonna watch my back tonight yeah?", he nudges me gently with a big smile and I relax slightly, laughing and rolling my eyes.

"How fuckin' old are you anyway?", I jolt from my smile as *Megs,* arms crossed and looking me up and down, directs her first question to me.

I feel my temper rising, I feel my Chopsy-ometer starting to peak as my lip curls and I hiss, "Old enough not to lose important shit like my handbag", as I raise an eyebrow and throw her a challenging look.

Obi whoops with laughter next to me, smacking Jay in the chest and muttering, "Happy fuckin' Birthday Wheels, this one is gonna be off the hook I reckon", he snorts again.

As *Megs* and her *Ma* exchange meaningful looks my way, D comes over, "Erin, been hearin' lots 'bout you from Wheels, hear my nephews are proper cute. Maybe you can get them over yeah? Meet their cousin, my little princess Kaydee?", D points to a picture of the gorgeous little girl on the wall.

I smile, "She's beautiful, I'd love the twins to meet her. Is she in bed?", I am relieved by his pleasantness but *Megs* quickly swoops in.

"Course she is, why, your *kids* usually up this time of night, eh?", there's real confrontation in her tone and feeling lost, I look up at Jay, silently pleading for rescue.

His face is frowning so deeply he looks like he's snarling, "Back off yeah Megan" but she smiles in a sinister way and walks towards him,

"Back off? That should be me sayin' it to you, yeah *Wheels*? I know you dragged him", she thumbs at D, "into shit again last week, he come back stupid late wiv' a fuckin' bat and I knew it was to do wiv' you but we're all gonna play nice, pretend like last year never fuckin' happened? She'll be there tonight y'know? After all the shit you put her through, all the fuckin' harm you did her and the pain you caused, she still wants to see you, wants to be your *mate"*, Megan crosses her arms over her chest and nods at her Ma, who is looking equally judgemental.

I am lost in what feels like a soap opera that I tuned into half way through the series. I have not the first clue what is going on here other than I am about as welcome as a dose of Herpes and Jay, or rather *Wheels*, comes a close runner up it appears. Right now, I don't think I have ever, *ever* wanted out of somewhere more than I want out of this flat.

I blurt out, "Jay, I'm gonna go. I.....I think I should leave", Jay looks down at me in confusion, as I pull away and walk back down the hallway towards the door.

"FEIST, you don't know this manor, where the fuck you going?", Jay trots after me, a restraining hand on my arm.

I go to respond but I hear shouting coming from the lounge, D is shouting at Megan and it sounds major. I suddenly realise that I would pay any amount of money for Gio Romano to walk through that door and carry me off from here. I would sell a few vital organs, I might even donate a twin depending on their behaviour. *I just want out.*

"Feist? Don't go", Jay looks a bit broken and when he raises those brown eyes to mine, I feel a throb of affection and concern for him as he whispers, "You're the only one on my side here, yeah? I need you girl", as he sweeps me into a hug that makes me wobble as my arms cling to his broad back.

I whisper in his ear, "What's her problem?", and he pulls back, chewing his lip.

"C'mon", Jay pulls me by the hand into a bedroom off the corridor and shuts the door behind us.

This is clearly D and Megan's bedroom, clothes and makeup everywhere and a strong mist of perfume still settling in the air.

Jay leans back against the door, his arms folded as he mumbles his way through my portal into his world,

"So, Megs and D been together since school days, like *forever*. Megs has a little sister, Case, er, Casey", Jay swallows thickly and looks at the ceiling as he continues, "When I moved down here from Mum's, Case was the first kid from my year that I met and me and her, we was like a team. The four of us an' Obi, that was it. Them girls, they lived with Sash 'cross the corridor from ours, we was like family, we are family now, wiv D and Megs havin' Kaydee", he sighs and closes his eyes.

"Me and Case, we got together when we were kids too, fourteen. She was the one that helped me, y'know, when it all went fuckin' to shit wiv' my Pops. She's.......she was the only girlfriend I ever had", Jay is nodding and looking at his feet now.

"But Case, she's a proper good girl, she did good at school like Obi, she never got in shit like me and D. She broke up wiv me when we was sixteen coz I was bein' a little prick and she didn't want the drama no more. That's when I got in with the boys nicking motors and stuff and I got sent down the first time", Jay takes a deep breath.

"I made her and my Iya promises when I was inside and when I come out, we got back together and it was proper good. I moved in at hers when we was seventeen, Sash let me move into their flat", I feel a stab of weirdness in my chest. I wouldn't describe it as jealousy, it's almost disappointment but Jay carries on, "Then Case started on 'bout bein' a midwife, going to Uni and shit. Nobody from her family never did that before, she was the proper star", his voice goes quiet.

"But in the end she never went far. She stayed local, she stayed here for Uni *for me* but I got myself proper prick jealous 'bout her new mates and that. We started havin' tough times at Christmas, rowin' and stressin' and that's when I went out wiv' them boys one night when we'd been proper screwin' at each other and I started with the dealin'", As he speaks, I feel a few jigsaw puzzle pieces click in my head.

"You started dealing at *her* Uni?", I whisper and he looks at me for the first time, his eyes sad as he nods.

"See, I'd used her student ID card to get into places wiv'out her knowing and when shit went down wiv' the Uni over me dealin' there, she got pulled in, put on warnings 'bout not bein' able to be a midwife student if she was *associatin'* with a suspected dealer, put on the banned list. Case, she ain't never been in trouble, she's a real good girl. It fuckin' *killed* her, she was proper shamed", Jay's shaking his head and he slumps slowly towards the floor.

"The week or so before that rave where you and me met, Case broke up wiv' me, she told me that she never wanted to see me again. I went to stay at my Iya's again. Case told me to get the fuck out her life, said she was going to look to go to another Uni and just get far fuckin' away from me. She meant it too an' it proper screwed me up, coz Case, she was…..her an' me...what we had", Jay's shaking his head, his face a study in abject misery and I am compelled to walk over to him, sitting on the floor by his side.

He reaches for my hand and looks at me, "That night, wiv you, you gotta know that it ain't somethin' I'd done before. Coz Feist, swear down, I'd only ever been wiv' Case before. I…….I was just so fucked off wiv everythin' and you, you looked so amazin' that night and you just didn't give a shit. You looked like how I felt. I liked that", he smiles at me and I press a kiss to his lips as his frown returns,

"Feist, you gotta believe me, I never meant to fuck things up for her, I…….she's….", he growls in frustration and bangs his head back against the door.

I reach for his hand again as he looks at me, "They went after her, them boys, when I got busted and lost their gear, they went after Case at the flat. They broke in at Sash's and trashed the place. They took all her stuff, took her computer wiv her Uni work on it and they…...they…...they fuckin' hurt her", and that is when I see Jay Watson break and it scares me.

He's got his hands fisted so tight and they are pressed painfully into his eye sockets but I know that underneath that fury, are tears. Panicked and out of my depth, I pull him into me, my body wrapped around him in a way that is increasingly familiar and I let my boyfriend take comfort from me because his stupid, foolhardy actions caused devastation and harm to the girl he loved.

Rapidly composing himself and looking embarrassed, Jay tells me how D, avenging his badly shaken sister-in-law on behalf of his incarcerated brother and horrified girlfriend, gathered up associates and called in every favour that he'd accrued during his misspent youth. Debts were repaid in kind, vengeance was sought but it thrust D back into a world that he and Megan had apparently fought so hard to leave behind. Megan blames Jay for the collapse of her sister's happiness and her bright future, as well as blaming Jay for Sasha's flat being burgled and the risks D placed himself in to clear Jay's debts. Casey left Uni. She has not gone back to her midwifery course and is instead working in a bank.

Jay left prison, his Iya having recently died, to find a family who blamed him for everything that had happened to Casey and D, a childhood sweetheart whose heart and life was in tatters because of his terrible choices and a stranger who had given birth to his twins.

And here we now are. *Jesus Christ.*

We've been in this bedroom for at least ten minutes and voices outside sound agitated and impatient. I'm still absorbing the enormity of the things Jay has told me, the mysteries that have shaped this boy that I sleep with. He looks ruined, his head slumped over his bent knees, his earring glinting in the gloom.

I clear my throat and whisper into the soft felt of his immaculately barbered hair, "Jay, you're not that person now. The mistakes you made, they…..they're not you now. You're this amazing Dad and this caring guy and I don't believe for one minute that you meant to hurt anyone. You're a good guy Jay", at my words his gaze meets mine, his eyes soft and vulnerable looking.

He croaks, "Me an' you Feist, we're like the *same*. We get into crazy shit, end up *causin'* shit when we don't fuckin' mean to", he shakes his head ruefully and I wince at the accuracy of what he's said.

He cups my face, "Them two babies, me an' you gonna raise them right and make them good people. Tha's our job, like a fuckin' team me an' you Feist, we're gonna stay out the madness and do right by those boys, not like my fuckin' Mum or my prick Pops. They're all tha' fucking matters, yeah, me an' you doin' right by them", my lip wobbles as I nod and Jay pulls me into a kiss that is part pact, part salvation.

We emerge from the bedroom, wobbly but clinging to our mutual team-mate like a limpet.

"Bruv, can we please get our asses up that club now? If I don't find me some action tonight, my dick's gonna give the fuck up and fall off, you get me?", Obi appears from the kitchen, scowling comically.

Jay snorts beside me as D approaches, his expression weary. He pulls Jay into a hug and then pulls back, holding Jay at arms length, "Megs, she's all fuckin' mouth. Them times, they're over bruv", D darts a glance at me before looking back to Jay, "Wheels, we're done wiv this shit, I can't have it no more. Past is past", he nods decisively and I feel Jay relax.

D slings a ridiculously large arm over my shoulder, "Now sweetness, you wanna tell me how little Wheels here landed this hotness *and* two baby boys? Little fucker gets all the damn luck an' me? I just get lost handbags, narky bitches and Princess Dolls and him", D jerks a thumb at Obi, "He gets fuck all coz he looks like a fuckin' wheelie bin wiv braids", with a roar of outrage, Obi launches at his bigger brother and I step out of the line of fire, laughing as the three brothers play-wrestle, banging doors and walls.

Sasha appears in her dressing gown, arms folded, "Go on you three, fuck off before you wake that little girl up and I have to skin the lot of you", and with a terse nod at me, Sasha goes back to the lounge.

The others, Megan included, headed to the club while Jay and I were in the bedroom so the four of us squeeze into Jay's Fiesta.

I'm shocked when D gestures at me to get in the front seat but as he, Jay and Obi banter, I enjoy listening to Jay's relaxed, funny chat with his brothers. He's definitely seen as the *'baby'*, the nickname *'Wheels'* the result of his first word and his life-long obsession with cars. His brief career as a car thief added a certain irony to the moniker.

"So sweetness, you reckon I need to wipe off that bat tonight, eh? You gonna take on any more big lads?", D's leaning forward and I turn to grimace at him.

I mutter, "I still can't believe you did that, that you went all that way just to wallop him", I shake my head as D tuts and I look at him,

D pats my arm, "Nobody messes wiv our family and you're family now, you gave this little twat two kids", he punches Jay's arm and he swears at his brother, smiling at me as I blush.

Jay pulls us into a roadside space, only a few minutes after setting off. The Club is an eclectic looking warehouse by a main road, covered in graffiti art and with a long queue formed outside the arched entrance. Jay, dressed in an achingly cool outfit of Moschino jeans, tight white t-shirt, black bomber jacket and thick gold chain, takes me by the hand and leads me across the road, Obi and D swaggering behind.

The boys get greeted by the bouncers and several randoms with fist and shoulder bumps, the queue bypassed as we are ushered in. The music is the loudest I have ever heard and the beat genuinely affects the rhythm of my heart. I cling to Jay and feel a warm glow when I feel his thumb rubbing the side of my hand, soothing me.

At a bar, Jay buys me a drink, laughing when I clearly have no idea what I want. He gets me luridly coloured alcopop although as I scan around, most people are drinking water. He leans against the bar, pulling me against his chest with his arms wrapped protectively around me as he chats with his brothers and introduces me to the people who were in the lounge at D's flat earlier, ex-schoolmates of the three boys apparently.

It seems that after fleeing a racist step-father and negligent mother in Birmingham, Jay moved into a complex paternal household which included Dion who is four years older than Jay and who had moved to live with his Dad a couple of years before Jay did. The household also included Obi but *not* Obi's Mum. Obi's Nigerian Mum has lived and worked abroad for years, her marriage to Jay's Dad somehow overlapping the entirety of his relationship with Jay and Dion's white British Mum.

Obi has always lived with his Dad, his Mum had moved to the States for work when he was very young. Obi is two years older than Jay and he works in marketing having got a degree at the old Polytechnic. The boys joke about how Obi is the 'Golden Child'. The boys gently tease Jay that he is regarded as anything *but*.

D wanders off and I see him approach another group, the admittedly stunning Megan easy to spot with her mane of blonde hair. Jay swears softly under his breath and I feel him nestle his face into my crazy curls. I see several brunettes in the group as Obi notes Jay's discomfort,

"Wheels, it's now or never bruv. You told Ginger here?", he nods meaningfully at me and I feel Jay nod behind me.

Casey.

I turn to an uncomfortable looking Jay, "Look, why don't you go over and have a chat with them all without me to start with, eh? I reckon Obi needs all the Wing Woman help he can get tonight anyway", I turn to Obi and wink at him, making him chuckle.

Obi nods, taking my hand with an elaborate flourish and leading me to the dance floor, Jay looking beseechingly as I leave. Obi shouts back at him, "Man the fuck up bruv", before leading me into the hot, sweaty wall of noise.

The music is *amazing,* the beat forcing me to move and although I get sweeping waves of anxiety about the twins and how they might be faring back at home, this music entices me and with Obi's jokey encouragement and friendly banter, we dance together for ages. I spot a particularly pretty Asian girl who is clearly checking Obi out and with some silent signalling, I manoeuvre us so that Obi ends up dancing next to her and *poof*, my work is done.

Dancing solo doesn't bother me. I wonder briefly if I should be more agitated by the whole Casey thing, whether my encouragement of Jay to approach her is weird. I ponder on the lack of jealousy I feel. When I see Gio kiss Carolyn, it *hurts*. It hurts in my lungs somehow, it makes it hard to breath. It makes me feel this rush of *loss,* unentitled as I am to feel any sort of claim over Gio but right now, I can't seem to tap into that sort of emotion with regards to the situation with Jay and Casey. I mentally shrug and I give my worries over to the music.

I open my eyes and see Obi with his arms wrapped around the grinning girl, he winks at me and I return it with a knowing nod. I catch the eye of a blonde lad to my left and although I offer no smile, he grins at me and approaches, dancing in my space. He's inoffensive and his face looks kind and in my solo state, I dance happily enough with him.

I look across the room and I see D first, his tall frame easy to spot. Jay's head is bowed as he talks with a brunette, it's all I can see from this distance. I suddenly feel like I want to leave, that I'm *intruding* somehow by being here. Smiling apologetically at the blonde lad, I head for where I presume the loos are located. In the dark, dilapidated and crowded toilets, I manage to grab a stall and sit on the loo, contemplating whether it would be acceptable to just fuck off and get on a train. *Gio would collect me from the station if I asked him.* I feel a wave of tears as I suddenly want to cuddle my boys, I want to hold their little sleepy bodies against mine and kiss their heads and feel that sense that I *belong*.

I am *never* more sure of myself than when those babies look up at me, when they lock eyes with me and the three of us are together. I can read them better than any book, I accurately predict their reactions to things, I know them like I know nothing else on the face of this earth, AJ and Jake Roberts are my Mastermind specialist subject.

I am plotting how best to extract myself from this club when I hear a voice on the other side of the stall door that even in our brief acquaintance, has become familiar in it's slightly shrill, nasal, Bristolian burr.

"He's so full of it Case, he gives you those pretty boy cow-eyes and you just fuckin' forget all the shit he's pulled. You met her yet? I ain't seen the fuckin' gobby little bitch since we got here, maybe she didn't get in, I don't reckon she's eighteen yet y'know. He ever tell you how old she is?", I hear Megs snort.

Then a soft voice, it's burr more gentle, "No, I never asked him but I think she is young, he said something about that lad punching her at her Sixth Form college so I guess yeah, she's eighteen max"

I hear another tut, "Fuck man, twins when you're just a kid? See, that's exactly the sort of shit that Jay pulls, he's fuckin' screwed up her life with his *mistakes* like he fucked up yours and he don't give the smallest little shit", I am not aware that I've jumped up and exited the stall until my door bangs.

Staring at a startled Megan, my arms folded, I growl out, "My sons are nobody's fucking *mistake* and

Jay, he *does* give a shit, he's a brilliant Dad. What if I called your Kaydee a mistake, eh?", Megan has the good grace to look embarrassed as she sucks her teeth and looks away.

"I didn't know you were there….we didn't mean", there's that soft voice again and I slowly turn to see what sort of threat I face.

She's beautiful, not surprising when you consider her similarly stunning sibling. Taller than me, slender, glossy brunette hair in a sheet down her back and her delicate features pinched in an agony of discomfort, Casey is the sort of pretty that makes you think she's a skincare model. She's dressed in a beautiful sort of draped mini-dress and in my trainers and basque top, I feel like a proper *kid* next to her. This is Jay's childhood sweetheart. This is Jay's *Case.*

She looks so uncomfortable that I worry the sparkle on her lashes is actually tears and I weirdly feel guilty that I have made this gentle looking soul upset. In typical fashion, I blunder on,

"Sorry, I didn't mean to y'know, *attack.* You're Casey yeah? I'm Erin", I smile gently at her, wanting to make her feel less awkward. I feel a wave of relief when she smiles softly and whispers,

"Yeah, I'm Casey, it's nice to meet you Erin", she smiles sadly and adds, "Your babies are gorgeous, we've all seen the pictures that Jay's got" and I can't help the grin I give her, my babies *are* gorgeous.

Behind me comes an accusing, "C'mon then, how fucking old are you, eh?", my grin turns into a scowl as I turn to an eyebrow-raised *Megs.*

Folding my arms over my chest, Chopsy comes out to play, "What the fuck does it matter to you? You got some alcohol you need me to buy or something?", I cock an eyebrow at Megan and I hear a gentle cough of laughter from Casey

Ignoring whatever comeback Megan may come out with, I turn again to Casey, "She", I thumb at her sister, "was wrong about Jay. He's still proper devastated about what happened with you…..the Uni stuff and the er, the dealers and you getting hurt", both girls gasp, clearly not expecting me to be this well informed.

I look at Casey, silently urging her to believe me, "He does care Casey, *a lot"*, as she lowers her head, nodding, I see her lip wobble and I feel like I need to give her privacy, even if that means leaving her with her bitch sister.

"I need to go, it was nice to meet *you* Casey", I throw a meaningful sneer at Megan who looks furious as I walk towards the door. I turn after a few steps, "I'm turning seventeen next week *Megan* so you'll need to find somebody else to buy your booze", and with a wink, I leave, an astonished hiss of *"Fuckin' hell"* following my departure.

I don't see Jay or his brothers anywhere, I grab somebody's wrist and their watch informs me that a train home is not an option any more. I am stuck here, feeling like an uninvited guest at a wedding. So I dance. I find a little corner, tucked away and I let the music take my body and my mind and I dance until I'm sweaty and my skin fizzes in bliss. I feel hands touch me, trying to invite their attentions but I don't even look their way and they back off. I am unconcerned that I have lost all and any of the people I came here with, I just enjoy the hard, heavy beats that this DJ is dropping.

In my head, my eyes closed, I see Gio's smile, my touch memory conjures his warm hand in mine and I remember his kiss as my visual memory throws me images of his bare chest that make me tingle. *Very inconvenient.*

"Feist, where the fuck you been girl?", I am jolted from my dance subspace by Jay, my eyes flying open to see his good-looking face slightly aggravated.

He gestures around, "I've been lookin' for you for like two fuckin' hours, Obi said you'd gone off wiv some blonde bloke hours ago, what the fuck?", Jay looks genuinely angry and I'm confused.

I shake my head, baffled, "Nooooo, I went to the loo but I left that lad on the dance floor, I dunno who he was. I met.....I met Casey and Megan in the loo", I smile weakly and I see Jay's face fall.

He gently pulls me against the wall, the music volume making chat difficult, "Case......she just left, she went to meet her mates somewhere else", Jay shrugs feigning indifference but you can almost taste his hurt.

He looks up at me, "Wha' did she say?"

I reach for his hand, "Jay, she's really sweet isn't she? She said that the boys were gorgeous and that was about it. She's really pretty Jay, you *used* to have good taste", I smile self-deprecatingly but he just looks sad, no smile forthcoming.

I sigh, my eyes rolling, "Megan seemed interested to know how old I was, I guess you haven't talked that much about er, *me?* ", I'm not really offended, I'm just interested.

Jay leans against the wall, hands deep in pockets, "Yeah well, they got enough shit to throw my way yeah, don't need to add in that I was a fuckin' cradle robber, eh?", he huffs out a breath.

I raise my eyebrows and shrug, "Well, they know now".

Jay kisses his teeth and looks at the ceiling, shaking his head ruefully.

"Are you *actually* having a good time tonight Jay?", the question bursts from my lips before I really process it.

He looks up startled, shrugging and looking baffled.

I throw my hands up, "Riiiight, well, it's your birthday so, y'know, you should probably be having actual *fun*", I look around and see Obi chatting up his girl at the bar, "C'mon you", I grab his hand and pull him reluctantly towards his brother.

In a series of events that makes Obi chortle, I demand that Jay downs two shots of tequila (I've never had it but I understand that it is a *thing* people do to celebrate) and I then start singing happy birthday to him, causing him to look *mortified* but then the whole bar queue joins in and he gets a free drink, downing it with a wry smile on his lips.

Introducing myself to Aisha, the girl Obi's pulled, I drag us all to the dance floor and using one of the large metal floor-to-ceiling posts as a prop, I channel the daftness that Lees and I engage in together and I faux-pole dance and mess about in a way that makes Obi roar with laughter and join in. Aisha, shy though she appears to be, also laughs and reluctantly joins us. Jay smiles and although he's *far too cool* to allow himself to look daft, he starts to dance and his whole posture relaxes.

"Obi man, wha' the fuck you doin' now?", a deep voice shouts behind us as D and bloody Megan approach.

Obi pulls me into a hug before lifting me aloft, making me squawk with shock, "THIS girl, she's fuckin' off the hook man, she's wild. Wheels, he's got himself a proper nutter", Obi lowers me down and dances animatedly as D looks boggled and Megan looks like she's sucking lemons.

I turn to Jay and see him smiling lopsidedly. He's *ridiculously* fit this boy I get to call my *boyfriend*, a quick glance around identifies at least three girls who are unashamedly checking him out but right now, he's smiling at me and he looks like he might *possibly* be having fun.

With Aisha back in Obi's arms, I cheekily beckon at Jay, who rolls his eyes but saunters over, wrapping his arms around me as we dance together. This is different, as the music takes me back towards subspace, I feel a heat building between Jay and I. He's a really good dancer and as our bodies move together, in a synchronisation that I didn't think we could replicate outside of my bedroom, he lowers his head to mine and pulls me close,

"I'm havin' fun y'know Feist", I feel his lips move against my ear as I smirk.

I turn slightly so that my lips brush his cheek, "Makes a nice change you miserable fucker", and with a chuckle of amusement, Jay Watson pulls me into a kiss that makes my knees weak.

We are proper snogging, our first affection since the flat. Jay feels familiar and oddly comforting which is weird frankly, given the mismatched hotness of him and the daftness of me.

He presses kisses to my lips and face as he whispers, "You an' me Feist, we handle shit together yeah, me an' you? Same team, yeah?", and the pleading in his voice makes me whisper, *"Yes"*, as he groans and deepens the kiss.

We separate eventually, turning to see Obi and Aisha having a snog of their own as D and Megan look at Jay and I with matching frowns.

Jay and I spend the rest of the night within touching distance. If we're not dancing together, he's cuddling or kissing me or I'm being held in the cradle of his legs as we lean against the wall, chatting to Obi who is at real risk of becoming one of my favourite people *ever*. Frowning Megan watches me the whole time, it would be unsettling if I didn't have lots of things to distract me.

The music is brilliant, at one point I drag Jay to a balcony and dance with abandon as he watches me smirking. I feel his hands snake around my waist as he whispers in my ear,

"You look like you did that night at the rave, Feist. C'mon girl,", and Jay takes my hand and forcefully takes me through to the back corner of the top floor and with a shifty look around, kicks open a fire door.

I find myself outside, the cold March air making my skin goosebump immediately as Jay's warm, firm body presses me against the damp brick wall of the fire escape balcony and he kisses me like he and I just got away with a bank robbery.

I grip at him, wanting this, wanting to be wanted, wanting to lose myself in the possibility that this is real. Jay's eyebrows raised in question, I nod as he gently pulls down my lycra trousers, a wholly undignified affair. He fumbles with his jeans as his other hand does *very* wicked things inside my knickers. As he moves them to the side and slowly pushes his sizeable length into me, he clutches me close, growling into my ear,

"Fuck Feist, me and you, we're so fuckin' good together. This here is so good yeah, you an' me together, it's the bomb yeah", and in that moment, I wonder who he's trying to convince.

In some ways, he's not wrong though. I struggle to believe that there are many lads who could make sex feel as good as he does and his gasps and groans as I squeeze and writhe suggest that I might not be without skills myself. His fingers twiddle my clit and despite the chilled arses and the precarious hold that supports my weight in his arms, we manage the elusive simultaneous orgasm.

Chuckling into each other's necks and eventually righting our clothing, we share gentle kisses and head back inside.

Later that night, as I lie in *his* bed, in the run-down bedsit that made me want to cry when I saw its bleak shabbiness, Jay Watson and I cling close.

He whispers, "We got a good thing, yeah Erin, this is real me an' you an' the boys? Family yeah?", and I cuddle closer, hoping that the action provides the answer he wants because honestly, I haven't got the first *fucking* clue.

Keen to get back to my babies and to escape the unsettling insight into Jay's reality that last night provided me with, I am on the earliest possible train, Jay having dropped me at the station on his way to work. I wonder if I should worry that aside from the slight wrench of saying goodbye to somebody that I like, my overwhelming emotion as my train pulls away is *relief* rather than grief at separation from my *boyfriend*. I eat my Mars Bar and try not to think about it.

Chapter Eleven

"Rinny, are you coming to this thing tonight?", Lees is powering across the common room, Ad in willing tow.

I sag in my seat, "Chick, I honestly cannot be arsed, Jay's staying tonight and we head to that sodding holiday park tomorrow so I don't reckon I'll have time even if I wanted to", I am distracted by my newly acquired despair, my minutes-ago discovery that I missed two *fucking* questions that were on the back of the modular exam paper making me despondent.

I cannot *believe* that I missed those questions. The last four months have been a full-on slog of juggling two teething, crawling piglets, job, parents, confusing feelings about Gio, dealing with the complexities of my sort-of-live-in boyfriend and endless school work and now I've ballsed up the bloody exam.

"Bring Jay, you *never* bring him to school stuff and honestly, it's weird. C'mon, this party is at the twins' place, they've got that marquee again", Lees looks at me pleadingly, "Plus Rinny, you have not been out with *us* for ages, are we not *cool* enough for you?".

Her eyebrow is quirked in a piss-take but I know that there is some genuine grievance underneath. Since Jay's birthday, I have been up to Bristol a few times. My boys have now met their cousin Kaydee, the most *gorgeous* five-year-old who regards the boys as her real-life dolls. They have met their Uncles, Obi's braids Jake's absolute favourite grab toy and even their bloody *Auntie Megan* does a good impression of niceness when they are around.

Casey has met the boys too, a brief visit to Obi's nice city-centre flat coinciding with her dropping by and an awkward ten minutes followed. Casey did a wonderful job of faking adoration and gentle playfulness but you could see the devastation on her pretty face. When I looked at Jay, I saw the pain echoed on his. Stood in-between them, AJ on my hip, I felt like that uninvited wedding guest again and I had to fake a shitty nappy to escape the awkwardness.

Obi however is becoming an honest-to-God mate. He even calls me for chats and advice about women, despite me providing limited help frankly. He confided, several weeks ago, that he had always felt left out by the foursome of Jay, Casey, D and Megan.

"But now that you're around Ginge, it's balanced, I don't stick out no more", he chuckled but I don't think Obi had any idea just how much I would ponder his words during the last few weeks.

Because on the nights out that I've had in Bristol, spare part is *exactly* how I feel and it is Obi's company that I seek to ensure that I don't *stick out*. Jay always gravitates to me towards the end of the night, a couple of drinks under his belt as he goes into kind and affectionate boyfriend mode but when we arrive, wherever we are, he and Casey immediately and inadvertently appear to gravitate towards each other, as if they've missed each other, as if the other person is their sole motivation for coming out. When Obi says about balance, I am certain he's referring to having *me* as *his* 'other half' in the six-some. Casey and Jay are still mentally paired together as far as Obi is concerned *and I'm not convinced that it's just Obi who thinks that.* I still worry about my lack of reaction to these thoughts, the absence of jealousy or outrage.

I compare this lack of reaction to how I feel when I observe Gio and Carolyn's on-off relationship. Seeing them together, it is like arthritis, this immobilising throb of pain that I have to try to ignore so that I can get through the day. When they are 'off', the pain of seeing Gio with whichever girl he's rebounding with, is genuinely sickening at times. Gio and I are mates, we hang out periodically, he pops over sometimes to see the boys or take them to the park but each time I see him, my chest hurts and I try to avoid comparing the intensity of this emotion with the flat, gentle throb of familiarity I feel with Jay.

I look up at my best mate, the Common Room noisy post-exam, "Lee, if I get the stuff packed in time, maybe I'll swing by for a bit", I roll my eyes as she grins.

Ad smirks, "You should come, get some Dutch Courage ready for a week with your favourite sister-in-law", they both laugh at me as I mock sob.

I am going to *fucking* Dorset for a week with *fucking* Megan. This was entirely D's fault, some mate of his has a static caravan on a Holiday Park in Weymouth and Sasha had been saving newspaper coupons for D and Megan, meaning that we could rent two caravans for £20 each for a week. Jay seemed keen to fall in with the plans for a 'family' holiday with the kids and I didn't want to hurt his feelings. Obi is coming down for a couple of days but when I asked if Casey would also be popping in too, everyone looked shifty and I never got an answer.

I look at Ad and Lees, reunited at Easter and I watch their playful affection, the soppy looks they give each other, the constant physical contact. Lees refused Adam's gentle, tentative advances which started a few weeks after the Kiron 'incident', loudly declaring that Adam was too nice for her, that she had betrayed him too much, that she was undeserving of a second chance. The drama got even sillier when she fixated on the decision that before she would take his heartbroken pleas for her to reconsider seriously, Adam needed to have had a dalliance with another girl.

"It's only fair Rinny, after what I did to him. He needs to even up the score, he needs to have been with somebody else too", I'd looked at her baffled as we sat on my bed just before Easter, her dribbling Godsons staring at her from their cot as she howled.

The next day, she'd reiterated this plea as we sat on the bus to school, Adam's boy-next-door face tense.

His voice was low as he spoke, "So Lees, what you're saying is that you'll only think about getting back with me if I've what, pulled someone else?", Lees looked up at him, her eyes damp and nodded sadly.

Adam huffed out a frustrated breath, turning in his seat to look around. Gio, travelling on the bus due to a car breakdown and sat next to his latest Year 11 rebound dalliance, had no warning of what was to come. Ad, jumping across the aisle, grabbed Gio's face between both his hands and snogged him. Well, he *tried* to. Gio initially made that same squawk of astonishment that I'd made those years ago when he hugged me after the incident with Daniel, before he rapidly extracted himself,

"JONES!! What the actual fuck?!", Gio was comically scanning the bus, looking for answers regarding his unexpected journey into LGBT community.

Ad however, pointing at Gio and ignoring his outrage, was addressing Lees, "Right, well now I've snogged Romano and it was fucking horrible so Lee, will you please, PLEASE get back with me because I know that there is nobody I want to be with more than you and I have missed you every fucking day since we split. I love you so much Lees, you're it for me", and as his gentle voice cracked, Lees let out a sob and nodded as Ad swept her into a kiss that made me cry.

Gio's voice bellowed across at me, "I dunno why you're crying Rin, I've just been fucking sexually assaulted, I should be the one crying", and I fell into a proper belly laugh at his horrified expression, Gio joining me as we snorted together.

With that, Ad and Lees were reunited and everything feels more *right*. When Carolyn is not on the scene, the four of us often ride to school in Gio's car and I feel a little wrench on Thursdays when I drive home with Jay instead.

Ad and Lee know all about the complex dynamics of my new Bristol-based *life extension* and they have listened to me grumble about Megan often enough. She's just so hostile, the most innocuous of comments greeted with sneers. Jay had to drag me out of D's flat the other week, when I heard her in her room, chatting on the phone about, *"Stuck up little bitches"* who she has to put up with because, *"My family can't keep their dicks in their pants"*.

Now I've got a week with her. *Aces.*

I get home to a quiet house, unusual for a Thursday tea-time. My little piglets are both crawling with *astonishing* speed and their ridiculous food intake makes my mother beam with pride, as if their rapid progress towards obesity is something to relish. AJ is very much the dominant twin, despite being younger. He babbles constantly and he is the instigator of all and any mishaps and misdeeds. Every surface in the house is padded, every cupboard is baby-proofed, sleep-sacks are specially restricted to prevent AJ's cot-Houdini tricks and yet on a daily basis, somebody in the house starts a sentence with, *"You won't believe what that baby did today"*.

Jake is my quiet, watchful little smiler. He watches his brother constantly but AJ will not go anywhere or do anything if Jake is not by his side. The other day, I had to take Jake for some hearing tests, a query from the Health Visitor worrying me half to death. I left AJ with my Dad for a couple of hours and upon my return, a worried Dad explained that AJ did not make a sound, did not move a muscle while we were gone. He just sat on his play mat, gripping his biscuit and waiting for his brother to come home. Jake's hearing is fine, he's just super chilled.

We were lying in bed at stupid-O'clock one Sunday morning, the boys chirping and wriggling in bed with us before Jay had to head to work, when Jay had looked at me,

"He's you, y'know? AJ, he's totally you Feist and little man here", he'd grabbed Jake and blown raspberries into his neck making him squeal, "He's me", Jay had looked at me, a small smile on his

lips,

"Feist, you an' me, we made another set of us", Jay pressed a kiss to my lips as he shook his head in awe.

In the deserted house this afternoon, I start to pack suitcases, grumpy still about potentially having banjaxed my exam. We're got a two berth caravan so I've been borrowing travel cots and playpens from anyone I can, the playgroup Mums warmer these days and more willing to include me in their circles.

As I cram nappies into the bag, I hear the boys babbling as they enter the back garden, Jay pushing them in the buggy. He's on his phone and I see him take a seat on Dad's bench, his head bowed and his hands clutching his phone and his face. Through the partially open window, I hear random words,

"I just don't get why you never said……..so who the fuck is he?.........How long?.........so you ain't comin' wiv Obi then?............that ain't……..messin' my head up…...I know………", I can see his frustration, I know Jay well enough now to read his body language. He looks like he's ready to lose it.

"Don't go…..we gotta get this straight…….it ain't nothin' Case……..it ain't the same…...Case? Casey? FUCK!!!", Jay jumps up and hurls his phone, I hear it thud against the fence.

The boys starts to grizzle, startled by their father's agitation. I see Jay slump as he approaches the buggy, unclipping them and pulling their warm wriggling bodies into his arms as he kisses their heads distractedly.

Me? I just feel a sort of resigned heaviness, a numb acceptance. I don't feel the urge to demand information or clarification, I don't have any sharp stabs of jealousy. If Jay wants to tell me about this, he will. *Meh.* I keep packing.

Jay puts the boys back in the buggy and he strides off with them again, agitation radiating from him as he heads off God knows where, the park probably. I go out to get some washing off the line to pack it and I spot his phone lying forlornly by the shed, its screen glowing green.

I know I shouldn't read it, I know it will only add to the list of things I'd rather not know. *But I do*.

"I had to move on J. You have Erin and those gorgeous boys, you have a new life and so what we had is in the past, I can't keep wishing that things are different. I don't reckon I'll ever stop loving you, I just need to try and love somebody else now too, because you are not mine to love, are you? Please understand, don't give me shit J. It hurts too much xx"

Shit.

Jay comes back from the park, the boys *hangry* and grumpy. Jay is monosyllabic and slopes off to the garden to retrieve his phone. Strapping them into their highchairs, I begin my twice daily battle of wills. Jake, oddly determined about this particular issue, always has to hold his spoon. It never goes well. I always have to prepare double portions so that he has fighting chance of ingesting one complete meal. AJ is OK to be fed but is prone to throwing and spitting and so I have to wear a protective tent of apron and t-towels that make me look like some sort of biblical goat herder.

"I'm gonna head home, I got shit to sort. I'll come back in the mornin' yeah, pick you all up", Jay's sullen, deep voice jolts me, this change in plans causing irritation to sweep my veins.

I turn to him as he stands awkwardly in the kitchen doorway, "What? Jay, I need to pack and I need your help", I play dumb, "What do you need to go home for? I thought you'd brought all your holiday gear here last night?", I concentrate on the boys.

I know why you're going back, I saw that text.

"I just fuckin' do, tha's all. Don't give me shit woman, I bought all that stuff on that fuckin' list you gave me today so I've done my bit. I'll be back tomorrow first thing", my jaw is clamped in indignation as he leans down and kisses the boys, whispering quiet endearments to them.

He kisses the side of my face and without further discussion, he runs upstairs, grabs his bag and he's gone. *Bye then.*

I feed the boys, I play with them, I eat with my family and fill them in on my exam catastrophe. I pack endless frikking bags of crap, filling my mother's hallway with luggage and causing conniptions. I bath the boys, I read them their stories, I pump them full of milk and I lie down with them on the bed until their cot-chatter turns to sleepy slurs and then snores.

My head is full of abandonment scenarios. He goes to Bristol, he chooses her. He never comes back for me and the boys, the hallway stays filled with luggage, my team-mate returned to the true owner of his heart which I *know* she is. I'm only seventeen but I'm not stupid. He still loves her, the look he shoots her sometimes is the same look Adam gives Lees. The look he gives me? It's warm, it's affectionate, it's…...nice. It's not love though.

Is it weird that we've never said it? We've got two kids, we've been sleeping together since February and we are officially a couple but in five months, not once have we quantified the emotions that connect us to the other.

I am not 100% what *romantic* love feels like. I know what proper, bone-deep love is, I have two milk-bubble blowing reminders lying in that cot of just how deep and visceral *that* sort of love is. I do remember the umbilical chord of emotions that tied my teenage heart to Daniel McNamara, the constant ache of unrequited love. I know that *whatever* it is I feel about Gio, it has physical

231

manifestations, tingles and aches. Yet I have no clue what it is that I feel about the *man* whose children I bore. If I'm honest, I'm not sure what being in love is supposed to feel like, I don't think I've got a clear expectation of that experience, my daily grind of parenting responsibilities make the giddy cinematic fairytale seem far beyond my nappy-ninja reach.

When I try to imagine Jay kissing Casey, holding *her*, telling her he loves *her*, the emotion that I feel is not crippling jealousy or the pain of betrayal. It's fear. *And loneliness.*

If the father of my children loves somebody else, who the *fuck* is going to love me? How will somebody else *ever* love my boys like their Dad does? How will somebody love me if a part of me always belongs to Jay? How will my boys have the family life they deserve if Jay and I aren't together?

It hurts now, it fucking *hurts* in my chest. I need distraction. Bags are packed, babies are full and deep sleeping and I need to be somewhere where my scary, big-girl worries are silenced.

A quick word with Dyls and I have a babysitter and with my lycra trousers, basque top and trainers, I make a few cursory face and hair improvements and I head out of the door. The last time I went to this end of term party, I was pregnant and isolated. Now, I'm a year older, wiser, stronger. I'm bloody *Feist*.

Lees squeals when I arrive, quickly dragging me to the marquee where to Adam's horror, we dance like complete *morons* on the as-yet-unoccupied dance floor.

"Roberts, it's a good job you're fit because *Jesus Christ*", I turn to see that Gio is stood with Adam, his eyebrow quirked in amusement at our ridiculous antics and his gorgeous face lit up by the disco lights as he calls out to me.

As the all the blood in my body rushes to my head, as my palms sweat and my heart painfully double beats inside my chest, I hear a cymbal clang of realisation.

I think I might be in love with Gio Romano.

"Oh Fuck", I whisper out my disbelief as my dancing stalls and in my alarm, I leg it out of the marquee, Lees and Gio's confused shouts following my exit.

I find the huge kitchen, smiling wryly as I spot the Bee Gees CD still propped by the stereo. I down an alcopop from the worktop bar and lean against it, contemplating my next step.

Do I love Gio Romano, the boy who held my hand as I gave birth and who has provided endless mixed messages for the last year or so? I don't see how I can when he has an endless supply of girlfriends, I have a semi-resident boyfriend and I have two children who need me to make the relationship I have with their father work out, to ensure their future happiness *but*………

"Oi woman, I wasn't taking the piss, didn't mean to upset you….", Gio enters the room clutching his beer and my heart swoops at the look of concern on his face.

I smile as widely as I can, "Nah dude, I was thirsty, see", I proffer my empty bottle as evidence.

Gio leans against the worktop next to me, I can feel his body heat and that wonderful scent of herbs and lemons that is *him* wafts over me as we chat. Gio and I, we chat and laugh and take the piss for *hours*. People come in and out of the kitchen, Ad and Lees joining us for a while before they wander off, probably for a sneaky shag but Gio seems under no compulsion to socialise elsewhere and I am just basking in his proximity as we perch on the worktop. God, I love pratting about with Gio like this. A near life-time of memories gives us ample piss-take material and things just flow. Tonight, it's as if the post-Jay awkwardness melts away and it goes back to how it was in that period between the boys being born and Jay's December reappearance.

"So, you're going on holiday tomorrow yeah?", Gio's staring at his bottle as I sigh and nod.

I tell Gio about Megan, about Bristol and about *always* feeling like an uninvited guest.

I see Gio frown deeply, "But Rin, you and him, you're together aren't you? I mean, well, aren't you?", Gio looks baffled and whether it's the alcopop or that text I read earlier that prompts my honesty, I tell Gio my newly realised truth.

"Gio, we're together but I'm pretty certain that he still loves his ex-girlfriend. Me and him, it's, y'know, *good* and we *need* to be together, we *have* to be together for the boys but if they weren't here? There's no way he'd pick me. I'm......I'm not in the same league as she is", I feel the heaviness take its place in my chest now that I've said it aloud, like a big, Christmas turkey coming in to roost its fat arse on my heart.

Gio just stands there, looking at me blankly and in my discomfort, I babble, "So, look, you've been here hours with me, you need to go socialise Romano. You're about due a re-match with Carolyn aren't you? You've been split up a while, isn't it time you got back together?", my smile is pained and my laugh hollow.

Gio takes a swig of his beer, his arm muscles tense and his strong body looking uncomfortable as he shakes his head, "Nah, we're not going down that road again. I realised the last time that I don't actually like her"

Gio looks up at me, those blue eyes making me feel sweaty, "Do you like him though Rin? Y'know, even if he's into that other girl. Do you really like him?", Gio steps closer to me and I feel a bit overwhelmed by the question and his proximity.

I look down at my feet, chewing my lip and fiddling nervously with my bottle as I shrug.

"Rin?", Gio's voice is whispered and croaky sounding suddenly and I flick my gaze up to meet his.

I hear the clink of Gio's bottle on the worktop and I watch him get closer, his ragged breath puffing against my skin and I think I might pass out, my head is pounding with blood.

A whisper, "Rin do you want to know who it is that I *really* like?"

In the last twelve months I've given birth, I've nearly died, nearly lost my sons to an infection and nearly lost Jake to a fit. Nothing scares me now so I look him in the eye and I nod shakily.

His hands tentatively reach for me, one cards into my hair at my temple as he gently holds my hip. As my heart beats its way out of my ribcage and he lowers his face to mine, his warm breath fogs against my lips as he whispers out,

"It's you Roberts, it has been for fucking years", and then he kisses me.

Those glitter explosions I felt when Jay kissed me at the rave were nothing, *nothing* compared to this. They were like cheap party poppers compared to this confetti cannon.

I have never, ever, *ever* been kissed like this, Gio is kissing me like he's offering me his soul. It's overwhelming and I'm giddy from the words he just said. His firm, soft lips nibble at mine as his tongue licks gently, begging for more which I willingly give as my hands circle his muscled back to pull him closer. I know I'm moaning into his mouth, his own groans match the gentle thrusts of his tongue and I feel desperate for more of him, I want to just melt into him and stay there.

He lifts me off the worktop, as if I weigh nothing and lies me down on the bloody sofa that's just casually placed in this massive kitchen.

"Fuck Rin, I want you so much", Gio's licking at the skin of my neck, his hands reverently stroking my bared skin, tentatively reaching for my tits as my hand goes under his t-shirt to feel those fabled muscles.

His weight on me is addictive, his scent making me soar and in the haze of this lust, I whisper my truth,

"I want you too Gio", as he gasps and deepens our kisses.

Time slips away as we stroke and lick and *absorb* each other, Gio's groans increase as my fingers slip under the waistband of his jeans, making their descent towards the contents of his jockeys.

"Oh my FUCKING God!! I knew it, I always *knew* it about you two. *Mates* my arse", a furious screech propels Gio off me like a rocket as I sit up in panic.

Carolyn is stood in the doorway of the kitchen, her finger pointing at us, her face a mask of outrage before she shrieks,

"Fuck you Gio", and she strides out.

Gio huffs out a weary chuckle but his wry smile falters as he sees the expression of horrified regret plastered across my face.

Getting swept away in hormone-drenched declarations in the privacy of a deserted kitchen is one thing. Having that exposed to the general populous, is *quite* another because *I am in a relationship*

236

with the father of my sons. I am not free, I am not unencumbered, I am not at liberty to see this through. I have just cheated on my *family*. I've just betrayed my sons' security.

I jump off the sofa, my panicked heartbeat pounding in my temples. Gio shoots forward, his arms looking to hold me, his face a question mark but I stick out my hands like a hostage negotiator and I back away,

"Gio, this was…..this was such a massive mistake. I'm so sorry, I'm so, so sorry but I can't do this", Gio's eyes go wide in panic as I stumble on, "I'm with Jay, I have to be with Jay, we're a team for our boys…..we're together", I dart over and grab my wallet but Gio stands in my way, his gorgeous, big body shaking.

"No, NO, Rin, he's not right for you. You should be with me, we'd be so good together Rin, I want to be with you *so* much", Gio's voice cracks as his hands stroke at my arms and shoulders, as they cup my face but I back away, I move out of his reach as my vision blurs with tears.

My own voice trembling and my mouth suddenly filled with saliva, I choke out, "But I love my boys Gio and I won't mess things up for them, I'm sorry", and without looking at him, I run.

Blinded by tears, I find myself at the knackered, piss-stinking phone box on the High Street, fumbling with coins as I dial a number with shaking fingers,

"Yeah?", he sounds stressed.

I blurt out without any form of greeting, "Me and you Jay, we might each have shit going on in our heads that drives us mental but AJ and Jake need us to try Jay, they need us to be a team because that is all we've got going for us. So you and me, we have to try, for them. All the other shit, we've got to step away. Do you understand Jay, do you know what I'm saying?", my sobs make me barely coherent as I hear his shocked breaths down the phone.

"Nothing is bigger than them being happy and safe, we can't fuck it up, no matter what we *feel*. Do you understand me Jay?", my sobs are out of control now as I beg,

"Please don't leave me alone with all this, I don't think I can give them the life they should have if you're not with me, you're their Dad", and I hang up before he can reply as my misery takes me over and I collapse, sobbing like I might die from it.

Lees and Adam racing down the road, find me. Shocked by the depth of my distress, they both hold me tight until I am calm enough to walk, their arms wrapped around me. Neither asks me any questions, neither pushes me to talk and in return I offer nothing. Silently parting from them, I let myself in the back door, my family all long gone to bed. I creep into my room and lie on my bed, fully clothed, watching two little tummies rise and fall with the effort of their deep, sleepy breaths.

Nobody is more important than you.

Two hours later, I don't even flinch as Jay skilfully breaks in, unlatching the open window and climbing into my room like a cat. Relief floods my bones as he climbs onto the bed and pulls me tight against him, whispering into my skin,

"Me an' you Feist, we're in this together. I'm right here, yeah", and as he pulls me into a kiss that tastes of tears and desperation and *loss*, we strip each other and take comfort in the actions and touches that are becoming so familiar.

Jesus, we are good at this. I have no idea if it's *love* between Jay and I but we can *make love* like it's the most natural thing. When he makes me come, sunk deep in me and his strong body pressed as close as he can get, I feel the tears start again. As he whispers out his own groan of release, I realise

238

that not all of the tears dripping onto my neck are my own. We cling to each other like shipwreck victims and we sleep facing the boys.

The next morning at breakfast, nobody mentions Jay's surprise re-appearance or my horribly puffy face. Jay and I stick to discussions on suitcase contents, nappy quotas and provision requirements whilst animatedly engaging with the twins by means of distraction. I know that something went down in Bristol last night, his neck *smelt* different as my face was buried in it. My clothes smelled of herbs and lemons when I threw them in the washing basket this morning and when I washed my hair, I smelt Gio again and it made me cry.

Jay kisses me, he pulls me into random cuddles, he pulls my hair affectionately but it feels a bit forced although I gratefully reciprocate. I look at him, this gorgeous lad and I wonder why my heart won't cooperate and just love *him*.

The twins are hilarious this morning, not the first clue why their father and I are engaged in such frenetic activity but clearly loving the sense that something fun is about to happen. As they babble and chuckle, Jay lifts Jake out of his baby walker to foist him into his car seat and at that moment, Jake reaches out and pats his Daddy's face and says, clear as a bell, *"Dada"*, with a look of absolute triumph on his little sticky chops.

The boys are eight and half months old and although they've babbled for ages, this is the first word Jake's said.

Jay turns to me, his grin incandescent as we both whoop and encourage repeat performances. AJ, slightly ignored in his baby walker behind us, bellows, *"Maaaaaaaaaa"*, making us spin around and stare at him. A gummy grin at the attention, AJ starts shouting *'mamamamamama'* like a football chant as I burst into happy tears and Jay whoops that his sons are, "Geniuses, my kids, they're fuckin' sharp Feist, them boys got sharp skills".

A baby each, Jay and I beam with pride at each other and with a surge of affection, I pull Jay in for a proper snog, tongues and everything, as the babies scream with delight at the giddiness of us.

Jay holds me close pressing a kiss to my forehead as he whispers, "We're doin' this together Erin, me an' you, you ain't gonna be on your own girl", and I close my eyes and nod gently, a soft smile on my lips.

We're meeting D and Megan at some petrol station on the A37 so with the boys readied and strapped in, I'm grabbing the last few bits as Jay loads the boot, when the phone goes. Huffing in frustration, I answer it and my heart stops beating,

"Rin, Rin it's me. What the fuck happened last night? We need to talk, please, I need to see you", Gio's voice sounds like he's been gargling gravel and his tone is sad.

My eyes immediately spring with tears and resting my head against the wall, I whisper, "Gio, I should never have kissed you, I'm with Jay, he's their Dad. I'm so sorry Gio, I've gotta go, I'm sorry, please can you just pretend it never happened?", I beg weakly.

"No! No, Rin, this is fucked up. I like you *so* much Rin and I know you feel something for me else you wouldn't have kissed me like that. Why won't you be with me? Talk to me, let's just talk, I'll come meet you. Please Erin, please don't make a stupid shit decision, I like you *so* much Rin, you're all I think about", his voice cracks again and I feel a little sob leave my lips,

"Gio, please don't. I......", but there is a strong hand on my waist and the phone receiver is gently removed from my grip.

I gasp and turn to see Jay, his face transmitting understanding, a gentle sad smile on his lips. He nods

240

very slowly and lifts the handset to his head,

"Bruv, me an' her we're a family yeah. You gotta back off now and leave her be. I'm fuckin' sorry bruv", and Jay hangs up.

I'm shaking as he pulls me into a gentle cuddle, kissing my hair before he leads me in silence to the car as I wipe my eyes and compose myself.

The distractions of map reading, managing the boys and mentally preparing for a week with *Megs* and her barbs means that my despair passes. Jay holds my hand in between gear changes and his gentle smiles give me hope that we will work this out somehow.

Waiting for them to arrive, sat in the petrol station forecourt, I turn to Jay, whispering due to our snoozing cargo.

"Jay…...is there anything I need to know, y'know, before Megan gets here? Is there…….is there something from last night that she's gonna be pissed off about?", my unspoken question is, *"What happened with Casey?"*.

Jay huffs out a slow breath, almost imperceptibly shaking his head, "I don't reckon so. I mean……..I mean I went to her mums to see…... and….I…..we talked me an'......she's got a new bloke…..I needed to talk…..she's wiv' him….", Jay's jaw is clamped so tight I wonder that he can actually make any sounds.

I understand. I reach across and turn his tense face towards me and I make him meet my gaze,

"I'm so sorry you're hurting too but me and you, we'll just work this out together, a team yeah Jay?", and as I gentle press my lips to his, I feel a little spark, a little sign that maybe we can manufacture something here.

We jump apart as a grinning D bangs the window and with a few minutes chat and a quick cuddle with gorgeous Kaydee who is full of holiday fizz, we head off. After the most confusing and stressful arrival at the Caravan Park, which saw *me* have to wrestle *Jay* back into the driver's seat when a particularly rude staff member got arsey with us for parking in the wrong place, we finally found our caravan.

Jay and I are a good team. We worked in calm cooperation, despite AJ's ear-bleeding screams because his lunch was overdue and we were unpacked and the boys munching messily within impressively few minutes. Jay smirked as we heard Megs screeching at D in the caravan next door, Jay muttering about how some things never change.

Jay left me clearing up and he returned with a giggling Kaydee on his shoulders, telling me that, "We'll all have an easier life Feist if I give them space, tha' bitch is easier to handle when she's had some dick", I snort with laughter and make Kaydee some lunch.

With no sign of D or a satiated Megan, we take all three kids out for the afternoon, exploring the site as Jay scowls at my enthusiasm for the organised entertainment. Pushing Kaydee on the swings as the boys snooze in their buggy, Jay and I chat happily about our own family holiday histories.

Jay has not had a holiday since he moved to his Dad's. His Dad, who I have only met once at the Barber's shop that he owns, paid his grandsons not an iota of interest during our only visit, standing with his arms crossed as Jay made stilted small talk. We left after ten minutes. Jay's Dad apparently spends his life either working at the barbers shop that he owns, hanging out there or trying to charm widows at his Church. I have rarely taken such an instant dislike to somebody. Jay's Iya never had the money to take him anywhere but he did go on school trips, paid for by his disinterested father when his Iya insisted.

I tell him about my Mother's insistence on Welsh holidays in cold, wet Caravan parks with beaches that would deliver frostbite and sand flea bites in equal measures. I tell him my favourite stories of Uncle Gethin, who would always come with us for those weeks in Wales, his summers absolutely filled with holidays as each of his siblings took him on their respective family breaks in turn. Gethin loves the boys *so* much, that it's rare for a week to pass without a woollen monstrosity plopping through the letterbox.

Jay smiles as I ramble on about my mad family and in a break in my monologue he quietly adds, "Tha's what I want for these two, y'know? A proper family, holidays and shit, wiv' people who love them like they deserve, yeah?", I smile back at him, nodding as I reach for his hand.

Jay doesn't find it odd that we've had Kaydee for four hours and yet her parents have not come looking for us. Teatime arrives, having spent a small fortune on the little amusement arcade games that Kaydee wanted to play. We feed her and the boys at the cafe and we take them to the little baby disco, Jay rolling his eyes and laughing as Kaydee and I storm the dance floor with our *epic* moves but then it becomes clear from matching sets of baby screeches that we must get the boys into bed.

D and Megan's caravan is dark and there is no answer at the door. Frowning, Jay makes a call but gets no response. He shrugs hopelessly at me as I hold an overtired Kaydee and an hour later, when Jay and I have got the boys bathed, bottled and into bed, there is still no sign of D and Megan. Little Kaydee loved the bedtime story that the boys had and Jay was forced by his gorgeous niece to read a further three stories to her before she collapsed into a snooze on our bed, wearing one of my t-shirts as a nightie and curled up to one of Jake's teddies as she sucked her thumb.

A few minutes later, as we sit watching the tiny, crap TV, we hear the roar of D's BMW and shortly afterwards, the slightly nasal dulcet tones of *Megs,* bossing D around. There's a knock at the door and Jay jumps up to answer it, Megan flouncing in followed by a slightly sheepish Dion.

243

I hear him muttering, "Yeah, cheers bruv, we just went into town and that, did some shoppin'. Megs she…..", but then Megan jumps in, tutting,

"Yeah, like Wheels here don't owe you enough favours D, don't come with that apology shit. So where's Dee-Dee?", Megan turns to me, no greeting or social niceties so I ignore her.

"Oi, where's Dee-Dee", Megan takes a step closer, frustrated with my lack of response. I ignore her.

"Oi *Erin*, where the fuck is my kid?", she comes closer again, arms crossed.

I smile sweetly, "Oh hi Megan, I didn't realise you were talking to me, bit tired from looking after three kids all afternoon see. Kaydee's had her lunch *and* her tea, we've been to the play area, Jay paid for her to go on a tonne of rides, we went to the disco and then we've given her a bath and she's had a milk and story. She's had a *lovely* day, no, no you don't need to thank us, Kaydee's happiness is all the thanks we need", I smile like I'm on medication.

She narrows her eyes at me but she's got nothing she can come back with so I keep going, "You're OK to have the boys tomorrow yeah? All day? I've packed all their shit ready for you. Cheers yeah", I grab another chocolate from the bag and turn back to the TV.

Jay snorts behind me and I just know that Megan's face would be worth a photo if I turn around but I make myself stare at the TV instead. D comes out of our room with Kaydee and makes noises that suggest he's thanking Jay. I shout over my shoulder,

"Y'know, Jay's an amazing Uncle, Kaydee's lucky to have him", and with a huff from Megan, I hear them leave.

Jay slinks back over to the sofa, chuckling softly and peppering my face with kisses as he mutters, "You ain't gonna really leave them poor little fuckers with Megs tomorrow are you?"

I smile broadly, shaking my head, "Nah, that miserable cow can barely look after a handbag let alone our two but it won't stop me knocking her door at 5am when they get up and asking her if she's ready for them".

Jay snorts and pulls me into a kiss which then turns into a sort of sofa cushion fight until, despite all of our complexities, we find ourselves having slightly frantic sex on the floor of the lounge, Jay making me laugh mid-shag when he gets cramp in his arse and both of us laughing and swearing when we realise that much of our lounge is visible through the open curtains.

Jay leads me by the hand to bed and I try, desperately, to forget what I was doing exactly twenty-four hours ago with Giovanni Romano and just how much I would give to be able to do it again.

Chapter Twelve

12th August 1997

I am so tired, I honestly can't work out if I remembered to put knickers on or not this morning, as I sit scanning shopping though the tills.

I am working full-time over the summer break, my amazing brother and Lees and Ads helping with childcare. I started as soon as we came back from the surprisingly good week in Dorset. It was good mainly because *Megan* only made an appearance after midday *every day* by which time, we were either off out doing stuff or we had made plans that did not include her. She came out every evening to the disco but spent most of the time on her phone or messing with Kaydee's hair.

Obi came up for two days, sleeping on our sofa-bed and I had genuine fun with Jay, Obi and the boys, wondering the whole time how a guy as nice as D could hold a life-long torch for somebody as annoying as Megan. Jay and I spent a lot of the holiday in the pool with the boys, who turn out to be proper, full-on maniacs, their slippery little bodies desperate for aquatic freedom at every opportunity, risking drowning and maternal conniptions. I puffed up with pride when I saw all of the lustful looks Jay got in the pool, sucking in my own belly and trying to pout seductively in an attempt to match his hotness. I fear I just looked constipated.

We had a couple of brushes with racist, mouth-breathing twats, my first proper encounter with *challenge* with regards to Jay and I and our children. At the disco one evening, I picked up on hostile, derisive looks being thrown our way by a large family group who looked like they'd struggle to operate Play-Doh. With an astonishing family gallery of misshapen bulldog tattoos on sweaty, sunburnt skin and sneering, potato-like faces that suggested a DNA strand or two had got lost somewhere along the way, it wasn't hard to miss some of the choice words being used to describe me,

246

my boyfriend, my in-laws or my *children*.

Interestingly, it was Megan who grabbed my arm as I leapt up, Jay and D distracted over at the arcades with Kaydee.

Her face tight and her jaw set, she'd stared at the DJ and growled out, "There's too many of them. It ain't worth the fuckin' aggro. Just look like you don't give a fuck, kiss your boy, fuckin' drink your drink and don't give 'em no reaction. That lot are all mouth, it's the ones that come and say it to your face you wanna save your energy for, yeah", she sipped her drink and stared blankly ahead.

She turned her immaculately made-up face to me, stunningly pretty as always, "You gotta pick your battles when it comes to this shit *Erin*. Your boys, they're gonna need to know when it's worth fighting and when you just gotta let the fuckers chat their shit, else you and them are gonna be having set-to's every fuckin' day and you can't live your life like that. It's knackering", she looked at me and nodded meaningfully, reaching out and affectionately stroking Jake's face as he snoozed on me.

When D and Jay returned from the arcade, they were both slightly staggered by the enthusiastic affection they received from their respective girlfriends, Megan and I offering matching smirks to the Bulldog Gallery as we headed out.

It was lovely to have a full-time additional parent on hand. Jay stays overnight on Wednesdays, Fridays and Saturdays now and that's enough for me but that week with him around 24/7 was genuinely nice.

Gio and Casey go undiscussed. We never mention them. *Blinkers on.*

Gio is in New Zealand, a last-minute plan made while I was in Dorset. He is spending the summer with Daniel McNamara and his family and it hurts so much to think about him that it's genuinely made me sick on occasion.

My sons are teething on an astonishing scale and my nights are filled with greasy sleeplessness, Calpol, Bonjela and frozen chew toys. Their nappies are also *off the chart*, even Mum heaved the other day and she nurses people with gangrene.

Now I'm scanning shopping and wishing I could just crawl into the bread shelves and snooze amongst the sliced white.

"Miss Roberts, what an unexpected delight", I jolt and look into the face of Mr. Gibson, my Head of Year.

I grimace an apology as I scan his collection of fruit, veg and breakfast cereal, praying that he has not got condoms or haemorrhoid cream hidden amongst it.

"Are you having a good summer Sir?", I stifle a yawn

He frowns slightly and sighs, "Relieved of the incessant presence of adolescents who are unable to appreciate the gift of learning or indeed employ basic impulse controls, I find myself enjoying my summer very much Miss. Roberts, thank you for asking", he frowns deeper, "Miss. Roberts, you do look somewhat fatigued, has your social life been that taxing?"

I grimace again, "Sir, I wish. My sons are teething and they're making a proper overblown fuss of it, little buggers", I smile weakly and Mr. Gibson shifts his face into one of sympathy.

"Ah Erin, I remember it well, my own children were indeed prone to the dramatics when it came to teeth growing", he smiles kindly and I nod in understanding.

"Erin, this might be a fortuitous encounter actually", Mr. Gibson hands me the cash for his shopping as he carries on talking, "The school has been approached over the summer by the local women's refuge who are looking for a responsible young woman to support the work they are doing with some of their younger residents, somebody perhaps to act in the role of peer mentor, to encourage their younger girls back into education", he takes his change from me and stands back, smiling wryly.

"For all the excitement you have caused in your school career, as a staff team we regularly comment on how much we admire your tenacity and your dedication to your studies, your parental commitments and indeed, on occasion, your commitment to securing the safety and well-being of your friends, even to the detriment of your own personal safety", his raised eyebrow suggests that he knows more about the Kiron incident than he let on.

He sighs, "In short Erin, *you* are the student that sprung to both mine and the Headteacher's minds when the refuge made the request and perhaps you can spend some time before term starts contemplating whether you can spare a few hours a week? With the challenges you have faced, I can think of nobody better equipped within your peers to empathise with young women in difficult circumstances", he nods at me and then smirks, "The notion of sending Miss. Gregory or her ilk gives me cold chills, I fear that those poor refuge residents would willingly return to violence rather than receive incessant instruction on the art of applying excessive makeup", he smiles as I snort.

He goes to leave but turns back, "Whisky on their gums Erin. Tell nobody, especially my wife but it did the trick when I was on tooth-duty", and with a wink, he heads off with his shopping.

I feel a warm glow and a bit of excitement, the opportunity to try something new sounds appealing. My next customer however has twenty-four tins of Spam and enough UHT milk to re-sink the Titanic and my warm glow is short lived.

At home after work, I open up my emails on Dad's computer in the corner of the Dining Room as AJ chews on my hand. Lees is in France on holiday with her family but she's found an internet cafe and on Day Two, she started sending me *hilarious* daily accounts of life in rural Brittany with her mental parents. She copies Adam in because he's in Greece and the three of us have been emailing daily, the messages getting funnier and more acidic as the days pass, my teething dramas eliciting significant comedy.

The bloody modem sounding like a strangled glockenspiel, I nearly drop my son when the screen flashes up with *"You have new mail from DannyMcnamara@kiwimail.com"*

"OhmyGOD AJ, OHMYGOD!! I think I've got an email from my Husband", AJ burps and grins at me, chewing on my chin in response.

Ridiculously giddy, I open up the emails to be greeted with the unexpected message title, *"What the fuck have you done to my best mate?"*.

Oh, marital relations have re-commenced somewhat frostily it appears. With a sense of trepidation, I open the message,

"Hi Roberts,

It's been a while, eh? I would ask how you've been, what you've been doing, how life panned out for you but guess what? I already know Erin. I know pretty much everything about you because my idiot best mate, he's been writing to me about you pretty much since I moved here so I'm all caught up with you and the rugrats (congrats by the way). I'm good if you were wondering, I'm pretty fucking mean, thanks for asking.

But see, G, he's doing pretty shit. He got here a few weeks back and I'd hoped he'd have cheered the fuck up by now but nope, he's still packing a proper sad and tonight, we were at this party. That hardout dickhead walked away from a girl from my college that is fit as, heaps of blokes want to get with her. She fell for that Romano charm but nope, he didn't see it through, not even. G just looked sad and walked off.

So here I am, back home after a belter of a party, pissed as and hardout mad at you.

See you've fucking broken him, he's pakaru and now I'm stuck babysitting the bastard when I could have got laid tonight Roberts, I mean proper, full-on dirty laid.

All I hear all fucking day is him talk about your dramas and it's getting straight-up old. What you got to say for yourself, eh Erin?

Danny (McNamara)

PS Got your email off that group one Adam Jones sent with the picture of the fucking Greek donkey, blame him. Mind you, he's done alright for himself bagging Morris, aye?

PPS Good work on the growing up, you turned out hot, Dickhead's got your photo in his wallet

PPPS Sorry if that sounded a bit sleazy, I'm not that guy.

PPPPS Nah, I am that guy. I'm that guy who could have at least got his dick sucked tonight but coz of you, I didn't. Cheers for that Roberts"

I have no words. I stare at my son who has now got his fist entirely in his mouth and on wobbly legs I go and bath my stinkers, wondering what on earth I do with this unexpected correspondence and the news the Gio has my photo in his wallet.

Boys settled for a few minutes at least, I speak to Jay who is pissed off after a shitty day at work and who has absolutely no chat whatsoever. I abandon the phone call, telling him to go out with Obi and cheer the fuck up.

Sat in front of the computer, Jake in my lap this time as the Calpol has yet to work its magic on him, I fire up my emails and taking a deep breath, I type.

"Er, hi?

I would say that it's nice to hear from you Daniel McNamara but I don't think that's the right response, is it? I mean, it is nice to hear from you but we're technically married (long story, might fill you in one day if I can be arsed) so I think your email detailing your hoped-for blow-job actually

constitutes proof of adultery. I'm going to take you to the cleaners sucker, I've got two kids to support

so my divorce settlement is gonna be HUGE.

If you're reading this sober, maybe near Gio, can you tell him this: I'm so fucking sorry. I never

meant to hurt him. Gio held my hand as my sons were born, he was there when I nearly died, he's my

friend and I miss him so much. He's also an astonishing kisser and is so gorgeous, it hurts to look at

him. There. Said it.

But I can't be with Gio because choosing him over my babies' Dad means choosing my own heart

*over my boys' hearts and I **cannot**, I **will not** do that.*

Danny (it's weird calling you that, it's like a teacher telling you to call them 'Steve'), I'm glad Gio

has a mate like you who sends random emails to girls to stick up for them. I've got my Lees and I take

down big, Roid-Rage sprinters for her in car parks so I'm glad he's got something similar (I can give

you pointers on the take-downs if you need them, I'm full-on savage).

I know that when I see Gio for the first time, it'll kill me. Tell him that. Tell him that I'll have to hold it

together but I'll be fucking dying inside. I have to put my babies first though Danny, they're all that

matters.

I need to go, I'm typing this holding one of my sons and he's just done the most horrendous shit that I

*am actually scared about dealing with. I might die before I sign off this email, it's **that** bad. Danny, I*

hope you get your dick sucked soon (more adultery= more alimony) and I hope that Gio has an

amazing holiday. I'm not worth being sad over, I'm just rank, ugly ginger Roberts and right now,

Gio's comments on my plaster cast when we were seven are bang on. I do actually smell of shit.

Erin

PS Adam has done well for himself but you stay the hell away from my Lees. Sleaze.

PPS Can you give that girl from your college a slap from me?"

I go and deal with Jake's nappy, it actually makes me vomit, my mother laughing at me until she gets

a whiff and then she goes quiet and opens every window in the house. The little horror goes straight to

sleep afterwards, his work for the evening complete.

As I go down to turn off the computer, I have a message. It must be mid-morning in New Zealand but Danny has already replied.

"Roberts,

Married? What the fuck are you on about? Never mind, I probably don't want to know. He never mentioned that you were funny by the way, I nearly pissed myself reading your email.

Look, I'll level with you. I have got a bruiser of a hangover and if G ever finds out I sent you that email last night, I'm a dead man and that bastard is twice the size of me. Mind you, you'd know exactly how big he is aye (I'm winking at you, just so you know).

Anyways, I'm not telling him any of that shit you wrote but if it makes you feel any better, part of my sleazy heart feels for you. You gotta wear Big Girl pants these days hey Roberts, heavy stuff being a Mum and all that, with that responsibility. Pretty shitty for a seventeen-year-old but hey, don't fuck drug dealers, there's a life lesson for you.

I reckon you'd be good value on a night out Erin but do us a favour, go and have a wash because you proper smell of shit.

Stay cool

Danny

*PS I'll look after the soppy prick, even if it means **my** prick suffers losses.*

PPS For what it's worth, he does get it y'know, the situation with you and that drug dealer, he's just fucked up about it.

PPPS Just so you know, when he sees you, I reckon he'll be dying too. Try not to look too hot, eh?"

I walk up to bed, smiling through tears.

21st October 1997

I did fail that sodding exam after all, those bloody missed questions were forty percent of the mark. I

253

retook it today and checked every inch of the bastard paper before I started, not wishing to repeat my mistake.

My sons turn one tomorrow. I actually cannot believe that we are a) a year down the line from that day of terror and joy and that b) I have kept two babies alive and healthy for that length of time.

I have got a party planned at the leisure centre on Saturday, a bouncy castle and a ball pit booked, both of which are likely to be enjoyed more by their father and their ridiculous Uncles than by them. Jake started to walk last week, an event that caused him terror and his brother unending glee. Jake wobbled across the floor like he was trying to flee a grenade, scared to death by the way in which the world had suddenly turned ninety degrees, his gorgeous face covered in tears as he howled in fear. AJ had whooped in delight as he realised that he now had his own personal two-legged courier.

Everyone from Bristol is coming down for the party, the first time that my family will have met Jay's. Even Jay's Dad is threatening an appearance, Golden-Boy Obi's offer of transportation having been an acceptable option to the miserable, selfish old goat. Casey has been invited too, Jay did not want to leave her out. I'm cool with her coming because I've also sent Gio an invite.

I saw Gio for the first time in six weeks, five days and thirteen hours on the Monday that we came back to school after the Summer Holidays. I had to bite my cheeks so hard to prevent me howling in pain that I briefly panicked that I'd need stitches. He looked *incredible.* Snowboarding all 'summer' in New Zealand had given him an astonishing tan and his hair was slightly longer than usual, curling around his ears. He looked taller somehow, broader too. Gio looked like a grown man. I had to wedge my feet between the legs of the tutor room tables to prevent me jumping to my feet and throwing myself at him. I heard nothing but the thumping of my heart and Danny's words in my head, *"He'll be dying too"*

Gio never looked at me once, not even vaguely in my direction. He laughed and joked with the lads, he winked cheekily at the girls and he engaged in banter with Mr. Dobbs, who was looking at Gio like he wanted to lick every inch of him but Gio never even glanced my way.

We have not interacted once which has killed stone-dead Carolyn's rumours that she caught us snogging. If we pass in corridors or rooms, he does this thing where he slickly turns away to talk to somebody, so that we have absolutely no interface. In tutor group, he always comes in last and he sits up on the Art Room sideboard behind everyone and away from any potential line of sight. Mr Dobbs, who now dribbles almost constantly in Gio's presence, does not scold him. Me? I just try to remember how to breathe until we are out of the same airspace.

I posted his invite to the party, stupid really. I made it especially, addressing it to him from AJ and Jake as opposed to being from me. The RSVP was to my Mum. He rang her the other day, knowing I was at school and said that he'd pop in for five minutes with Adam.

Mum knows about Gio, I got really tearful one night watching a soppy film and I told her that we'd kissed but that I am choosing to be with Jay. She looked genuinely sad, holding me in a gently affectionate hug as she told me that she was so proud of the way that I prioritise the boys in my decision making. She never commented on my actual decision to choose Jay over Gio.

I accepted Mr. Gibson's offer of the voluntary placement at the refuge, my interest piqued but also my CV in need of some serious padding. My age means that it has to be deemed 'work experience' and the training that I have been given earlier this month was aimed at this level.

"OK Erin, so I see you've completed the Health and Safety, Confidentiality, Safeguarding and Staff Conduct training modules so how about we set up an introduction session with the girls", Sinead is the Refuge Manager, a kind but terrifying lady whose whole demeanour speaks of a life fraught with overcome-challenges. She has zero tolerance for shit and is the most vigorous advocate for her 'girls' that anyone could ever wish.

Sinead has explained that she currently has two sixteen year old girls in the refuge. One has a child of her own and is fleeing violence and the other is the daughter of a refuge resident. Both girls have had to uproot from their home areas and are a bit lost in terms of plans and direction. My role is to spend two hours a week with the girls, having a cup of tea at a local cafe and chatting to them to discuss their plans, as a Peer Mentor. We'll meet next week

Christ, they must be desperate.

22nd October 1997

Their first birthday starts like a dream. Jay and I sit with the boys in bed as they tear at the wrapping of their present, entirely thrilled with the cardboard boxes in which their toy train set came in leaving the train and it's lurid coloured tracks casually discarded on the floor. Jay is belly laughing at the boys aggravatedly tussling with the box, each trying to topple the other off the bed as Jay and I have to dive to catch them in turn. When a particularly animated catch by me sees Jake and I fall off the edge, Jay's deep laugh makes me grin through my bashed shoulder and I find myself being covered by the warm, gorgeous weight of my muscled boyfriend, his Colgate smile and his cheeky scarred eyebrow making me tingle. As our two mobile little terrorists squeal and clamber all over us as we lie on the floor, Jay leans down, his biscuity morning breath oddly familiar to me as our lips are within millimetres of touching,

"You an' me Feist, this, is the fuckin' bomb, yeah?", he's looking at me as AJ attempts to mount his face and he as he removes the intruding gnome, he kisses me softly, before we both swear and grab Jake as he tries to ingest Jay's loose change.

Chapter Thirteen

25th October 1997

Introducing Bronwen Roberts to *anyone* when she is a bit stressed, is never a wise plan. Introducing an entire family of in-laws, when her sister's cake-making skills have *again* resulted in a mouldy offering and her forty-one year old brother with Down's has taken up residence in the ball pit and is refusing to move out of the way for the toddlers it is *supposed* to contain, just added to the *friction*.

The leisure centre is a noisy venue. The breeze-blocked walls do a fabulous job of amplifying the screams and tantrums of the fifteen little people invited to this jamboree and the bouncy castle pump is bloody loud. The odd thing is that adults outnumber the kids three to one and my goodness, aren't we the eclectic bunch.

My Welsh family make up 50% of the attendees, my Cambridge-residing paternal family politely declined this little festive soiree. As Jay's brothers, Megan, a slightly uncomfortable looking Casey, Kaydee and Jay's Dad Kel arrive in the hall, you can cut the awkwardness with a knife. Casey looks beautiful, she's wearing jeans and a simple top but with her hair loose and her pretty face immaculately made up, I watch as Jay looks *pained* when their eyes meet.

My family are loud, obnoxious and *entirely* without any regard for political correctness or social sensitivity, the ethnic diversity of their Valley towns and villages extend to the owners of the Chinese takeaway, a Curry House and The Iraqi family who run the grocers. Even as a teenager, the words my Aunties use to describe my Uncle make me wince sometimes. While I was getting the boys dressed, I heard my mother lecturing her siblings and their offspring on words they are not allowed to use today. I cried tears of silent laughter at my Aunties' and Uncles' bafflement,

"So beaut, are you saying that I can't call the boys 'my little Allsorts' no more? I dunno Bron, that seems a bit much"

"But I do always call our Jake half-caste, how comes I can't no more? Mixed-Race? That do sound like he's in a little baby Olympics by there? I mean, our AJ, he do look like he's just got a little touch of sun, you'd never know his Dad was a coloured lad.....what? I can't say coloured no more either? Bron, this is proper fucking ridiculous"

My terrifying mother has frightened them all so much, that upon the arrival of Obi and his father Kel, the Welsh Contingent stood in fixed-grinning inertia, looking a bit mental. Jay, who has not met two of my Uncles, is over enthusiastically greeted by them both, shooting me baffled looks as my Uncles try to ply him with pints and demand to know if he watches Rugby.

I am busy greeting the ten sets of 'playgroup babies' who I invited, my weekly attendance at one of the nicer, more chilled playgroups earning me a few proper 'mum friends' finally. They are stood, clutching the shitty urn-tea that my mum foisted upon them on arrival, trying to look like they are cool with the fact that their toddlers are currently sharing a ball-pit with an obese Down's man who is having the *time of his life.* I thank them all for coming, take the generous gifts, tell them to help themselves to the mountain of food and we allow the babies to toddle wild for an hour.

My Mum takes a shine to Obi, charmed by that smile and his willingness to help with the teas. She's blushing as he play-flirts with her and I shoot him a look of incredulity as he tells her,

"Mrs. Roberts, I can see where Erin gets her stunning looks from". Obi just winks at me as I snort into a sausage roll watching my mother simper and giggle.

A Dinner Lady by trade, Auntie Di has cornered a stiff and uncomfortable Kel, who has only said

'Hello' to me and has barely acknowledged his grandsons or his youngest son. *Bastard.* Mind you, revenge is being served as Auntie Di has started talking to him about how chuffed he must have been,

"When that A-party-ed nonsense finished in South Africa and that nice Mr. Nelson got made Prime Minister".

I watch as Obi sticks his fist in his mouth and has to walk away, choking on laughter.

I'm so busy hostessing and preventing my sons from committing fratricide on the bouncy castle that I don't initially get a chance to greet D, Megan and Casey. Kaydee rushed up for a cuddle earlier, before immediately launching herself onto the bouncy castle with my nine-year-old twin cousins but I have not spoken to the others and I decide to put that right.

I approach, ignoring Megan's raised eyebrow, "Hiya, thanks so much for coming all this way, I know that Jay was really chuffed you could all make it", I make a point of smiling at Casey, keen for her to know that she's welcome.

D smiles, "It's cool Erin, Kaydee was proper excited to see the boys and tha'. Man, wha' the fuck is Wheels doin'?", D points at Jay across the room.

People don't always see my *favourite* side of Jay but today, messing about with his two sons, his teenage brother-in-law and his equally daft older brother, Jay is chasing the twins on all fours on the bouncy castle, making every tiny occupant of the inflatable boxing ring squeal and shriek like they are being murdered. Jay is beaming, his laugh is deep and warm and he looks relaxed. Jay is not somebody who willingly draws attention to himself, he is often found frowning quietly, not risking looking daft or making himself vulnerable to piss-taking. Jay is pretty serious but more frequently, I see the daft side of him with the boys, I see him messing about with them when it's just us. When he's like that, it's the closest I come to thinking I could fall in love with him.

D looks astonished, Megan's eyebrow is off the chart but Casey, her pretty face is a whole flicker show of emotions. She's smiling broadly at Jay messing about but her eyes are brimming with tears, her lip trembling as she watches him, gasp-laughing as Jay starts to make those duck noises that send Jake *frikking mental*.

Casey turns to me, her eyes shining and her smile wobbly, "Erin, I haven't seen him laugh like that since…….since before he got sent down that first time. He hasn't laughed like that for so long", I hear the emotion in her voice and with a gesture, she pretends to head for the loo but given the speed at which Megan follows her, I suspect there is limited wee-ing going on.

We do the cake, the boys' wide-eyed delight at the possibility of unrestricted sugar requires Jay and I to grasp them both tightly to prevent them launching themselves into the icing. It's then that the cameras come out and demands are made for 'Family Photos'. Holding a twin each, Jay puts his arm around me, both of us grimacing slightly with embarrassment at being the focus of so many lenses. Snap after snap is taken.

"Give her a kiss boyo", my Uncle Gareth shouts and with embarrassed smiles, Jay leans forward and plants a soft kiss on my lips.

I look up as we pull apart and at the back of the room, I see Gio stood in the doorway, his coat still on and his whitened knuckles gripping two matching sized parcels. My heart genuinely misses a beat as we lock eyes for the first time since that kiss at the party. His expression is hard to read, he just looks like he's carved from stone. As my gaze shifts slightly, I see Casey stood a couple of feet away, her face similarly blank but rigid.

I watch, ignoring shouts for me to smile, as Gio slowly places the two parcels on the table and walks back out, Adam following him. Casey makes a similar move, Megan on her heels.

Mum got the photos printed a week later. In amongst the tens of pictures, some of them with me and Jay kissing, was the final shot she took. In it, the twins are smiling as Jay and I are looking off camera, towards the retreating figures of Gio and Casey. On our faces are matching expressions of mournful loss.

11th December 1997

"Well Miss. Roberts, I have a great deal of pity for the poor unfortunate souls who may be landed with you in their hour of need but as Social Work is such an understaffed profession, I'm sure they'll be grateful for whatever they can get", Mr. Gibson's Careers Advice is, as always, inspiring and motivating.

Today is my UCAS Application Appointment. An hour with Mr. Gibson to decide my University choice, my future career and manner in which I will propel myself into both.

I've been meeting with sixteen-year-old refuge-residents Abi and Chloe for two months now, sometimes at the refuge, whose secret address I am sworn to protect with my very life and sometimes at a cafe nearby. Chloe has had a tough time in recent weeks following her decision to leave the refuge and return with her baby to the boyfriend who beat her. She lasted a week until he put her back in hospital after he scalded her with a kettle of boiling water, leading her to require significant medical care and endure horrific pain which is ongoing. However her return to him, albeit brief, has seen Children's Social Care get involved and tiny baby Lexi is on the Child Protection Register.

Abi is just angry at *everyone* and I'm always astonished that she turns up for our sessions but turn up she does. Abi has spent a lifetime watching her mum jump from one arsehole boyfriend to another, unable to prioritise her daughter over her need to have a man around, however much of a twat that man might be. Abi has lost her home, her place at a familiar college, her friends and her home area because the last boyfriend, a charming gentleman called Carl, slit her mother's throat during particularly nasty row. Abi had to stem her mother's wound with her bare hands as she dialled '999', Carl fleeing the scene.

At nearly seventeen, Abi is deemed 'too old' to need to go into Care so she resides at the Refuge with her mum but she angrily repeats, at every session, that she wishes she had been taken into care as a child. I am also told that she and her Mum have screaming rows which may see them evicted from the refuge if they are not careful.

When we meet, we just chat. I have no expertise to offer other than being a year older, a mum myself and somebody who sees the world from a slightly more stable bedrock than they have had the privilege of enjoying. Now that Lexi is 'on the register', I'm helping Chloe with college application forms because she wants to show people that she's looking for a better future. For Abi, she just seems to like ranting and having me nod and make suggestions with regards to how she can approach her mum with her grievances. I don't feel I'm necessarily making anything better for them but Sinead seems happy enough and I like our little weekly meet-ups, Mum watching the twins for me while I get the bus into town.

It's what has led me to contemplate Social Work as a career.

"So, looking at this, you've listed the three main local establishments, that's what you want to do Miss. Roberts, study locally?", Mr. Gibson asks as I nod slowly.

I realised, on about Day 20 after my sons were born, that there was no way on God's Green Earth that I would be able to cope without Mum and Dad's help until I am able to earn enough money to pay for babysitters, nurseries or Christ knows what else. I have also come to realise, in a painful journey over the last few months, that my A Level Grades are not going to be *earth shattering*. I just don't get any time to study, make a decent job of assignments or invest 100% in my work because the whole time, I

262

am juggling bigger commitments. I am coasting, pretty well I might add but coasting nonetheless. If I get three C's I'll be ecstatic but I predict a sprinkle of D's in my future. It makes me sad in my bones when I think about it.

My friends are all clever arses. Lees will do Sport Science at a *proper* Uni, no doubt about that. She and Adam, joined at the hip in an adorable but pretty healthy way, have got the same three Uni choices on their UCAS form, Manchester, Leeds and Exeter. Gio........well, as far as I know, Gio is planning a pretty mega Gap Year with my email pal *Danny* before he does the Town Planning Degree that he has decided on. I can't think about him not living down the road and not seeing him every day because it hurts too much. Even though we barely look at each other, even though we never speak, seeing him every day that I'm in school makes me *warm*. The days when I'm at home with the boys and I don't see him, I feel like I'm missing something.

My three choices for the Sociology Degree I want to do, consists of the two local Poly's and a College of Higher Education.

Jay, who has become somebody that I look forward to seeing, has dropped massive hints about me studying in Bristol and for a while, I did genuinely contemplate it but there is a truth that I struggle to acknowledge, nearly a year into our relationship.

I still feel like the uninvited guest.

I don't want to move to Bristol, I don't want to move in with Jay because I still feel *unwelcome* at times when I'm there with him and his family and friends. Obi is my ally, I never feel this way when he's chatting and messing about with me but with everyone else, I feel a bit.......tolerated. D is kind and polite but there's a slight sadness that coats his face when he sees Jay or I share any sort of affection. The result is that I mute myself, I self-censor, I try to blend into the background. *I'm not me.*

"Right Miss. Roberts, I think that concludes our appointment. Your personal statement sufficiently highlights your attributes whilst playing down your troublesomeness and therefore, I declare my work here done", Mr. Gibson raises his hands in mock surrender as I smirk at him.

He clears his throat, "If I can ask you to please go and collect Mr. Romano, his appointment is my next tribulation", I jolt and wince, *bloody alphabetical register.*

Mr. Gibson frowns as he sees my response, "Miss. Roberts, I understood that you and Mr. Romano were particular friends, I believe he was present at the birth of your sons, or so staffroom gossip suggested?", he watches as I nod reluctantly.

He sits back in his chair, folding his arms over his chest,

"Miss. Roberts, I would rather eat Year 7's cookery class offerings than get involved in any sort of trivial, teenage melodrama but I would like to offer you this morsel of disinterested observation: On the afternoon that you engaged in a Car Park brawl with a mystery, disappearing pugilist, I observed Mr. Romano's concern, alarm and dare I say, *devotion* to your securing your safety and well-being. It was.......impressive", he looks directly at me.

"Go and fetch Mr. Romano, Miss. Roberts", and he nods, dismissing me.

I know Gio's timetable as well as my own. *Obsessed much, Roberts?* As I enter the unfamiliar territory of the maths classroom, all eyes are on me. When I mumble that I am here to collect Gio, I see him jolt in his seat from the corner of my eye, his big frame filling the desk where he sits.

I spin on my heels and flee, I cannot speak to Gio because the last time we talked, he ended up giving the hottest kiss of my *life* and my lips do this stupid tingle thing when he's close but I have made my choice and my boys' security is dependent on my keeping to it.

"So that's it, yeah? That's how this goes now, you and me?", Gio's deep voice behind me is harsh, echoing down the deserted corridors.

I stop my stampede, my head bowing as I feel sadness sweep through me.

I mumble, "I don't want it to be like this Gio", as I stare at my feet.

I hear footsteps, I smell lemons and herbs and then he is in front of me, his beautiful face scrunched in a frown.

"So we haven't talked in like, *months* Rin. Not since…...not since that night", he looks down at his feet, his jaw tight.

I nod, looking out of the window as I whisper, "You just ignore me, I thought….I thought it was what you wanted?".

His lip curls in a snarl, "Yeah, well, what *I* want doesn't fucking matter does it? Your *boyfriend* made it pretty clear where I fucking stand and so I'm just doing what you want, right? Staying away from you is what you *want* isn't it Roberts?", he starts fiddling with the wall display.

I need to pull the ripcord, his proximity is unsettling me. *Jay, Jay, Jay. Remember Jay.*

"Mr. Gibson is probably….", I start to babble but Gio moves closer, cutting over my rambling.

"Rin, what do *you* want? Eh? Him? *Jay*? Just do me a favour, cut the bullshit about what you *need* to do. These appointments with Gibson, they're about what we *want* for the future yeah, so tell me Erin,

265

what do you *want*?", he holds his hands out in a plea.

I look at him, this boy I've known almost my whole life, since we were three years old and started playgroup together. The bane of my existence for years, my friend who looked after me and my unborn boys and now the one thing I can't stop thinking about. *I want you.*

Every muscle and nerve ending in my body wants to throw myself at him, my fingers are aching to touch him, my lips wants to kiss him, my voice box is itching to scream the words, *"You're what I want"* but I grit my teeth and I fight it, my heart hurting as I say,

"Gio, Mum always told me that *"I want, never gets"*. I think for me, that's pretty true. What I want doesn't matter, it just doesn't fucking matter. I'm going to get my crappy A Level grades, get on whichever Degree course will take me and just see what happens while I keep my babies happy and give them the *family* they deserve. I've got no room for *wanting* anything apart from making my boys happy and safe. Any time you *want* to see the boys, just ask Lees and I'll make sure she or Ad bring them round to see you. They love seeing you, you're their Godfather, they love you Gio", I sob on the last words.

I look up at him, his mouth hanging open slightly as his eyebrows crease into a deep frown as he shakes his head angrily.

I start to back away, "I'm not worth getting aggravated about, I'm just rank, ugly ginger Roberts. Go see Gibson, he'll be pissed off already. I'll see you around Romano", and I turn and walk out of the door and towards the bus stop, my heart in tatters beneath my ribs.

21st January 1998

I'm not sure when I started to feel this *inkling*. I can't pinpoint an event or a date but something is *different*. As I look at Jay, the outline of his sleeping features illuminated by the boys' night-light, I ponder the fact that he and I have not had sex in over two weeks.

We had a big row, a couple of days after Christmas. It was horrible actually. I'd finished, signed and sent off my UCAS form and when I confirmed to Jay that I was definitely not going to study in Bristol, he got unexpectedly angry. He accused me of being,

'Too scared to grow up and fuckin' move out Feist. You're all mouth, innit? You got a sweet deal at your folks so while it's just me gotta haul my arse everywhere to come see you, you're gonna stay put. It's fuckin' selfish Erin'

It was the first time that he'd used that accusatory tone and it unsettled me. I was also *fucking* furious, how *dare* he spout such total bollocks. I tore into him, pointing out that without my parents' on hand, I cannot afford the childcare that I need to do my degree, even with the grants and bursaries I'd get as a parent. I pointed out that he has to work full-time, I would have to study AND work to earn money, that we could not afford the size flat that we would need, that he was an *ignorant shit* if he had any doubts over exactly how brave I have had to be to survive the last twenty-two months or the things I have sacrificed.

We were nose to nose in his *shitty* bedsit as we screamed at each other.

"Anyway Jay, why the fuck would I want to live here, surrounded by people who see me as the fucking shit *second choice*, the girl who trapped you by having your kids, the girl who keeps you from being with *beautiful, perfect Casey*", Christ, it went dark a lot quicker than I thought it would, a couple of post-club alcopops well and truly loosened my lips.

Jay looked absolutely stunned. He gasped for words like a beached goldfish but then his face turned to thunder and he growled out,

"Don't you chat any shit 'bout Case, y'hear?", there was real menace in his tone.

Ginger Feist reared her head, "Oh God forbid I mention Casey or the fact that you don't ever stop staring at her when we're out, *like you were doing tonight* or the fact that you look at her like she's magical. I heard Megan say she broke up with that lad she was seeing, you must be pleased, eh Jay?", I considered for the first time that I might be a nasty drunk. I'd only drunk this much once before and that time I retired meekly to bed without any of *this* nonsense.

Jay stepped even closer, his breath puffing against my face, "Don't. Fuckin'. Start. This. Shit", venom trickled unexpectedly from his words and I felt a shiver of fear.

I stepped back slightly, feeling a bit woozy from the booze,

"What do you feel about me Jay, eh? What am I to you?", my tone was genuinely questioning as opposed to pathetic.

He looked baffled by the change of direction, huffing and shrugging awkwardly, looking a bit jittery,

"You're askin' me *now*? Fuck woman, I dunno. You're my girl, yeah? Me and you, we're together, we're raising those boys together, innit? Girlfriend and boyfriend, parents and that. Fuck's sake Feist, why you askin' me this shit now when we're screwin' at each other?", he huffed over to the bed and sat down, shaking his head at me.

My voice was low, "Those are just labels, they're the things we call ourselves. What do you *feel* about me? Do you love me Jay? I think I want to know, I never have before but I think I want to know now", I wobbled slightly as I walked over the bed, sitting beside a wild-eyed Jay who looked as if he was in actual physical pain.

I patted his hand and tried to wink but I think I probably looked like I had palsy, "Jay, you don't need to freak out, I mean, I care about you, I like you so much when you're not being a fucking twat who shouts at me", I kissed my teeth at him as he shook his head.

I took a breath, "Jay, what do you feel about me?", now that *did* sound pathetic.

He swore a bit, paced round, muttered incomprehensible and borderline offensive things about *'crazy women'* but then he turned and threw his hands in the air,

"I care 'bout you Feist, 'kay? I care and I think you're proper fuckin' sexy and I love tha' you're such an amazin' Mum. I mean, you are hardcore mental and you talk proper shit but when I see you wiv' the boys, I.....I *feel* stuff, yeah", he closed his eyes, a bit embarrassed.

He turned and looked me in the eyes as he smirked, "You crack me up, no girl ever made me laugh like you do an' when me an' you are together, it's.......it's hot", his smirk became a bit feral.

I smiled and it was a genuine smile but I felt the need to push,

"But you don't love me, do you Jay", resigned curiosity is how I'd have defined my tone.

Jay'd scrubbed his hand over his face, pursing his lips and frowning until he allowed his gaze to meet mine and he whispered, "I guess, it ain't yet......but maybe wiv' time an' tha'? I.......I care, a whole lot.....just......time yeah?", he reached out and grabbed my hand, his gaze gentle and worried.

I nodded and smiled but I had more drunken words, "Jay, don't you.....don't you want to ask me, y'know, how I feel?", I saw his face stiffen as he jerkily shook his head.

"Nah, I ain't somebody asks questions they know the fuckin' answer to already Feist, nobody got time for tha' shit", his look my way was hard, his face guarded.

I felt a bit sick suddenly and I frowned in confusion as he added, "You reckon I look at Case like she's magic? You ever seen the way you look at *him*?", his words were clipped as I felt the ache in my chest.

Jay had come to midnight Mass on Christmas Eve with me, Mum and the boys, she didn't really give him a choice. Gio was there with his family, Mum patting my hand and shooting me concerned looks. Afterwards on the way out, Sofia and Gio's little sister Aurora cooed over the twins and Gio, he stood, arms folded, watching. As Jay took AJ to the car with Mum, I wrestled a recalcitrant Jake back into his winter coat and led him by the hand, his little legs wobbly because he was so tired, out of the door.

Spotting his beloved Gio, Jake yelped and toddled off towards him, Gio turning just in time to catch him as he tripped. Gio pulled faces, making Jake whoop with laughter before looking up at me and nodding tensely. He kissed Jake, pulled more faces and then handed him back, me gasping in an overly dramatic manner when our hands touched.

Awkwardly walking together down the path, Gio's arm bumped mine making both of us jolt. Emerging out of the church gate, we both paused and turned.

Gio sucked his teeth as he looked up at the frosty sky, "Merry Christmas yeah, Roberts. Have a good one. I hope you get everything you *want*".

I looked at him, pressing a kiss into my sons soft, baby-smelling head as I held Gio's blue-eyed gaze,

"I can't have what I *want* Gio. Merry Christmas Romano", I started to walk away.

Gio called out, his voice wobbly, "I still feel the same Rin, nothing's changed for me. What you want? It's always been yours, you've just got to want it enough" but with my heart doing a weird icy-beat thing I kept walking, over to Jay who was watching us with a frown.

A few weeks on, as the noise from our post-Christmas row echoed in our ears, we'd sat in an awkward silence on Jay's bed in his crappy studio flat. I looked at his frown and I'd asked,

"Jay.......we're doing the right thing aren't we? For the boys I mean, making this work?", my certainty was suddenly shaky.

Jay jerked his head up, scowling, "Feist, I ain't gonna play them boys like my piece of shit Pops played me an' D. I'm wiv' their Mum and we're a fuckin' family, 'kay? They ain't havin' the life I had, you got me? D and Megs, they got their issues but they make it work for Kaydee. So you stay wiv' your folks for a while longer, do that Uni study shit an' then we're gonna get a decent place together yeah? Safe an' that", Jay punched the bed and stared at the ceiling as I bit my lip and smiled tightly.

That night, Jay and I lay under the covers, my head tucked into his chest as we both pretended to sleep. We'd started to fool around but somewhere along the line, the lips and fingers and gasps lost their momentum and in an unspoken agreement, it tapered off into nothing

You ever seen the way you look at him?

Now, three weeks on and lying in my bed, things are definitely different. Jay is a bit *taut*. His smiles don't reach his eyes, his body is sort of stiffer when we hug and with the boys, he's less *silly*. It's nothing that I can quantify but it's there. As I lie on his chest, the sound of our sons snoring the gentle backing track, I feel like I can hear a clock ticking.

10th February 1998

It's knocking on for midnight and I'm finishing an entirely dull Social Policy essay when a ping on the computer alerts me to a new email.

"Roberts,

Congrats on still being a proper headfuck, G is as screwed up as he was in the summer so, well done there, eh. Anyway, who gives a shit, apparently he's messing with some right little goer so I guess he's coping. Right, although it's making my balls retreat back into my belly, I think I need your advice. Jesus, it hurts to even write that, I need a beer now.

Roberts, what the fuck do I do about this scenario? I reckon you gotta have some insight, I mean, you've got tits and you've had kids so you must be semi-useful I reckon. Here we go: Boy likes hot girl from school but girl is goodie two shoes, never hangs out anywhere good, has mates that don't go to the same school, mystery girl. Girl wasn't always hot, girl has suddenly acquired hotness. Boy is astoundingly good-looking player, stud muffin and all round chick magnet. The guy's hot. Really hot. He's a school legend. Goodie Girl should be sacrificing goats in thanks for the attention Boy is trying to give her. But girl doesn't give the tiniest shit, girl ignores boy's debonair approaches. Girl is ignoring Boy so much that it's actually starting to, y'know, piss him off. Boy has tried different approaches: funny, chat, piss-take, small gifts, shagging her mates but nothing gets his foot in her door.

C'mon Roberts, help a guy out? Come up with some ideas to turn this around for Boy. I can't ask the lads, it'll destroy them to see their idol laid so low. You can't have much of a life, sat there with your nappies and your drug dealer. Plenty of time to think of some useful advice, aye?

Remember, the guy is super hot, so y'know, factor that into your planning.

Stay ginger,

Danny

PS Oh yeah, those kids good? You still keeping them alive and that?

PPS In light of the PS above, you should probably factor in that the boy is sensitive, caring, good with
kids and is y'know, sweet and shit. Chicks are into that crap yeah?
PPPS The boy is me, just making that clear in case sprog-popping has dulled your brain. It's been a
while Roberts, you might have had a brain injury since the summer, how would I know?
PPPPS I reckon G would still give you a poke, even if you were proper retarded"

I am snorting in outrage, hiccuping in laughter and frowning in disapproval. *What a twat.* I mean, he
can't be entirely serious but at the same time, even a small degree of belief in anything he's just
written renders him a proper knob jockey. *I'm sort-of-married to you.*

Smiling, I start to type,

"Dear Dickhead
Well that was quite a treat for a Tuesday night, cheers for that. There's now two pairs of pissed-
through knickers sat in my washing basket, thanks for the hilarity McNamara.
Sit your arrogant butt down, c'mon, park that pretend-Kiwi tushie on a chair and listen to your Auntie
Erin.
As my not-a-drug-dealer-thank-you-very-much boyfriend would say, ***"She don't fancy you bruv".*** *Or*
at least she doesn't fancy the up-his-arse school legend, mate-shagger version of you. You might be
good looking still (confession time, proper fancied the arse off you when we were fourteen, don't let
your head get any bigger) but if she's pushing such a ***catch*** *away, I think you need to accept the fact*
that you, McNamara, do not float her boat in your current incarnation.
Time for a change.
You can't manufacture attraction but what you can do, is alter the variables. Be less of a dickhead.
Stop shagging her mates. Stop show-boating around her. You have got glimmers of hope, you left a
party to look after your mate, you emailed me to give me shit for hurting him and I'm willing to be bet
that you aren't anywhere near as much of a prat in reality as you are on paper. Gio's a good guy,
he's the best actually and I don't reckon he'd be mates with an inexorable (I do English A Level

273

sucker) twat.

Valentine's Day is coming up (it's the same date down with you isn't it?) so here's some pointers for free. Find out who she actually is, what she likes doing. Bands she likes, things she enjoys doing, hobbies. Do something genuine, low key and thoughtful. For Gods sake don't throw cash or glitz at the situation, you have probably been flash enough. Brace yourself for rejection because you appear to have pulled a lot of crap that has probably pissed her off. Keep going with the genuine, low key and thoughtful. If we're still in the same position in a few weeks time, you'll need to move on dude. Thus ends the advice. I would say 'good luck' but in all honesty, that's probably better directed at this poor cow you're pursuing. Jesus, I feel like this email is betraying each and every one of my worldwide sisterhood.

It's been emotional dude, off to wash my pissed knickers

Erin

PS Maybe you're just really shit in bed and the mates of hers that you've shagged have told her that. Ooooh, did you think about that? Christ, there's a burn waiting to happen, eh?"

I trot on with my essay and then forty-five minutes later, up he pops again.

"Roberts,

All your crappy advice is duly noted and I would offer my thanks but honestly, I don't want to delay you washing those wet knickers (mind you, typing that has given me a bit of a chubby so I might keep going while I rub one out....kidding.........sort of).

Her name's Adrienne by the way.

Gotta go, need to grab the wank sock quick. Talk dirty to me Roberts.....quick....oh...ohhhhhh.....ah well, too late for that fucking sock eh?

Danny

PS How very dare you Roberts, I am an awesome shag.

PPS I think I like chatting to you Roberts. Don't let it go to your head"

14th February 1998

It's been a year since Jay and I got together. A year. Twelve months as a couple. As I stock supermarket shelves with the same nappies that I will need to purchase on my way home with the money that I have been paid for stacking them in the first place, I sniff away some unexpected tears of self-pity because tonight, I will not be celebrating with Jay. He's not here. He's *with her.*

Casey turns twenty-one tomorrow and it is her Birthday celebration this afternoon and tonight. She is having a massive 'get together' at the pub on the estate and it will be followed by a huge night out in Bristol. Jay, to give him credit, had initially said he wasn't going to go. I'd felt uneasy about making any demands on him, weird though that sounds, as there is a strange sort of tension between us at the moment. However, Dad and Mum are going out tonight, Dyls is on a *date* and I have no babysitters.

The idea of spending a night in alone with Jay, with the pressure of Valentine's Day and it's associated romance hanging over our tense heads, it made me uncomfortable. Then Dad bought Mum a Photography Session as an early Valentine's gift and she booked to take the boys with her, wanting some photos with them. Jay's Saturday childcare duties relieved and with pressure on him from his brothers not to miss a huge night out, I told him that I thought he should go,

"Honestly Jay, you should…..you should go, spend time with your mates without me hanging around. I've….I've got revision to do anyway, those modular exams are after half-term", I tried to make my smile as wide and genuine as possible.

He didn't take much convincing, he could have perhaps resisted a bit longer. He came up last night, a bit surly from a long day at work. Handing me a bunch of flowers that he had clearly bought at a petrol station, he played distractedly with the boys, ate the tea that Mum had cooked him and then headed to bed. We had quick, heart-not-in-it sex and fell asleep. He dropped me at work with a distracted peck on the lips. That clock in my head has been ticking all day.

I keep the boys up later than normal this evening, playing their favourite games ('Shut Mummy in the coat cupboard', 'Who can bang the saucepans the loudest', 'Mummy jumping out of doorways and doing crazy dancing') and they furnish me with the hugs and kisses that my sore heart needs. I got in the bath with them, a bubbly-jamboree that saw me half-drowned as my sons delighted themselves in drenching my hip length hair with endless cups of water.

Dried, dressed and cups of milk guzzled, I threw on my PJ's and to their entire delight, I put the boys in my bed, bundled on top of the duvet in their sleep-sacks with my restraining arm preventing them from going anywhere. I am in bed at 9pm on Valentines Day with two gorgeous boys that I love more than anything else in the world. As I drift into sleep, I beg myself not to dwell on where Gio might be tonight. *Or who he might be with.*

Jay doesn't call me the next day. I tell myself he must have a stonking hangover as I focus on revising and playing with the boys in the park. He doesn't call me on Monday. I tell myself that he must be very busy at work as I spend my first day of half-term taking the twins swimming with Lees, Adam and Dyls. Tuesday comes and I'm too busy with my coursework and the boys to pay much attention.

I throw out Jay's half-dead flowers.

18th February 1998

Today, Day Four of no contact from Jay, I start to feel sick as panic slowly rise up from my toes, gripping my limbs and stalling my heartbeat as I sit on the bus with my double buggy which provokes the usual raised eyebrows and frustrated huffs from my fellow passengers. The boys need new shoes and there is a sale on at the sports shop. AJ is being an absolute stinker today. Both boys were awake at 4am and AJ threw his breakfast at me this morning, pretty much setting the tone for the days' behaviour. He is screaming and *'Mummeeeeeee-ing"* at a piercing level. Nothing I am doing is stalling the noise as I rock and jog the buggy and when Jake decides that he will provide the sidekick support, his querying calls for *'Dadada'* are what makes my lip wobble.

An elderly lady shoots me sympathetic looks but as I frantically offer the little stinkers snacks from my bag in an attempt to silence their noise, the first tears fall.

I make it through the fractious shoe purchases and they fall into snotty-faced slumber as I manage to navigate the purchase of some clothes for them and stuff for school. Then AJ wakes and I realise that he's actually a bit poorly. His eyes are gummy and judging by the truly, horrendous smell coming from him, he's got a poorly tum too. Jake wakes in the same state and they are screaming as I race the buggy through the shopping centre towards the loos.

We are in that baby-change toilet for the best part of half an hour using every baby-wipe I own, they've got shit *everywhere* and I come out feeling like I've been engaged in warfare. I dose the feverish pair with some Calpol, which has the unfortunate effect of re-invigorating them, their subsequent demands to exit their buggy driving me to madness. On reins, they're a *fucking* nightmare and we must look like some sort of travelling circus as I desperately try to herd them and the buggy to McDonalds where we are meeting Lees and Ads for lunch, when honestly all I want to do is sleep.

Lees takes one look at me and whispers to Adam as he heads to the counter, *"Buy her one of everything Ad. Seriously, everything",* as she gently takes Jake and ushers me to a table.

They are staring at me while I sit in heavy-eyed silence, the boys having finished the picnic lunch I'd made at 5am this morning as I slowly navigate my mountain of fast food.

"You OK babe?", Lees' pretty face is scrunched in a frown.

I nod and wipe AJ's face, "Uhuh".

She darts a glance at Ads, "Er, OK. So, Jay's coming down tonight, yeah? You fancy doing something tomorrow with us, him and the boys?", Lees' tone is gentle but worried.

I reach for Jake, wiping his little cheese-covered paws as I shake my head and purse my lips.

"Rinny?", Lees whispers and reaches for my hand, Adam sweetly stroking my arm in synchronisation.

I shake my head and whisper, "I need to get the boys home, I think they're coming down with something", and at that exact moment, my sons decide to validate my statement with a matching set of projectile vomits.

I go into efficient robot mode. The mess is beyond description. No fewer than five restaurant staff members are despatched to the clear up as I calmly retrieve my screaming sons from their vomit covered environs and begin the clear up in calm silence, changing and re-dressing them in the new clothes I have just purchased whilst dealing with nappies.

I efficiently cleanse their hair of vomit in the too-small sinks, inadvertently setting off the hand dryers and scaring the boys half to death. With my weird twin-mum arm-strength, I clutch my cleansed but hysterical sons to my chest as I exit the loos and calmly apologise to all of the staff, get the boys in the buggy despite their protests and bid a very concerned Adam and Lees a thanks and farewell, as they reluctantly head to the cinema.

I'm doing OK. *I am*. As I walk through the town centre towards the bus station, I'm OK. I can do this. If Jay is gone, if he has left me and our boys, if this is the rest of my life, managing every day on my own then I can do this. The boys might smell of shit and vomit, I might cheerfully sell them to the circus any moment soon but *I can do this*.

I'm almost there, the route to the bus station taking me through the bottom half of town near the car park, when I see him.

Gio's with a girl called Jessica from the year below us, a pretty blonde who is on various sports teams and has an annoying healthiness about her. She's tucked safely under his shoulder, his warm strong arm wrapped around her, protecting her from the cold and from any of the shit life might want to throw her way this afternoon. She's grinning up at him adoringly as he smiles down at her. That smile. Those blue eyes, She can probably smell the herbs and lemons. He's probably going to give her kisses today and she might not realise just how amazing those kisses are, she might not appreciate what it is that she has. She may not appreciate the freedom she has to have what she wants.

They dive into a shop, thankfully not seeing me and my bedraggled cargo. The don't see the way that my body slumps as my heart just gives the fuck up. They don't see me push my sons towards the bus that will take us home to the place where their father has not called for four days, my face slick with silent tears.

At home, it turns out that Jay *has* rung, a message left with Dyls. He isn't coming tonight but he'll be here in the morning apparently. Dyls said he sounded tired. I nod and zombie plod through the rest of the day, managing two poorly, demanding toddlers giving me enough things to occupy my brain.

At midnight, I creep down the stairs and turn the computer on.

"Danny

I think Jay's leaving me. He hasn't called for four days. He went to his ex-girlfriend's 21st on Saturday and now he's not staying tonight like he always does. He's coming here tomorrow and I'm so scared that he's just going to say that he's leaving me on my own, that he doesn't want to be with me, that I'll have to handle everything alone, that he'll be in Bristol. I don't know if I can make life good enough for them on my own, I don't know if I'm enough to make their life the one that they deserve without their Dad being with me. I'm so scared, I'm so scared that I'm fucking everything up. I'm proper, proper scared and nobody knows.

I saw Gio today with his girlfriend. Danny, It hurts so fucking much, why does it hurt so much? There is nothing I can do about it though and nobody I can tell because my boys deserve a family with their parents together so I'm trapped but now I think I've lost Jay anyway. I am so scared. Nobody knows the shit in my head, nobody knows how hard it is seeing Gio with other girls. I don't tell anyone, not even Lees.

Nobody knows but now you do. What do I do? What happens to me and the boys if Jay's not with me? What if I'm not a good enough Mum on my own? I'm scared Danny.

Erin

PS I'm too scared for a PS"

I go and get a drink and as I return to turn off the computer, there's the ping of a message

"Erin,

You're enough on your own. He's a cunt if he leaves you. A proper cunt. Do better. Be less scared. You're fucking enough Roberts.

Danny

PS I'm going to see some shit band tonight, because she'll be there. Totally your fault.

PPS You're enough

PPPS With G, if there's any moves to make, you've got to be the one making them now woman. The boy did his best Roberts, ball's in your court"

I stare at his kind bluntness.

"Night McNamara"

Two seconds later, *"This band describe themselves as 'Industrial Noise'. Fuck you Roberts"*

I chuckle all the way up the stairs.

19th February 1998

I'm stunned when I see that the boys and I have all slept in until 8.30am but then I realise that the room smells of vomit. It's *everywhere* in their cot and I'm crying with relief that they didn't choke in their sleep. Dyls is asked to help, he lasts two seconds before he has to retreat, his face green. I don't even notice Jay come in the room. I genuinely don't. He's just suddenly there, picking up babies, running baths and helping sort it, a silent, cooperative presence by my side. I don't even acknowledge his arrival.

The boys are washed, changed, beds stripped, room aired and as Jay has wordlessly carried the boys downstairs to their playpen, I'm in the shower. I reach for the shampoo and realise that my hands are shaking uncontrollably. I stare at my hands and look up to see Jay stood the other side of the shower screen, looking at me. I am naked and soaking wet and yet it's him that looks vulnerable.

"I had to get my head straight", his words are soft and nervous.

I look at him defiantly, as I step out of the shower and wrap myself in a towel, "And did you? Get it straight?", my voice is stronger.

He bows his head as he nods.

"You love her", it's not a question that I ask.

His deep brown eyes look up at me, that scarred eyebrow suddenly making him look young, that gorgeous mocha-toned face arranged in a pained expression.

He nods, he bites his lip and he nods. *There.*

"Did you fuck her?", my words are spat out and he steps forward in alarm, protesting,

"Nah, nah I wouldn't play you like that Feist. But……..me an' her…..I stayed at hers after the club. We…I…….we talked Erin, we got so much history me an' her, we got so much. I've been at hers", I think my heart has stopped as I see his lip wobble.

But then he reaches out and slides his hand around the back of my head, fingering my shower-damp curls, "But you know what proper did my fuckin' head in Feist, you know why I've been gone these days?", his tone is a bit angry as I look confused.

He lowers his forehead against mine, his eyes closed, "Ask me that fuckin' question again Feist, ask me what I feel", it's a whisper and I'm momentarily confused until I realise what he's asking.

I whisper in return, "What do you feel about me Jay?", my heart is thumping under my towel.

He looks me in the eyes, "I love you Feist, I love you as well as Case an' I got no fuckin' idea what I do 'bout that. Tell me, tell me what to fuckin' do?", as he clenches his jaw impossible tightly, his eyes look fierce but there's a glistening on his lashes that makes my breath hitch.

In a panic, I pull him into a kiss, a frantic one, which sees us stumble until my back hits the ensuite wall. I'm swamped with too many pieces of information, both painful and reassuring and so I use the most straightforward language that Jay and I speak to try to communicate comfort. I use sex. Our touches are frantic, hands pulling rather than stroking, grabbing rather than caressing. Our desperation for some sort of answer to this complex situation makes us claw at each other.

As he releases his dick from his jeans, my towel long discarded, he slips into me and groans into my skin, "It's you too Feist".

We come with our hands clapped over each other's mouths, conscious belatedly that Dyls is in the house although my parent are thankfully departed to work. Panting our post-coital exhaustion into each other's skin, our sons with their perfect timing, start yelling for both of us, making Jay snort. I gently stroke his face as he looks anxiously at me, he can see the question in my expression.

I whisper, "Jay, who made the decision that you would…..that you would come back here? Did you choose to leave or did Casey tell you to?", I need to know this.

Jay sucks his lip and shakes his head, looking torn, "It was me. She…...she told me that I gotta choose. She told me that she couldn't let herself be wiv' me unless I was *hers* again", he shakes his head wincing, "It fuckin' killed me coz honestly, I been wanting that since me an' her split. She's all I figured I wanted. Then, Sunday mornin', I wake up, on the floor in her room an' I realised tha'...tha'.....I didn't feel like I figured it would. Somethin' was missin'. *You*. You and my boys", his eyes are desperately sad.

"Me an' her talked. She proper gets me, y'know? It was her that made me see that it…..that I….tha' it's love, what I got for you. It's love Feist", and he kisses me gently.

"She told me that it was only me that could choose. I've spent three days screwin' myself up thinkin' an'.....", he shrugs.

I whisper, "You chose me?"

He nods and smiles weakly. I return his smile but need to distract with humour because I cannot have him ask me what it is I feel about him. *I have no fucking clue.*

I raise an eyebrow, "Well, just so you know, you missed your sons filling a shopping centre with shit, filling McDonalds with vomit and then screaming like banshees for a whole day. You *owe* me Watson", he swears inventively and makes me laugh.

I will try to love you, I will try.

Jay stays the night. He takes me on a belated Valentines Date to a proper restaurant, he holds my hand and he makes me laugh again, an odd sort of peace settling on us. In bed that night, the sex is slow and tender and Jay's reverent almost in the way he touches me. When he comes, he quietly groans *'I love you girl''* into my neck. As I stroke his skin and kiss him gently, I convert panic into determination.

I will make myself love you.

Chapter Fourteen

3rd April 1998

Lees has been no help, if I'm honest. None whatsoever. Today is my 18th Birthday and weeks ago, I told myself that I would tell Jay I loved him *today* or not at all. After his return and those first declarations, Jay hasn't said it more than a couple of times since and those have either been orgasmic exclamations or chuckled throwaway comments when I've made him laugh hard.

It's now three minutes past midnight, I am officially eighteen but as I look across my pillow at Jay, his face relaxed in sleep, I realise that I am no closer to knowing whether what I feel for Jay constitutes love.

I've done a secret list, to try to hone my decision making:

1) He is an amazing Dad. I mean, *properly* amazing. My Dad and he went out for a drink one night and apparently, according to a slightly startled Jay, my father hugged him and told him that he was proud of the father that Jay had become. Dad got choked, Mum would later tell me, when Jay had mumbled, *"I just watch what you do, innit"*.

2) My boys adore their father, they *worship* him. They behave for Jay so much better than they behave for me, I could throttle them for it.

3) Jay makes me feel comfortable, I feel like I can breathe a bit easier on the days when he's by my side.

4) Jay is incredibly fit. Girls stare at him constantly and it makes me feel stupidly proud that he says he loves *me*.

5) Jay chose me over the girl he has loved for his entire adolescence. He chose me and I owe him my loyalty for that.

6) He's brilliant at sex. I have no comparison by which to measure but honestly, an orgasm is an orgasm and he gives me a lot of those. His penis is lush.

7) I like making him laugh and we have fun together when we go out as a family or as a couple. He's funny and he's kind.

8) He goes out of his way to make my life easier. He has started to support my decision to stay local for Uni.

9) He compliments me and makes me feel attractive.

10) He gets on with my *mental* family and although things are tense with he and Megan at the moment due to the fact that Casey no longer comes on nights out, when we are in Bristol he no longer allows me to feel like the uninvited guest.

That's my list.

In my despair last week, a decision no clearer to me than it was weeks ago, I showed Lees the list, pointing accusingly at it and demanding that she tell me,

"Lees, does this look like love, eh? You love Ad, you and him are *in love* so you *must* know? Does it? Does this list look like love?", she'd looked slightly frightened by my wild-eyed, frantic questioning.

She'd read it, frowning slightly, "Er, well, honestly? Rinny, it's not setting the world alight with passion is it? I mean, where's the affection? Where's the desperation and the romance? What about how he makes you feel, where's that on the list?", she'd winced slightly as she awaited my response to her feedback.

I tutted and pointed at the list, "There! He makes me feel safe, he makes me feel attractive and he supports me. He makes me laugh and we have fun", I'd nodded encouragingly at her.

Lees lowered the list and looked anxiously at me, "Rinny, you could be describing that multi-way bra you got stuck in in Top Shop that time…...I mean, that was safe, supportive, made you feel attractive and then when you tried to get it off, it was completely funny and it definitely made you laugh. This list Rinny, it's not exactly, er, *gushing* is it?", her face could not look less convinced.

I saw her take a deep breath, "Rinny, have you asked yourself this question: What would Gio's list look like?", I saw her wince slightly.

Snatching my list from the duvet, I jumped to my feet, "Well, that's just ridiculous, there is no list for Gio, there will never be a list for Gio because…….", I'd aimed for outrage as inside my head, I was screaming,

"Because that list would never end at ten things. It's infinite. It's a novel. It's every fleck of blue in his eyes, every smirk, every deep laugh, the way his lips felt like silk, the way that I can feel every pore on my skin tingle when he's in the same room as me, the way that his voice is what I hear when I'm scared, it's the way I have imaginary conversations with him when I see something funny on TV, it's the way his arm muscles move like ripples under the soft tanned velvet of his skin when he stretches in lessons. It's the hurt when he ignores me, it's the way I don't bath my sons on the days when he has seen them because I want to sniff their hair and smell his scent. It's the way I see him everywhere, it's the way I fantasise about sex with him in a way that makes me impossibly wet. It's how I can list every one of his visible scars and tell you how he got them. It's how I can recall an entire childhood of memories and incidents that involve him. It's the way that my heart hurts acutely when anyone says his name. It's the way that a part of me dies every time I see him holding Jessica's hand because that warm, strong, big hand is mine to hold when I'm scared or dying. It's those things and a thousand

more".

I stared at Lees,

".....because that would be a pointless waste of my time", and with a firm nod, I'd told her I'd see her the next day at school and I stomped home.

Leaving my three sleeping menfolk in my room, I sneak downstairs, needing to solve this riddle now that my birthday deadline is upon me.

"McNamara, are you there? Please say you're there and not shagging Adrienne…….… Remember who brokered those shags and to whom you owe gratitude….ME!! Please be there…..."

The glow from the computer screen is all the illumination that I have in Mum's dining room.

"We don't shag Roberts, you fucking heathen. We make sweet, beautiful love that has the angels weeping over my skills as a lover. It's midnight there isn't it? What the hell you want now?"

Danny has become my real life, real time, pen pal. We email almost every day now, even if it's just to insult the other person or to send them a one line message about something funny or astonishing. Danny tells me the stuff that I am sure he never tells the lads or Adrienne and in turn, I use him as my confessional.

"Is it love? Danny, do I love him? Today's the day, I either tell him today or I………"

"Or you what Roberts? What will you do if you decide you don't love him? Release him into the fucking wild? Return him to sender? You have got two kids with this stupid twat, he's going nowhere from your life, together or not. Anyway, I think I know the answer, you wanna hear it, eh?"

"No, I'm already regretting asking you"

*"Tough shit. Adrienne says hi by the way, she's sat here, says I need to be nice to you. Gonna ignore that. Right, here's the truth. You're asking the wrong fucking question. You love him already, you daft ginger. You love him. **That** was never the issue. If he died, you would mourn him like family. He is the father of your children. Love is part of the deal. If he was hurt, it would hurt you. If he was wronged, you'd be pissed off. That's love, you daft cow. The question you should be asking is, are you IN love with him and Roberts, the answer to that is a big fat fuckin' **NO**. Sit for a second. Process that"*

I stare blankly at the screen, processing.

*"You done processing? Right, Adrienne's got that top on that makes her tits look like fucking perfect puddings with cherry-nipple toppings. I've got twenty seconds before my dick gets strangled by my jeans zip so here's what you need to know before I go and rock that girl's world. If you were in love with him, you wouldn't need a fucking list. You wouldn't need emails. You'd need that one second, that one moment when the bolt goes through you and you realise it all by your little baby-popping self. In over a year with him, if you've never had that moment, you're not in love. You love him, you're just not **in** love with him.*

Roberts, you are lucky to have my wisdom at your fingertips. I gotta go, My dick's too hard to keep typing.

Danny

PS You can tell him you love him because it's true. Then admit to yourself that it's not enough to keep sleeping with the guy.

PPS Then admit to yourself that your old mucca Danny is a love God.

*PPPS Roberts you know there **is** somebody that you're in love with, even though we're only 18 and that is pretty ridiculous. Admit it, stop pissing about and do something about it. That soppy dickhead is still hung up on you.*

PPPPS I'm in love with Adrienne. See? See how when you know it, you know it? No fucking list needed. Happy Birthday Erin Roberts. Don't get pregnant again"

I sit, staring at his words for over two hours.

As I creep back into my bed, a pair of deep brown eyes flicker open, staring at me with a questioning expression. I shuffle closer, sharing his pillow as I press a gentle kiss to his lips and I whisper those words, those words that are actually true,

"I love you Jay"

His eyes go impossibly wide in the darkness and the kisses that we share, musty breath be damned, make me tingle with warmth.

He gives me a lopsided smirk, "Happy Birthday Feist", as we both drift back into a comfy slumber.

I get breakfast in bed, I get gifts, my sons are giddy with the wrapping paper that I discard and as I sit amongst *my boys,* I think that McNamara has got one thing wrong.

I might not be in love but I think that what I've got here might be enough for me.

10th July 1998

I'm done, we're all done. It's over. Finished. Today, as I sat my final A Level exam paper, trying desperately not to memorise every hair on Gio Romano's head as he sat less than two feet in front of me, I felt an overwhelming sense of loss as opposed to relief.

I'm not going to see him every day any more. He's not mine, he's *never* been mine, he appears to currently belong to yet another Lower Sixth girl called Amy but now, I won't have any link to his life other than his regular interaction with my sons, which mainly takes place at Mass when Mum takes them or when Lees has the boys for me and she spends time with Adam and Gio.

Gio is going to New Zealand in three weeks time and from there, he and Danny will be launching themselves into a Round-the-World working Gap year, both of them deferring their respective Uni places in Sheffield and Auckland. The thought of Gio being so removed from my life, of him being lost to me so entirely by disappearing into the world at large, hurts in ways that make me squirm.

Danny is torn between supersonic excitement and panicked heartbreak over being separated from Adrienne. I have not been able to tap into the bluntness that he breathes like oxygen but I want to tell him that I think Adrienne is losing interest. He's been describing her being 'a bit busy' and his words have conveyed a hurt-masking bravado that makes me wince when I read his emails. I see his first every heartbreak in his near future and I'm weirdly grateful that Gio will be with him when it happens because I have grown very fond of Danny 'Cheeky Fucker' McNamara and I want him to have a mate with him when his crude, wannabe Kiwi, cocky heart takes its first bruising.

In one my late-night exchanges, I'd asked him a question that weirdly, I'd never asked before,

"Danny, does Gio know that you and me have got a whole pen-pal thing going on? Me and him don't really speak much so I've never told him.....have you?"

"Well Roberts, as he's not my keeper or, y'know, my parole officer, I don't generally snuggle up in my jammies and tell him the details of every single person I talk to. Also, over the last few months I reckon G's finally shagged himself over you, like a sex-orcism, so he's probably not all that fussed. Anyways, gotta go Roberts, afternoon surfing beckons, stay ginger. Danny"

I'd read the words and felt my heart shrivel. Taking a deep breath, I'd stomped back up the stairs and woken Jay up with a blow job, his comical gasps of astonishment from being awoken thus making me smile around his dick.

G's finally shagged himself over you.

It's our 'Leavers' Ball' tonight, a posh do at a local Hotel having been organised by the Practically Perfects and their Social Committee. Jay, when I mentioned it back in April, had genuinely looked like I'd offered him a plate of dog shit, he could not have looked less keen. It didn't hurt or upset me *per se* that he did not want to come, I wondered if it was weird that I did not have a stronger desire for him to come with me. What it did was just make me feel a bit *heavy*, a bit *meh*.

I'm going as the third wheel with Lees and Ad and I'm starting to genuinely look forward to it. My Mum's friend is a dressmaker and following a falling out with a bride-to-be, she had a beautiful 1920's style, silver-sequin covered silk dress going spare. It's strapless and is full-length and it's just *gorgeous.* It's totally OTT but I *love* it and I've never, ever worn something so grand. When I tried it on, Mum got weirdly tearful, muttering something about Jay that was less than complementary.

I watch Gio and the lads head en masse to the pub after the exam, a gaggle of the girls in tow. Gio has Amy by the hand although I note that he does not smile at her and looks slightly pissed off. As I watch his tall, built form leave the school premises for the last time, I find myself gulping back sobs as I gather my bags and head for Adam's car, Lees frowning when she sees my blotchy face.

It's Friday night but Jay will not be staying over as he's going out with his brothers for D's birthday. Casey will be there, Jay told me that whilst looking a bit sheepish. I smiled and nodded my unspoken understanding of his discomfort.

Gathering up my boys into a massive squishy cuddle when I collect them from the nursing home where they have been 'helping' their Nana by entertaining the residents, I fill the afternoon with things that keep them occupied.

As soon as Mum gets home from work, I am able to invest time, effort and sanity into trying to style my hair and do my makeup. It is however pointless. My crazy curls resist all and any attempts to restrain them and in the end, Mum gets involved (with a wooden spoon at one point as a styling tool) and we manage a cascade ponytail which is frankly more luck than skill.

Stupid gravity-defying bra on, dress on, shoes on, face on, I grip the handrail and head downstairs, my silver satin shoes making me feel like Bambi.

Mum cries, the boys look stunned and Dad swears as I walk in, making me snort with laughter. As I grab last minute bits and kiss my babies, I hear Mum in the kitchen muttering to Dad,

"I just don't understand those two Fred, I don't understand it. I mean, a boyfriend would kill to see his girlfriend all dressed up, wouldn't they? You always loved going on nice nights out with me when we were kids. Those two, they're like, I dunno, kissing cousins or something. I don't see that giddy, soppy stuff when they're together. They're…..they're, oh I dunno. They're just not *right* together, are they? I mean, she's going by herself Fred, she's all dressed up beautiful and where's he? Hey? Where's the giddiness of being young and in love, eh? I just don't see it with them. Oh Fred, I want her to have *more*", I hear my Mum sniff.

Feeling *heavy,* I plaster on a smile as Dad drives me to Ad's. Lees looks *amazing,* her teal dress has a sort of corset and it falls into heavy jersey pleats around her toes. She looks gorgeous. Ad literally cannot stop staring at her, he's trying but he can't. Her squeal as she sees me is a bit of an ego stroke but it has the undesired effect of attracting another resident of the house. *Ryan.* Home from Uni for the holidays, he strolls cockily into the kitchen and with genuine aggravation, I note that he's managed to get even more good-looking over the last two years. *Bastard.*

He scoffs out an astonished exclamation when he sees me, "Fucking hell, Erin Roberts? Jesus, what the fuck happened to you? Shit, you never looked this good when I knew you. Maybe you should get yourself knocked-up more often, eh?", he sneers at me as his gaze rakes up and down my body, making me shudder.

"We're going now!", Lees' yell is loud as she grabs me by the hand and tows me away, she saw my knee moving in readiness to neuter that bastard again.

I turn and yell over my shoulder as Lee drags me out, "Show us your pixie prick Jones, I could do with a good laugh", and as the front door slams behind us, I hear him shouting abuse at me.

Adam and Lee have booked a room at this hotel for the night, much to Lees' mum's consternation and so I'll be getting a solo cab back. As Ad parks his car and the two of them go to check-in, I head to the loos. I can hear the noise from the function room already, suggesting that many of the Sixth Form attendees have already arrived.

I'm sat in the loo, wrestling with my dress when I hear a kerfuffle outside the stall door.

"....I should have listened to those rumours. I mean, that Jessica told Mina that she thought he might be gay. You know he wouldn't sleep with her, did you hear that? Two months they were together and he never made a move. Now he doesn't want to stay over tonight, I mean, I've booked that room, it's paid for. Is it me? Am I that gross?", I hear sobbing and multiple voices soothing.

I feel a proper ache for whoever this is outside the door. The pain of rejected affection is savage. *Poor girl.* I'm wrestling my stupidly small knickers out of the ball they rolled into when I hear her start again,

"Do you think he is? Do you think that's it? I mean he's got that amazing body and gay guys are always buff in the films and that, aren't they? Do you think Gio's gay?", more sobbing.

Me, I've just accidentally dropped my knickers in the loo.

Somebody tells the girl, who I now presume is Amy, that maybe it's because he's going away for a year, he doesn't want to get in too deep. She accepts this explanation, after a bit more sobbing. I wait for them to leave, my heart beating through my throat as I see Danny's words,

G's finally shagged himself over you.

I'm not sure that's entirely true.

I exit the loos, sans knickers as they are now travelling through the plumbing and on shaky legs, wash hands and go to find Lees and Ad. They are having their photos taken by the lobby of the Function Suite and as I watch them smile and stare lovingly at each other, I feel a massive wave of envy sweep me.

They beckon me over and we have daft photos with the three of us pratting around, the laughter attracting the attention of a group of lads from our year who are heading towards the bar. As I turn and bend down to fix my shoe strap that's come undone, I hear whoops of greeting, Adam's lovely laugh and lots of banter about how fit Lees looks and how pissed everyone plans to get.

"Roberts? Is that you down there?", oh Jesus, bloody Liam Merchant.

With a resigned sigh I slowly rise to standing and turn around, braced for ridicule but it doesn't come. Instead, to my bafflement, I see a dozen or so astonished looking faces turned my way, the lads all looking like they've seen an alien.

I conclude in that instant that I have either forgotten to zip myself up or I have got something smeared all over my face. I do pats to check my dress, I rub my hands over my face. Nothing. I turn to Lees who has a nauseating look of pride about her as she waggles her eyebrows and I shrug in confusion, silently requesting an explanation for my zombie-peers behaviour.

She leans in and whispers, "You hit that twelve Rinny, I knew you'd never stay an eight-out-of-ten", I roll my eyes at her.

Then Liam whistles under his breath, "Fuck me, Roberts".

I open my mouth to tell him exactly why I will not be doing *that*, when I'm jolted by a voice to the group's rear.

"I can't see your boyfriend Erin, where is he, eh?", my heart beats out of my chest. *Gio.*

Like the parting of the Red Sea, the boys stand aside, revealing Gio, dressed like a fucking supermodel in his achingly cool suit. Hands thrust in his pockets, he's looking at me through his lashes, his head bowed and his gorgeous curls slightly shaggier than usual.

I meet his stare and my wobbly voice is little more than a whisper, "He's not coming tonight, he's out with his brothers".

I watch as Gio kisses his teeth and shakes his head slightly, before he raises his gaze and looks at me directly, "You look fucking amazing Rin and he's a clueless twat if he's not here with you", and with that, he walks off.

I hear people chuckle comments and the whispers of, *"Well that was awkward"*. I'm just standing there, shaking and trying not to cry. Lees and Adam are looking at me worried and Lees leads me away by the hand to go and get a drink.

The night is actually really lovely. The DJ has half a clue and the music is great. I manage *not* to drop my dinner down myself earning praise and a toast from Lees about how I am 'finally growing up', making me pinch her as we spend time chatting with our year group in a way that is far more relaxed and indeed pleasant than I can ever recall.

Perhaps we are all growing up.

Photos taken, shoes removed for dancing and Malibu consumption significant, we are all on the dance floor when there is an explosion of applause as a deeply uncomfortable Mr. Gibson takes to the stage. With an acerbic and hilarious introduction that makes us all weep with a mixture of amusement and nostalgia for all that is about to end, he informs us that the staff have decided that the class of '98, formerly the GCSE class of '96, are deserving of some awards to befit the level of chaos that we have wrought over our seven years at this school.

He proceeds to hand out, with accompanying speech, awards for things like 'Person most likely to appear on Crimewatch', 'Person most likely to be convicted of White Collar Crime", "Person most dedicated to the art of makeup application", "Person most likely to proceed through clearing", "Person most likely to be recruited by MI5".

Once the laughter fades and the awards are handed out, Mr. Gibson takes to the microphone for the final time.

"Now, before I allow you all to re-commence your disco and its accompanying aural assault on my elderly eardrums, I have a final award to make. This award is one which was oddly a unanimous request, noted on every staff member's voting slip in the 'any other suggestions' box. Mr. Romano, I require your assistance on this stage please", Mr. Gibson points out to Gio in the crowd who smiles in

297

his usual good-natured way, shrugs and makes his way on stage, through a sea of jibes and patting hands.

"Right, Mr. Romano, you just stand here a moment. You see, this award is being presented to a student whose inability to tread a sensible, straightforward or, on occasion, law abiding pathway through her school career has led her to become quite literally, the bane of my life at times. But this inability has also led her to achieve things that few others her age could do. She is both a source of huge pride to us as staff members as well as a source of unending indigestion and hair loss. There are not many students would could cope with a double dose of early motherhood and still remain dedicated to their studies", as he says those words, I feel every face turn to me.

"...nor are there many who could prove themselves to be a dedicated and capable parent, a loyal friend, a mentor in their spare time or indeed an unending source of inadvertent amusement for us as a staff team. This award is simply entitled, "We wonder what on earth she will do next?", because with this student, you can never be sure. What we are sure about however, is that whatever she does do, she will do it well and she will do it with her usual astonishingly calamitous energy. Erin Roberts, this award is for you. Mr. Romano, can I ask you to hand Miss. Roberts these flowers please".

I feel Lees push me forwards, my mouth gaping open as my peers begin to clap and cheer. I feel the hot burn of tears in the corner of my eyes as I mount the steps carefully in my knickerless state, walking the three steps towards Gio. Gio's eyes are wide, frantically scanning my face as my lip wobbles with the emotion. His arm reaches out to give me the really gorgeous bunch of flowers and with a shaking hand, I take the offering, our skin touching and making my whole body sing. Mr. Gibson gently smiles at me and I leap forward, giving him a nervous hug and pressing a kiss to his bearded cheek as he scoffs and shakes his head, patting my arm as I pull away and offer my thanks.

Mr. Gibson takes hold of the microphone as I take a step towards Gio, our nervous darting glances at each other making me want to exit the stage *rapidly.*

"As is nauseating tradition at such events as this, I believe that requests have been made for some sort of slow-paced dance and at this point, the DJ has been instructed to perform his duties accordingly. Mr. Romano and Miss. Roberts will start these proceedings off and for those of you hormonal, teenage reprobates who find yourselves here with your paramour, please follow suit", and Mr. Gibson strides off the stage. In shock at his instructions for Gio and I to slow dance, my careful descent down the stairs from the stage falters and I feel two large, warm hands grab me around the waist and hold me safe.

My body is pulled flush against Gio's as he guides me down the stairs. I feel his hands tense on my waist as he dips and his breath tickles my ears.

"You don't have to y'know, dance with me Rin. I can just go to the bar or something. Gibson's full of shit", Gio's proximity makes me shiver and I cover his warm hand with my bouquet-free one as I look over my shoulder at him, his face so close.

I mumble, "I want to dance with you Gio", because I *really* do.

He nods, his face tense. Taking my flowers from me and handing them to a startled looking waitress, Gio ignores catcalls from his mates as he leads me onto the dance floor, both of us with heads bowed in embarrassment. I gesture furiously at Adam who rolls his eyes and reaches for Lees' hand, dragging her onto the dance floor with us.

As the opening bars of Bryan bloody Adams wafts across the speakers, I am turned by a directive pair of hands and everything else, *everything else* just melts away because all I see is Gio. He's so much taller than me, even in these daft heels and as I look up into his face, I realise that Danny McNamara is an absolute, smug bastard. That Kiwi dickhead was totally on the money because when you are *in love* with somebody, there is no need for lists or pros and cons. You feel that bolt go through your heart and you *know*. As I look at Gio, a full year on from that party, a full *fucking* year since I felt his lips on mine, I admit the truth that I have been trying to deny for too long.

I am in love with Gio Romano

His arms slip around my waist, those amazing strong arms and he gently pulls me close, forcing me to bite my cheeks to stop the tears from flowing as I smell lemons and herbs and feel his warm heart beating under my cheek. My arms reach up, smoothing over the fabric of his shirt as they rest on his shoulders, the tips of my fingers touching his hair.

He lets out this sigh, this gentle sound of pleasure and I feel his hands rhythmically stroking the sequin-covered fabric at my hips, his finger-tips making contact with the bared skin of my back as I fizz with pleasure. We sway slowly together, holding close.

His head resists against the top of mine as I search desperately for something to dilute the intensity of what I'm feeling, as Bryan growls out over the speakers. I mumble,

"Are you excited about going travelling?", his fingers grip me a bit tighter.

His voice is so deep, it rumbles through his chest, "Yeah, y'know, it'll be amazing but it's gonna but hard to leave stuff behind for all those months"

I nod gently, rubbing my cheek against his warm chest and I feel his hands moving, stroking my hair in the ponytail that is barely holding itself together.

I smile sadly and mutter, "I'm so jealous, think of all those amazing things you'll see", my fingers are reaching further, stroking into his hair.

Gio's resultant gentle groan is a problem because it causes a reaction in me that knickers would really help to er, *absorb.*

It's barely a whisper but it leaves my lips before I can fetch it back in, "I'm going to miss seeing you every day Gio". *Shit.*

Bryan's still going at it as Gio pulls away slightly, his hand leaving my hair. His forehead against mine he mumbles,

"Rin, we haven't talked for like months but you need to know, I need you to know…..it's you I'm going to miss the most…...it's you Rin, it's always been you", his voice cracks as he moves one hand up to cup my face, "You look so fucking beautiful Erin, you are *so* beautiful. I can't…...I have to get past…...coz you're with…..and it's……. I've gotta…..", as his voice gets louder and more insistent, my heartbeat is deafening in my ears.

His jaw clenched in what looks like determination, he huffs out a frustrated breath and pulls me closer, leaning so that our noses touch and his lips brush mine as he closes his eyes and drops his voice to a whisper,

"I love you Rin, I love you so much", his breath is warm and as my eyes close in bliss, I feel a flood of warmth sweep my body, from the top of my scalp to the tips of my toes.

Every synapse fires and my hands move of their own volition, skimming his shirt-covered arms and feeling the muscles beneath them shaking with tension.

The words are there in my throat, they move up to my mouth without any sort of hesitation and as Gio opens his eyes and we hold each other's gaze, I open my lips to finally set the truth free.

I'm in love with you too Gio.

But before the words can be given form, a forceful pat on my shoulder makes me jolt. I turn, perplexed by the interruption, to see my Dad.

"Dad?", my heart is falling through my feet as I realise that my Dad can only be here if there has been an emergency. *With my babies.*

I wrench myself from Gio, "Dad, what's happened? Ohmygod what's happened to the boys, where are they? WHAT'S HAPPENED", tears are already starting and I feel Gio's strong warm hand take mine as my Dad holds my shoulders and forces me to meet his gaze,

Dad looks at me anxiously, "Erin, sweetheart, the boys are fine, they are at home with your Mum and Dylan, they're *fine* but poppet there's…..there's been an incident in Bristol", my heart restarts and then plummets again, as I whisper, "Jay?".

Dad nods slowly at me and I see Lees and Ad rushing over from behind him, "Sweetheart, I need you to stay calm but you need to know that Jay has been…...he's been shot at a nightclub Erin and at the moment, all that Obi could tell us is that he was alive when they put him in the ambulance. We need to get to Bristol sweetheart. C'mon, get your coat, let's head there now", I clap my hands over my mouth and I know I'm repeating, *'He's got to be OK, he's got to be OK, he's got to be OK",* because my babies *cannot* lose their Daddy.

Gio fetches my coat, Lees and Ad rush around fetching my bag and answering the questions of bystanders who clearly smell some *sensational* gossip.

As I am ushered out by my Dad and Mr. Gibson, who has been very sweetly supportive in the last three minutes, I look back over my shoulder. Gio is stood with his hands thrust in his pockets again, his head bowed in what looks like despair. I'm leaving him behind. *Again*. For Jay. *Again*.

Even in my panic, my heart throbs its loss.

My mother is a wonderful woman. I bloody mean it. As my father and I arrive at this busy hospital, filled with Friday night humanity in all it's alcohol soaked glory, I could not be more grateful to her for having the presence of mind to send my father to collect me armed with a pair of jeans and a t-shirt to change into. Arriving in an evening gown would be a cliché that I do not need.

Dad has been like a parrot the whole way here, irritating me as the motorway lights zipped past the car windows like orange lightning bolts, repeating *"He's a fit and strong lad, he'll be fine Erin. He'll be fine"*, until I wanted to smack him.

The journey here gave me time to analyse my emotions. I was tearful and terrified but at the core of my terror was not the risk of losing my *boyfriend*, my *lover*. The fear that was making me nauseous was the risk of losing my sons' father, their Daddy who they adore. It was the possibility of my sons losing something *so* precious that made me sob.

Upon arrival, my use of Jamel's name was enough to immediately prompt the receptionist to flag down a nearby police officer. They asked to see some ID for both of us before we could be given any information. Our shaking hands proffering bank cards and drivers' licenses, the police officer's posture visibly relaxed and we were ushered into the bowels of the hospital.

Dion had apparently named me as Jay's next of kin upon arrival and as we are taken up to a family room, I spot Obi's sturdy figure in the distance as I run ahead of Dad and shout Obi's name,

"Oh Ginge, fuckin' hell girl, he's been shot, Wheels got *fuckin' shot*", Obi's deep voice is wobbly as he pulls me into a tight cuddle, his whole body shaking.

"Where is he Obi, where is he?", I am frightened by Obi's shaking.

Obi shakes his head, "Surgery, they took him down a while ago, we ain't heard nothin' yet", Obi distractedly greets my Dad with a nod.

Obi leads me into the family room, a surly looking Police Officer standing outside the door. As I step through the door, I jolt a little from the volume of bodies contained within. Dion, stony faced and shaken has his arm around a tearful Megan who in turn is embracing a sobbing Casey, who has her head buried in her hands.

All of them are dressed for a night out and a pathetic sliver of me wishes I'd kept the bloody dress on, I look like a cleaner compared to their glamour.

I look at D, "D, what happened? How the fuck did he get *shot*?", my swearing makes my Dad cough uncomfortably but I ignore him.

D gets up from his chair, both Megan and Casey now looking at me, although Casey avoids my direct gaze. Darting meaningful glances towards the Officer outside, D lowers his head and whispers but his tone is harsh and raw,

"Erin, we was at the club when it went down, we'd only been there like an hour. There was, there was some hassle wiv' some of them boys from Pops' manor, them Dealers that Wheels hung wiv' before he went down", D's jaw clenches and he punches the chair next to us, making Casey jump and sob into her sister's shoulder again.

"It was *me* they was after though, not Wheels, they been lookin' for some reckoning after me an' my boys worked that payback after what happened wiv' Case", there's more sobbing from the girls as D

304

shakes his head.

I think I'm holding my breath as D carries on, "He pushed me out the way Erin. He.......Wheels took it. They got him twice, neck and chest. He........pushed me out the fuckin' way. He saved me an' now he's fucked", and with that, D looks like he's going to lose it and I see Obi swoop in and gather his brother into what looks like a rugby tackle but in reality, it is simply the most raw of hugs. Obi holds his brother as D sobs on his shoulder, tears running down Obi's face too as Casey and Megan whimper.

I'm mobilised into action, suddenly feeling like the uninvited guest again.

"Dad, I need to go find out what's going on. Can you....can you go and ring Mum? Tell her what's happening? I need to find his doctor", on wobbly legs I flee the family room, not feeling like I have a right to be there.

I grab any nurse or Doctor that I encounter, none of them able to tell me much other than the surgery is expected to last at least another hour. I have no real religious belief, despite a lifetime spent in a Catholic household but I sit on a seat in the corridor and I *pray*. I pray that my boys do not lose their Daddy. I pray that I do not have to spend a lifetime referring to their lovely, funny, shy, moody, fit-as-fuck, foolhardy-brave father in the past tense.

I feel a presence next to me, as I sit with my head in my hands. Expecting to see my Dad, I'm shocked when it's Casey who I find sat beside me. We smile warily at each other and both simultaneously lean back in our chairs.

I mumble, needing to fill the awkward silence, "He'll be OK you know, he has to be. He'll be OK".

I see Casey nod, her pretty face smudged with tear-spoiled makeup and I belatedly realise that she is splattered with blood. *Jay's blood.*

I hear a sob leave my mouth as Casey shifts in her seat and wordlessly grabs my hand, her own face re-soaked. Obi joins us in the corridor, sitting the other side of me and taking my other hand. We sit, in scared silence. *Waiting.* The police are speaking to the others, their presence almost continuous and Dad joins us, taking his seat across the corridor, winking at me whenever our eyes meet and offering teas with an annoying regularity that even makes sweet-faced Casey look a bit murderous.

Ninety minutes later, two weary looking women in scrubs approach us with an air of authority that makes us all jump to our feet, the Police Officer joining us.

Identified as Jay's next of kin, they direct the information at me.

"Jamel suffered two gunshot wounds as you know. The most dangerous wound was not actually the one in his neck, as this wound missed his arteries but did come a little too close for our liking so we have done some repair work. However, the gunshot wound to his chest caused some significant damage to his right lung, resulting in some bleeding and a condition we call a pneumo-hemothorax. Unfortunately a couple of his ribs were shattered and the shards of bone caused further damage internally which has given us quite the jigsaw puzzle to fix", the kindest looking surgeon, a young woman in her early thirties steps closer, smiling kindly, "But what you need to know now is that Jamel is stable and we have repaired everything that we need to", I feel a gush of relieved carbon dioxide leave my lips as she smiles.

"Give the guys in recovery enough time to get him all settled and stable and we will be transferring him to Intensive Care, where you can go and see him Erin", she pats my hand and we all jump in to enthusiastically thank them both, Obi's hug startling her slightly.

We immediately transfer the news to D, who leaps around beaming broadly. As I watch them all, a thought strikes me,

"Where's your Dad Obi?", and the temperature in the room plummets about fifty degrees.

Obi looks more angry than I have ever seen him look as he sneers, "He can't be troubled to come down to the hospital just now, it's in God's hands and will play out in all its due course", Obi's mimic of his father's accent is done so bitterly that I wince.

"Cunt", it's out before I can stop it.

"Erin Roberts!", my Dad is horrified but he smirks.

Casey is unable to sit still, her agitation makes me feel inadequate as I bask in my relief. *My boys still have their Daddy.*

An hour later, a kindly looking nurse turns up and tells us that she can permit two visitors in the ICU with Jay. In my head, I'm fourth in the pecking order, just above Megan but as all three faces turn to me, I feel a bit startled.

"Oh, er D? You want to come with me?", D nods curtly and together, we follow the nurse but I still feel uneasy. On impulse, I turn,

"Casey, do you, do you want to come too? I'll just pop in and say hi and then I'll switch with you, OK?", I know I've done the right thing when I see everyone smile softly.

Nodding furiously, Casey trots to catch up with us.

He looks so young. Surrounded by beeping machines and with a grim looking chest drain hanging from the bed, he's ventilated and unconscious with big dressings on his neck. D stalls, his face a mask of horror but I strap on a *'My Kids have been in the NICU and nothing scares me''* face and I approach his bed, taking his cannula-ed hand and telling him that he is a prize dickhead who really does need to be less attention seeking, as I stroke his face and hold his hand between my own. D looks wary but smirking at the hassle I am giving an unconscious Jay, he joins in with his own soft ribbing, telling his unconscious brother that he'd better get well soon because there's a *'beating'* that D needs to give him for the *'fool nonsense hero shit'* he pulled.

I see Casey loitering at the staff desk, tears pouring down her face and as I press a gentle kiss to Jay's hand and his lips, I realise that her need is more pressing. I beckon her over, as I move from the bed and in the seconds that follow, everything falls into lucid place.

Casey runs, she *runs* at the bed, sobbing as she gently and reverently kisses Jay's forehead, strokes his hair, strokes his face, his arms. Her entire posture screams devotion. There is no piss-taking, there is no sibling banter, she is entirely focussed on Jay and checking that he is OK. I hear her murmur barely discernible endearments, telling him how much he scared her, how he's got to get better.

That's when I realise. *This* is what Jay deserves.

I love Jay, I love Jay in the same way that D loves Jay. That piss-taking we just did, it's *friend* love, it's *family* love. The love that Casey's got for him, that's *'In Love'* love and who am I to deny this lovely lad *that*? Jay, whose own father cannot be fucked to visit him when he's been *shot*, whose mother allowed his step-father to racially abuse him and then rejected him, Jay who is a wonderful Dad himself, a fantastic co-parent, a lovely boyfriend and a good man, he deserves the *real* deal.

He chose me out of loyalty to our boys. I chose him because I want my sons to have the best and I genuinely believed that it was only possible with Jay by my side. As I look at Casey pressing kisses to Jay's hands as she strokes his arms, I realise that I am being another abusive force in his life if I continue to allow us to pretend, if I deny him a life with the girl I'm almost certain he's still in love with and who is clearly in love with him in return.

Those boys will always have the best, because Jay is the best Dad I could ask for and I am a *cracking* Mum. It doesn't matter if we not together as long as we work together to give them everything.

I feel so foolish suddenly, I feel so short-sighted. Jay loves me and I love him but that is not enough for us to be together *romantically*. It is however a fantastic basis for us to work as a loving *family*.

Unbidden, it's Gio's face that suddenly flashes through my mind and I choke back sobs as I realise that if he was lying in that bed, if a Gio was the one whose life hung in the balance, my terror would be entirely focussed on losing the person that *I* could not live without. My fears would be for the loss of the person who holds my heart, who is precious to *me*. I would look like Casey does right now.

I'm so lost in my thoughts that I don't realise that D has come to stand next to me, his gaze wary as he watches me watching Casey.

"Y'know sweetness, they just got a lot of history y'know? You an' him, you don't gotta worry coz Wheels, he's loyal an'....", but I cut D off shaking my head and smiling softly.

"D, I love Jay but I'm not *in* love with him. We're family, me him and the boys but I think I've just realized that we don't need to tie ourselves into a relationship to be amazing parents. Casey…...she loves him like he deserves to be loved because she's in love with him, isn't she?", I look at D, hoping that my tone and my face transmit the genuineness of my question.

D looks wary for a moment but then he nods slowly. I nod in return and ask in the same tone,

"D, Jay told me a while back that he loves Casey. Please, before I go into this like a car-crash, can you

309

tell me the truth? Is Jay in love with Casey? Is he properly in love with her? I don't want to pull this ripcord if I've got it wrong", I reach for D's hand as he scans my face.

Clearly seeing whatever confirmation he needs to allow his confession, he croaks out, "I don't reckon he ever fell out of love wiv' Case y'know, even when they went through shit. He was just.....he was just a bit messed up back then, young, dumb and a dickhead. Yeah Erin, he's in love wiv' her. I'm so fuckin' sorry girl", D steps forward to offer comfort but I shake my head,

"D, you don't need to be sorry. You see, I love Jay but I *totally* understand what Jay has been going through, we have been fighting the same daft battle and the whole time, we've been on the same fucking side", I shake my head, looking at the floor and trying not to think about Gio and being in his arms earlier tonight.

D raises by chin with his finger, making me look up into his stern face "That Godfather? I seen him once girl, he come to that party yeah, big guy?", I raise my now wet eyes and nod slowly.

D nods in understanding.

I sigh and look at the ceiling, "Let's get the daft fucker healed and on his feet and then him and me, we're gonna have a little chat", I look over at Casey again, as she strokes Jay's face.

I smile sadly, "I really like her D, I think she'll be a brilliant step-Mum to my boys", and with those words, I fall apart in the arms of my enormous brother-in-law as he rocks me and tells me I'm a *'fuckin' legend'.*

Chapter Fifteen

11th May 2000

"Mummeeeeeee, noooooooooo, I nots eating it….noooooooooo", AJ is pointing accusingly at his broccoli as if it has gravely offended him.

His brother, smugly pointing at his own clear plate lisps with an enthusiastic nod, "I ates mine, I did. Cake?"

AJ, at the mention of cake, cocks an eyebrow and lobs his broccoli at his brother's head as he announces, "Ates it now. Cake?", with such an innocent look, I fall about laughing.

My personal tutor at my Uni, a lone parent herself, got me applying to a whole bunch of local charities when I started Uni a year-and-a-half ago. These charities were all offering grants and bursaries to 'local students in need' and armed with a humorous application letter and copies of that photo Jay took on the day that the boys pasted themselves (and the cat) in nappy cream, I happily wrote off to all of them asking for support with childcare costs for twin monsters.

When the first cheque arrived, it was like I'd won the lottery. When another eight plopped through the door, I realised that with my existing student funding, child benefits and some of the in-house support for student parents, I could actually afford for the boys to go to the Uni subsidised nursery four days a week, easing some of the guilt that Jay and I feel about imposing on my Mum. I love the boys being so close by to me and the boys love their nursery but I fear it may not be reciprocated. My standard feedback from the frazzled nursery workers at the end of the day is that my two have had *'a lively, busy day'*.

I got two C's and a D at A Level securing my place at my first choice local Uni to study Social Policy. The Uni is about a forty minute drive on an average journey and I commute four days a week, no lectures for me on a Wednesday.

Jay has got the boys this weekend, I have my end-of-second-year exams to study for and he and Casey are planning to take the little monsters to some digger theme park, near their place.

I can't lie, it does hurt still, deep in my chest when I say *'their place'* but big girl pants on, I have to suck it up because Jay and Casey have been living in their nice little flat in Clevedon since this time last year. Jay was in hospital for seven weeks after the shooting, it was a slow and painful recovery and he had a couple of setbacks with a bone infection. It was a horrible period of time, the boys missed him so desperately and with the knowledge that he and I needed to have *that chat*, it just felt like an agony drawn out, quite literally in poor Jay's case, as his body fixed itself. I could only really get up to see him in hospital twice a week and in that time, nature took its course with he and Casey, as we began to slowly switch places in the pecking order of his life as her daily visits became his norm.

Gio Romano flew out of the UK one week and six days after the Leavers' Ball. He came to the house, just as I was leaving for a hospital visit with the boys, the week after the shooting. In possibly the most painfully dishonest two minutes of my life, he stood in my hallway silently scowling as I parroted the script that I'd been practising for days. I told him that all I could focus on was Jay's recovery, that I wanted him to go and see the world and enjoy every single second and that he and I would always be mates. I told him that I *cared* about him and that I wanted him to have amazing adventures. His jaw clamped tightly, he'd nodded his head, mumbling that he loves his Godsons and would be sending them cards and presents from his travels.

I could not and I will not be selfish again. I nearly trapped Jay with my anxiety about coping solo and if I had told Gio the truth, that I loved him so deeply that I could not see the bottom of it, he might not have gone travelling or at least he would have gone with the burden perhaps of guilt or regret. I have two small sons, no money and the burning need for a degree, I could not even have offered to go travelling with him, if indeed he had wanted me to. I felt that to tell him the truth would potentially have limited his life chances. It might have ruined his opportunities, spoiled his enjoyment. So I lied to him and I let Gio get on that plane, believing that nothing had changed for me, believing that I still chose Jay over him.

I cried every night for weeks, months even. I missed Gio so much, I went off my food. It was *that* bad. I still miss him. Every *fucking* day.

The chat with Jay took place on the third day after his release from hospital, my Mum having insisted that he stayed with us, where she could nurse him. I told him I'd only supported this plan because the thought of my mother nursing him would probably speed up his recovery in order that he might escape her clutches. He'd laughed gently, told me he'd missed me and I launched us into the chat about our *future*.

We were both in tears, hours of talking, some disagreements, emotional exhaustion and finally a mutual sense of absolute and blissful *relief*. Mum said that she and Dad came back from their Day Out with the boys and found me and Jay fast asleep on top of the duvet, hand in hand and looking like best mates.

He was with Casey within the fortnight and when I first saw them together, at Obi's city centre flat where Jay moved after his recovery, I was initially *giddy* of all things, a bit like the happiness I felt when Ross and Rachel got together on Friends. Then, just when I thought I'd pulled off the *'ex girlfriend of the year'* award, I saw Jay kiss her and I got hit with a wave of loss so powerful, so *acute*, that I literally had to run from the building, I had to run from the pain.

I was sprinting through the city centre, like the world's least athletic shoplifter until a pair of strong hands grabbed my shoulders and Obi pulled me into a hug that saw me wailing in grief. When he eventually got me back to the flat, Jay was stood in the building doorway, his face a mask of distress as he scanned the streets for us. When he saw the state of me, he lost it too, swearing and raging at himself and the pair of us ended up in a total tizzy, clinging to each other and causing Obi to have to apologise to countless startled neighbours who had to clamber over our huddle of madness to be able to get into the lifts.

Jay could not live back in their home area, the stress of potential risks and reprisals were just too much. Jay initially lived with Obi but then when D and Megs moved to Clevedon because they did not wish to risk Kaydee's safety living on the estate after the shooting, Jay and Casey found their own place nearby.

Jay and D refused to engage with the police investigation into Jay's shooting, denying all and any knowledge of their assailants identity, refusing to give statements and generally, driving the poor police officers spare. However there was some significant CCTV evidence plus other witness statements and as a result, the case went to court. Jay and D were called as witnesses but maintained their position that they could not identify the assailants, they were intoxicated and it was a dark club.

The shooter and his accomplices received significant jail terms but Jay and D do not discuss the shooting *ever* and as a family, we have learnt to just skirt the topic. My parents went through a sort of delayed shock, postponed until Jay had recovered. It saw them not sleep on the nights that the twins spent at Jay and Casey's flat, terrified that *something else* was going to happen. They talked to their friends in horrified tones for months about *'our Jamel having been shot'* and my mother still frowns and fiddles with her rosary beads whenever I make plans go out in Bristol. I have an odd recurring nightmare where I'm telling the boys that Jay died but the photo next to the coffin is Gio's. It makes me howl every time.

Jay strokes his neck and the angry scar it bears when he's nervous and Casey no longer allows Jay to go clubbing. To be fair, he avoids crowded places now anyway. The physical scars are somehow less noticeable than the emotional ones that we all carry.

However, the last almost-two-years have seen us move on to a place where Jay and I are genuinely and truly, the best of mates. I can see him and Casey kiss, I can leave my children in his and Casey's care and the pain is a manageable dull throb.

The boys spend every other weekend in Clevedon, *loving* the beach and the pier. I drop them off after Uni on a Friday and Jay brings them home on Sunday evening. My driving test passed pretty hastily before Uni started despite the stress of Jay's hospitalisation, I am the owner of a small, unattractive Volvo, my father's insistence that I drive the 'safest possible car' slightly offensive given the shade it cast over my driving skills.

Jay still comes up mid-week too for tea with the boys, sleeping on my sofa when needed and it's not uncommon for him to pop in on my weekends with the boys, especially now that Casey is back at Uni doing midwifery and she often has to work weekends. Jay's new job does not allow him to do a days childcare mid-week, something that he and the boys miss. I'd encouraged Casey go back to Uni, Jay's guilt over her abandoned future posed a genuine risk, I felt, to their future happiness. Having done a year at Uni myself, I felt I was well placed to push her. She started back there in September.

I spend my 'twin free' weekends in a combination of Exeter, where Lees and Adam are at Uni, or in Bristol, where Obi and I go partying together. Obi and I have become close mates, to the surprise of many and the bafflement of his younger brother who seems torn between amusement and suspicion that there might be more to our friendship that we let on but Jay's wrong about that. I am Obi's most effective Wing Woman when it comes to helping him pull in clubs, my success rates for him are *off the hook*. In turn, Obi loves to dance, he is as much of a dickhead as I am and he is a wonderfully effective bodyguard. Our nights out have become legendary- we woke up on the floor of a posh flat in

London one Sunday morning, having got a lift to a celebrity party with a DJ who was doing a set at a Bristol club we were in. We jumped on a train back to Bristol as soon as we woke up, giggling like idiots and with a roaring hangover.

My weekends with Lees and Ads are the best sort of fun. Chilled, familiar, cosy and comforting. There are some nights when I sit on my sofa, watching the TV alone and I have a little weep over how much I miss my friends.

Yup, it's *my* sofa because the boys and I have our own place, we moved in last summer between my First and Second Year at Uni. Mum and Dad had started to talk about bloody loft conversions and needing more space and I began to feel like more and more of an imposition, especially when the boys grew out of their cots.

In the May, I spotted an advert in the newsagents for a two bed flat above the sewing shop on the High Street. It was cheaper than the average rent because the second bedroom is up in the eaves and nobody over five foot three can comfortably navigate the room. I am five foot two and my sons reach my thighs, we are essentially a family of Hobbits. The flat was ideal although I won't lie, watching Jay crawl around their room, swearing as he bangs his head, is the best free entertainment I could ask for.

Despite being bone-chillingly terrified, moving out was the most amazing confidence booster and I now *love* having my own space. My mother and father are daily visitors, only being five minutes away and Dyls is over most evenings although his apprenticeship with a local graphic design firm keeps him busy.

When Mum has the boys for me on Wednesdays, I work at the refuge on a long shift, in my paid role as a play worker. My job is to run three parenting groups and to also do one-to-one work with the girls who are parents, essentially building their confidence as Mums. I love it although if I'm honest, I wing it most of the time feeling like a bit of a fraud but Sinead seems happy with what I do.

As I give my sons their undeserved cake following Broccoli-gate and I lean against the worktop of *my* kitchen, in *my* house, feeding *my* sons, it feels pretty bloody good.

I just need to not think about the things that I am missing, the people that are not around me. *The person that I still dream about.*

He did not come home after his gap year. Having travelled to enough countries that his postcards to the boys fill an entire shoebox, he decided that he would not return to the UK but would instead join Danny at Auckland Uni, having somehow sweet-talked his way into a scholarship.

Danny McNamara and I email almost daily still. He has become my Jiminy Cricket, he is the voice in my head. Since my split from Jay, I keep my *relationships* low key and commitment free. I guard my boys and their familiar world fiercely, nobody I'm seeing ever sets foot in my sons' house, nobody ever meets my sons, few are told about my boys. I rarely mention any of these *dalliances* to my friends or family, they are passing fancies and yet, I always tell Danny and he always gives me blunt advice.

The first guy I slept with after I split from Jay, was a fellow First Year that I met at the Uni Christmas Ball. He was good looking, a bit cocky and he had blond hair that actually reminded me of teenage Danny's hair. We snogged, we shagged back at his Halls of Residence bedroom and when he came, he squealed. I mean, pig-stuck-in-a-gate, twelve-year-old at a pop concert sort of squeal. I nearly burst a blood vessel trying not to laugh.

Then I cried. Driving home in the Volvo, at 4am, I was sobbing. I might not have ever been *in love* with Jay but I loved having sex with him and now I was condemned to perhaps a lifetime of squealers, whose bodies I don't know, whose eyebrows don't have scars and whose children I have not borne. I snuck in the back door, still living at home at that point and I got straight on the email to Danny, who was travelling with Gio in Australia at the time.

"Roberts, what the fuck did you do to him to make him squeal? Oh Jesus, not the finger-in-the-arse thing? Christ, a girl did that to me last month without any sort of lube. I nearly hit the fucking roof"

"I just made him come McNamara, honestly, it was just a bog-standard orgasm but with this astonishing sound effect. Danny, I don't want to have sex with people who squeal, how do I spot the weirdos? I don't want to have sex with anybody I don't know. I've only ever had sex with Jay and I don't want to do it with strangers. I feel so sad Danny, I feel really fucking sad and I can't stop crying"

"Roberts, man the fuck up. Here's the lesson that somebody should have given you years ago: you don't have to have sex if you don't want to. Now, you've only been with one guy up until tonight so you're kinda new to this but that's the mantra Uncle Danny needs you to repeat. If you don't want to do it with strangers, then don't. Right, gotta go, Romano's been left in charge of the scuba rental shack in my absence and he's a dickhead who can't tell Coral from seaweed. Stay ginger Roberts. Danny
PS Seriously, what the fuck did you do to that guy to make him squeal? Have a think and let me know, I'll get that fit barmaid to do it on me.
PPS Just in case you are interested, G whispers your name when he wanks. It's fucking pervy.
PPPS The first time I had sex with somebody after Adri dumped me, I cried. There's probably a girl in Brisbane who emailed a mate asking if it's normal for guys to cry after sex. She didn't make me squeal though, lazy bitch. Chin up Roberts, you're still fucking fit"

Since what Danny refers to as Piggy-gate, there's been a fair few guys but I only sleep with people that I fancy enough to not care what noise they make when they come. I have had three *boyfriends* in that time, lads who I've seen for a few weeks at a time but none of them really *captured* me. I feel a

318

bit numbed to romance if I'm honest.

If I'm *really* honest, I know the real reason that I'm numbed but I can't think about *him* because it makes my heart hurt and I need to get a grip. *He* and I have never done more than kiss, *he* has not spoken to me for more than a few sentences in years and *he* has been the other side of the world for long enough that I sometimes wonder if *he* was actually a figment of my imagination. *He* also has a very pretty girlfriend, Danny broke the news to me about five months ago. It's love apparently. There've been mutual declarations.

I feel a tug at my dress and I look down to see two chocolate-cake-covered monsters staring at me. AJ's caramel curls are, as always, filled with food and dirt and his incredible perma-glow skin tone makes him so beautiful, belying the true roguish nature of my cheekiest son. My Jake, more like Jay with every passing hour, has Jay's gorgeous mocha skin-tone but his hair is slightly lighter, shot through with browns and russet. Jake's eyes are mine though, russet-gold.

"Mummy, why's you looks sad?", Jake takes my hand in his, looking pensive.

AJ nods knowingly as he whispers, "You gots brocklilly for tea too Mummy? Tell Nana you'd ates it but then puts it in the bin when she's nots looking", he gives me the cheeky wink that his father taught him and I snort with laughter as I sweep the sticky horrors into a hug.

With an hour or so to kill before bedtime, we walk to the park near the Fire Station, the boys running wild as always. Living in your home town when the majority of your mates have headed off on their own adventures, is *weird.* My Uni mates are a lovely bunch and I have a wide circle of people to sit with, eat with, chat with and even go out with. However, I never lived in halls, I miss out on student living and my social life has to be planned far in advance. I inhabit a sort of Netherworld, betwixt and between identities. As a result, I find it hard when my worlds collide.

Jay came to meet me for lunch at Uni early on in my first year, his new job as a tyre courier takes him all over the place and he happened to be coming past my hallowed halls of learning.

"Jay, don't take this the wrong way but you being here, I feel a bit tearful. I don't know why, it's like......it's like I suddenly really miss being us, I feel like I've lost something. I just want to go and crawl under the duvet with you and not in a kinky way. Shit, am I going mental?", I'd looked at him wide-eyed as we scoffed overcooked curry.

He'd smiled softly and put his fork down, shifting closer to me.

"Feist, I'm gonna tell you somethin' that you can't never, EVER tell Case, 'kay? She might look all quiet and shit but that girl's full out savage when she's on the rag", I snorted loudly and a grain of rice went up my nose making me cough and sneeze.

"Tha's well sexy Feist", he'd rolled his eyes but carried on, "You gotta know that there's some mornin's, when I wake up and I reach out and I get a proper shock when I see Case next to me. An' the thing you gotta know girl, that shock? Some mornin's, that shock is fuckin' disappointment tha' she ain't you", he looked at me warily, those brown eyes soft as he took my hand.

He whispered, "It weren't never a straight, clear cut thing y'know, me goin' to be wiv' Case. You gotta know, you left a big fuckin' hole in me Feist, you're in here for keeps and I fuckin' miss you", he patted his pec as my eyes filled with tears.

Jay leant forward and kissed my hair softly as he murmured, "I know you ain't in nothin' serious right now but when you get wiv' someone for real, you need to know, it's gonna fuckin' proper pain me", and with a peck to my forehead, he carried on with his food as I sniffed and used a curry-covered napkin to mop myself up.

Jay looked up, rolling his eyes and tutting, "You got Korma on your face now you daft cow", as we sniggered and I smacked his arm.

That's it really. I'm in bits. Not in an emotional wreck, overly-dramatic kind of way but in a very literal sense. There are bits of me all over the place. The biggest bit of me sits in a nursery on campus and in the slightly lopsided maisonette that I rent. My sons, they own the biggest bits of me, they are the Freeholders of my entire self.

There's a chunk of Erin Roberts that is on leasehold in Exeter with my best friend and her boyfriend. That part of my identity is left there in a box, to be reclaimed whenever I visit. A big slice of me now lives in Clevedon too, the part of me that Jay will always own, the part of my heart that will always have a Jay-shaped dent in it.

My Uni self resides within the confines of the campus, separate from both my Mummy Identity and my past in its academic bubble.

Then there's the painful, jagged, raw chunk that lies literally the other side of the world. The part of my heart that will not *fucking* heal, despite the passing of years and the lack of direct contact. It's the part of me that fills my head when I can't sleep, it's the part that hurts when I see couples kiss and it's the part that makes me cry in the dark.

So I'm in bits. Scattered everywhere. Exhausting if I'm honest and it makes me wonder if I will ever feel 'whole' again.

"Mummeeeeeeeee pussshhhhhh usssss", I turn with a smile to see my pickles trying to clamber aboard their swings whilst gripping their ever present footballs, grinning like the toads they are. Three years old, sturdy and covered in muck, there are is nothing I love more in the world.

They adjusted like flowing water to the change in their world after Jay and I split. Kids are astonishingly accepting. They love Casey although her quietness unsettles them at times but it does make them more gentle around her which is a bonus. They do, being three, ask horrifyingly awkward questions on occasion.

"Mummy, can Daddy come sleepses in your bed? Isss cold and we wants cuddles in beds nots on sofas"

But as I push this squealing pair of miscreants on their swings, I smile. Life, it's pretty good.

9th August 2000

"I don't understand why we can't stay over at yours? I mean, it's not like I've never seen your kids, is it? I've seen you with them in town loads over the years and anyway, you said they were away with their Dad this week?", after a long day working at the refuge, his pleading tone is a bit irritating if I'm honest and as I re-dress after our surprisingly good sex, I try to smile placatingly.

"Liam, look, don't take it personally, I don't let anybody stay over at the flat or meet the boys. It would confuse things too much. Sorry dude but this is all I can do right now", I re-tie my trainers as I go to head off.

This summer, all my friends home from Uni *except the New Zealand contingent*, the social life has been pretty decent. Lees and Adam dragged me to *another* party at the Bronson twins' palatial home back in June, the annual celebration of everyone's return from their Uni studies.

It was at this party that I found myself chatting to, of all people, Liam bloody Merchant. Two years at Uni appeared to have somewhat matured Mr. Merchant who, far from being the obnoxious *cunt* I had labelled him previously, he had turned into a funny, slightly self-deprecating, good-looking guy who had decent chat and who was suddenly being attentive and flirty.

What threw me a little bit was the intensity of the lust that suddenly sparked between us. Up in an attic room of the Bronson's massive house, Liam Merchant and I shagged ourselves into a coma. We lay there, after about the fourth round, chuckling and sharing our mutual astonishment that this explosion had taken place, given our past animosity.

"Roberts", he'd chuckled slightly embarrassed, "You in that silver dress from the Leavers' Ball has been a staple of my wank bank for a long time and now, now I've got the 'under the bonnet' visual to go with it", he roared with laughter as I thumped his chest and before we knew it, round five was under way.

I have spent this summer having incredible, sneaky sex with Liam, whenever I can fit him in around summer fun with my boys, study, my additional summer job at the pub and just life in it's mundane chaos. Fitting him in generally seems to occur immediately after my shift at the pub ends, in the twenty minutes grace I have before my trusty babysitter Mum needs to get home. Luckily, Liam also lives on the High Street too so we can get fairly sneaky with little hassle. He does not set foot in my boys' home though. *Nope.*

Jay has taken the boys on holiday this week, the longest I have ever been separated from my children. He and Casey pushed for me to come, offering Obi as bait, knowing how greatly I fear the 'third wheel' scenario. I declined, feeling oddly achy about the idea of observing a whole week of Casey and Jay's domestic bliss. They're at Prestatyn Sands and me, I worry constantly about whether the boys have brushed their teeth and if Jay has locked the caravan door at night so as a distraction, I fuck Liam, leave his Mum's house afterwards and cry myself to sleep because I miss my babies and I miss…...I miss being loved.

"Erin, what do you…..what do you tell people we are? I mean, when I go back to Manchester for Uni, what do you see happening?", Liam is sat up in bed, his very lovely torso still tanned from his recent lads week in Greece, his tousled tawny-blonde hair making him look like a fallen angel.

He sounds anxious and I flush with humiliation, *shit have I come across as the desperate, clingy single mum?* Genuinely, I don't see a future after the summer with Liam. I like him, he's funny and we have a laugh and the sex is pretty amazing but I'm a twenty-year-old mother of two, I can barely plan past the end of the week.

I feel a need to reassure him that he is not anchored down, that no guilt is necessary, "Dude, this has been a great summer but that's all it is, I know that, don't worry. You'll go back to Manchester and I'll crack on here, nice memories and no….harm…...done?", my words peter out as his face falls. *Oh bollocks, I've read this wrong.*

"Oh, right, 'kay. Got it", he shrugs and fiddles with his phone. He flits his gaze up to me as I hover in the doorway, unsure what to say, "I'll see you tomorrow night I guess?".

I smile weakly and nod, heading off and leaving this car-crash conversation. In the forty-five seconds it takes me to walk from Liam's house to mine, my phone rings. It's Ad's number and I smile, wondering what my mates have been up to tonight.

"Hey Roberts, whatcha doing?", Ad's voice is a bit odd.

I frown slightly but joke, "Well, been rocking Merchant's world again my friend, this girl's got skills".

I hear Ad groan, "Jesus Rinny, I don't want to know, Merchant was always a bit of a prick at school, I have no desire to hear about what you're doing with his *equipment*", I snigger but then he sighs,

"Rinny, the reason I'm ringing is I just bumped into Aurora Romano at the pub and she said Gio's coming home for a visit in two days. Did you know?"

I didn't. As my knees give way and I sit on the pavement abruptly, I hear Adam add, "Rinny, he's bringing his girlfriend to meet the family. Rinny? Erin? You still there love?"

I find the oxygen I need, "Yeah, cheers for the heads up Ad, see you tomorrow mate", and I hang up abruptly.

I don't even process the thoughts. I get up, turn around and when Liam opens his front door, confused in his t-shirt and boxers, I throw myself at him and let him fuck me like a jack-hammer in his deserted house. I stay the night in his bed, sleeping in his arms for the first time ever as I watch his clock tick through every minute of the darkness and I try and focus on the feel of his bare skin rather than the pain in my chest.

10th August 2000

Back in my own flat before Liam even wakes up, I am clutching my tea in my eerily quiet home and I am *fucking* furious as I turn my computer on and start to type.

"McNamara

What the fuck dude? I thought we were mates? I thought that after these years of us emailing, of being each other's 'Dear Diary' that we maybe had each other's backs. I thought that you gave a shit about me? You see, I give a shit about you. I cried y'know, when you sent me that first email the night Adrienne dumped you. I cried because my mate was in so much pain and I couldn't give him a hug.

I'm wrong to think what we've got is real aren't I? I'm such a dickhead Danny. I've always been a dickhead, I always wind up getting into shit and making a fool of myself. Me and you, we're just words on a screen. I don't think we've spoken more than a few full sentences to each other face-to-face in our lives.

There's probably a reason that we've never spoken on the phone, isn't there? I last saw you when you were calling me 'ugly' and 'ginger' outside a nightclub when we were kids and yet I was stupid enough to have faith in this email bollocks, to believe that you were somebody I could trust. I tell you things sometimes that I've never told anyone, even Lees or Jay. I told you that I loved…….I told you things that are deep in my head.

Danny, he's coming home. He's coming home and he's bringing the girl he fucking loves and you never told me. You never warned me. I am here, stuck in this fractured life of mine and I am shagging Liam Merchant and he's coming home and you didn't tell me.

Bye Danny, I don't want to play this any more"

I cry in the shower before pulling myself together and ringing my babies, AJ's gushing stream of consciousness about all of the fun he's having making me laugh. Jake is a bit wobbly, tears start and he tells me that he wants to come home and that he wants me. Jay takes the phone and I hear him reassuring Jake and kissing him, Jake's sobs stalling and then Casey's soft voice offers him pancakes making him whoop. Smiling, Jay and I chat for a bit, it's comforting hearing his voice and we joke about the boys and their crazy ways.

"You 'kay Feist, you sound a bit fuckin' quiet?", I hear Jay walking as he talks, a door shutting behind him.

I swallow down a sob, "Jay, he's…..he's coming home tomorrow and…..and he's bringing his girlfriend from New Zealand. He….he loves her", I concentrate on breathing.

Jay's voice is a low rumble, "Don't see him Feist. Don't fuckin' put yourself though that. Stay clear yeah? Come stay wiv' us here till Saturday?", his kindness is lovely.

I sigh, "I've got work mate and I want to paint the boys' room with Dad before you get back. I'll just stay busy, look I need to get to the pub for work. I'll ring the boys before bed tonight yeah? Sorry if I set Jakey off"

Jay chuckles, "Tha' sneaky little bastard turns on them tears coz he knows it gets him treats and shit. Boys got moves!", we laugh together over our sons before I ring off with my usual *'love you dude'*.

I hear the smile in Jay's voice, "Love you too Feist".

I'm getting my shoes on when my phone rings. The number is a foreign one and I roll my eyes, an Indian call centre the likely culprit.

"Hello?", my tone is curt.

"Roberts, put down the fucking paracetamol, step away from the noose and for God's sake get your ginger butt away from whatever bridge you're on. Jesus Christ, what do you mean *'you don't want to play this'*? Fucking hell you've got kids, don't top yourself over Romano", the deep voice sounds a bit frantic, a Kiwi twang flattening and shortening the vowels.

"Eh?", I'm baffled.

"I'm sorry, 'kay? I would have told you but honestly, I didn't think it was that big a deal for you? It's been ages since you mentioned G and straight up, I thought you wouldn't give many shits coz you're fucking that dipshit Merchant but for the fucking record, I *do* care, you *are* my mate and I *give* a proper shit about you", he pants for breath at the other end.

"Danny?", I'm still a bit stunned.

He sighs, "Roberts, you are a *lot* more intelligent on email".

I laugh and reassuring him that my typed melodrama was not a cry for suicide prevention, Daniel McNamara and I have our first proper conversation, making me horribly late for my shift at the pub and sending my pub landlord into a conniption but it is totally worth it. Danny is fucking hilarious. For the whole twenty-five minutes of our ridiculously expensive phone call, I don't mention Gio but when I explain that I *really* need to leave for work, it's him who brings it up.

He sighs, "Roberts, I didn't know you were still into him love, you never said, eh? He had to let you go though y'know, it was fucking him up. We were just kids, we're *still* kids but the way he felt.........it was messing him up and that's fucking *ridiculous* for a guy our age. I know you were *there* too but you had all that grown-up shit to distract you and dilute it. He didn't. He had to let it go. Emily......Emily is easy for him to be with", I'm nodding as he talks, biting my lip to hold in the tears.

I hear him take a breath, "Roberts, I've seen your pictures, seen you in that one with the Silver dress that he keeps in his sock drawer. I'd pick you over her any day girl, you're fucking hot Roberts", he snorts as I tut.

Smiling sadly, I mumble, "My best mates call me Rinny, y'know?".

"Well, *Rinny*, get your ginger, mum-butt to work, eh? Good talking to you, yeah?"

I smile, "Good talking to you too McNamara, I'll email you tomorrow"

"You do that dickhead, see ya", and he's gone.

I fill my time effectively, ignoring the sound of a countdown in my head, my twelve hour shift at the pub a fantastic distraction.

11th August 2000

Dad and I paint the boys' room, my landlord giving very few shits what I do to the flat as long as I pay my rent. As Dad and I paint the messy Navy Blue backdrop for the space and rocket wall stickers that I've bought, we chat about life. Dad and I rarely get time alone and these seven hours in undisturbed isolation are just lush. We chat about the future, about my hopes for the boys, about my life goals. Dad asks me whether I have a 'young man' and I tell him that I am dating an ex-classmate but that it's just a summer fling. He nods a bit sadly.

Rearranging the room, Dad stumbles across the brightly coloured shoebox that contains all of Gio's postcards to the boys. I see Dad smile as he flicks through them, reading the short comments that Gio writes which always made the boys gasp wide-eyed when I read them. *"Saw a crocodile as big as a bus today boys, he had teeth as big as my hand"*, *"A snake was in my toilet today boys. He'd have bitten me on the bum if I hadn't spotted him first"*, *"Saw a massive palace in the jungle today boys with monkeys swinging from the trees. They were nearly as cheeky as you two"*.

There's one he sent from Belize, with a gorgeous hummingbird on the front, that I keep in my bedside drawer. It's the only one he ever sent that mentions me. *"Saw this beautiful hummingbird today boys. It was nearly as pretty as your mum but not quite. Nothing is as pretty as her"*.

Dad puts the box down gently and looks at me, "Erin, it's my greatest hope that if you decide to spend your life with somebody, that they realise how lucky they are to have you and my grandsons", he smiles sadly and gestures at the box, "Giovanni always was a good lad", and without further discussion we lift furniture into place.

A few hours later sees me working at the pub on my last child-free night and my friends are all here in the bar. Lees and Ad have rounded up a bunch of ex-classmates and I feel increasingly uncomfortable about the fact that Liam makes a point of hugging and kissing me every time I leave the bar to collect glasses, putting on a proprietorial show for our peers. It's pretty common knowledge that we're *seeing* each other but this feels a bit *clingy*. I shrug him off a few times, smiling sweetly but his frown tells me he's miffed.

A group of lads enter the pub, slightly older than us and dressed up for a proper night out. I'm serving them when their chat starts to get a bit cheeky, a bit suggestive and I have to wag my finger and read them the riot act, despite the fact that the cheekiest one is actually *quite fit*. I chat with them but spot an aggravated-looking Liam come over, posturing slightly which immediately puts my back up.

"Hey sexy, you staying at mine again tonight babe?", his voice is louder than it needs to be

I smile tightly as the group of lads look on in interest, "Er, I dunno, maybe? I've got the boys coming home tomorrow afternoon and I've got stuff I need to crack on with. We'll see, eh?", I whisper the last bit and serve more customers.

"That's a *'no'* then mate", the fit lad from the group snorts and his mates jeer.

I see Liam bristle and to my horror, he loudly responds, "Lads, when she's gagging for it and riding my cock like a pro every night, the last thing she ever shouts is 'no'", before he grins like an idiot and walks off, as if he's just won an argument.

I feel that red mist rise, I feel that ire build, that chopsy little madam never far from the surface. Throwing the bar gate open, I grab the nearest pint to hand and storm over to where Liam is high-fiving some of the morons from the Practically Perfects group.

Lees spots the danger and I hear her call out my name, causing Liam to turn just in time to get a full-on dousing in snakebite and black. As it drips down his astonished face, I snarl out,

"I think that's a 'no, I won't *ever* be fucking *you* again', *mate*. We're through you prick", and I knee him in the bollocks.

Ignoring Liam's incredulous gasps of pain, I turn around and three things occur simultaneously: I see Obi and Jay rushing towards Liam like a pair of bulldozers, intent on some sort of damage, I see an astonished Casey stood in the main doorway of the pub holding both of my sleepy looking babies by the hand with Jakey's face tear blotched and snotty and I see an open-mouthed Gio Romano stood in the other doorway at the back of the pub, holding the hand of an extremely pretty girl.

It turns out, I have a new skill to offer the world. *Crisis creation and immediate diffusion.*

Ignoring the fact that the sight of a Gio seems to have actually stopped my heart, I manage to grab both Jay and Obi and at least halt their progress even if their verbal threats directed at Liam are loud and truly menacing.

"I'm gonna kill you, you fuckin' prick. Who are you? What the fuck you done to Feist, eh?", Jay is pointing his finger accusingly, his tone sinister.

"You're a dead man walking boy, dead man *fucking* walking", Obi is actually terrifying.

"Who the fuck are you two?", Liam looks like he might shit himself.

Me, I'm pulling both of them away, desperate to prevent catastrophe but also aching to hold my babies, who are straining at Casey's hands. I gesture to Casey to grab the two biggest problems while

I run towards the two smallest ones, scooping them into my arms and peppering their warm, sleepy bodies with kisses. I have no idea why they are here but my heart feels like it might burst from the pleasure of holding them.

"We missted you soooooo much Mummy, so much. Jakey, he got all sillies and was cryings too much so Daddy and Casey said we's come home to see you. I love you Mummy", AJ kisses me frantically as I clutch them both close.

Jake is indeed sobbing furiously and I pepper his snotty little face with kisses telling him how much I missed him and how much I love him and his brother.

At this point, we have moved away from the doorway and we're in the Inglenook fireplace. With a smile at Casey, she explains softly what happened, whilst maintaining an iron-like grip on Obi and Jay's shirts as they continue to eyeball Liam who has retreated to the back of the pub, away from the doorway and my large *enforcers.*

It turns out that Jake did indeed get himself worked up to the point of no return after a long day in the swimming pool, even managing a hysterical vomit or two, such was his distress. With the stuff already packed and no seeming end to Jake's meltdown about wanting his Mummy, nobody saw much point in prolonging the agony. Jay had tried to call me but my phone is on charge at the flat and so I never answered.

After kisses and reassuring cuddles, I give Casey my keys as she offers to go and put the boys in their beds as I have some, ahem, *clearing up* to do here. She smiles, her pretty, kind face amused and Obi offers to help her,

"You're telling me 'bout the hassle with that prick over there before I go, yeah", Obi gestures towards a wary looking Liam as I roll my eyes and nod reluctantly.

Jay stands in front of me, his face almost angry as he nods towards Liam, "You really fuckin' tha' prick Feist?", he's grinding his jaw, that oh-so-familiar face pulling at my heartstrings like it always does.

I wince and nod, Jay banging the table closest to him in anger before he walks off, following Obi and Casey, "See you back at the flat, yeah?", he mutters over his shoulder.

I've managed to delay my reaction to Gio's presence with these last four minutes of chaos but as I turn, I know that the likelihood of collapse is high. As I force myself to look over, I see hands being shaken, hugs of greeting being offered, gestures of introduction being made over at the slightly shell-shocked table of my friends and peers.

I see Gio Romano for the first time in two years, four weeks, three days and nineteen hours.

I see his wide, white smile, I see the dark curls, the freckles, those blue eyes, the warm hands and that big strong body. I hear his voice, it coats my whole internal audio-system with treacle as I listen to him chat with Ads, as I hear him laugh and as I watch him gripping the hand of the pretty, smiling girl that he loves. My heart is simultaneously ripping and warming with each beat, schizophrenic in it's cluelessness about what it is supposed to be feeling with Gio so close but belonging to another.

I turn to Bill the landlord, who looks a bit boggled watching me from the bar. Getting a bit of banter from the group of lads that I was serving, I apologise to Bill for the rukus and he smiles kindly and asks if I want to head off early. I gush my gratitude and grabbing my coat and bag, I take a final glancing look at Gio, his gaze still firmly on our assembled school friends and I leave. As I head out of the door, I smile as I hear Bill shout,

"You! Yes, *you* the gobby blonde twat who got his bollocks rearranged by our Erin. You're barred now son, fuck off".

Back at the flat, after a bit of a chat about Liam, the holiday, the journey, my babies and all the usual mundane stuff, Jay, Case and Obi decide to drive home tonight rather than stay over in my cramped little maisonette. The boys *lost their shit* when they saw their room and we spent ages all crammed into the tiny space as they pointed out every sticker and asked questions about every planet and rocket, Jay grinning at me as Obi laughed at my crap space knowledge.

As they went to leave, I gave Casey a massive hug. I genuinely like her, any aches I feel about her and Jay have never been directed at her. She's sweet and gentle and I am grateful for how kind and lovely she is to my boys. I tell her this as we hug, I thank her for looking after my babies so beautifully. I see tears glistening in her lashes as she grins broadly and tells me that it was 'her pleasure'.

Obi heads out, plans made for a night out next weekend. He hugs me and whispers in my ear, "Pick somebody better to fuck, eh Ginge? He looked like a proper twat", as I snort and nod.

Jay swoops me into a slightly urgent hug, kissing my hair and not releasing me for longer than I expect. When he pulls back, he's looking shifty and I raise an eyebrow seeking clarification. He shakes his head and mumbles, "It hurts y'know Feist. If I never see the blokes, I can sort of handle it, you, bein' wiv' somebody else……..", he shakes his head again, huffing out a breath, "Never gonna be simple, you and me", it's a statement, not a question and I nod, fighting a lip-wobble that I can't allow right now.

Jay presses a kiss to my forehead again and whispers, "I saw him in the pub, the Godfather. Stay away, do yourself a favour and don't put yourself through it coz it fuckin' hurts Feist", and with that he walks out.

I sleep on the floor in the boys room, all three of us cuddled together in a massive duvet pile, underneath their new ceiling of glowing stars.

My loves.

Chapter Sixteen

18th August 2000

Gio Romano is home for two weeks allegedly. Taking on board Jay's advice and with no desire whatsoever to run into Liam, I resign myself to a hermit-like existence for the duration. My shifts at the pub always see me hyper-alert to any potential Romano visitation but thankfully it never happens. I work at the refuge on Wednesdays as usual and all my spare time is spent entertaining the boys at places and days out where I am certain I will not run into him.

Lees and Ad have been watching the boys for me a couple of days a week over the summer while I work and Gio has seen them several times on these days. The boys came home from the first visit, furnished with a crazy number of presents, toy Kiwi birds, t-shirts and Auckland Uni memorabilia as well as sweets and toys. I wrote a 'thank you' letter from the boys, decorated in their hand prints and their drawings. I also copied two of the most up to date photos of the twins, put them in frames and gave them to Lees to give to him.

The other day, Danny told me that he had never really bought into the reported chaos of my life until he started to get first hand accounts and now that he has, he cannot believe the entertainment value that I provide. He said the image of me dowsing and neutering Liam Merchant will keep him warm at night.

"So Roberts, you spoken to the Italian Stallion yet, aye? He's been over there a while, you grown a pair of those balls you're so fond of assaulting?
Danny"

"Danny,

Nope, won't do it. Can't do it. Jay said not to and I think he's right. Seeing Gio for those few seconds
in the pub was hard enough and he never even looked my way. It's better he just gets back on that
plane without drama. See how mature I'm getting, SEE! Avoiding drama, it's my new motto.
Rinny x
PS He looked fucking amazing. You could have told me that he looked that good. I looked like
hammered shite.
PPS She's pretty.
PPS I still love him Danny. What a pain in the arse"

"Rinny,
You avoid drama like I avoid tits, as in, you don't........If you're gonna be a pussy then own it, don't
make excuses. I need your advice although honestly, I've got no clue why I'm asking, your love life is
a car crash. Adri texted me. It's been two years y'know? She is asking to meet for a drink, she's in
town. What do you reckon?
Danny
PS He doesn't look that good, you've just got desperate. The wanker flosses his toes with his socks
when he's watching TV, still fancy him now, eh?
PPS Yeah she's OK. You're hotter though.
PPPS He's texted me every day since he's been over there. Pretty much all the texts are about you. He
saw you Roberts, he's seen you quite a bit actually but I guess you haven't spotted the stalking creep.
I don't think you're the only one with that pain in the arse"

"Danny,
Only meet up with Adrienne if you know 100% that if the night ends with polite goodbyes and
pleasantries exchanged, that you will be satisfied. If what you're hoping for is declarations of love,
devotions and/or jack-hammer shagging on every flat surface in your condo, then don't fucking go.
I can't see Gio, I can't talk to Gio because if I see him and have to actually acknowledge that he's
really here, my heart won't recover when he gets back on that plane with the girl he loves. If I pretend

he's just a mirage, I'll be OK. I can't cope with polite goodbyes and pleasantries so I am staying my ginger arse the hell away.

If Adrienne hurts you, I'll kill the bitch.

Rinny.

PS Honestly? I'd probably lick those toes and suck on his sock. Yup, that's where I am.

PPS Thanks dude.

PPPS The other day, the boys made me go to the park in Lees' neon pink wig, silver hot pants, a pair of Moonboots from the 80's and my arms wrapped in tin foil. I was an alien apparently. Please, PLEASE tell me this was not one of the days he saw me?"

"Roberts,

Your advice is noted, pretty fucking useful actually. Yeah, I'm after the jack-hammer shit. Maybe I'll bail, aye? Dangerous times. Stay ginger,

Danny.

PS SUCK HIS SOCK?! What the actual fuck? You need professional help

PPS The sock comment has changed things. You are no longer hot.

PPPS Yeah, he saw. It made him laugh. He said you're 'still this hardcore nutter". I think it was a compliment. He followed with flattering comments about your tits and your arse if that makes you feel any better. I know I felt better after hearing about them……..might have a little imagine now actually……it's been a slow month….."

This weekend, the boys are at Jay's and so Obi and I have decided to branch out, keen as I am to avoid anywhere where Gio or Liam might be. A few years ago, a new club opened up in a nearby town and it's starting to attract some big name DJ's and national press. I've fancied going for ages so Obi and I are having our first *local* Friday night out, I've even set aside some of my wages and spent it on the new mini-dress that Jake and AJ helped me choose, their comments causing hilarity amongst my fellow changing room occupants,

"Jakey, I see mummy's pants, MUMMEEEEEE I SEE YOUR PANTS!!"

"Mummeeee yous look so pwetty, yous the pwettiest mummy evers. I have choccy buttons now?"

"Mummy!! I see your bare bits Mummy!!"

Obi's adamant that he's going to drive, a heavy week celebrating some big commissions for his team has seen him rendered a little bit *delicate* so no alcohol for him tonight.

Obi is massive, a fact I often forget. Ribbed by his brothers in the early years of knowing him for being 'cuddly', Obi has worked hard on his diet and fitness. He is a solid lad and will always be prone to putting on the pounds but at the moment, this solidness is primarily muscle. He ditched the braids back in the 90's and he now has cornrows, another source of amusement for me as upon his arrival, it's clear he's just had them done as he can't smile or close his eyes properly, his hair is *that* tight. He's got some cool lines shaved into the side of his head and with his new clothes, Obi looks *good*.

"I'm gonna find her tonight y'know Ginge? I am. My African Queen is gonna be powerless coz could you resist somethin' this fine? I fuckin' couldn't", he puffs and pouts in my mirror as I try not to laugh.

Obi turned twenty-five earlier this year and had some sort of 'Quarter Life' crisis. He is absolutely convinced that he can only find love with a girl from Nigeria, his bloody Father and Mother's whispering in his ears seems to have started to take root and so each night out that we have sees me scouting for his fabled 'African Queen'. I have as yet failed, with a Kenyan girl and a beautiful but slightly weird girl from Guadalupe my only offerings so far, both of us having to consult the map when we got home having neither heard of Guadalupe.

The pub goes silent when Obi walks in for our pre-club drinks, the ethnic diversity of our town as limited as you might expect for rural Wiltshire. The silence is so *loud* that we both get uncontrollable sniggers and Obi adopts a thick Nigerian accent and talks loudly, making me snort Diet Coke out of my nose at one point as he loudly tells me that he is looking to procure wives for all of his brothers back in the village. However, our amusement wears thin as despite my status as a regular barmaid here, the frosty looks and thinly veiled racism piss both Obi and I off. Nodding at each other, we head off, Obi slinging his stupidly heavy arm over my shoulder, sneering at the offenders.

Obi growls as we walk towards his car, "Jesus Ginge, you live in a right MilkyBar town, eh?", as I grimace and nod.

I have had a few confrontations over the years regarding Jay and my sons' ethnicity. I am a pro at belittling racists but each time it happens, I feel this heaviness deep in my bones that I will not always be there to defend them and to knock down the petty people who hold prejudiced views. I tell Obi this as we drive into town and turning in my seat, I tell him the thing that I haven't said out loud before,

"Obi, it's like despite being their mum and knowing every single thing about them, reading them like I can and predicting them like I do, there's these two things about me that mean I can't really understand what they're going to face. I will never really understand what it's like to be a mixed-race lad growing up in our town. I have no reference points on which to draw and I'm scared shitless that I won't get it right, that I won't support them in the way they need to be supported, to teach them how to handle dickheads like those guys in the pub. I'm scared Obi", I look out of the window and fiddle with my fingers.

Obi indicates and pulls over into a lay-by, turning off the engine and turning to me, his large warm hand gripping mine earnestly,

"Rinny, you listen the fuck good to your Uncle Obi. My Mum and Pops, according to you, should have been amazing then at helping me deal with discriminatory shit from ignorant twats, because what, when the lights go out you can't find them unless they smile?", Obi winks and flashes his Colgate grin making me snort in appalled amusement.

He carries on, "My Mum and Pops, they might look like me, they might have talked the talk about strong black men, proud heritage, Nigerian identity but neither of them were *there* when I got bullied at school, eh? Neither of them were there to give me love, make me feel OK when people said shit or did shit", he shakes his head and looks at me,

"I don't look that much like my brothers, I don't look like Sash or the girls or you but who are the people who make me feel good about being me, who make things fuckin' OK when life is shit?", he raises his eyebrows as much as his cornrows will allow him to.

I smile at him as he smiles back, "It's them, it's you, it's my mates. It sure as fuck ain't my missing Mum or my clipper-cunt Pops. Love is love little Ginge. You don't need to understand exactly what those little buggers might go through, you just need to be *be* there, you need to love them like they deserve and you make them feel that it's brilliant to just be them. Me and their Dad and Uncle, we'll do the stuff you can't. You just love them, 'kay?", he nods and then winces as the cornrows fight back.

I snort and reach across for a big Obi-hug as I say in his ear, "You are AMAZING Obi Adeyemi, you know that?".

He winks as I pull back and re-starting the engine, we head off.

"Clipper-cunt?", I snort in amusement as I turn to him for explanation.

Obi smirks, "When I was sixteen, I had a set-to wiv' Pops and told him that he was just *'a cunt wiv' a pair of clippers'*. He strapped me good but since then, if he pisses us off, me, D and Wheels call him

'Clipper', he don't get it but me and the boys crack up", I laugh loudly and turn on the stereo.

The club is incredible, the music just *spot on.* Obi blags us into some sort of VIP area and despite us not knowing anyone, Obi's loud, friendly chat soon attracts us a crowd of new mates,

"Your boyfriend is proper funny", a slightly pinched looking girl with overly-gelled hair and an overwhelming cloud of perfume shouts in my ear as I down my soft drink thirstily.

I smile as I watch Obi, "He's not my boyfriend, he's my brother", I grin at the words.

Her look of utter astonishment as she swivels from my transparently-pale ginger face to Obi's deep, rich, ebony-toned smiling visage, makes me snort into my bubbles.

Love is love. Family.

We crawl in at 3am, laughing at my failed attempts to locate Obi a potential wife. He deserves the most amazing girl and I decide that I will start looking beyond our nights out to find somebody worthy of my lovely mate.

Obi heads off mid-morning and I find myself with pretty much a whole day at my disposal before my monsters return. I potter about until a call from Lees inviting me to an afternoon at the local open air pool gives me a plan for the day. Armed with my elderly swimming costume and the boys' inflatable ring, I arrive at the pool ready for a chilled day with my mates until I see Lees sprinting towards me through the turnstiles, a worried look on her face. She pulls me into a hug and gabbles,

"Chick, I didn't know Ads had invited them, silly wanker didn't tell me. It's…...Gio's here chick, with Emily. I…...I know you wanted to avoid seeing him", Lees looks crestfallen and I feel disappointment trickle through my body.

I shrug and give her a squeeze, "It's OK Lee, I needed to pop into town for some bits anyway so I'll just head to the shops I think. Say hi to Ads and er, everyone from me", giving her a kiss on the cheek, I smile and head off. *Oh well.*

I'm nearly back at the very grubby Volvo when I hear the sound of somebody jogging to catch up with me. Expecting Ads coming to apologise, I turn with a smile on my face but startle when I see that it's *not Adam.*

He looks angry, his big, strong frame dressed in a t-shirt and board shorts, his coal-coloured hair wet and dripping and in bare feet, he looks pissed off.

Gio gestures at the car, "This is it now yeah? You don't just walk away from me, you drive off too now? Motorised fucking avoidance? Two years it's been, *two years Rin* and you can't even be bothered to say hi, to come and have a chat, catch up? You just fuck off, like….like I mean nothing, like *we* mean nothing, like you don't give a shit?", I stand like a stunned mullet in the face of his justified accusations as he shakes his head and starts to walk backwards again.

"I get the message *Erin.* Got it. I'm so over this shit with you", and raking his hands through his hair, he turns, shoulders slumped and walks off.

Nodding to myself like a lunatic, I climb in the car and drive to the supermarket wondering if I can still class Gio as a mirage if I technically didn't speak to him.

I see Mirage-Gio the next day though. We're at Mass, Jay brought the boys home yesterday because Mum's making me bring the boys for some Kids Blessing Service bollocks at church, knowing that with all the favours I owe her, I cannot refuse.

Gio's mum Sofia is beaming widely, her expensive wardrobe even more jewellery adorned than usual as she introduces *Emily* to Father Eamon and as many members of the congregation as she can, *"This is my Gio's beautiful girlfriend Emily from New Zealand", "Margaret, have you met Emily, she's Gio's girlfriend from University in Auckland, such a bright girl, doing Medicine".* Emily looks so clean and pretty, so neat and put together in her knee length skirt and smart vest top. Her smile is sweet and her voice soft. I can't imagine for one moment that Gio ever has to worry about her throwing up on him or starting fights in car parks.

I can't look at Gio. He's wearing a plain white cotton shirt, a thin blue tie and a pair of chinos that make me want to bite his arse. He looks like some sort of preppy model. I am wearing a summer dress from New Look circa 1997 and the Adidas trainers that Jay bought me when I was sixteen. *Classy.*

My boys however are wearing little short sleeved shirts, cargo shorts and bow ties. They look so adorable, I may actually cry. I'm doing OK, the boys are distracted by cooing old ladies until Mass is just about to start and then AJ clocks Gio across the room,

"Gioooooooooo, Mummy, I want Gio, he's there Mummy, he's there. I go see him, yeah?", AJ is trying to exit the pew like a dog pulling at the leash.

Gio turns around, not looking at me but instead gesturing to AJ to come over, which he does at high speed. Gio swoops him up, holding him at arms length and making him giggle, Sofia batting at Gio to tell him to be quiet as Mass starts. I watch as the man, not a boy now, the *man* who occupies all my spare thoughts holds my son in a cuddle and reads him his book as Mass drones on. Emily, sat next to him, is smiling tightly.

Jake starts to fidget and with a sort of dawning resignation, I am unable to hold him as he too makes a dash for Gio, clambering over immaculate Sofia in his desperation to get to his hero. Gio smiles and with a strong arm, hoists Jake onto his lap. As the minutes tick on, I feel as if I'm imposing on Gio, I feel I should go and retrieve my sons. During a particularly loud hymn, I sneak down the aisle, gesturing silently to AJ from the pew behind that he should come back with me. The little stinker pouts, shakes his head and wraps his little arm tighter around Gio's neck. I silently try Jake, indicating that I may have chocolate buttons in my bag if he comes with me. Nada, the kid stays put.

I swear under my breath as Emily turns, her pretty face a bit wary as she spies my crouching, swearing form in the pew behind.

I take a breath, "Er hi, I'm Erin, sorry if they're…" but she cuts me off.

"I know who you are Erin", there is a tinge of steel beneath that polite smile and those blunt Kiwi vowels.

I grimace-smile, "Oh, er it's nice to meet you, it's Emily isn't it?", she nods curtly.

"Go back to your seat Roberts, they're cool here", Gio does not even turn to look at me as his hissed, clipped words put me in my place. I slope back to my seat feeling like a chastised child. Mum rolls her eyes at me as I park my bum, my sons beaming triumphantly at me from Gio's shoulder. *Traitors.*

Mass finished, I can already hear the boys begging with Gio about something as he manhandles them out of the pew, dangling them both by the ankles as they shriek with delight. Underneath their yells, I catch an exchange between Sofia and Emily, the odd word here and there, *"Such a shame….only sixteen….always been a bit wild…..Gio was very kind to her….sympathy…..less fortunate……had a teenage crush…..glad left…..more suitable………brighter future"*. Lovely.

"Gio, you gots to come see the rockets on the wallses in our bedroom. Mummy's sooooo clever, you gots to come see them. Pleeaaasseeee Gio", AJ as always is the more vocal one, Jake nodding his support of his brother's request.

Like bloodhounds, they sense Gio's reluctance and immediately they matching lip-wobble at him and Gio, the sucker, visibly melts.

When Gio's eyes meet mine, I hear Jay's voice in my head telling me to walk away, to stay away, to not put myself through *this* but then I look at my sons, re-attached as they have become in a short space of time to the man who was there at their birth and I feel my poor, battered heart physically reach out from my chest to try and touch Gio. *Shit.*

"Gio, you're welcome to pop over if you have the time", my voice sounds a bit weird.

"I don't think that's possible Erin, Giovanni is taking Emily to a restaurant for lunch, we're meeting family there", Sofia sounds a bit flustered but I can't tear my eyes away from Gio, I don't think I can breathe, I am drowning again in my feelings for him.

Gio doesn't break my gaze, "Ma, I'll just be five minutes, you go on with Em and I'll meet you there. OK?", but it's me he nods questioningly at.

"Gio, I can wait for you........", Emily takes a step forward, her brow creased in a frown but Gio has the boys in his arms and he's already moving towards the door, the boys whooping in delight at their victory.

"It's OK Em, go on ahead and order me a beer, carrying these two herberts is thirsty work", and he starts to jiggle the boys in an animated jog, the boys insensible with giddiness. Emily follows Sofia but anxiety is written all over her pretty face.

As we walk up the High Street, Gio chats at the boys, making me smile as they chirp like birds in response. He is *here*, Gio is *here* and I cannot pretend that he is a mirage. His deep voice, his hair, that smile, the chicken pox scar, the lemon and herbs scent of him. *Here*.

He stops outside the door that leads up the stairs to our home, as if he's been visiting here for years. As I turn the key, the boys bundle past me, scrambling up the stairs in their usual madness, leaving Gio and I at the bottom, in an awkward silence.

I sigh and look at the carpet, saying what I should have done at the swimming pool, "Hi Gio, it's really good to see you Romano"

I hear his smirk conveyed in his voice, "Hey Roberts, still a massive pain in the arse I see", and without any further words, I turn and bury my face in his chest, my hands reaching around him to rumple his immaculate shirt as I hug him and pray that my heart does not actually just give up from the degree of aching it is currently doing.

I mumble into his tie, "I'm sorry I was a dickhead and avoided you. I just couldn't.....too hard, y'know?", Gio's arms are frozen to his side, no reciprocation and I stand back a bit embarrassed, staring at the carpet.

A voice yells, "Mummeeeee, bring Gio to see our rockets", I shake my head and look up.

I feel my heart crack as I realise that Gio is fighting tears, *actual* tears, his lip is wobbling and is jaw is doing that side-to-side thing that boys do when they're trying not to weep. I panic momentarily until Gio takes a ragged breath, clears his throat and starts to walk up the stairs ahead of me, calling out in a slightly tight voice that, *"There'd better not be stinking socks on that bedroom floor",* making my hooligans screech with laughter.

Still shocked from his near-tears, I watch Gio risk his posture and concussion in their tiny room as the boys show him every single toy and wall decoration. Gio is amazing with them but then again, he always was. He responds to all their questions and he plays along with their daftness, making them scream with laughter as Gio shoots me furtive, unfathomable looks across the room. Jake fetches the shoebox of postcards and Gio looks shocked as he asks me in a whisper,

"You kept them all?", he looks stunned.

I nod and smile weakly as my own lip threatens a wobble, "It was pretty much all I had of you".

He looks around the room awkwardly and checks his watch, "Oh Christ, I need to go boys, I've got to go and eat a truckload of food", he goes to stand up, carefully under the eaves.

AJ turns to me with his mouth agape, "Mummy, Gio eats TRUCKS!", I laugh out loud.

Bidding the boys farewell with hugs and hair ruffles, Gio follows me out of their room as we leave them playing happily.

Gio stands awkwardly in my hallway, hands in his pockets as always. He looks around, through the doors to my kitchen and living room, into the open door of my luridly painted bedroom,

"You made them a proper home Roberts, you did it", he smiles at me but as the awkward silence returns, I ask,

"You've had a good time, y'know, visiting your family and that….with Emily?", I pretend to rub marks off the wall but instead appear to be *creating* some new ones.

Gio nods, head down, "Yeah, it's been cool. Mum, Dad and Rora, they've been over to see me a few times but it's expensive and my housemate, you remember Danny McNamara right?", I feel a flood of guilt as I realise that Gio has absolutely no clue about the fact that Danny and I know each other's darkest secrets and 'speak' almost daily.

He carries on, "Well Mac is a massive twat who got us locked into this contract on an expensive apartment and so the rent makes it hard to save for air fares", he shakes his head smiling. *I know, Danny told me last year actually.*

"I should go", he sounds uncertain and my ears prick up. He said *'Should'* not *'have to'* or *'need to'*. *'Should''* always suggests reluctance.

I nod, sucking in a breath. Gio pauses and in that second, a thousand different scenarios and fantasies go through my head, mostly influenced by 80's Teen Movies. *Passionate kisses, declarations, arguments, accusations, furious goodbyes.*

What I don't imagine is him suddenly jolting and gabbling out, 'See you then Roberts' followed by his astonishingly rapid descent down my stairs and out of my front door, before I even get a chance to draw breath. Door slam. *Gone.*

Gone. Gio's gone.

I slowly slip to the floor on my landing, shaking oddly and wondering why my chin has sprung a leak as something drips off it and into the cleavage of my summer dress. I hear the key turn in the lock and as my mum comes up the stairs, a massive bag of Maltesers in her hand, she sighs, crouching down and pulling me into a cuddle that screams understanding.

"Oh my lovely, lovely girl, I thought I'd find you in this state by here, as soon as I saw you leave Mass with Giovanni. I knew no good could have come from it, not when he's spoken for", Mum presses kisses to my hair as she strokes my arms.

Resting her head against mine, she whispers, "Love is out there sweetheart, it's out there somewhere, you just need to give it time. We do find it in unexpected places and with unexpected people. I never thought I'd move to England with a lanky, English softie but there we go", she winks and I smile weakly.

"MUUUUUUUMMMMEEEEEE, wipe my bum Mummy, I dones a big poo", as AJ's yell from the bathroom makes me snort, Mum pats my knee and hands me the Maltesers as we clamber to our feet.

"How about your Lisa's Adam, doesn't he have a brother?", Mum asks as she starts to head down the stairs.

My face must say it all, as my Mum tuts and rolls her eyes,

"I should have sent you to confession more bloody often Madam", she rolls them again as she shuts the door behind her.

AJ shouts from down the landing, "I don't need you now Mummy, I wipedted my own bum........wiv da towel".

I'm already running.

24th August 2000

It's the Bank Holiday weekend and this Thursday night has seen the pub rammed to the rafters, running me ragged behind the bar as people warm up for their three-day bender. Lees and Ads are babysitting the boys for me, their opportunity for *alone* time having been a bit limited whilst living back home with parents over the summer break.

As I finish mopping the bar and straightening up, I am trying desperately not to think about the fact that Gio flies back this weekend. We have not spoken or even seen each other since last Sunday's weird little interlude and his subsequent abrupt departure but just knowing that he is up the road makes me feel like things are aligned right.

I told Danny what had happened. He too was a bit sharp with me.

"Rinny,

What the fuck do you want the boy to do? Eh? He's with Emily, you're being your usual loony self and he's got to just deal with seeing the girl that broke his heart for the first time in two years. No wonder he legged it.

Danny

PS Women are all fucking mental bitches. You're the exception in that you're just mental"

"Danny,

Broke his heart?! He clearly recovered and moved on but mine's still breaking you bastard and I will have you know that I was perfectly normal and not at all loony.

Rinny x

PS You met Adri, didn't you? You wanted the declaration. That's why you're being a twat to me?"

"Rinny

I did. I do. She didn't. She left. I fucking feel like I'm burning.

Danny

PS I've got no PSs left in me. I'm PS'd off. Wish you lived closer, would love a hug right now"

"Danny

I'll kill the bitch. How fucking dare she. She has no idea what she's missing, you are amazing and I will shank her in the twat for being such a cow.

Rinny x

PS I'm PS'd off enough for the both of us. I wish I was closer too. I give fucking awesome cuddles. I reckon it's the massive tits"

"Rinny

"I will shank her in the twat???!!!" I bloody love you heaps Roberts. And your massive tits. Stay Ginger.

Danny

PS He's a dickhead, always has been, I've tried my best with him. It's your fault his pakaru, you broke him all those years back"

Mopping and cleaning done, I bid landlord Bill goodnight and head the few hundred yards up the High Street to my home. There's an unfamiliar pair of blokes' trainers in the hallway as I open the door and both Lees and Adam's shoes are missing. *Jay.*

As I plod slowly up the stairs, I'm gabbling, "Jay, have you got the day off tomorrow then? I wasn't expecting you, this is a nice surprise, the boys will be well chuffed. Did Lees and Ads head off? I've had a shit night at work but I've got Ben and Jerry's in the freezer if you want to share? Jay I need a proper fucking cuddle, I swear this week......", but my voice fades out because it's not my ex that is sat on my sofa watching TV.

It's Gio.

He stands up slowly, looking a bit sheepish but so gorgeous in his jeans and a well worn t-shirt and my heart bungees around my rib cage from his proximity.

He smiles apologetically, "I....I had to see you Rin, before I go back. I had....I felt like.....like I should explain", those blue eyes are so wonderfully familiar.

As I stand there like a stunned mullet, Gio takes a breath and launches, "Possums are like fucking mutant rat-hamsters, they're everywhere in New Zealand, d'you know what a possum is Rin?", Gio looks a bit wide-eyed.

It's a novelty frankly to be the sane, rational person in a conversation but it seems I am. I shrug in alarmed bafflement and he carries on,

"They make these fucking awful noises at night, they scared the absolute shit out of me when I first arrived there, Mac would take the proper piss. Then we went to all these rainforests and jungles in South America and there are things in those places that make sounds like somebody is getting murdered, I mean full on axe murdered, right by your tent", he sounds a bit like Jake does when he's describing something astonishing that's occurred at nursery and I feel a smile pull at my lips.

He carries on, taking a step closer to me which makes my skin prickle, "But I realised, after the first couple of nights, that those noises didn't freak me out any more. You know why Rin?", he takes another step closer to me and instinctively, I step back slightly.

His blue eyes are imploring me to understand, "You see, I realised that I'd already heard the scariest noise in the world and these animal sounds, they were nothing compared to that. You know what that scariest noise was Rin?", his voice lowers slightly and I watch his Adam's Apple bob in his strong throat as I shake my head dumbly.

He swallows thickly as his eyes bore into mine, "That noise, it was the sound of the girl I love *bleeding to death* from having twins right in front of me when I was seventeen, it was the sound of those machines screaming out flatline beeps, the voices of those doctors so fucking panicked and the *silence* of her, this girl who usually never fucking shut up", his voice cracks and his eyebrows furrow as he looks down, "All those times in the jungle and with the sodding possums, I figured that if the noise of her dying didn't kill me, then these furry bastards had no chance", he holds my gaze as I swallow down the brick in my throat.

All I can hear is my heart thumping.

It's a croak, the words that leave my mouth, "You said *love*. You said *love*, not *loved*", and I see those endless blue eyes widen in response.

He winces and then he looks defiant, "I learnt a long time ago Rin that when it comes to loving you, there is a difference between being *brave* and *backing off* when the risks are too big", he looks at me sadly now, my own face crumpled in confusion.

He softens his tone, "You won that award, at the Leavers' Ball, you remember? They called it something like the *"What the hell will she do next?"* award. That was the night, after you left with your Dad, when I realised that I wasn't brave enough to keep on being in love with you", I gasp at his words as he bites his lip and looks at the carpet shaking his head.

"Loving you Rin, it was like this obstacle course that I was never, ever going to get to the end of and Jesus, I was only a kid", he huffs out a breath, carding his hands through his hair as he walks over to fiddle with the boys' toy castle in the corner of the room.

His head is bowed, those dark curls hiding his eyes as he sounds a bit angry, "Every few minutes, I was getting walloped by something else or something would pull the rug out. I mean you were with Ryan fucking Jones and then you got pregnant. Then we're cool for a bit and although I was with that Carolyn, I dumped her for you because I needed to tell you how I felt, just before that party that time, d'you remember?", Gio looks up and I see his jaw tick as his eyes narrow before he continues,

"You were pregnant and you came to my house to walk there together and I asked you how you'd feel if somebody asked you out but you flipped and told me that they'd be a 'fucking idiot' for getting involved with you, you threw a right eppy. We fall out because I let that dickhead Merchant be a twat to you and we don't speak for ages even though I knew I *fucking* loved you, we didn't speak. Then you're in labour and the babies arrive and we had this moment, this tiny kiss but then you DIED, in front of me, you fucking DIED", he's pacing around gesturing furiously now, those strong arms filling my tiny lounge.

"After the boys were born, it was so amazing. I…... I loved every minute of hanging out with you those first few months. Christmas party arrives, I *finally* kiss you properly, like I'd always wanted to and BOOM Jay turns up. Then at the next party *months* later, you tell me you want me too and *that* kiss, that *fucking* kiss Rin is all I ever had of you because BOOM you're gone again, and again and a-fucking-gain. Babies, boyfriends, fights, shootings, drama, chaos, *pain*", his tone is accusing as he stands in the room, arms outstretched and I stare gormlessly.

His tone quietens and the wind leaves his outraged sails, "It was like self-harm being around you Rin, it killed me watching you with Jay all those months, watching and wanting and never fucking getting, even though I *knew* you had feelings for me. I *knew* it", his lip wobbles and his voice cracks,

"I went travelling and I was proper fucked up about you, in some ways I still am", he shakes his head as he toes the carpet, "Y'know, I've fancied you since we were kids Rin. I used to watch you moon over Danny and it did my head in. There was this disco at the youth club when we were about fourteen, I remember that you looked devastated when he pulled Carolyn, do you remember?", I'm so stunned by this new version of my life history that I just shrug as he smirks ruefully.

He carries on, "You stood there, bloody crying over my best mate and I felt like I wanted to punch something. You came over to talk to me, we played pool or some shit and I was an absolute bellend to you, I regretted it for *months"*, I am wide eyed in astonishment.

"Then we are at some shitty Under-18's night a few months later and you're there looking *gorgeous* but you're mooning over Mac, AGAIN. You were dancing with Morris, having a proper fucking laugh and I was so pissed off about you fancying Mac and about him moving, that I snogged Carolyn to get back at him. It was shit. I just wanted to snog you. So I did that too, only I bolloxed it up and then you told me, loudly I should add, that you didn't want me, you wanted Mac", I flop onto the sofa, stunned by this new version of past events as Gio still monologues wildly,

"Can you see now Roberts, can you see why after bloody years of this shit, after years of wanting what I could never seem to fucking have, I just had to give the fuck up? I went to New Zealand and it was as far away from you as I could get", he seems to lose all his bluster at that point and he flops onto the sofa next to me, catching his breath after his tirade.

I turn slowly to him, "But......but I ended it with Jay, we split....", I turn to him as he spins in his seat, his blue eyes wide,

He throws his arms out again, "And what? What difference would that have made, eh? Your life Rin, it's complicated and you.....you never make the easy choices. I figured that yeah, I could come running home. Weirdly it was Mac that told me you'd split, he said he'd heard it from somebody back here, he told me I needed to get back on a plane and go see you but what if I had? You'd never told me what, if *anything*, you felt about me and so I figured it would just be a waste of my time. Plus Rin, you've got all these people in your life pulling you in different directions, you're in so many different *parts,* there are so many *bits* of you that I could never pin you down and I'm a simple guy, I like things straightforward and pretty organised", I feel my eyes sting as he whispers,

"Ems, she's the most straightforward, easy person, what you see is what you get, no hidden complications. I love that", he smiles a bit wistfully as I feel something tear in my chest. As Gio carries on, my chest starts to feel tighter and tighter,

"I mean c'mon Rin, we arrive home to find you brawling, *again*, only this time it's because you've been shagging Liam Merchant of all fucking people and you're causing chaos, *again*", he scoffs with derisory laughter and I feel Chopsy Madam twitch.

He turns to me with this irritating, slightly patronising smirk that makes me want to *knock him the fuck out* as he hammers in the coffin nail,

"Rin, I'll always love you but I know the difference between being *brave* and being *reckless* with my heart now. That's why I'm with Ems and it's why I needed to come here tonight to put everything, y'know, *straight* between us. I wasn't sure how this would pan out, coming here tonight because it's been so hard seeing you again and feeling the way I do about you but talking it through like this, it's helped actually. I know for sure that it's Ems I need to be with", he's smiling into the middle distance, nodding to himself like he and I have just solved a complex coursework question.

I feel a sense of disappointment in Gio surge through me, I see flashes of Jay confronting him in a carpark for his lack of fealty and it's underpinned with a most peculiar feeling of self-congratulation. *I knew he couldn't be trusted.*

I growl, "I'm *so* pleased that my total lack of response to all this *stuff* you've said, helped you with formulating that conclusion Giovanni", my voice is like shards of glass and Gio jolts, his smile wiped off as he looks at me warily.

I stand and move towards the door, "Gio, I think you need to hurry back home to Emily, y'know, escape my *complicated, chaotic* life before I do your head in more or cause you more damage with pulled rugs or perhaps even just overwhelm you with my many *parts,* you poor, simple soul", my tone is *vicious* and Gio now looks horrified, he's trying to find words, his hands flapping placatingly but Chopsy is on her horse and she's not dismounting.

I snarl, "Tonight has helped me *work out a few things* too y'know", I fold my arms over my chest and kiss my teeth as I continue,

"All those years ago when we argued at school, you asked me what it was that I *really* wanted", I glare at him as he swallows and nods imperceptibly, those blue eyes piercing.

I snarl on, "Well, I reckon I know what I want now", Gio looks torn between astonishment, panic and intrigue as his eyebrows raise.

My voice is a low growl, "I want you to go down those stairs, put on your shoes, shut the door and never, ever fucking come back Gio. You think I don't make *straightforward choices*? You feel like *you* were the one who never got what they wanted? You immature, selfish prick. You have travelled the world *unburdened,* you have had *adventures*, you've had a *life* and part of that is because I kept my *fucking* mouth shut about how I felt about you. I kept it hidden so that you would go travelling without feeling *torn or burdened* by my feelings. *That* was one of the not-straightforward choices that I made and I made it because I fucking *loved* you more than you will ever know Gio", Gio visibly gulps as we both get to our feet.

I step forward and he's the one that steps back as I point a finger to his chest, "The whole time I was with Jay, it was because I was trying to be a fucking good Mum to my boys, putting them first and I'm sorry if my near-death has left you with lasting *noise trauma*, I guess I should have gone into that operating theatre solo after all, eh?", I walk over to my living room door and I point at the stairs,

"Fuck off Gio. Take your lovely simple life, your straightforward shit, your very pretty and very perfect girlfriend and go back to New Zealand. I am so sick of getting punked by heart-shit, I feel like on my grave they're going to write, *"Here lies Erin Roberts, she was eternally Love Punked but bore it like a friggin' trouper"*. Go Gio, just go. We're so fucking done here", I feel my heart crack right the way through its core.

I watch as he takes heaving breaths, he goes to say all sorts of things judging by the waves of different emotions that cross his good-looking face but nothing comes out. When resignation finally coats his features, his posture slumps and he starts to move. I watch as all six-foot-two of my preoccupying fantasies slowly walks out of my lounge, down my stairs and after a brief tussle with his trainers, he opens the door and walks out of my life forever.

I don't really know how long I stand inert in my hallway. It's after midnight but I hear a knock at my door. Heart in my mouth I open it and my best friend is already stood on my doorstep looking at me with love and concern.

"I thought I'd hang around Rinny, y'know, thought it might not go *smoothly*. I just saw Gio leave and he……..he couldn't talk…….he was too upset. I *knew* letting him come in was a fucking mistake, I'm so, so sorry babe", and with that I fall into her arms as she coos and rocks me, stroking my back as I muffle my howls of misery into her shoulder.

Lees sleeps in my bed, holding me tight all night. In the morning, she looks after the boys for me as I zombie plod my way to work. Shift over at the pub, I drive my gorgeous, excitable piglets to Clevedon for a weekend with their Daddy who has clearly had a phone call from Lees because he hugs me for so long that I nearly fall asleep on him.

I go out with Obi in Bristol, he seems to understand that my lack of chat and vivacity is no reflection on his company and when I pull a ridiculously muscled by bouncer-type with curly black hair and a cheeky smile, Obi simply asks for his address so that he can collect me safely in the morning and he watches me leave with him.

I fuck this stranger into blissful, orgasmic oblivion. I ride him like I am trying to catch up with that plane that I know is taking off at 6am this morning and in the middle of the night, when he asks me if

359

I'm cold because my entire body is shaking, I nod. I don't tell him that it appears that my heart has simply stopped beating and that's why I'm shaking. I also tell him that my c-section scar is from appendix surgery.

Obi rings the stranger's door at 8am, collecting me with a bacon sandwich in one hand and a hot chocolate in the other. He also looks so worried, I could cry again. I drive home and stay in bed for twenty-four hours.

Sunday, I wake up, put two feet on my carpet and declare the entire episode concluded. I plaster a smile on my face, I look around the flat at all that I have achieved and I start to accept a new narrative.

Gio Romano was simply a guy I used to go to school with.

When my babies come home, we mess around and Jay smiles warily at me, his good-looking face concerned. I wink at him and poke out my tongue, making him smirk and I figure that I've got it pretty good. I've got it pretty fucking good right here.

Chapter Seventeen

August 2002

"Ginge, this is a Red Alert. Davvo broke his leg", it's very quiet in my office and as a result, I am forced to whisper my incredulity down the phone.

"Obi, who the actual fuck is Davvo?", I honestly do not have time for this.

I have got exactly eight minutes to finish writing up this Care Plan before I have to dash to get the boys from their football camp and mystery Davvo's fracture is the least of my worries.

I've been working all summer as a Social Work Assistant. I'm one year into my two year postgraduate Diploma in Social Work and my placement this year was in this very lovely Early Years team based in a Children and Family Centre here in Bristol. They offered me full-time paid work over the summer, which I took gladly as the boys have been on at me for *months* about the expensive football camp that I had no clue how Jay and I would afford.

Therein lies a hilarious twist in my life: I appear to have given birth to two football prodigies. I, Erin Roberts, who had a 100% unbroken record of PE avoidance, whose sporting endeavours have been limited to occasional wheezing training runs with my athlete best mate, all-night stints on the dance floor or running for buses. My brother, the sprinter, was a genetic anomaly as far as Team Roberts was concerned. Jay is equally baffled, having never set foot inside a football ground *in his life*.

This nonsense all started a week after The Godtwat (Lees' new moniker for Gio) returned to New Zealand. I'd taken the boys to watch Dyls' first post-summer training session. The Athletics Stadium has a massive inflatable cushion for the High Jumpers to practice on and the coach had said the boys could come and leap around for an hour or so, an offer I'd snatched up as the boys' energy is entirely without limits.

Some of the sprinters had been messing about with the twins when one of them set up a 'race' on the track, intending for the toddlers to be allowed to beat the teenagers. Only, it didn't pan out the way they intended. The speed at which my two little bandy-legged three-year-olds shot off up that track caused the staid, very straight-laced coach who was stood next to me to mutter, *"Fuck me"*, under his breath.

As I watched people's jaws dropping, I'd turned to the coach and said, "Er, is that not normal?", because honestly, the little buggers have *always* moved at that speed, from about ten minutes after they learnt to walk.

Dyls, grinning from ear to ear, ran over with the boys in his arms, "Coach, did you see that? Did you see these two run?", his Uncle Pride was off the chart.

As we stood there, chuckling as the twins raced around giddy with the praise they were getting from the other sprinters, somebody tossed a football over and without pausing, my two fell upon it, their love of kicking balls superseding any activity in their life apart from eating. As I watched them do their usual back-and-forth kicking runs the whole length of the field, I'd turned to see more astonishment on the faces of the coach and his team.

I'd rolled my eyes and huffed, "Okay, what am I missing? You lot look like those boys just shat gold bars", I turn and point at my two speeding goblins, "They've always done that, haven't they Dyls? Eh, they've always been kicking balls and running like that, we go to the park every night before bed so that they can do it", I'd looked at my enormous brother for his confirmation.

Coach cleared his throat, patting me on the shoulder as he muttered, "Erin, I think you need to get those two onto a football team and quick. I, er, I am no expert on football but those two boys, well, let's just say that I've never seen three-year-olds move that fast or kick balls with that sort of precision", and he'd walked off, shaking his head ruefully.

I rang Jay who sounded as baffled as me, "But Feist, I figured that's just what kids do? I mean, yeah, on the beach and that when we was at the Caravan park, people were tellin' me that the boys were amazin' but I thought that was, y'know, just wha' people say about cute kids and shit? D'you reckon that coach was serious, I mean, they're only like three?"

I'd laughed, "Dude, I have got no clue but honestly, that whole group of lads and the coach looked like the boys had just pulled the winning lottery numbers out of their little butts. Maybe we should have a look at sending them to a Saturday club or something?"

So we did. The kids Football coach at the leisure centre watched them for two minutes before he asked me to *'pop in for a chat'*.

Two years on, my now nearly-six-year-old boys play football three times a week. They are both on the school Under 8's Team and they also play in the Under 8's for a local kids team, having been asked to move out of the age groups below because nobody ever got a chance with the ball. They are also being 'watched' by the local Premier League team Youth Squad, a stony-faced scout with an improbably large coat pops over to watch their matches occasionally.

Quite honestly, I hate football and if I had to supervise all these matches solo, I would be driven to kill. Jay is far more keen than I am to go and so we share the burden. It's a good job we live so close by and therein lies *another* development.

The Godtwat gone, I went through a period of misery and numbness after his departure. Despite him having been absent for two years prior to our combustion, it was astonishing how much time I spent daydreaming or thinking about him. With his departure, I forced myself not to do this any more and it freed up an alarming amount of mental space. This freed up space gave me clarity. I realised that I was being selfish living in my home town. With Jay the most important non-resident person in my sons' lives, it became clear to me as I started the third and final year of my Degree, that my reliance on my parents had waned enough that I could look at a move closer to Jay and Casey, allowing my boys more time with their beloved Daddy and maybe, *just maybe*, allowing me to start to gather together the remaining scattered parts of me and start to build a *whole* life.

Using Jay's address, we made the boys' school applications and as I entered 2001, I was house-hunting on the *Bristol Riviera*. Lees and Ads had already organised their post-Uni plans, moving to London for their respective Graduate Jobs and with that, my links with home town became reduced to my family and a couple of scattered playgroup and school acquaintances.

Mum and Dad were actually pretty positive about the move, *tearful* but positive. Jay was ecstatic at the idea of his boys being so close, Casey and I *wetting* ourselves over the fact that he was trying to play it cool but would ring me at least twelve times a day telling me about houses and flats he'd found for me. He came on every viewing and if possible, it made me love him even more, this lovely mate of mine.

Casey and I actually went out together a couple of times during this period of planning and home-hunting. Typically, it was me who drove a very blunt and up-front conversation about how I needed her to understand that in moving closer, I still pose no threat whatsoever to her life with Jay. I love him, I think he's stupidly fit and yes, Jay and I have a significant under-the-duvet history but I was not, I am not and I will never be *in love* with him.

Casey burst into tears, hugging me and telling me that she'd always wanted to thank me for the decision she knows I made after Jay came out of hospital,

As she sobbed, she blurted out, "He would have stayed with you y'know, if you'd not been the one to end it. He's so loyal and he loves his boys so much, he loves you so much too. I know why you did what you did Erin, D told me about what you'd said to him in Intensive Care and Jay talked me through the chat you guys had afterwards. I could see it was you releasing him. I…...I can never thank you enough for what you've given me and him. It must have been so hard for you to choose that", and with a very tearful hug, Casey and I became genuine friends.

Me and my boys moved house the day after my last exam for my Degree. In hindsight, it was a *terrible* timing decision because as we filled the cars and Jay's works van with all our worldly possessions and furniture, I realised that I was still pissed from the celebrations with my Uni mates the night before. I whispered to Jay that I was still drunk at which point he fell about laughing, my mother had a conniption and like a small child, I was relegated to the back seat of *my own car* with my squealing sons, as my brother drove us to our new house.

We live in a gorgeous two bedroom bungalow on a quiet residential road in Portishead. We have a garden, the boys school is only a ten minute drive towards Jay's house and I am doing my two year Diploma at a nearby Uni. The boys spend every Tuesday, Thursday and Saturday night at Jay's, he collects them from school on a Tuesday and Thursday and depending on who's covering football duty, they have either a Saturday or a Sunday daytime at Jay's too. It's brilliant. Jay comes to every school meeting, every assembly, every event, *everything.* He and Casey pop round whenever they're passing and we do the same. We feel like a proper family.

Courtesy of the boys starting school, I now have a really lovely bunch of Mum mates, I hang out with Jay, Casey, Obi and their friends and I see my own parents, brother and mates as often as I can. Jay helps with the rent, offset by the fact that he no longer has to drive up the motorway several times a week to see his boys and my little stinkers *love* their school.

"Ginge, *Davvo* is Dave you daft cow, he's trying out a new thing ready for Ayia Napa", Obi is tutting down the phone.

I cannot contain the peal of laughter, "Dave?! Fuck's sake Obi, it's tragic enough that two twenty-eight-year-old men are going to Ayia Napa with every teenager in London, now you're developing nicknames? What are you? Obi-Dog? Snoop-Grandad? MC Black Magic?", I make myself laugh, snorting really loudly and I have to retreat to the loos as my colleagues shoot me evils.

Obi tuts at the other end, "Yeah, laugh it up Granny Knickers, when was the last time you fuckin' had it large? Eh? You been like a hermit this summer ANYWAY that's not why I'm calling", he sounds exasperated, "Look, *Dave* broke his leg last night, came off his bike in town"

"Shit, is he OK?", I like Obi's best mate Dave, he's sweet and funny and we had pretty decent sex one drunken night that Obi can *never* know about.

Obi sounds impatient, "Yeah, yeah he's cool but he's gotta have surgery and he won't be able to fly out Saturday"

"Oh no, that's really crap, you guys were looking forward to time travelling back to your lost youth", I laugh again as Obi swears at me,

"GINGE! Shut it yeah. Look, he's rung his insurance, they're gonna pay out for his room and his flights so he won't lose out but that leaves me with a two bed apartment and no mate to be on holiday with. So you're coming", Obi doesn't draw breath as he carries on,

"Wheels says he'll have the kids at his for the week, you just gotta find £200 to change the name on the flights and that's fuckin' it! A weeks holiday girl, come party it up wiv' *MC Black fuckin' Magic* you cheeky bitch. You ain't had a holiday on your own *ever*, I know it", Obi's tone is pleading.

I have one minute before I will officially be late collecting the boys. I run through every argument in my head, every reason why I cannot go, why I should not go, why it would be silly to go to Ayia Napa at my age…...and then I remember that I am twenty-two. This is *exactly* what people do aged twenty-two, they go on daft holidays and have fun. They *don't* stay in washing muddy football kit and reading bedtime stories, freezing their tits off in playgrounds and parks trying to tire out their twin sons whilst juggling work and a Diploma course. Twenty-two-year-olds don't forget that they are *only* fucking twenty-two.

"I'm coming", it's a whisper but Obi whoops in response.

"Wicked, call you tonight yeah. You're a legend Ginge", and Obi's gone.

I walk back into the office and over to my bosses desk, smiling placatingly,

"Anna, can I have a word with you about next week……..?"

Later that night, as always, I email Danny.

"Dude,

I'm going to Ayia Napa for a week with Obi. Ayia-fucking-Napa. I may return with a new MC identity and an affinity for Nike Trainers and a lot of gold chains. How's things this week? Work any better? A mum came into the office today, pissed off that her contact with her kids was cancelled because she was high as a kite on crack. She called me a 'Boot-faced ginger cunt-fuck". It's without exception my favourite new phrase. I might get a tattoo in Napa, it's what people do yeah? It'll read, "This boot-faced ginger cunt-fuck will shank you in the twat". Hope you're good Danny.

Rinny xx

PS This thinking about holidays today has made me think, we should meet up. Will it be weird do you

reckon, face-to-face? I might still have a crush on you. Maybe I'll get a 'I heart Danny' tattoo

instead.

PPS Just realised, I have no holiday clothes. I have no clue where my passport is. I must go and

panic. And wax things. Christ, there are definitely things that need waxing. SHIT"

"Rinny

HAHAHAHAHAHAHAHAHAHAHAHAHAHAHAHAHAHHAHAHAHAHAHAHAHAHAHAHAHAHA. You

in Ayia Napa? Fuck me, they're in for a tough summer. Get that awesome tattoo or I will lose what

little respect I've got for you.

Yeah, work's shit. Fucking hate this grown-up crap. Uni was mean, this is bollocks. The Lead

Architect I'm working under is a hardout, heavy duty dickhead. Me and No-Name, we're thinking of

bailing on this and doing some travelling again. He's pissed off with his grad placement too.

Look, I'm not talking to you if you've got a feral muff that needs sorting, woman I've got standards.

Go and wax the fucker NOW. Stay ginger (Do the curtains and carpets match? Never asked you....)

and give Napa hell for me,

Danny

PS We should meet. Might come to the UK actually, escape this architect dickhead and his 'integral

ethos of the structure' crap. You will still have a crush, I'll try to tone down the hotness of me.

PPS No-Name dumped her, did you hear? Miss. Perfect-stick-up-her-arse-prissy-twat-joyless-bitch

told him to ask her to marry him or she'd end it. He took the third option and binned her. Thank fuck.

It's been a long two years.

PPPS I'm guessing you're not taking Pele One and Pele Two? They staying with their Dad? Say hi to

the little bastards from their Uncle Danny who's never met them and won't be meeting them until they

can be taken to pubs and used as bait for barely-legal totty"

I sit and digest the email for a moment.

No-Name dumped her.

Danny has called *him 'No-Name'* since I sent him a very long, rambling account of our combustive *discussion* almost exactly two years ago. I wanted Danny to have my side of the story, I suddenly felt a bit territorial over McNamara and didn't want him to think badly of me.

I'd told Danny that I never wanted to hear *his* name again, that I was moving on from my romantic preoccupation with somebody who viewed having feelings for me as some sort of *burden*, something that was *harmful* to his *emotional wellbeing*. The fact that Danny quickly started to refer to *him* as *'No-Name'* in our emails seemed to imply some *unfavourable judgement* towards *him*, although they have of course remained the best of mates. Danny finished his Masters in Architecture this June and *No-Name's* four year Urban Planning course finished at the same time.

Danny has been increasingly hostile towards *No-Name's* Emily, who it appears had everyone fooled with her *chilled, straightforward, pleasant* demeanour and who has gradually let her guard slip, revealing her shrew-like interior. Danny hates her, he has done for about twenty months now. It makes me pettily happy to read his bitches about her.

I try and analyse what it is I feel about *No-Name* being single again but realise that it's a waste of my valuable time.

Twenty-minutes later, my sons are knocking on the bathroom door, tearful voices asking if I am OK.

"Mummy, what are you *doing*? Are you hurt? Why are you shouting?", Jake's lip is wobbling as I open the door, clutching a towel to myself. Unbeknownst to my sons, attached to my overgrown pubes beneath the towel, are four strips of wax that will not *fuck off*.

I press kisses, I hug, I tell them that Mummy is giving herself a tricky *haircut* but that I am fine and that I will just do one more shout and then it'll all be finished. Rolling their eyes and smirking *just like their father,* they troop back to bed.

There's isn't a shout, when I eventually brace myself and yank all four strips at once. *It's a scream.*

21st August 2002

I can't do it. I am a truly unnatural shade of angry red and I can no longer pretend that it's simply because I'm hot. I am spending the day inside today, *end of.*

This week has been *brilliant.* The apartment turned out to be lush and combined with amazing weather and the Cypriot Government crack-down on excessive partying in the resort, everyone is playing a slightly more gentle game than they have been in previous years and it's *ace.* The clubs are still rammed, the Square filled with noise and neon every night but Obi and I keep it chilled, no agenda, no big group logistics needed with just two of us. We go where we want, when we want and if it's shit, we move on to another place.

I bloody love Obi. The first night here, we got a bit wasted at a massive beach-side bar and examined exactly *why* neither of us has any sexual attraction to the other. Obi says that initially it was loyalty to Jay that meant I was placed in an 'off limits' box but that he has just come to accept that troublesome gingers do not float his boat but that he *'admires the view',* nodding drunkenly at my boobs, making me wallop him.

"You're family, woman and only a twisted twat fucks his own family", Obi had slurred out and when we stopped laughing, we agreed that this feeling was mutual.

Obi sits in a place in my heart and in my life that sex does not come near and for that, I love him.

We have both pulled while we've been here. My repeat-offender, a gorgeous lad from Manchester called Aiden, has actually wormed his way under my skin. I *like* Aiden. We met on the second night here and actually didn't do more than snog that night. We met, during the daylight hours the next day and spent a proper fun day with Obi and Aiden's mates at the massive water-park. After lunch, I told Obi, in a shocking lie, that I was going to head home early because I *felt a bit of sunstroke coming on.* He was happy to stay on with Aiden's Manchester mates and nobody commented on the fact that Aiden quietly left with me. Aiden and I did not leave my bed until 11pm and when we did leave to go to the club with Obi and the others, we managed an hour before returning to the apartment for some more shagging.

Aiden is twenty-four, a builder who owns his own house in Hale. He's got tawny brown hair and a cheeky earring (I'm such a sucker for a lad with an earring) and his green, sparkly eyes are always filled with kindness. He's got a lush body, God bless those bricks and I knew that I must really like him when I told him within two hours of meeting him that I had kids. He'd smiled and asked me interested questions about them, grinning indulgently when I gabbled about my boys.

When he left my bed to head to the airport to fly home yesterday, I actually cried. *Completely pathetic.* I was absolutely certain when he pressed a soft kiss on me and finally left the apartment after a few false starts, that I would never see him again. However, a text flashed up on my phone within three minutes.

"God I'm gonna miss you woman. Can I come see you when you get home? Sunday? Aiden xx "

Obi said he liked Aiden, he also told me that, *"Wheels will be fuckin' spittin' Ginge, you like this one don't you? I can see it. I've not seen that look since....since ever actually. Shit man, Wheels is gonna be pissed",* he's smiled sadly and I'd grimaced.

Today though, I feel so gutted that Aiden's gone, I'm also too hot and burnt and when Obi said he was spending the day by the pool and that he planned on going nowhere, I left him to it and retreated

371

to the shade of my favourite bar with my book and a large Diet Coke.

An hour in, I'm starting to get a bit pissed off with the loud group of girls sitting at the table behind me. About my age, they are trainee teachers judging by their conversation but they are also loudly discussing their holiday sexual exploits. I am no prude, Jesus I am in no position to judge *anyone* but they are making public certain details and preferences that honestly, I doubt anybody wants to hear.

"Aretta, you're quiet, how come we never get anything juicy from you? It seems a bit unfair, doesn't it? You know all about our sex lives and we know nothing about yours!", the girl talking has an annoyingly whiny voice and I have had enough experience of bitchy girls to recognise an implied slight when I hear it.

Then a soft voice, quiet and measured with a slight Nigerian twang if I'm not mistaken, speaks, "Charlie, I have never requested this information from you but I am furnished with it nonetheless. If I choose not to disclose intimate details of my life, maybe it is because I do not feel that we are closely enough acquainted", I smile softly at the implied rebuke in her words and I decide that I *like* whoever *Aretta* is.

There's a little twitter of an exchange and then declarations that everyone will head off to the beach, a slight chill in *'Charlie's'* tone. *Aretta* softly informs them that she will be staying at the bar for a while.

Following their loud exit, I hear a soft sigh behind me and a voice gently whispering to nobody in particular, *"Why on earth am I here?"*.

I turn around to see the most stunning girl sat staring out of the bar window, a look of exasperation on her beautiful heart-shaped face. She has the most *immaculate* braids I have ever seen in my life, all swept up into an elegant swirl on top of her head. Dressed in a modest swimsuit but with a stunning figure, she shakes her head gently as she looks into the distance.

I initiate chat, I feel a bit sad that she is here with such a bunch of nightmares. Initially a bit wary of the strange, violently-sunburnt ginger girl with a mismatched bikini and a slightly weepy look about her who invites her to join her table, Aretta soon starts to smile as I give her my sympathy regarding her travelling companions.

We chat for *hours*, Aretta no more keen to sit on a beach or poolside than I am. She's a trainee teacher, the girls are all from her shared student house in Reading and she was bamboozled into coming on holiday with them because she genuinely couldn't face spending the next few months reliving it endlessly *second hand*. She has regret about her choice. When she tells me that her parents are Nigerian, I hear the first gentle 'ping' of a tick in my head. I tell her that my sons' father is half Nigerian, she smiles sweetly. As we talk and I tell her about Aiden and a potted history of my past, she tells me that she too has had bad experiences and has sworn off lads until she meets somebody that she can actually see a future with. She talks about how she felt like her *soul* was being chipped at by shitty, machismo-pumped boys who treated her like crap and that she has decided that the next lad she's with, has to pass a lot of tests before she will even contemplate a relationship.

As we talk, I find myself feeling a little bit dreamy over Aretta. She has this melodious voice and she is so, so poised and precise, her words carefully chosen and her whole being is *gentle* and *measured*. It doesn't hurt that she looks perfect, I mean *actually* perfect. I scan her face as she talks and note not a single blemish on her smooth black skin. I think I might be developing a crush.

"Erin, we have talked for so long but I have not asked you who you are here with. Your friends, I have been monopolising you with my troubles and yet I have not considered them. Who is it that you have come on holiday with? You are not here alone surely?", she pats my hand and looks at me gently.

I beam at her, "Ah, no. I'm here with my mate but he's by the pool all day today. I'd really, really like you to meet him Aretta, I think you guys definitely need to meet, I think you'd get on", I grin at her but I must look a bit shark-like because I see her face crumple with wariness.

She smiles politely, "Ah that is very kind but I think I should be…..", her words trail off and I lose her concentration. Baffled, I follow her line of sight and have a little snigger to myself.

Buff Obi has decided that it's not enough that he has ruined countless knickers poolside, he has decided it seems to arrive shirtless at the bar too, doing some dry-land underwear-destroying judging by the looks on the faces of the women around me.

Obi is *built,* gym-honed and with that Colgate smile, knickers have been dropping since we arrived here. He pulled the first night we arrived, forcing me to spend the early hours of the morning with my headphones on as *Charlene from Lincoln* loudly made us all aware of Obi's proficiency between the sheets. As I look back at Aretta's face and then back towards Obi, I grin like a moron.

"Oi, MC Black Magic, mine's a pineapple juice", I smile as I bellow at him across the bar, "And my friend Aretta will have another of these fruity cocktail things", I reach over and grab Aretta's glass as Obi goes through a hilarious mime of reactions.

Firstly, he smiles when he sees me, then he flips me the bird when I demand a drink. Then he sees who I am with and he drops his wallet, his mouth hanging open and his eyes widening as he looks at me in inquisitive-shock.

"That...that is your boyfriend?", Aretta is looking back and forward between the two of us clearly boggled.

I smirk and wink at her, "Nah, that's my mate", and I snort Diet Coke through my nose at Aretta's look of undiluted astonishment.

I am a *legendary* wing-woman. I don't just deliver 'pulling' opportunities. Judging by the devoted look on Obi's lovely face, I deliver *love*. He sat at our table with the requested drinks and we have been chatting as a three for *ages*. I have been able to work into the conversation every single positive achievement, attribute and personality trait that my lovely Obi has. I have basically pulled a subtle, "This is Your Life" on Aretta and in turn, I have got Aretta talking again about her exhaustion with fruitless, upsetting dating.

When they start syncing, when their questions and comments are directed solely at each other, I know that I have done all that I can. I fake tiredness at 8pm and mentally howling with laughter at the lack of chuffs Obi gives about me leaving, I make a move.

"Aretta, it was so lovely to meet you. If you're free tomorrow morning, Obi and I were going on a boat trip to the caves. Do you fancy it?", I smile innocently and have to bite my cheeks when Aretta nearly falls off her chair as she nods animatedly.

My work here is done.

I go back to our apartment. I ring my boys, I chat to Jay who takes the piss over the news about Obi and the amazing girl I have found him and hear all their news. I'm sat quietly on the balcony when my mobile rings,

"Hello?"

"Erin, it's Aiden", I smile like a soppy schoolgirl.

"Hey you", I can hear the smile in my voice.

"Erin, would you judge me love if I told you that I just dropped £300 on a flight back to Cyprus because I met this girl that I really fucking like and I didn't want to wait until Sunday to see her?", he sounds stupidly nervous, his accent a bit thicker on the phone than in person.

"Er, what?", I'm boggled.

"Please open your door love, I feel a right twat out here", and as I run through the apartment, I fling open the door to see a very sheepish looking Aiden, his lopsided grin a bit shy as he holds up a bunch of very droopy looking flowers and a small holdall. His nose and cheeks covered in cute freckles, that strong body and that adorable rumpled tawny hair. *Gorgeous.*

"I know this is a bit fucking mental but do you reckon I could stay here? I got on the plane but I didn't think to sort out……..", he doesn't get to finish because I have thrown myself into his arms and I am snogging the words right out of him.

I don't go to those caves the next day. Obi does, with Aretta. I don't see Obi again until we meet with our packed suitcases in the apartment hallway, on the day we're going home, both of us grinning like idiots.

8th February 2003

"Case, I don't know what to do, me and Jay have *never* disagreed over anything to do with the boys before but *fucking hell*, I've been seeing Aiden for six months and I was only being polite asking Jay's opinion…..I wish I hadn't bothered", as I clutch my hot chocolate, freezing my *arse* off on the touchline, Casey looks over at Jay, who is having a *Dad Discussion* with the other team dads by the goal posts.

Casey pats my arm, "Erin, he's being a total twat about this, I can't make him see sense. Aiden *should* meet the boys, you guys are serious but all I get out of Jay is, *"I don't trust him"*. Honestly, I know it'll cause shit for a bit but just do it. Just invite him over and do it. Jay will go nuts but it blows over with him, you know what he's like and he loves you too much to be pissy with you for long. Just do it, don't risk blowing what you have with Aiden", Casey pats my arm again and walks over to Jay.

I have never, ever introduced a man to my boys but I really want Aiden to meet my amazing babies. I'm so proud of how incredible they are and I want the man I think I'm *in love with* to meet them.

I mean, I'm pretty sure I'm in love with Aiden. He's so funny, he's so cheeky and the time we spend together gives me aching muscles from laughing and well, aching *other things* as well because *hot damn*, that boy knows his way around a duvet.

It's been mental these last few months. I was on a placement with my Diploma, spending four months with a Child Protection Team in Bristol. It has been an incredible experience but so, so stressful, so intense, so devastating at times and there have been weekends when Aiden has come to see me when the boys are at Jay's or I've gone up to Manchester and all we've done is watch DVDs and sleep because I am *knackered.*

I worry that I'm a boring girlfriend but Aiden says I'm not and his acceptance of our long-distance relationship, with no pressure on me to make any changes in my life at this point, makes me feel at ease.

Now, my placement is over and I want to establish something *firmer* for Aiden and I. I haven't told him I love him yet and he hasn't made any declarations but there are these moments when it feels like he's going to tell me something but then he pulls back and just smiles and kisses me instead. I feel like he's *there* too but honestly, I have limited experience to base this on. The whole love thing still boggles me and I have no template to act as a comparison, no clear benchmark upon which to draw conclusions.

I told Jay that I wanted to introduce Aiden to the boys and I asked him what he thought two weeks ago.

"Nah, no way, don't mess with their heads Feist", his blunt statement was topped off with a head nod.

I was flummoxed, not expecting the usually chilled Jay to have much of an opinion.

"Oh, er why? I've been with him ages now and it feels like we're serious. I, er, I think I love him Jay and I want him to meet the boys. He plays football too, he was really good when he was younger, he could be a bit more use than you or me", my eager smile faltered when I saw Jay's frown deepen.

Jay had pulled his most mulish looking face, "You asked what I think an' I told you. I don't reckon it's a good idea Feist, if you don't want my opinion, don't fuckin' ask, eh?", and off he stormed.

My eye roll was so severe, eye-related things nearly got detached.

Mum likes Aiden, Dad too. It's just Dyls that is a bit less 'gushing' about him but I put it down to the fact that Dyls will always hero-worship Jay and nobody will replace Jay in his estimations. Lees and Ads like him, we went to London for the weekend Christmas Shopping and we all went for a night out. Ads took me to one side and told me,

"Rinny, he seems a nice guy. If he makes you happy, I am so fucking pleased, Lees too. After all that shit with Jay and with…...well, with others, this guy seems decent", and Ads had hugged me tight.

Danny is Team Neutral. He takes the piss, gives me advice but ultimately offers no opinion, even when asked, about what he 'thinks' about the relationship I'm describing. He's almost *too* cautious in what he says.

The boys are staying with Jay today and as the match ends, the boys having yet again scored a number of goals in their synchronised play that has their coach weeping with joy, they run over and give me muddy cuddles and blow-by-blow re-tellings of their victories. Kissed, hugged, scolded for messing around and then packed off with Jay and Casey, I sit in the car and ring Aiden.

"Hey you! What do you fancy doing tonight when you get down here? D'you want to go out somewhere? Bit of clubbing?", I'm smiling as I watch Jay trying to de-mud two wriggling, giddy, mud-covered six-year-olds before allowing them into his prized BMW and I can see Jay's *'I'm pissed off'* vein standing out in his bullet-scarred neck.

Aiden sighs down the phone, "Oh babe, work's mental. We've hit a fucking nightmare with some steel beams and we're gonna be all day at this, can't leave until it's sorted and it might be a late one. I don't reckon I'll be able to get down tonight. How 'bout I make it up to you next weekend? Valentines yeah? Me an' you, we'll do something yeah?", he sounds fed up and my heart is sinking,

"Oh mate, I've got the boys next weekend, Jay's taking Casey out but we could do something chilled here? Maybe you could meet the boys…..? I'll make us decent food, maybe get a film or something?", I try and sound encouraging but he's silent at the other end, I could swear I hear a tut but I ignore it.

I sigh, "Look, how about I drive up to yours now, I've still got that key you gave me last time, when you were going to be late back. I could just, y'know, wait for you at yours?", I really want to see Aiden, I love spending time with him and it'll be two weeks since I've seen him if I don't go up today.

His voice sounds tired, "Babe, it's gonna be a shitter of a day and I dunno when I'll get back. I don't reckon I'll be at me best when I eventually get in. Let's leave it this weekend and make it up to each other next week", he sounds a bit distracted.

I feel the burn of disappointment in my throat, "Oh, okay mate. Speak to you later, yeah?"

"Yeah, gotta go babe", and he's gone.

I sit in the car-park, watching my ex-boyfriend strip both of our muddy sons down to their pants as they sit in his boot, the boys hysterical with giddiness at their public semi-nudity as Jay finally seems to deem them clean enough to set foot in his car. I watch them drive off, feeling grumpy that Jay gets to go home with his *girlfriend* and his *children* but me? I'm going home to a ready meal because I got stood up for a bloody *beam*.

Nope, I'm not having this. Aiden always says that deciding to get back on a plane to Ayia Napa was the riskiest thing he's ever done,

"I mean, you could have fucked off or have pulled some other bloke or just, I dunno, not given much of a shit but I knew I had to see you Erin, I knew I couldn't just leave you behind"

It's stuff like this that makes me think I am probably in love with him and I decide that I will drive to Manchester and I will wait for him and then tonight, when he gets home after his shitty day, I will try to cheer him up and I will tell him that I'm pretty sure I'm in love with him and that I want a future with him. I will take the same sort of risk that he took getting back on that plane in the summer.

I rush home, pack a bag with all my sauciest underwear which mainly consists of the one bra and knickers set that has not gone grey or frayed and I head off up the M5.

The traffic is pants and by the time I get to Aiden's cute little terrace house in Hale, it's nearly 8pm. As I let myself in the front door, it's dark but the house smells like his aftershave, it makes me feel giddy. His little two-bedroom house was bought by him last year, a deposit provided by money he got from his Grandad's will. His house is tidy for a lad's house, I smile as I remember how disgusting Jay's bedsit used to be or how filthy he and Obi would routinely make Obi's flat.

I eat the pizza I grabbed on the way, I have a shower, I get in my posh undies and I fall asleep in his bed, waiting for him to get home, sniffing his pillow and grinning at the scent of his shampoo on the fabric.

Since the boys were born, I sleep incredibly lightly. Jay would always laugh about the fact that I can fly out of bed and be upright and functioning within a millisecond of hearing a noise, no sleepy befuddlement for me. I hear the sound of footsteps on the front path and my eyes fly open, suddenly giddy like a child at the prospect of surprising Aiden. I look at the clock and to my slight shock, see that it's midnight. *Jesus, that's a long day at work.*

Then, I hear a noise that makes me feel chilled. I hear a coquettish, flirty female giggle and the low, bass-heavy rumble of my boyfriend's voice. It's the rumble he uses when he's saying something filthy and Aiden, he is pretty filthy at times. As I sit upright, I hear a sound that I have not heard for a long, long time.

It's the sound of hooves and a horsey bray. It's the sound of Humiliation Palmer-Smart, older, portlier but still cantering through my life.

They open the front door and as it shuts loudly, there is this awful moment when the footsteps still in the hallway and I hear breathy thumps and muffled moans and the sounds of heavy, deep kissing. I move slowly, my limbs feeling disconnected as I process what's going on just a few feet away from me.

When I hear Aidan's voice groan out obscenities and the mystery woman declare that my boyfriend, *"always knows"* how to make her come, I am forced to accept that this is not a one-off lapse of judgement.

I am suddenly desperate to get out of this situation, I cannot face confronting head-on this latest humiliation. Silently, I throw on my jumper, wrestle my jeans and my shoes on and I grab my bag. The sash window of his bedroom looks out over the slightly recessed bathroom roof and from there, there is a solid looking drainpipe, illuminated by the streetlights. The hallway noises are getting more x-rated and I feel a sob rising. I hear his voice, I hear *her* gasp his name as he mumbles something, seemingly muffled against her skin.

Looking around, I see a big black permanent marker pen lying next to a set of structural drawings, probably from a project he's working on. I take this pen and I write, all over his pristine painted walls and his immaculate Ikea furniture, *"Cheating Fucking Cunt"*. Judging by the noises they're making downstairs, I've got a little while. I unscrew every toiletry bottle I can find in his room, including all of his expensive aftershaves, and I tip them onto his duvet and carpet, giving the particularly 'stain inducing' potions a good shoe rub, to *really* grind it in.

Then I open the sash gently and climb out, bidding a silent goodbye to the life I had started to picture. For somebody with zero athletic ability, I get over that roof and down the drainpipe easily enough but once safely on tarmac, my knees start to wobble and I throw up into a hedge, my body trying to purge itself of the shock it's experiencing.

I'm reaching for my car keys, sobbing as I approach the increasingly-knackered Volvo when it hits me.

Who the fuck is *this*? Who is this pathetic, vomiting, drainpipe-coward? What have I become? I haven't needed her for a while, I suddenly realise how greatly she's been missed but I hear the sound of hooves and it's not Humiliation on her sodding horse that's riding towards me. It's Ginger Feist and *she is fucking furious.*

Aiden's first mistake was to open the front door. His second was to do so in just his pants, with lipstick marks all over his neck and torso. The pants just made my life easier if I'm honest and the lipstick marks made my muscles just that little bit more motivated.

Grabbing his handily accessible dick and yanking it with the force of a bell-ringer made me realise that I genuinely *can* turn lads into squealers, it seems to be a gift I possesses. That action only required one hand though. The other one, pulled back in a piece of kung-foo artistry, landed upon the bridge of his nose a punch that I will take pride in until the day I die. I released his dick and my trusty *'neutering knee'* finished the job for me.

As I left him groaning and howling in the foetal position on the doorstep in incomprehensible agonised fury, I heard an irritating voice shouting down the stairs, *"Babe, what the fuck has happened to your room?"*.

It took a good handful of junctions on the M6 before the cackles of laughter turned into the inevitable howls of pain from my freshly Love Punked heart.

I feel so devastated, this is potentially worse than any of the past twenty-two years worth of cock-ups. I've told people I might love him. I told them that I could see a future with him. FUCK, I told Jay I wanted him to meet our boys. As I writhe in the agony of humiliation, parked up the motorway services, I decide not to tell anyone just yet, not even Danny. I think I need to be a bit stronger before I can handle *pity* on top of heartbreak.

As my sobs run away with me, their volume increases as I belatedly become aware that it's not Aiden's name that I am blurting out in amongst the snot.

It's No-Name's.

I get home at 5am, beyond knackered and exhausted by the whole débâcle. I sleep until lunchtime and upon waking, I put my feet on the carpet, plaster on a smile and look around at the home I have created for my boys and I try to ignore the searing pain in my chest

Chapter Eighteen

14th February 2003

This week has been hard, I wasn't lying to myself when I said I thought I loved Aiden. I miss absolutely everything about him, well, apart from the lying cheating scum-bag parts. *They* can sod off frankly. I miss his smile, his phone calls, the daft in-jokes we had, I miss his body, his scent, the feel of being wanted by him. I miss him. He has rung me so many times that he filled my voicemail. I don't listen to any of the messages, they can say nothing that puts this right or makes me feel better. At worse, they will deepen my pain, cheapen and denigrate that which was becoming so precious to me.

In an admirable attempt at denial, I have taken to singing loudly to distract myself whenever the voice in my head tries to point out that the pain I feel over Aiden is nowhere near the viciousness of the agony I felt after *No-Name* left my flat over two years ago.

Valentine's Day is upon us and all my friends have plans, even Danny has a date with a girl from his office, his first *proper* date in several months. I never directly ask about *No-Name.*

Me and my babies are having a massive Valentines Blow Out. They *love* Chinese food and so we'll have a takeaway, we'll eat loads of sweets and I have, because I love them more than anything, bought a *'Greatest Goals in the World''* DVD that they have been nagging about. I sit and watch it with my little monsters despite the fact that I would rather eat my own feet than watch two hours of football.

I'm trying to muster up AJ's level of enthusiasm for the DVD but I cannot. He's throwing himself around the carpet, in paroxysms of delight about various goals, his brother gleefully cheering him on as I eat Maltesers and contemplate the fact that six years ago tonight, Jay and I had our first proper date.

At that moment, a text pops up from Aretta. Smiling I open it and see, *"We're engaged!! Oh Erin, Obi proposed".*

I scream in delight, hugging my sons who look at me like I've gone mental just as Obi's text comes through, *"I'm gonna be a married man Ginge and it's all your fault. Best. Wing Woman. Ever xxxx".*

I text them both my happiest of congratulations, sensing that ringing and interrupting *whatever* is going on at their end right at this moment, may be inadvisable.

I'm just about recovered, the boys now recreating the 'Best Goals Ever' with my sofa cushions and a foam ball that I just *know* is going to break something when another text pops up. It's Lees this time.

"Rinny, what colour bridesmaids dresses go with ginger hair? Should I just get you to shave your head? My fiancé says that's just harsh, I reckon it's pretty fair. Maybe we could dye it? Let's discuss xxx"

I've dialled her number before I've even finished reading the text and when she answers the phone *screaming,* my corresponding scream puts Jake right off his aim and Auntie Eileen's horrendous Christmas-gift vase meets its more-than-timely death.

My first words of congratulation down the phone consist of me yelling distractedly, *"Thank Christ it wasn't anything I liked, you stinkers".*

Tears, whoops, screams, my threats to dress the boys as Princesses if they don't stop kicking the *bloody* ball in my lounge and celebration, our conversation is a lovely one to have. I tell Lees that she and Ads are so perfect, I can't imagine her being with anyone else and that their engagement is amazing news. The sudden rush of renewed heartbreak that I feel as I remember the future I had *hoped for* with Aiden, means I have to pretend that there is an emergency and cut the call quickly, to prevent sobbing down the phone and ruining her happiness. Composing myself, I text Adam and tell him that, *'It's about time dude xxx'.*

Recovered, the boys eventually stowed in their beds and feeling a little bit sugar-sick, I sit on my sofa processing the nights' events. When my phone rings again, I roll my eyes and jokingly mutter, *"Jesus, who's getting married now"* but then I see Jay's number flash up and my heart genuinely falls into my pelvis.

He tells me that he did it at the bowling alley where they'd gone for their first date when they were fourteen. He'd even bought them the exact same Slushies that they'd had. He'd picked the ring weeks ago, he was going to tell me but the right time never came up, I've seemed a bit *distracted* this week. He got down on one knee, she cried. He took her to a lovely restaurant and they gave them free champagne. But you see, the funny part is, *hahahaha*, Casey can't drink the champagne. Because she's pregnant. So can he have the boys tomorrow? Is that OK? They'd like to break the news to them together at the boys favourite pizza place on the seafront, it'll give me an afternoon of peace.

That GCSE drama teacher was full of shit, I am a fucking *brilliant* actress. I whooped, and squealed and congratulated with proper gusto. I spoke to Casey, I asked Jay to hand her the phone and I gushed and 'oooh-ed' and told her how pleased I was, how amazing and perfect this is. I even fooled myself. She sounded genuinely touched, telling me that she's so glad we're a family, that she can't wait to get my advice on raising babies, because I've raised two such lovely ones of my own. I smile and the call ends with declarations of love and arrangements for them to collect the kids tomorrow morning.

Like a zombie, I plod to my computer.

"Danny

Hey, I dumped Aiden dude. I had to really, I caught him shagging another girl while I was waiting to surprise him at his house. He brought her home and shagged her in his hallway while I was waiting upstairs. Not my best plan in hindsight, should have factored in cheating when I looked at the pros and cons of the surprise visit. Hey ho, you live and learn. Heart is actually fucking broken again though. No-Name did it first, I don't think it has ever recovered from him although I thought I'd repaired the bastard thing but looks like Aiden cracked it along the joints and now it's fucked once more. Not sure it's salvageable this time, I think it's done y'know. I think it's giving up.

So I spend tonight with my boys, usual shambles of chaos and food. All lovely. Then my six closest friends all simultaneously get engaged. What an incredible thing, can you believe it? I can't. I'm genuinely chuffed for them all, thrilled actually. I love them all, they are all perfect for each other, three little units of perfection, sealed with rings. If I sound sarcastic, I don't mean to. I am honestly thrilled.

One of those units is Jay and Casey. They are getting married and Case is pregnant, with Jay's baby. They're having a baby.

But I've already done that see, I've had my babies, maybe the only ones I'll ever have but the problem is that I had them with the wrong boy. I didn't know back then, on that Argos Patio chair that I was sealing my fate but I that's what I did Danny. I sealed it at sixteen. That fate means that I have too many parts of me, did you know that? No-Name was right. I have parts I have to juggle, things that bind me and tie me and split me. Babies, children, ex-partners, family, friends, Uni, house, job, school, childcare, pressure, pressure, pressure, demands, competing needs, pressure.

There will be no ring for me because you can't put a ring on bits, they have to go on a whole person with a whole hand that somebody can hold. My hands are in bits, in all different places, spinning all different plates. And nobody wants that. Nobody has ever wanted that. Nobody. Jay gets the whole though Danny, why the FUCK does HE get to be whole and I just get to be fucking broken, pulled parts. It's so fucking unfair.

I'm twenty-two and I feel about ninety. I don't feel good Danny. Right now, I feel proper shit and that is such a selfish thing when everyone's got such lovely news.

Aiden didn't love me, I feel so unbelievably stupid for thinking that he did. I don't imagine I was anything other than a guaranteed weekend shag. I think I loved him but to be honest, what the hell do I know about love eh? I was with a guy for eighteen months without actually being in love with him. What do I know about love? Bugger all, that's what.

That's not strictly true actually. It took me a long time to work it out but I know that I loved Gio. That's his name, I forget sometimes. I loved Gio so much that I think it's spoiled me for anyone else but the thing about Gio is that he didn't want my many parts, he went out with lots of other girls and then he ran away to the other side of the world to get away from me because I was too much aggravation to love. He bent my heart all out of shape so that I think it only fits him and then he fucked off to an easy life with a supposedly perfect girl. Aiden he doesn't want my parts either it appears. Shame, I'd thought my parts were pretty decent.

Hope your night was better than mine mate, hope you're finding something that is whole.
Rinny xx"

I press send and I go to my bed.

15th February 2003

The boys clamber into my bed at 5am and we have the best sort of bed-cuddles. We each find the comfiest position, they are perfectly angled so that no bony limbs poke into delicate flesh, they are lying still, they have equal duvet, the TV remote is within my reach so I can flick it on if needed. *Perfect.*

Then the phone goes. *Shit.* Perfection is ruined, the eldest child has moved and now it's all gone to cock because there's little knees in my back and sticky hands all over my face. Huffing, I reach across the bed,

"Now, good girl, I know it's early but your father has some news", my mother is not one to break things gently

I yawn, "If either of you are engaged, pregnant or likely to be either of those any time soon, you can both bugger off, I've got enough of that going on", I yawn again.

My mum tuts, "Erin Hannah Mary Roberts, the day you make sense will be a lovely day indeed. No, your father have been doing those competitions still, although thank Christ there's been no more of those bronze head sculptures. The other day, he did send off the funniest little ditty about some Airline company and do you know? He have won a flight! New Zealand it is now!", Mum sounds thrilled but I have some initial questions,

"Mum, Dad doesn't fly", I use my best social worker voice, the one I use when a parent is *really* kicking off about something I've said/done/decided/written/implied, "Dad hates planes and he would never go on one for like twenty-four hours. Why did he enter that?", I separate my warring sons with my patented 'twin squash' technique on the bed as my mother scoffs down the phone,

"You daft apeth, it's not for us. It's for *you*. Emma McNamara have been over visiting, staying with the Romanos. I *would* ask if you remember Daniel McNamara but Emma told me at Mass that you two have been pen-pals for *years* and *apparently* Daniel do talk about you when he's home", I can actually hear my mother's eyebrow rise as she talks in an affected sing-song voice.

Daniel told his Mum about us writing? How odd. Does Gio know now then too?

"Hmmmm, anyway, he's a good Catholic boy Daniel, I remember your First Communion together you two, so sweet although as always, you looked like you'd been dragged through a hedge backwards, Lord, that broken arm, Erin you have always been…..", as my mother winds herself up, my father removes the phone from her, his voice deep and a bit sleepy,

"Sweetheart, your mother and I will come to yours for the week, it's half term isn't it? You've got those study weeks too, in between your placements? Anyway, we will come and stay with the boys so that Jamel and Casey don't need to make any changes to their week. You are to go to New Zealand for nine days holiday and you are to go today. We will be with you in about four hours, you fly from Heathrow tonight and your mother and I are paying for the airport taxi. Go, ring your friend Daniel and have an adventure. Lord knows, you deserve it poppet", Dad's voice makes me teary.

I told my parents that I'd split from Aiden. I had to, my mother rang earlier in the week because she wanted to know his address to send his birthday card next week. I didn't give her the details, I just said we'd agreed to end it. Mum didn't push me for more info, unusual for her. I asked them not to tell anyone else, I said I was a bit sad about it.

As I finish the call to my parents, I have a call waiting and I answer, the Kiwi accented voice immediately launching into a rant,

"I'm gonna kill the fucking cunt, if that Aiden had a twat, I'd be shanking him in it Roberts, I swear I would. Mate, are you OK? I only just got your email, the internet's screwed in the apartment. I'm worried, are you OK? Jesus, that's the most genuine I've been in *years*. I think I've strained something Erin, Christ, that *hurts*. Fuck being genuine, I'm sticking to sarcastic. You OK though?",

Danny's words are frantic, his Kiwi vowels soothing.

I smile, "Danny, where is *No-Name* this week? Is he still on that project in Wellington", I cannot stay with Danny if Gio is there, I just can't but I know he's been working away a lot.

He's confused, "Er, are we having a little 'Love Connection' relapse Roberts? Why the fuck you want to know, eh? Yeah, he's away for another three weeks, thank God. He gets pissy with no internet. C'mon, you sound weirder than normal, do I need to ring somebody? Can you smell violets? Is your arm going numb?", he sounds genuinely perplexed and I snort.

"Danny, can I come and stay with you for a week or so?", I am smiling.

He whoops, "Fuck yeah! When you thinking Roberts? You gonna bring the Mini-Pele's?"

I laugh, "Er I was thinking of coming now actually…...you got space for just me?"

Danny's laugh is deep, "Roberts, you are far out, batshit crazy and I fucking love it. Yeah, get your ginger arse over here and let's have a proper laugh"

I fill him in on the circumstances of my unexpected visit and it makes him whoop even more.

"I'll be there at the airport to pick you up. Brace yourself love, I know you've seen photos but they don't do me justice. I am a fucking work of art", he sighs and it sets me off laughing.

He sniggers, "Can I snog you at the airport, y'know, like some shitty film?"

I snigger, "If you slip me the tongue, I'll neuter you in the arrivals lounge".

I'm seeing Danny McNamara in about forty hours. My inner fourteen-year old *loses her mind.*

The next five hours are sheer lunacy. The twins are surprisingly distraught at the prospect of my absence, lots of tears and clawing hands and I actually start to cancel the trip in my head as their little, skinny frames cling to me. Then my mother arrives, bizarrely brandishing a still-hot roast chicken and an apple crumble. She quickly extracts my sons from me, soothing and distracting them beautifully as she ferries them to football and gestures at me to get packing. I am literally throwing random crap in the case, no idea what late summer in New Zealand will require me to wear.

Jay arrives with a beaming Casey and there is an explosion of information, declarations, updates and congratulations. My mother, hugs, kisses, offers her congratulations and then she makes a pathetic excuse to get me on my own in my bedroom, she shuts the door and she holds me in the tightest of cuddles as I weep away the top layer of my very complicated emotions about their news.

She whispers into my hair, "Look at the life you've built *cariad.* Look at what you've achieved love. A future filled with good things is all yours sweetheart, you focus on that", I pull back and see her wipe her own tears away.

We put our faces to rights and head back, sharing the news about Lees, Ads, Obi and Aretta, the house giddy with celebration. My Mum shoots me kind smiles and my Dad puts his arm comfortingly around me as we chat.

I hand Casey her birthday gifts from me and the boys and when Casey asks me what Aiden got me for Valentine's Day, my parents turn to me, slightly startled. I smile weakly and say that we're swapping presents when we're together next, I don't want to bum-out their happy news. New Zealand plans explained, I spend ages kissing and cuddling my boys, never having been so far away from them before. I actually feel physical pain as they head off for pizza with Jay and Birthday Girl Casey, I am going to miss them so much.

The afternoon is a blur of chicken, crumble, frantic packing and endless lists for my parents. When the taxi arrives at 3pm, I feel like I've been hit by a tornado. Clutching my bag like a lifeline, I wave my beaming parents off and start my journey to be reunited with the boy I sort-of-married fifteen years ago.

17th February 2003

So it's been two days on that sodding plane, two nights technically because I set off on Saturday night and I'm landing on Monday morning but my body is so thrown by the entire performance that it could give bigger shits frankly, it would just like to sleep.

I have tried to do all of the things magazines tell you to, to guarantee that you arrive at your destination looking like you stepped off a photo shoot. I think the photo shoot I look like I've been engaged in would be classed as bit *specialist*. I'm all shades of a shambles. Long curls have lost the plot, skin is now so over-moisturised that I look like a greased weasel, clothes feel oddly tight as my body has expanded with air-travel and the tiny loo's lighting has led me to over-apply the makeup. In short, I am a horror show. Maureen, my finger-knitting companion, shot off that plane at LAX, never to be seen again. I spent the second leg of my trip next to a large man with sharp elbows and an aroma of wet carpet. I am bruised and slightly nauseous.

The airport is huge and clean and a bit overwhelming when you've been in a flying metal loo-roll for the last two days. I feel wobbly and plane-greasy and as I step through passport control, the brevity of my trip raises eyebrows from the border guards but I am granted access to this very clean and very sunny looking place.

Arrivals is *heaving* and I can't see anything that looks McNamara shaped. I loiter by the end of the barriers, watching people reunited with their loved ones and feeling a bit wobbly about missing my boys when I feel a presence behind me, warm breath puffing against the back of my head,

"Hey there Roberts, fancy seeing you here, eh? Out of interest, is there a reason you haven't grown since we were kids? You never mentioned any medical conditions that cause short-assedness", I hear the chuckle in his voice as I turn, a grin plastered across my poorly-made-up face.

Fucking hell. Daniel McNamara is *here*, he's here for *me* and my fourteen-year-old-self faints with joy. That face, *that face,* it's all grin and healthy tan and good looks. As I spend a millisecond appraising the view, I see the blond hair that has become surfer-dude bleached with the sun, I see a cheeky grin, I see the boy who knows all of my secrets. He is shorter than I pictured, maybe five-nine but the self-obsessed wanker was right. He *is* a work of art.

With a yelp, I throw my arms around him, any initial awkwardness railroaded and he holds me tight, spinning us in fast circles as he laughs loudly. He stands still and holds my over-moisturised face in his hands,

"Roberts, just so we get this clear, you are officially the best thing to happen to me on a Monday Morning in a long fucking time and you were totally right, it *is* the massive tits that make you a good cuddle", he winks at me and laughs as my funny email friend is reborn into real life.

We stand in a cuddle for longer than is perhaps warranted but it is so, so nice and neither of us seem keen to part. Danny smells like expensive aftershave, salt and oranges. It's lovely.

"C'mon then Rinny, we've got a week and a lot of fun to be had. I've booked off work and you get this", he gestures up and down himself, "at your disposal as tour guide", he's grabbed my bag and is towing me by the hand through the airport.

His hand is large and warm and I feel giddy from the prospect of a week of fun with this mate of mine. Our chat flows as freely in person as it does through a keyboard and as he drives me towards his and *No-Name's* plush apartment, the one that has financially crippled them for the last few years, I feel a weird sense of things *clicking together*. I can't explain it so I just chat and smile.

As we park up in the underground car-park beneath their apartment, Danny's telling me about he and *No-Name* got proper fed up of living in crappy student places with people who annoyed them. Danny's pretty wealthy Dad coughed up some extra cash each month and they found this place being rented by a naive and somewhat easy-to-manipulate investor. This poor landlord, a flamboyantly gay guy, spoke to them on the phone and then both of them, the bastards, turned up shirtless and tanned to the viewing and proceeded to flirt outrageously, securing the flat at a much reduced rate although it remained stupidly expensive. I am crying with laughter at Danny's re-telling of this event and I tell him about how *'no name'* could manipulate our teacher Mr. Dobbs in a similarly shameless manner. Recalling these memories makes my chest ache.

Our laughter peters out and Danny turns to me, "Rinny, I know….I fucking know that the stuff with you and him got far-out messy and sore but I need you to know, he's my best mate. I mean, I'd kill for the stupid bastard. I would. I'd twat-shank for him", we both laugh loudly at this shared joke.

He smiles kindly, "Before he went off to Wellington last month, we...we went on a bender as a sort of farewell bollocks and somehow I went off on the fucking deep end at him, telling him he needed to get himself together and stop you doing something stupid with that Aiden twat, needed to stop you making a massive mistake by moving in with the dickhead or some other bollocks. He was proper pissed too but not enough to not work out that you and me must be mates and that I know everything that goes down with you. I had to bloody fess up that you and me are email-buddies and to be honest, he got hardcore weird about it, he was still chewing when he went to Wellington. I rang him last night coz I had to tell him Rinny, I can't not tell the dude that you're staying here, that's fucked up", he looks at me pleadingly.

"You are this sassy little ginger dwarf-person who has muscled her way into my life and who I'm kinda hoping will stay there but he's my best mate and despite him being a heavy duty dick right now, I can't keep doing my mate down. Calling him *'No-Name'*.....", Danny winces and looks uncomfortable.

I smile and pat his hand in a mock-patronising gesture, "His name's Gio, fucking hell McNamara, not too bright are you? You've lived with the bloke for this long, you should know his name. Did you get to Uni just by flashing your muscles too?", and as he swears at me and laughs, we make an unspoken agreement that Gio is allowed back into the conversational fold.

The flat is lush. Cream carpets and slick tiles in a huge open plan kitchen and living space with a big balcony that gives you a glimpse of the harbour in between buildings, this is a *nice* place. There is a big bathroom and as Danny shows me his palatial room, it's clear that the landlord has been properly *robbed* by these shameless morons.

Danny chats as he leads me to the final door, "So yeah, this is G's room, you wanna see? It's always tidy, the bloke's got OCD or something", as I wince and nod slowly, a portal into Gio's world opens to me.

His big room is lush. It's covered in photos, there are frames and pictures and canvases everywhere. There's a beautiful, seascape picture on his wall that I remember being one of his A Level art coursework pieces. Taking a little gasp of breath, I walk into the space, overtaking Danny. So many photos, his face is everywhere. There's a big one of him with Danny, holding up some gigantic fish on a tropical beach, both of them wearing coconut bras and showing off those ridiculous landlord-flummoxing bodies. I reach out and stroke his face, an unconscious movement.

I see frame after frame of pictures, people I don't recognise, arms slung around each other in friendship. Gio's whole life that I am no part of, the world he inhabits that has no trace of me. I see a collage of school photos, I feel the first tears prickle as I spot myself in a large number of them, pregnant in some. I see how my smile is wary, how my posture is a bit frozen, how *guarded* I look.

I see pictures of older Gio with various girls, hugs, kisses being pressed to cheeks. I wander further into his room and I see his bed, where his big, strong body lies every night that he's here. I don't realise that I'm doing it but I reach out and pick up his pillow. I smell it and the lemons and the herbs stab my heart and my brain simultaneously. I drop it like it's on fire. Then I look at his bedside table and I see it. I see the small, almost miss-able frame containing a photo of me, him and the twins at their Christening. The boys were so tiny, I forget sometimes how tiny they were. We've got one each and Gio is smiling down at me as I look down at my babies. We look like a *family*. We look like a *couple* with their newborns.

My legs give up and I plop onto his bed, staring at the frame.

Danny's voice breaks the silence, a sad tone, "He changes it, y'know? The night I told him about the emails, he switched it to this one. It was you in the prom dress before that. Sometimes it's one of you sat on some grass, smiling next to Morris and Jones. When he was with psycho-bitch, it was a group photo but you were in it. It's always been a picture of you Rinny", Danny nods and leave the room, he leaves me to contemplate this information.

I am struggling to process the notion that thousands of miles away from me and my dramas, the boy I *loved* has been sleeping with pictures of me by his bed for years.

There's a shout from the main room, 'C'mon you, we've got a fucking mountain to climb and you need to wash your face Roberts. Was the plane crashing when you put that makeup on?", his evil cackle makes me race from the room to batter him.

The bastard does take me up a mountain, I trail behind his annoying athleticism, huffing and puffing as he lures me with a picnic to the top of Mt. Eden. It's beautiful and although my jet-lag makes me feel like it's the middle of the night, I appreciate the view.

We sit and chat for bloody hours. We reminisce over our years of email interactions and I finally tell him the story behind our presumed marriage,

"When did you last watch that video your Dad made?", Danny is smirking and shaking his head.

"Jesus, I've not watched that thing since I was little, it was humiliating enough the first time", I roll my eyes.

He shakes his head again, "Right, before you get back on that plane, we're going to my Mum and Dad's and we're watching that video, they've got a copy too, and you will see why me and you are definitely *not* married Roberts, you freak", I batter him laughing.

I ask him about Isla, the girl he took on a date on Valentine's Day. He's not fussed really, that's clear but given the sheer volume of texts that he gets from her while we're sat on the mountain, she's fussed about him.

I tell him about my teenage crush on him, some of the memories I have of that time and he brutally but hilariously confirms that I held the allure of a stamp collection as far as he was concerned.

I tell him about the Foam Party and my broken heart and he looks genuinely remorseful, telling me that he had no idea about my crush and that he was understandably preoccupied with his parents' snap decision to move to New Zealand and the loss of his life in the UK. Chatting we merge our accounts of that night with the one that Gio gave me the night we combusted.

"Well, I'm a shit best mate and you're, well, you're just shit Roberts coz I had no idea he fancied you back then and you were clearly as gormless as you are now", I smack him again.

We head back into the city, my jet lag starting to bite. Danny has got us tickets for the Sky Tower and with a reviving couple of energy drinks, I make it up the tower and we enjoy a few cocktails as we rotate nearly 200 metres above Auckland's sprawl.

Starting to slump as my jet-lag hits a critical point, Danny pulls me into a cuddle as we head down in the lift. His lips brush my forehead in a very sweet way as he says, "Glad you popped by Roberts, you're definitely my favourite ever ginger".

I fall asleep in the taxi and I don't feel Danny carry me up to the apartment or lay me on his bed, as he takes his temporary spot on the futon in his room. I'm sharing a room with Danny McNamara and my inner fourteen-year-old may *never* get over it. My twenty-two-year-old self groggily acknowledges, when she wakes for a wee in the middle of the night, that it *means something* to her to be sleeping in Giovanni Romano's home.

18th February 2003

"Love, you're sure this is what you want me to put on your bum?", Terrance, a cigarette clamped between his lips, looks torn between amusement and pseudo-paternal concern as McNamara guffaws in the corner and makes lewd comments about my bare arse.

Today has been, without any doubt, one of the top five days of my life. After ringing my babies as soon as I awoke, hearing their tales of Nana's indulgences, Danny took me down to the harbour where we got on his mate's boat. We had an amazing breakfast as we sailed out to turquoise bays and multi-coloured beaches, circumnavigating islands and pausing to swim in the sea when we fancied a dip.

The owner of the boat, Stevo, is a mate of Danny's from Uni.

"So you, m'lady, are the legendary Erin Roberts, aye?", a huge Maori lad, Stevo's cheeky grin was friendly as we were introduced.

"Legendary? What in God's name have you told people Danny?", I was wide-eyed with trepidation, Danny has years of blackmail material in his inbox.

Stevo snorted, "Nah love, not this dickhead, the other dickhead, G. He's talked about you heaps over the years. It's good to meet you Erin", he winked and set to doing boat things.

We were on the boat until tea-time, Stevo returning us to the harbour so that he can collect his nightly booze-cruise paying customers. I'd thanked him for the amazing day and Stevo had grinned and pulled me close, whispering "Don't go back home without seeing the boy, eh? He's a good bloke that Romano. It was good to meet you Erin", and with that he scuttled off below deck as Danny shouted his thanks.

A bit wobbly from Stevo's words, I'd followed Danny from the boat to bar after bar after bar. Now we're here, in Terrance's tattoo parlour. I lost a frankly ridiculous bet with Danny tonight regarding headstands, after I'd disputed his claims that he was the headstand king in primary school. He was not, it was Wayne Matthews who once held the pose so long, he actually had a convulsion. We lined ourselves up in front of a jeering crowd in a harbour-side bar and I fell over before he did. I am now Terrance's first victim of the evening.

"Terrance, I want you to write this on my arse because it is a place that I hope neither my sons, my mother nor my father will ever lay their eyes on. Do it Terrance!", and with my girlie squeals and screams as his soundtrack, that's exactly what Terrance did.

Danny got a pretty neat old-school Rockabilly flaming-heart on his shoulder. He tried to play it cool but he went very pale and had to hold my hand. He smiled weakly when I kissed his forehead and called him a *'giant twat'*.

I wish I'd considered the fact that tattoos hurt like a bastard *afterwards* as well as *during*. Danny cried with laughter when I had to kneel backwards on the taxi seat on the way back to his to avoid any pressure on my *burning* arse and when I had to position myself on my front to sleep, his sniggers went on for ages.

In the dark, Danny's voice is slurred and sleepy from the futon, "Jesus you've got a fucking good arse Roberts. I reckon old Terrance might have seen some flaps from the angle he was at, old perv probably had a proper chubby", I throw a pillow in his vague direction and hear a satisfying *'whoompf'* as it meets its target.

His voice gets very slurred, "Rinny, I'm gonna dream about your arse. G's been doing that for years y'know? Poor, sad bastard", and his snores are almost immediate.

Despite my inebriation it turns out that the endorphins from my newly-branded arse and constant thoughts of Gio make sleep impossible. Before I really know what I'm doing, I find myself padding across the hallway and into his dark room, my heart thumping as if I'm breaking and entering.

I flick on his bedside light, running my fingers over things that he touches daily, his things, his life. My conscience screaming at me for the invasion of his privacy, I open the top drawer of his dresser. His clothes are neatly laundered and folded, I take out a t-shirt and I stroke the fabric. I sniff his aftershave but it's not really familiar, I don't recognise it. Opening his wardrobe I smile at the neatness, the contrast with my own chaotic *boudoir*. On a shelf, folded immaculately, are a pile of hoodies and I spot one that looks familiar. Pulling it gently out, it's a black one with 'Hockey Team' printed on it. It's the one from that day, the day that I threw up on him. The day I found out I was pregnant. The day I trusted Gio and he looked after me. The first day I smelt the herbs and lemons.

As my poor, throbbing arse silently protests, I sit down on Gio's bed, hugging the hoodie and looking around at the pictures of him and me and *us*. I don't feel sleep claim me but it does, as I lie face down in a pillow that smells of the boy I loved *so much.* My last thoughts are of how lush it feels to be in his bed.

When I wake the next morning, I can hear Danny on the phone. I crack an eyelid at the urgency in his voice, this conversation with whoever it is, is *not* going well.

"Don't be a fucking tool, I can't let you do that……..Why not? It's her stuff too, I can't just hand them all over to you to read just to prove a point…..mate, you've gotta believe me when I say……...always been best mates……don't be a prick, when have I ever….get your arse back…..you need to see her……this fucking nonsense has been going on for too many years……...best fucking laugh I've known….the way you feel about her you stubborn wanker……fucking ridiculous…..whatever….yeah? Right back atcha you prick"

I hear Danny swear as the call ends, pots and pans being mistreated as he mutters to himself. I ring the boys, they are giddy still about their Daddy's news, about their baby brother or sister. AJ's asking me if he can teach the baby to play football and Jake's wary voice is asking me if the baby will take his bed and if so, where will he sleep because he likes his bed. I reassure, I joke, they chuckle, it's lovely. I tell them how much I love them, how they are my babies and always will be. They snort and deny that they ever wore nappies. I assure them that they really, really did and they filled them with astonishing regularity. I end the call promising toy possums.

"How's that gorgeous arse this morning Roberts, need me to kiss it better?", as I pad into the kitchen in my vest and shorts, I realise that my boobs might be a little more on display than I intended as Danny's laughter halts, his eyes go comically wide and he nearly drops his toast.

Grimacing I shoot back to Gio's room and grab that black hockey hoodie.

As I emerge, he's smiling weakly, "You slept in there, huh?"

Walking over and stealing his other piece of toast, I look up and shrug apologetically, "It seems so, I didn't really plan to. How's the shoulder?"

He winces, "Hurts like a motherfucker. Honestly Roberts, you and me together are a bad bloody influence on each other, in twenty-three years I've avoided tattoos and headstands in bars. You arrive and within a day, my unblemished record is shot to hell", he snorts and I grin toast at him.

As we sit on the balcony, I ask him, "So who was on the phone earlier? Didn't sound an easy call", I see Danny grimace, his lovely form bare aside from a pair of jockey shorts making the view a good one.

He looks at me, shaking his head, "Yeah, stupid Italian prick has got this theory that you and me are cracking on *behind his back* or some shit. A fucking *lifetime* of being mates isn't enough to make him believe me when I put him straight, he's still hardout pissed off that I never mentioned the emails all this time", Danny tuts and stands to lean on the balcony rail.

Danny turns to look at me, his salt-bleached hair adorably rumpled but his face tight, "He wants to read the all the emails Rinny", he shakes his head and rolls his eyes.

I feel the blood drain from my face, "But….but there's so much in them about…...about how I feel about everything and…...and…..shit, Danny I don't know if I can let him read some of…..I don't want him to know some of that", Danny steps forward, rumpling my hair affectionately.

"I know Roberts, me too, y'know. I tell you shit I can't ever have the boys knowing. You're my little secret keeper too, yeah?", he winks and sighs as he sips his coffee and looks over the view.

My voice is a whisper, "Why's he bothered? I mean, even if you and me were having mad, rampant sex, why would he be worried? We've not spoken for two years and we were like *estranged* for two years before that. Honestly, why on earth has he got a face on?", I fiddle with my cup.

Danny's face is crumpled in an incredulous sneer when I look up, "Roberts, don't play fucking innocent, it doesn't suit you. He's bothered for the same reason that *you* sniff his bloody pillow and sleep in his room. You're both big fucking pains in my arse", he snorts and takes another swig before tutting and repeating incredulously, *"Why's he bothered?"*. I look at the view and ignore him.

We decide to spend the day at some caves, a couple of hours journey from Auckland and somewhere that Danny has never been. Chatting as we drive, we tell each other about our hopes for the future. It's nice to share the prospect of *possibility* with somebody who is so unburdened, it makes me think that anything is possible, allowing me to temporarily ignore the multiple anchors that limit my options. He tells me, in a little throwaway comment, that he's not sure that Gio plans to stay in New Zealand long term, he's increasingly missing his family. Danny's pretty certain he'll return to the UK permanently after the boys do the Europe trip they've been planning. My heart does a painful double beat at the prospect of Romano back on UK shores.

The caves, when we get there, are lit by glo-worms and it is *incredible*. As we ride underground boats and gasp at the incredible beauty in the darkness, I grip Danny's hand and whisper my thanks for allowing me to have adventures. He raises my hand to his lips and tells me not to be a dickhead as he whispers so as not to interrupt to the tour, *"Every fucking day with you is an adventure Roberts, you're straight up nuts"*

Chapter Nineteen

20th February 2003

The days go past in a blur of fun. Danny uses me as an excuse to do all of the things he's always fancied doing but never got round to in the city. Today though, he's taking me camping overnight at Waitakere and we walk frikking miles through incredible scenery before I humiliate myself for hours on a surf-board on a stunning black sand beach. I am entirely rubbish at surfing but I love bobbing about in the waves and I run about on the sand like a lunatic, missing my babies as I behave just like they do.

Privacy is a bit lacking in the tent and it's intense as we lie, side by side in the dark, giggling like school kids as we play *'I have never'* with the marshmallows we brought.

I'm still cracking up at Danny's confession that after repeatedly watching a nun-based porn film when he was fifteen, he now gets a Pavlovian erection whenever in the presence of a Bride of Christ, regardless of their age or attractiveness.

I'm still snorting as I say, "D'you know what, I wish I could go back in time so that I can tell my fourteen-year-old self that her *desperate* crush on Danny McNamara will die a brutal death as she lies beside his half-naked body in a tent and hears that he beats his meat to old ladies in wimples", I grin.

I hear the smirk in his voice, " *'Desperate crush'* eh Roberts? You wanted me bad, eh?", he sniggers like a school boy.

I roll my eyes in the dark, "Get over yourself McNamara, my taste was dubious at best, I thought that East 17 were *fit as* too", he laughs.

There's a pause as I snaffle a few marshmallows and I hear Danny sigh and he says, "Y'know, you might want to tell that fourteen-year-old that in a few years time Danny McNamara develops a pretty massive crush on her too", I hear him swallow and he reaches for my hand over the sleeping bags, his fingers stroking mine as my heart rate raises.

"Oh", my mouth is stuffed with marshmallows.

He sighs dramatically, "Yeah, see she turns into this funny-as-fuck, fit as hell, hardcore lunatic that makes me laugh like a twat and is the only person I tell my secrets to. She's bloody cool as, *perfect* actually, I could see myself getting into real trouble over this girl but there's this problem", in the dark, Danny turns to face me, I can feel his breath wafting over my skin as I remain prone on my back, not even daring to breathe,

"The problem is that my best mate has been in love with her, like straight-up, deep-shit love, since we were just kids. He's a fucking dickhead, always has been and they have messed each other's heads up heaps but despite all of their nonsense and the years that have passed, he loves her like nothing else. And her? She's right there too. Isn't she?", Danny's voice is just a whisper.

I stay silent, I can't say anything because I don't know what words to use.

I hear him tut again as he turns onto his back once more, "Tell that fourteen-year-old that Danny McNamara thinks she might turn out to be pretty fucking perfect for him but that he's gonna stand back and be the bloody hero of the piece and fix this shit because the two of you need your heads bashing together", he tuts.

"Danny…..", I try to find words, "Gio said that there were too many *bits* of me, that I was too *complicated* to love and he was probably right. Plus, most of the time dude, I'm boring as fuck and juggling all these mundane, everyday things just to stay afloat. You wouldn't have a crush on those bits, they're ridiculously dull. Here with you, well, I guess I can just leave those behind for a bit, escape reality", I hear my voice wobble but Danny sighs softly beside me.

"You're not in bits y'know. You're not Roberts", I make a soft noise of protest but he carries on in the dark, "You work hard to keep people in nice little boxes in your life. It's why you never lived with Jay when you were 'together' and it's why you never really let him mix with your school mates. It's the reason you never let blokes meet your sons, it's why you liked that bloody dickwad in Manchester because he was neatly packaged away during the week until you wanted to play with him", I sit up in the dark wanting to protest.

Danny sighs and sits up too, I feel him crossing his legs as he turns to face me in the blackness, "That *Aiden*, he played along pretty bloody well, until he *didn't.* He played along so well that you told yourself you were falling in love with him but any twat could see that you were just happy that your rules were being obeyed", he leans forward and grabs my face.

"Roberts, you don't have faith that you won't get hurt so what you do is keep guys in a neatly fenced section of your life, that way, when it goes wrong, you can just shut the door on that *part,* without it affecting the *whole",* I'm shaking my head in the dark.

My voice is wobbly as a refute his claims, "Mate, that's not true, that's not true. I was falling in love with Aiden, I don't keep boxes, it's…...it's bollocks that, it's bollocks", I fiddle with my fingers and feel a bit wobbly.

Danny reaches across in the dark and cups my face gently, "You know what girlie, I've got an exception that proves the rule. There was somebody, somebody that was a part of every bit of your life. They were in your past, your present and they would have been in your future. They knew your family, they knew the mini-Pele's, they knew every part of your life. They knew what it was like to kiss you, they knew what it was like to love you, they bloody watched you give *birth*…", but I'm shaking my head, dislodging his hand, my lip wobbling,

"No, no don't Danny, you know, you know *everything*, please don't, please don't go there", I feel the tears.

But he keeps going, "He was all those things but you couldn't trust it, could you? You didn't trust him did you?", he pulls himself onto his knees in the tent, clearly thinking aloud.

"Oh FUCK!", his shout makes me jump, "You said you chose Jay for the boys' sake but really, you chose Jay because you didn't trust G. You did it so that could put Romano in a bloody box that you could shut a door on! Fuck, I should be like bloody Oprah or some shit, I am *good* at this".

He turns to me again, grabbing my face, "You still love him, you love him but you don't trust him not to hurt you so you keep him in the box and that *stupid fucking knobhead* came home and spouted shit that made it easy for you to stay thinking that way when he said what he did about Emily and your *bits*", Danny snorts as he builds to his finale.

"But Rinny, all the poor bastard sees is the box you bloody put him in, you never let him see the *full picture* so he thinks it's all complicated and shit. Trust him, let him get close, tell him how you bloody feel about him and he'll see there's no mystery, scary bloody *complications*. It's just you, it's just *you* Roberts, you and the mini-Pele's and that is all he's ever fucking wanted. Jesus I am *good* at this stuff", Danny chuckles with self-satisfaction but I can't contain the confused sobs and I start to properly bawl.

"Fuck!", Danny moves and pulls me against his warm bare chest that smells of salt and sweat and camp-fire smoke.

I make a lot of incomprehensible, snotty noises and Danny tries not to laugh at me. With a rueful chuckle he whispers,

"In any other scenario Rinny, I'd be making a move right now while you're vulnerable and I'd bloody *rock your world* but I think I'd be the easiest thing in the world for you to keep in one of your bloody boxes and I'm not playing that game. If I get any deeper into this, I'm proper fucked, just like that stupid bastard and I don't want to sit in one of your boxes on the other side of the world", he pulls me tighter and I hug him back, pressing a kiss into his salty skin.

"C'mon woman, lie down and get some sleep, you've got a few more crimes against surfing to commit tomorrow", he manoeuvres us back down, his arm still around me as we lie next to each other, my hiccuping breath slowly calming.

I whisper, "I still think you're wrong about those stupid boxes you're going on about but thanks Danny, for, you know, *everything*. You're pretty amazing McNamara, I had good taste as a fourteen-year-old".

He snorts, "Yeah? Well you just remember how *amazing* I am before you kick off when you wake up and find me fondling your tits while you sleep. Jesus Roberts, I would *kill* for a play with those puppies".

As I snigger in the dark, I take one of his hands and place it under my vest top, upon my bare tit.

"Call it a freebie McNamara", I grin.

There is a groan of agony behind me, as we both shift onto our sides for sleep, Danny's warm hand firmly clamped upon my bare boob.

"You Roberts, are the best fucking mate I've ever had", we chuckle ourselves into slumber.

21st February 2003

We do indeed surf and I manage some brief seconds of upright-triumph before plunging to my doom. Danny is an amazing surfer, I sit on the sand and watch him. Jesus, he's fit. I mean, *proper* fit but what he said last night sits heavily upon me, his Oprah-like insights into my behaviour and my psyche sting a little bit more this morning and a tiny voice inside me is starting to pull like a magnet. *I want to talk to Gio.* I watch Danny slide between the waves like a bare-chested eel and I wonder how far it is to Wellington.

We head back, stopping off at all sorts of sights and views, New Zealand is a truly incredible place. Danny's taking me to his mum's for tea today, I've not seen Emma McNamara possibly since our Holy Communion but she has invited me for tea, having only returned from the UK a couple of days ago.

Emma is warm and welcoming, she and Danny are obviously very close and from our conversation it's clear that she has a good insight into Danny's life, his romances and even some of the things he confessed last night. Every time Gio or the Romanos are mentioned, which is frequently, I see her watching me and it makes me nervous.

"Mum, you still got that video of our First Holy Contraption or whatever it was called?", Danny's shouting from the 'family room' as he wanders back from the loo.

As it's located and Danny pulls me onto the sofa to watch it, I am plunged back into my childhood. There we stand, the three of us on the screen. Danny's blond hair immaculately groomed, his smart suit and tie on point and his posture stiff but bored. I'm there, *Jesus Christ*, my hair sprayed into some sort of ginger helmet, my fringe thick and sheep-like. I'm all freckles and missing teeth, with a plaster

411

cast that is shrouded in bandages. *Gio.* How did I never realise how cute he was? Coal coloured curls, those blue eyes and looking terminally bored, picking his nose at one point but every so often, his gaze comes back to me. I'm staring at Danny like some sort of stunned-mullet and Gio's *looking at me*.

The priest mutters a lot of questions off camera, the boys mumbling as I bellow out the (wrong) answers. Then he asks us a whole bunch of questions which require an *'I do'* response and it is at this point that Danny jumps up from the sofa and runs to the TV, pointing and grinning.

On-screen Danny does not utter a word, Gio and I are *'I doing'* like pros but McNamara utters not a syllable. Gio says them animatedly and he says them facing the side of *my* head, where it is turned to Danny. I'm grinning at Danny like pig spotting a truffle but then Gio shuffles awkwardly and seems to step on my toe. In the video, I stop gazing adoringly at an oblivious Danny and I turn to Gio, looking murderous like I'm about to lamp him. As we hold each others' gaze, my expression furious and his wary, we exchange the last set of 'I dos'. Looking at each other.

Danny's hopping up and down by the TV now, "You married Romano you daft cow, not me. See? You married G!", and as the truth stares at me from its 'paused' position on the screen, I feel that weird feeling of *clicking into place* sweep me, I feel like pieces of my body realign after a lengthy dislocation.

I'm looking gobsmacked as Danny comes and sits next to me on the sofa, patting me on the hand,

"Fancy a weekend in Wellington love?", he waggles his eyebrows at me as I look baffled.

Emma, who has been stood behind us watching the video from the doorway with a glass of wine, speaks in a soft gentle Kiwi-Scottish hybrid, "Erin, you had to grow up much faster than the kids around you and I'm not sure many people realise how hard that must have been for you. But growing up fast means that sometimes, you forget that the people around you might not be quite as mature or able to understand complicated things. Especially lads. They're pretty bloody dense no matter their age", she walks over to her outraged looking son and ruffles his hair, before continuing,

"Don't judge people too harshly for things they may have said or done when they were younger, for not being quite as adult as you had to be. Sixteen, eighteen, twenty, twenty-two….. It's all still *horribly* young Erin, this dingbat here still messes up constantly", she kisses Danny's head as he swears softly under his breath.

Emma walks towards the doorway and smiles at me, "It's been so lovely to meet you again after all this time, I couldn't believe it when Danny said he'd been emailing you for so long but you have already been a familiar name in this house for years Erin, ever since Gio first started writing to Danny. I think maybe you should go to Wellington, perhaps catch up with your other friend while we have you in this hemisphere, eh? Take care sweetheart", and with a very kind smile and a head nod, she leaves the room.

Danny tuts, calling his mum a *'cheeky bitch'* under his breath before he turns to me, rolling his eyes,

"If you hadn't got the gist of that, y'know, with your little ginger brain addled by sprog-popping, what my mother was *trying* to tell you is that G was a massive, clueless, *immature* dickhead when you guys fell out and that maybe, you need to speak to him because that massive, clueless dickhead *is and has always been* pretty bollock-deep in love with you Roberts. The question is, what do you feel 'bout him eh, pillow sniffer?", Danny quirks an eyebrow at me.

I look at Danny and honesty is, yet again, my best policy, "Danny, I was maybe in love with him from about the time when the twins were born right up until he brought Emily to the UK. Although I didn't realise it, I was in love with him while I was with Jay and while he dated bloody Carolyn Gregory and umpteen others. I loved him when he left to come here and when he found a girlfriend that he *loved.*

Then he *hurt* me, he proper *hurt* me with those things he said and I trained myself to forget about him because what the fuck was the point? He didn't want me then, I was too much *aggravation* for him, he told me as much", I stand up now, pacing as I wave in Danny's direction,

"You know all this dude, I wrote it all in emails", I feel exhausted.

Danny rolls his eyes, "Oh stop being a bloody dramatic tart Roberts. NOW, what do you feel *now*?"

I look at him, "I'm in love with the Gio that I *used* to know, my friend who held my hand and made me safe. I don't know Gio Romano now, I haven't known him for years. He's almost a stranger now I guess. So to be honest, I am in love but I don't know if the person I'm in love with still exists", I look up and smirk, "Maybe I need to go to Wellington and find out?".

"YESSSS!", Danny jumps on the sofa, fist-pumping, "Fuck, this is like that film, c'mon Roberts, we need to go find G and mess him up even worse over you than he was before now", Danny leaps off the sofa dragging me by the hand as we shout our thanks to his mum.

But see, in my life, nothing works out the way it should.

We're pulling into the apartment car-park to grab our bags, Danny having decided that we'll drive the bloody ten hours to Wellington through the night in shifts, when my phone goes.

"Erin, oh sweetheart I'm sorry to wake you up", it's Mum who is clearly clueless about the time difference.

"Mum, you OK?", I feel skin prickles of dread.

Mum gabbles, "Everyone is FINE Erin, you don't need to worry, it's all sorted and everybody is

FINE…...now", I instantly know that everyone is *not fine*.

"MOTHER!", my shout is shrill

"Sweetheart, our AJ have had a bit of a tumble this morning and he have broken his little collar bone and we've had a few stitches in his forehead but he is FINE", there's a whooshing sound in my head and my heart starts to pump acid.

Mum carries on, "Jamel is here with him in the hospital but we thought we should call and let you know but he's FINE Erin", I feel sick. *My baby.*

With my Batman-esque Mummy hearing, I can hear crying in the background, I can hear pleas for *'Mummeeeeee'* and I know instantly that this is my son, my broken, stitched son who is thousands of miles away from me.

I order Mum to pass me onto Jay, who sounds a bit shaky as he tells me that he had to hold AJ down to have his stitches. I sob as he tells me that AJ is fine now but that he is desperate to see me and that they are having, *"a bit of a fuckin' ball-ache Feist tryin' to calm him down".* When AJ and Jake go into one, it is a challenge to get them back down but I have an arsenal of techniques at my disposal.

As Danny strokes my arms, his face a mask of concern, I talk to my wounded baby who is an incomprehensible, hiccuping wall of sound. I tell him that Mummy is coming straight home, that I am going to get on a plane and come straight back to him. I am going to get his stuffed possum but he needs to be a good boy, calm down for Daddy and Mummy will be home really soon. I use the secret weapon,

"Dude, I need you to be the bravest boy and not be sad any more, OK? Coz Jakey gets scared when you're sad and we don't want Jakey to be scared, OK? You do that for me, yeah mate?", I close my

415

eyes praying that this works.

I hear jagged breaths and a resolute huff of determination at the other end, "Mummy, I'll look after Jakey, don't worry Mummy. I'll look after him", I smile through my tears

"You are my AJ-Legend. Right dude, I need to get on that plane. Can you put Jakey on the phone?"

Danny shakes his head in disbelief as he hears me chat to my other, sobbing child, "Jakey, I need you to be the bravest boy and not be sad any more, OK? AJ's arm and head hurts and if you're sad, it'll make it hurt him more and we don't want that, do we? So you be brave for me, yeah mate? Help look after AJ, yeah?", I hear more sniffs, more resolute affirmations.

Jay gets on the phone, "Feist, what voodoo shit have you just pulled? Eh? Them boys ain't stopped crying since it happened, now they're asking for food and to watch DVDs…….woman, you scare the shit out of me. Fuckin' love you Feist"

I close my eyes as a tear rolls down my face, "Love you too Jay. I'm getting on that plane, I'll be home in a couple of days yeah? Keep them safe for me, OK, keep them safe".

As the call ends, I stand head bowed and tears dripping as Danny takes a step towards me. I look up and hold my hand out in a warning gesture, halting his progress.

I feel angry suddenly, like I've been missold something, like I've been led to believe I can have something that is genuinely not available to buy. Right now, Danny is the salesman who deceived me and I turn on him,

"You still reckon I've not got *pieces* Danny? You still reckon my life's not that complicated? You reckon those *boxes* are still my bullshit creations to keep myself protected from hurt?", I am shaking my head as Danny looks a bit thrown.

"I can't go to Wellington Danny. I need to go home. I've had the most amazing week", my tone softens and I take a step towards Danny, my bitterness evaporating.

"I can't thank you enough, this has honestly been the most fun five days of my life but do you see now, do you understand why I have to leave Gio *the fuck* alone? What I *want*, what I am *in love with,* it means bugger all. Those boys will always, ALWAYS come first and it's not fair to expect any guy to happily play second fiddle. The only guy who would have been happy to do it is their father and he, well, he's not mine and that's OK but it leaves me with *nobody",* My voice cracks as I look up at Danny who looks a bit broken too.

"I need those boxes Danny. I need them. Because those guys, they'll always get put on a shelf when my boys need me and *boxes* are neater and easier to lift", I smile sadly at my friend as he sighs and pulls me into a hug, kissing my hair and rubbing my back.

At the airport an hour later with my flight changed, I'm sobbing my thanks, telling Danny how amazing he is, how glad I am that we're friends, how grateful I am.

"I am going to properly bloody miss you Roberts, you are the most ginger fun I've *ever* had. And you let me feel your tits…..I'm welling up Rinny, I'm going to miss those tits so *fucking* much", he wipes away imaginary tears as I laugh and smack his chest.

We hug our goodbyes and before I head towards security, I feel the need to tell him something,

"Danny, I don't think I've got anything to hide any more. If showing Gio those emails means he stops being a twat to you, then show them to him. I don't mind him reading them. Even if he moves back home, I don't reckon I'll ever see him again. Me and him, it's just best left in the past where it belongs so what does it matter if he reads them, eh?", kissing him gently on the cheek and winking, I back towards the scanners.

"Stay ginger Roberts, you are FUCKING awesome", Danny yells, scandalising the airport crowds

I beam back at him, yelling "Yeah, well, my arse doesn't lie", I pat my still-sore bum as Danny creases up, blowing me kisses and saluting.

Thirty-four hours later, I am buried under a bundle of small boys in my hallway as their father and my parents look on, shaking their head at the chaos we're causing.

My parents steer the boys back to the lounge, AJ's arm in a sling, as Jay hugs me and mumbles into my forehead, "Why the fuck didn't you say nothin' bout you and that shady prick Aiden splittin'? Eh?", he pulls back and looks at me worried.

I smile gently and look him in the eye, "Mate, he doesn't matter, he's not important to be honest. I didn't say anything because it's nothing", I shrug.

Jay frowns, "But Feist, you said…..you said that you figured you might love him?", Jay's tone is confused.

I shrug and look away, "Nah, I don't think love came into it. He was just a convenient box", and with a swift kiss to his cheek, I head into my lounge to hand out stuffed possums, ignoring Jay's concerned stare.

Chapter Twenty

4th April 2003

I didn't mean to pull the face, I honestly didn't. It was so kind and thoughtful of Case but honestly, the idea of drawing any attention to myself at this event had filled me with horror. Jay'd shot me evils as Case looked hurt by my ejaculation of, *"Jesus Christ no!"* and so I'd apologised and back-tracked, telling her that having a bloody birthday cake at her wedding would only remind me that I was a year older and uglier. I thanked her but declined more politely, flicking Jay the bird behind her back.

They have planned and arranged this wedding within six weeks of getting engaged, which is bloody impressive. Case is exactly fourteen weeks pregnant today, the scan photos confirming that their baby is healthy and due in late September. The hotel offered them a massively discounted package if they had the wedding on a Friday and with Casey's desire to wear her dress before her belly is noticeable, we've all been on Defcon Six planning duties since I got back from New Zealand. Megs, Casey's mate Shanice and I are the bridesmaids, our dresses are pretty lush ones from Coast. Casey, her slim elegant frame an easy one to flatter, found a beautiful dress at a Bridal Samples Sale and well, here we are.

I'm trying to be invisible today. My sons, the Best Mini-Men, are partnered by their two Uncles and I have been trying to hide behind their little three-foot, gorgeously be-suited frames all morning. It's a small wedding, only forty guests but there are still people here who do not understand that Casey and I are friends. There have been baffled looks regarding my inclusion in the wedding party from Casey's extended family, her decision to include the *'teenage harlot'* who briefly ensnared her sweetheart boggling some people.

The hen do was a fucking nightmare. Megs, absolutely *vile* with jealousy that both Jay AND Obi proposed to their girlfriends whilst D, after an astonishing *fifteen years* with Megs has yet to muster up a ring, was on truly horrendous form on the night out. She was rude to everyone, she got messily drunk, she started a fight in the club which *I* had to diffuse and in the end, to prevent Megs from actually ruining Casey's big night, I took her *by myself* to another club, lying to her that we were all heading there. On our way out, I whispered to the bouncers not to let her back in under any circumstances and I went with her to some truly awful Garage club where we 'waited' for Casey and the other girls, who were obviously not coming. Megs tried to start a fight with me and when I pinned her by the shoulders to the wall and called her a *'Fucking spiteful bitch'*, she wobbled off, pulled a completely random bloke and spent the taxi ride home sobbing on my shoulder. *Aces*.

Jay bought me jewellery the next day, a really pretty necklace. I looked boggled as he stood on my doorstep with the gift-bag but he kissed my cheek, told me I was a legend for rescuing Casey's big night and promised that I'd never need to go clubbing with Megs again for as long as he was breathing. I'd laughed.

I turned twenty-three yesterday, I'm going to London for the weekend with Lees tomorrow morning as my birthday treat, my parents are having the boys because Jay and Casey are having a week in Fuerteventura for their honeymoon.

As I herd my giddy sons into position in the ante-room, Obi winking at me and D looking a bit stressed, I am grateful that the chaos and jitters prevent me from contemplating the fact that I am about to witness the father of my children, the first boy I slept with, my first proper boyfriend, pledge his love and life-long fealty to the girl who is going to bear his next child. I am going to watch him start his future.

As the boys go off with Obi and D, Jay and I have a moment of peace. He looks so incredible in his suit and with his freshly barbered hair. Jay is even more gorgeous now than he was at nineteen. I look up at him and I smile indulgently, reaching up to stroke his terrified looking face.

"I love you Jay. You are a lovely guy, a wonderful Dad and you are going to make Casey a fantastic Husband. I'm proud of you dude", I smile as his lips twitch and he looks a bit bashful.

He pushes an escapee curl behind my ear cupping my cheek in his palm, "You an' me Feist, we been on a proper journey eh? You gotta know, I'd never be here wiv'out you. You.......you saved me girl. When I come out of lock up, I had fuck all but then I saw that message and.......and my life, it fuckin' changed. You ain't never gonna know what I owe you coz givin' me my boys, makin' me a part of their life, makin' me a part of *your* life, you gave me everythin'. You even gave me Case, don't you ever think I don't know what you did woman", he smirks at me, that scarred eyebrow raised.

"I love you Feist. I proper fuckin' love you", and he presses a gentle kiss to my lips as we hold hands, nodding in understanding.

As he walks towards the door to the ceremony room, he turns back with his dangerous smile on his face, "You're hangin' on yeah, you'll be here for the disco an' that won't you? You'll be here till late?", I nod, looking a bit confused.

He winks, "Good", and turns and walks into his future.

I take a jagged breath and I go and find my fellow bridesmaids and my sons' soon-to-be-step-mother.

Five hours later, I'm surviving. The ceremony was beautiful, the boys behaved impeccably, Jay's father managed to be almost civil to us all, Megs kept her mouth shut and Kaydee was an enchanting flower-girl. The vows didn't crush me as much as I feared they would and my tears were genuinely of happiness as I watched Jay and Casey beam at each other, their love just *radiating*.

We've done the speeches, Obi the nominated Best Man speech maker and a fine job he did of it. Eternally shy Jay did not want to make a speech so instead, our boys read out a little letter that started with *'Our Daddy has loved Casey since he was only eight years older than us'* as I crouched behind them and prompted them when they got stuck. They almost combusted from the cheers and praise they got, various Nigerian Aunties stuffing £1 coins in their little sticky fists.

Cakes have been cut, dances have been danced and we are now at that stage in the evening where there's a lull before the second half of the wedding really kicks off.

Mum, Dad, Dyls, Lees and Ads are arriving any minute now and I'm looking forward to seeing them all, feeling that a few additional friendly faces will soothe my slightly frazzled nerves. My sons have been kidnapped by Obi and Aretta, both of them so comically broody that their wedding next month is likely to be rapidly followed by their own babies. The four of them are dancing on the dance floor like nutters.

I turn around, looking for my drink when I spot Lees, making me shriek and start lolloping towards her, my high-heels slowing me down and giving me a chance to spot that the look on Lees' face is furtive at best, shifty at worst. Something is definitely *up*. I slow down, frowning in confusion.

When I see Jay approaching from the sidelines, looking similarly *shady,* I feel a growing unease, strongly suspecting that my requests for no birthday cake or fuss have been ignored.

"Roberts, I've got some blank flesh needs decorating, where the fuck is Terrance?", and with those words, I spin risking a cricked ankle, to see Danny McNamara emerge from the crowd.

I scream and launch myself into his arms, laughing like a drain and shouting my astonishment. As I kiss his cheek and pull back with *a thousand* questions to ask him, I quickly note that he too is shooting furtive looks at Lees and Jay.

What fucking now?

Ads appears and I smile in greeting but Ads looks so nervous that my hackles rise. Panicked, I look to my left, where McNamara is still holding my hand and then Jay's voice rumbles in my other ear,

"Feist, you gave me my fuckin' future with the person I love so I figured it was time I returned the favour yeah? I reckon it might be a few years overdue but y'know, I reckon you both needed to get shit straight first so I invited him here", I turn to Jay whose gaze seems to be directed at Danny.

Feeling a bit sick from what appear to be *calamitously* crossed wires regarding my feelings for Daniel McNamara, I turn to Danny to try to straighten this God Awful misunderstanding out when I see that he is not looking at me. He's looking over to the doorway and in that moment, *I know.*

Gio

Shaking off Danny's hand and blindly turning a hundred and eighty degrees, I walk as fast as I can away from all of them. I walk past my dancing sons on the dance floor, past all of the friends and family and I head out through the large patio doors to the terrace beyond, my entire body shaking. As I flee, I hear my sons yelps of excitement behind me, I hear them call out the name of the Godfather who sends them birthday and Christmas gifts without fail, the man who still sends them postcards occasionally.

I have no idea what I feel. Sick is the predominant feeling, panicked, startled, angry, frightened. *Scared.* I'm scared. I'm *so fucking scared.* All of my worlds are in this room. Kids, family, parents, friends, ex-boyfriends, past, present, future. All my *parts* are here. There could not be a more complete audience for whatever humiliation or rejection I am about to face. There will be nowhere I can hide when he rejects me again, when he confirms yet again that I am not worth the headache and the drama. I will have no boxes left to put him in. *There will be nothing left of me.*

I hear the patio doors shut, the music muted and I hear footsteps behind me.

I hear a shaky inhalation close by, as a low bass rumbles, "Hey Rin, it's really good to see you", it's wobbly from what I guess are nerves but his voice hasn't changed. It really hasn't. No Kiwi twang adopted, no change in tone over the last two years, four years, *years*.

I hear a soft sigh, "I read them y'know, the emails?", his voice wobbles more in its questioning tone but I can't turn around, staring out instead over the gardens of this mid-budget hotel with the sound of the motorway in the distance, the April evening chilly as I nod, shaking.

He takes a deep breath, "I sat there for like a whole day Rin, I mean, you two didn't half write a lot of shit", I smile at his words but I don't turn around. I nod again.

His tone is soft, "The pair of you are fucking hilarious, d'you know that? You could sell some of those emails, they are that funny. But it was kind of hard to laugh when mixed in with it was stuff that made me cry like a pansy. Do you know how hard it is to read a computer screen when you're full-on crying Roberts?", his tone is jokey but I hear the earnestness, I hear his honesty.

I look up at the clear, cold sky and I try desperately not to collapse.

I hear him take a step closer, "I told you once Rin that I always felt that I was apologising to you, that I felt like I was always being accused of not being on your side and that I felt like it was so unfair because you didn't want me on your side so why should I bother putting myself into shit for you. Do you remember that?", his voice is even closer and I feel my body respond, I feel my synapses tingle at his proximity.

I nod and he carries on, "See, reading all those emails, reading the bits where you were in pain, where you were so hurt by shit that life threw at you, where you were so hurt by stuff *I'd* done, it fucking killed me. You were just a kid but you were handling this massive *life* stuff with babies and degrees and shitty blokes and tough-as-hell placements and you had nobody to share how you *really* felt about it all with apart from some obnoxious moron Kiwi whose advice was suspect at best. Reading how strong you were having to be, it made me scream. I've never felt so fucking ashamed of myself, never felt as guilty as I did reading those emails", I feel the tears start to fall and I cram my nails into the palm of my hand in anger at my own weakness.

He carries on, "But I felt like such a thick bastard too because the first thing I think of, every *fucking* morning when I wake up, is *you* Rin, even when I was with bloody Emily, even after all these years. But in reality, I had no clue what your life was really like, the reason you made the decisions you did or what you were going through. I have thought about you every day since I was about fourteen and yet it turns out I knew nothing about your life Rin"

He's close now, I can smell the herbs and lemons and his voice is little more than a whisper, "See Rin, what I've figured out is that when you love somebody, when you love them so much that you spend fucking years missing them and thinking about them constantly, there is no *side*. You don't stand by their *side*. You should be standing there in front of them, surrounding them, protecting them when they are vulnerable or scared or sad or just fucking *eighteen* and alone with two babies. When they sacrifice shit to make *other* people's lives easier or better, you don't stand by their *side*, you should *hold them up* and I didn't do that. I hurt you Rin, I walked away when things got too hard. I let you down by leaving you behind on your own when I should have *fought* for you and I am so, so fucking sorry"

I hear his voice crack and I feel his hand gently brush the skin of my bare arm as my skin *sings* from his touch, "I was the biggest prick in the world Rin, I have honestly been the biggest prick. I read those emails, the ones you wrote about when I was over with Emily and I wanted to scream, I wanted to knock myself out for going on about needing things to be *easy* or *straightforward*", I hear his agitation but I can't turn around yet and I hear him moving in circles behind me.

He's back though, his hands tentatively stroking my arms again, "I asked you the wrong question all those years back and I came here tonight to just ask you the right question Rin, can I ask you the right question this time?".

Taking a jagged breath in, I finally find the courage to turn around, my heart hammering in my ears and I look up into the face that has filled my thoughts and daydreams and fantasies since I was sixteen years old. His dark hair is cropped shorter than I expected, the curls thwarted slightly. He's as tall and as strong looking as always but he looks tired and his tanned skin is a bit dull looking, his freckles standing out.

I look into those blue eyes, they're entreating me to agree and slowly, I nod.

"I'm not going to ask you what you *want* because I know that all you ever wanted is to be a good Mum, to give those boys the best life they can have. I *know* that you will always, *always* put those boys first and that is exactly how it should be", I feel my lip tremble as he steps forward, taking my hands in his big warm ones.

I feel those hands, the ones that held me so safe and I close my eyes from the pleasure, from the *rightness* of feeling his skin against mine.

His voice is hoarse as he whispers, "The question I should have asked you Rin is this: Whose hands do you want to hold while you're putting those boys first? Who do you want to hold your hand and stand behind you, *beside* you, in front of you? Who do you want next to you when life is shit? Who do you want lying next to you when you're scared or sad?", he looks at me and a tear rolls down his face.

I reach up without thinking and wipe it away with the pad of my thumb but he moves, nestling his face into my hand, making my breath hitch with the sweetness of the gesture.

I break my silence and my voice sounds rusty, "We don't know each other now Gio, it's been years since we spent time together. So much has changed, hasn't it?", I feel his head shaking in disagreement under my palm, I feel his jaw clench as he looks up and pulls away from my hand.

He's shaking his head resolutely, "Not the important things Rin. Yeah, we've both grown up, I had more of that to do than you I reckon", he smirks but carries on, "We both had relationships with people that weren't right for us and had experiences that have shaped us but honestly, Rin, I'm still the same person", and that's when he takes my face in both of his hands,

"Rin, I still love you just as much, more even, than when we saw each other every day at school. I am so fucking in love with you Erin Roberts and I don't know how it's possible when we haven't spoken for so long but I think it's because I've always loved you and I don't know how to do anything else. So please, can you try and answer that question? Who do you want holding you hand? Coz if you say it's Mac, I need to go and get a head start on battering the twat", his joking tone sounds forced but it makes me smile.

I close my eyes as flashes of memories from our twenty year history flicker through my head. I see the *boy*, the *teenager*, the *man* who has been a part of my life and my heart for so long and as my brain wrestles with identifying the safest course of action, my impulsive heart and lips jump in and let honesty guide them,

"It's you Gio, it's always been you Romano. I never stopped loving you", I open my eyes and stare into his wide blue ones as a tear tracks down my cheek.

I see his lip wobble as he croaks, "Rin, thank *fuck* for that", and with a gentle sob of breath, I feel his arms pull me against his warm body and I feel his soft lips press themselves against mine as the explosion of glitter cannons in my head makes my legs weak.

427

The feeling of being kissed by Gio makes every part of my body sigh with happiness. As his satin-soft lips stroke gently against mine, his hands clutching at me as I lean into him, I feel my own hands go up his back, I feel him shaking. His tongue softly licks at my lips and with a mutual groan, the kiss deepens and I am *snogging* Gio, proper full-on snogging and it is so delicious, I wonder if you can pass out from pleasure. His tongue strokes mine, soothing me, exploring me as his soft groans and moans do wicked things to my knickers.

He's got me held so tightly, so safely. I've never felt so *supported* by somebody since…..since Giovanni Romano carried me to the sick bay.

As his lips move to my skin, his hands ruining the elaborate French plait containing my unruly curls, he whispers against my neck, "I've never wanted anything as much as I want you Rin, *never*. You'll never know how sorry I am for hurting you, I love you so fucking much woman, you are *it* for me", and his lips claim mine once more.

I did not know that kissing could be like this. It's like communion, its like some sort of renewal. The more we kiss, the more healed I feel. Judging by Gio's unrelenting enthusiasm for the activity, I'm guessing it's having the same rejuvenating effect on him. When he pulls me even tighter into the cradle of his legs, leaning as we now are against the brick wall of this balcony, I feel the rock-hard evidence of his rejuvenation and it makes me melt.

His hands, so respectful and reverent until now, start to wander. They cup my secretly-branded arse, squeezing hard. They wander around the edges of my dresses beaded bodice, fingertips brushing forbidden territories and delicious though it is, I start to feel panic rising.

These emotions are so strong, this turn of events so unbelievable that I suddenly feel overwhelmed by sensation. Tearing myself away from a startled looking Gio, whose well-snogged lips are almost comically red, I stand three feet away, wrapping my arms around myself protectively and possibly looking as terrified as I feel.

Gio's voice sounds panicked as he holds his hands up in surrender, his face agonised, "You don't need to run Rin, it's OK. Just take a breath, it's cool. Whatever you're feeling, it's OK, we'll just back off a bit, process it yeah? Don't run Rin, please, *please* don't run away from me again. *Please*", Gio's voice cracks.

I turn away and my jittery eye is caught by an entire sea of nosy faces, pressed up against the glass of the reception suite windows. I see my whole tribe of assorted eejits- Jay, Case, Lees, Ads, my bloody mother, Dyls, Obi, Danny, Aretta…..they are all there and when they see that they have been spotted there is a comical scrabble from the window, limbs tangled and curtains tugged in their haste to disappear.

I feel the bubble of a chuckle rise up from my chest and before I know what I'm doing, my overwhelmed nervous system converts all the emotion into laughter. I am proper, full-on belly laughing and I see Gio's lips twitch although he still looks scared to death.

I turn to him, his dark head bowed and his strong body a bit slumped and slowly hold out my hand, "I'm not running Romano but slow yeah? I need this….I need this to sink in a bit. Let me process it? Okay?", I gesture for him to take my hand.

He smiles, it's a slow burn across his face but it turns into a real blinder of a grin, "I can do slow Roberts, it's already been years, what's a bit longer, eh?", and that warm, safe, lemon and herb scented hand takes mine as we walk in to face the crowd of muppets that make up the pieces of me.

Three hours later, we have spent most of our time chatting with our mates and my family. Gio seemed to instantly understand that our incredible *reunification* on the balcony was not the whistle-start of immediate relationship status. As we got to the patio doors, he'd kissed my hand so sweetly and then gently let me go, seeming to understand that we have a journey to take before publicly declaring *anything*. We've sidestepped everyone's raised eyebrows, smirks and pointed comments and the only confirmation I have given that Gio and I are the cusp of something, is when bloody McNamara dragged me for a dance and drunkenly accused me of,

"....being a total pussy. The boy loves you, you love him so what's with the polite friends bollocks? Shouldn't you be sucking the bloody faces off each other?", jet lag and a decent quantity of Jack Daniels have got McNamara swaying dangerously.

I roll my eyes at him and kiss him on the cheek whispering, "I don't know what has gone on here tonight or how or why you two turned up at this but honestly McNamara, I know you had a big part to play in it and I can't thank you enough", I kiss him on the cheek again.

He tuts bashfully and then flashes me a feral grin, "Tell you what, hook me up with that fit as, hard-faced bridesmaid and I'll consider your debt paid", he nods drunkenly at Megan who is dancing somewhat provocatively nearby.

I snort and point at D, chatting with his Dad by the bar, "See that giant lad with the cornrows by the bar? That's her long suffering boyfriend and the father of her child. Want to risk pissing him off?", I turn to Danny who swears wildly and looks alarmed,

"Bloody hell, he's a big fucker. Nope, find me some less dangerous pussy please Roberts", Danny winks and I pat his shoulder as we dance.

He mumbles against my shoulder, "Y'know, I hope that dickhead knows how lucky he is Roberts. I mean, you're a pain in the arse but you're a legendary laugh and those tits...Christ those tits....does he know I've had hold of them?", I pull back ready to berate him as I see Gio approaching us, his eyebrow raised in question.

"Dude, your missus has INCREDIBLE tits, I should know, I've had a proper bare handful", Danny shouts to Gio and then stumbles, Gio grabbing Danny's smaller frame and holding him up,

Gio looks at me smirking, "Have you indeed Mac? Well dude, consider it a one-off coz they're off limits to you now", Gio winks at me, "Rin, I'm gonna take this wanker up to our room, I'll be back in a mo", and with a heave, Gio leads a shambolic Danny out.

I find myself being dragged to dance by two sleepy little Mini-Men, both absolute in their refusal to go to bed but both of them struggling to stay conscious. It's a few seconds later that I find myself carrying one in each arm, their now substantial six-and-a-half-year-old bodies a proper weight and I am struggling. Jay smiles and comes over, taking a now nodding-off AJ from me as the four of us sway in a huddle on the dance floor. I see camera flashes going off as Jay and I hold hands and stand close, our babies in our arms as I whisper to him my thanks for his role in whatever machinations brought Gio and Danny here tonight. He kisses my head and tells me that it was nothing more than what he owed me.

I see Casey smiling at us and I poke Jay, indicating that he needs to have a dance with his *wife.*

"Pass me a God Goblin dude, I'll take one", a deep voice from over my shoulder causes me to smile.

Jay looks up, a slightly guarded look on his face as he glances down at his sons, across to me and then finally up into Gio's face. I see a flicker of sadness cross Jay's features before he nods and slowly hands a now snoring AJ over to his Godfather, who lifts him effortlessly and presses a gentle kiss onto AJ's caramel hair. Jay smiles at me and nods before turning to Casey and taking her off for a dance.

Gio's strong, warm arm wraps itself around my waist as I lean my head on his chest and we dance together for the first time since that Leavers' Ball. I see more camera flashes but I ignore them, as I stand in the arms of the three boys who claim my heart.

Gio comes with me as I take the boys upstairs, their night at an end as they snore loudly. Smiling self-consciously at each other as we deal with a twin each, I wonder how such an unexpected set of events can feel so perfect. Gio gets AJ into his PJ's with surprising skill (*'I've had to get Mac into bed more times that I can count when he's pissed, bloody lightweight'*) and as we tuck my monsters into their beds, snoring like sugar-filled piglets, I stand and look at them, Gio's warm hand slipping into mine.

His voice is soft and warm too, "This is all I ever wanted Rin. You and them with me. I kinda fell in love with them too you know, when they were born. I've missed them so much. Does that sound proper creepy?", he chuckles and shakes his head but I am reaching for him, turning his face to mine as I go up on tip toes and press a slightly urgent kiss to his lips, our first one since the terrace.

The man I love loves my sons too.

His response is immediate, hands grabbing me and pulling me close, breaths urgent, tongues stroking and teasing as we groan into each other's mouths. *God I want you.*

At the sound of banging on the door, we fly apart like we've been shot, blushing and rolling eyes. I walk over to the door and am a bit surprised to see Lees bowling in as the door opens.

She smirks as she sees a slightly rumpled Gio, "RIGHT! Romano, I've put Ads in your room with Danny. Ads is so pissed I can do nothing useful with him tonight so they can be two pissed morons together. I will be sleeping in here with my two little God Angels and *you two*", she throws me a set of room keys, "You two can have mine and Ads room", she winks and pretends to yawn, flopping onto *my* bed.

She cracks open an eye, "For God's sake, bugger off before I change my mind", she points at the door as Gio nods and taking my hand, he pulls me towards it whispering, "I owe you Morris".

As Gio tows me around the hotel corridors looking for the room, we don't speak. I can see the blush on the backs of his ears and his neck and I feel like I did all those years ago driving to the rave with Ryan Jones. I know where this is heading and I'm so nervous.

Locating the door, Gio lets us in and I follow him into a truly massive room. We wander in, looking around at an astonishingly enormous bed, various tables, chairs and dressing areas and what is probably the bathroom door.

"Holy Shit Romano, you ever been in a hotel room as nice as this?", I'm distracted as I take off my shoes, not wanting to to mess up the room's perfection.

Gio doesn't reply though, he's stood stock still, turned towards the bed, his big, strong body rigid, his hands clenched in fists.

"Gio?", my voice reflects the panic I feel. *Shit, he's already regretting everything.*

He shakes his head and my heart takes the umpteenth pelvis-plummet of its life but then he whispers,

"Rin, I'm so fucking nervous. I'm so scared. Just being here *alone* with you, it's been what I've dreamt about since…..since far too long. If I spend tonight here with you, even if all we do is chat and I sleep on that sofa", he turns to me and I see how anxious his gorgeous face looks, "I don't reckon I'll ever be OK if I have this time with you tonight and then you walk away from me again", I see his lip wobble as he carries on,

"I can't share a room with you, be here with you if you might leave tomorrow Rin, if you might change your mind. I just can't, it'll fuck me up too much", he's looking at the floor as he shakes his head and he doesn't see me move towards him.

As I get within touching distance he looks up and I step closer, whispering in his bowed ear, "Gio, don't share a room with me then", he jolts, pain transmitting all over his features as he raises alarmed blue eyes at me and I quickly finish what I need to say as I hold his gaze, "Don't just share a room with me. Share my *bed*, share my *life* Gio. I'm yours, I've always been *yours*", and with an agonised sob, he's on me.

These aren't just hot kisses, these kisses *brand* us, they *meld* us together. Hands caress reverently, as gasped breaths declare love. His tongue licks my skin and I whimper, my hands undo his buttons and zips as he gasps and groans. As my lips explore that lemon and herb scented olive skin, my whole body thrums with *rightness*. With each stage of undress, we stare at what is revealed, stroking gently like we can't believe that this is real. Down to our underwear, our kisses get deeper, touches get bolder. Gio groans against my bra covered nipple as he kisses the covered flesh before releasing the catch and biting his lip as I show Gio Romano my boobs for the first time,

"Oh fuck Rin, OH FUCK, they're amazing, ohmygod, I've dreamed of these for so long and they're fucking amazing", I giggle into his hair as he kisses and strokes my tits with a wide-eyed look of wonder.

My hands manage to wander *finally* into his boxers and as I hold Gio's sizeable dick, stroking it's impressive length gently and making Gio groan loudly, I get a terribly unfortunate case of the giggles, making Gio huff and sit back on his haunches, an eyebrow raised.

I am giddy with silliness as I blurt out, "Do you remember flashing your dick at me in Home Corner at playgroup? I showed you my *fairy* and you *cried*", I snort with laughter, as Gio's frown turns into an eye-rolling grin.

He looks at me, smiling, "Roberts, you show me it now and I promise you, the only crying I'll be doing is in happiness", he waggles his eyebrows and Chopsy Madam makes her entrance.

Smirking, I reach down and as Gio's jaw drops, I slowly roll down my knickers and sitting up, I let my legs fall akimbo, trying to look innocent.

"Holy Fuck", his voice is a croak before he winks and launches himself onto me, his blissful heavy weight pushing me backwards as exploratory fingers and hands cause each other all sorts of bliss.

He makes me come on his tongue, his broad, muscled back scratched under my fingernails as I detonate, moaning his name and giddy from the fact that I am *naked* with *Gio*. I discover that I have never loved sucking somebody's dick as much as I love sucking Gio's, his loud shouts of pleasure and astonishment fuel my ingenuity and the taste of him is addictive.

"Don't make me come yet Rin, please, please, I want to come *inside* you the first time, I've wanted you for so fucking long", his kisses are deep and longing as I reach into my bag and offer undeserved thanks to Aiden for the infidelity that left me with an unopened box of condoms.

'Wrapping up' Gio gives me more opportunity to torture the poor lad, as he groans desperately under my rolling fingers, those amazing muscles rippling under his skin as I play with the *perfect* dick that I've wanted to see for *years*. As soon as I'm done, he flips me onto my back, cupping my face as he whispers against my lips,

"You have got no idea how much I've wanted this Rin, been dreaming about doing this with you for *ever*. I love you Rin, I love you so fucking much", and with a mutual groan of pleasure, Gio slides into my slick heat and we clasp ourselves tightly together, whispering our love as he *makes love* to me.

This is somebody who I am *in love* with and who is *in love* with me, *making love* to me. It's breathtaking. The feeling of Gio inside me is perfect and as his strong body moves under my hands, his muscles shifting with every thrust and caress, I float in bliss.

We both cry, it's a bit ridiculous really. As we gasp our incredulous climaxes, gripping each other like we're scared to let go, I feel his tears on my cheeks and mine smear against his skin.

I don't know when we stopped kissing, it must have been as we fell asleep but I know for certain that despite jet-lag, mild inebriation and emotional exhaustion, we used three more of those condoms before it happened.

In the morning, I wake up grinning and wrapped in Gio's arms. As I stretch my sore muscles under the duvet I turn to face Romano, his coal-coloured hair adorably rumpled and his face sleep-creased and gorgeous as he whispers across the pillow, "So Roberts, you'll never believe it but it turns out I'm moving to Bristol. Do you know anyone who might have some place I can crash, a bed that I can maybe share?", as I grin and nod, we're both beaming as he pulls me in for a proper, deep snog.

Two hours later, I wonder if I should send Aiden a thank you note because honestly, that condom packet is bloody empty now. As a naked Gio opens the shower door, intruding on my watery haven with a smirk that could set ice on fire and a body that makes me whimper, he asks, "So, tell me Erin Roberts, are you ever going to explain why, out of all the things you could have chosen, you've got, *'This boot-faced ginger cunt-fuck will shank you in the twat'*, tattooed on your gorgeous arse? Eh?", he sniggers against my skin as our hands roam the long-dreamt of topography of each others bodies.

Chuckling, he soaps the offending graffiti as I kiss the fabled six-pack and I hear the faint sound of horses hooves and a posh bray retreating into the distance, their work here finally done.

February 2006

"So Mrs. Romano, let's have a look here shall we? I understand that your previous pregnancy was fraternal twins, is that right?", the sonographer looks at me kindly as Gio grips my hand like a vice, his nerves making him shake.

The gel, the potato masher, the screens and the darkness, it's all oddly familiar and I get a tearful flashback to Madhoo and my Mum as I nod.

Gio's thumb strokes mine as he stares, clueless, at the screen. I'm not looking at the screen though. I'm looking at Sarah, the updated version of Madhoo. I'm watching her because I know her face will tell me more than any grey-toned screen.

My breath hitches as her eyes widen, as the eyebrow tilts, as the shaky exhalation leaves her lips.

"You need to just pop and get someone, don't you?", my words are a whisper as Sarah nods jerkily and reassures me that she just wants to get a second opinion, it's *nothing to worry about.*

She leaves and Gio is frantic, questions, panic, confusion, "Are they OK Rin, is the baby OK?", his hands clutching at me, kisses pressed to reassure.

I just smile gently and whisper to him, "Yeah, it's all normal but sit down dude, I think it's probably best you sit yourself down", the speed at which that bite-able, muscled arse hits the seat is almost comical.

A man comes in, surprising me slightly in this female-centric space. Much as his predecessor before him, we have curt introductions before the masher is stroked, the screens are examined and the heads are nodded. He gets up and leaves and I can sense Gio's confusion, his big, strong body rigid in the seat next to me, his warm hand holding mine safe.

Sarah smiles warily, looking like she wishes she'd called in sick, "So Mr and Mrs. Romano, the fantastic news is that they all have strong heartbeats and your three babies all look to be developing well, they're not sharing an amniotic sac so we're looking at fraternal triplets………..".

I didn't know you could fall off a chair from a sitting position, kudos to Romano.

Me, I place my hands over my belly as my husband groans from the floor and my smile is wide.

Ah girls, don't scare your father, he has a hard enough time coping with your mother.

As Gio grimaces and stands, taking my hand once more in his lovely big warm one, he looks at me in blue-eyed terror and whispers,

"Roberts, there's boys in there yeah? Tell me you reckon some of them are boys? If there's three of *you* in there, I am so fucking screwed"

I pat his hand and wink, whispering his long ago words of comfort, "You just look at me, just look at me and hold my hand and it'll all be fucking OK Romano, y'hear me?", I look up into the gorgeous face of the man I've loved for over ten years.

Gio pulls me gently towards him, smirking slightly as he leans in for a proper snog, scandalising poor Sarah as those soft lips and the freckled olive skin that I get to kiss *every day,* fill my vision.

He murmurs against my lips, "Yeah Roberts, *I do*", and we grin at each other.

36450412R00255

Printed in Great Britain
by Amazon